Hope Is a Waking Dream

Kimberly R. Cimorelli

Published by:
K R Cimorelli
Lulu Edition

Hope Is a Waking Dream

© 2012, Kimberly R. Cimorelli. All Rights Reserved
ISBN 978-1-105-70315-7

Published by K R Cimorelli
Second Edition: 2014
Lulu Edition

Dedication

To My Mother,
The things you've struggled through in your life have become my inspiration.
Your enormous support and belief in me has been my guiding light.
Everything that you are, and have become,
Is everything I aspire to be.

Chapter 1

"Welcome Home"

Looking out through the tiny window, my future seemed as opaque as the clouds I was staring into. I couldn't describe exactly what I was feeling. I wouldn't have even known where to begin. There was so much going through my mind. Pain. Fear. Excitement. Grief. Longing. Confusion. Each emotion that I could identify seemed more terrifying than the last. I had never felt so lost. And to think that it this was only the beginning...

My flight was scheduled to land in less than an hour. From that moment on, my life was starting over. Everything I had known no longer existed. My home, my family, my friends... gone. I had no idea what I was walking into. Why? Because my mother felt that it was better I knew nothing of her past. Apparently she had never anticipated the possibility of suddenly losing her life one day and leaving me behind to fend for myself. She was unaware that there might come a time when her mother and stepfather would need to step in, and take over as parental guardians.

I never understood why she refused to divulge the details of what happened to her during her childhood. She wouldn't tell me what made her so bitter towards her mother, or why she fled home when she was seventeen. The same age as I was, now. All I knew was that she had gotten pregnant with me, and then ran away from her home with just a single suitcase and her boyfriend—my father—Jeremy. Still, there were many holes in her stories—what little she had told me. Holes I wished she had filled. Now, I may never know. I only knew that now I was going to the place she had run away from. A place that made her eyes water when she would think about it. A place that left her so much pain that she refused to speak of it.

I saw a picture of the house, one time. I say "*house*," when in all actuality, "*castle*" would more accurately describe it. My mother kept a wooden chest in her closet, and in that chest were the only items she had taken with her when she left home. A few articles of clothing, some pictures, and a rag doll she had torn a small hole in to hide money she had collected, were among its contents. But the items that fascinated me the most, were the three pictures at the bottom. I was so drawn to the mystery of her past, that after I first discovered what was inside that chest as a child, I would continue to steal visits with its contents, any time my mother wasn't around. On the one day she walked in and caught me, I happened to be gazing at one in particular, of her as a teenager with a man and a woman on a hill. The amazing castle was off in the distance, behind them. At first she was startled to find me in her room, amongst her most sacred possessions. For a brief moment, her eyes beheld a touch of fury. I sat frozen, flushed, and wondering how much trouble I was in as we stared wordlessly at one another. But her eyes softened instead, and she picked up one of the two pictures on the floor before me.

"Hope, this is your grand-father." She held the picture out before my face, and I stared at the handsome, smiling man with sparkling eyes and perfect teeth. "He was a wonderful man. The best... He loved my mother and I, with all his heart. And I truly believe he'd still be here today if she hadn't taken me away with her, and left him for someone younger, wealthier..." Her eyes shone with tears. "He died of a broken heart."

Surely, you would think a person couldn't die of a broken heart. But to hear her tell the story, it seemed he really had. My mother went on to tell how Lawrence Anthony Van Steenburgh suddenly appeared in her life, and how her mother connived him into marrying her. "She didn't love him," she went on with bitterness softly spilling with her words. "My mother never loved anyone but herself." While all of this happened, and even after the divorce, my grandfather sank into a deep depression. He let his business go. He neglected himself. He turned to alcohol for comfort, and ultimately he drank himself to death.

I glanced down at my watch. Approximately forty-five more minutes until this plane lands.

I will never forget walking down the hallway, and past my parents' bedroom, catching a glimpse of my mother sitting at her vanity table. She was getting ready for a dinner banquet she and my father were attending for his company, and for a moment I just had to stop and admire her, drinking in all that she did to make herself more exquisite-looking than she already was. She was humming softly while she sprayed a subtle scent onto herself, and as she put the finishing touches on her make-up, she glanced over to find me standing in the doorway.

"Hello there, Hope." She held her hand out towards me, and smiled. "I was so lost in my own little world for a moment that I hadn't noticed you standing there!"

"You look so pretty," I gushed, entering the room. She stood up in her elegant black gown, and that's when I noticed the sparkling diamond necklace she donned around her small neck. "I don't think I've seen that one before," I pointed out.

In her other hand she revealed the matching set of earrings that glittered in the light of her bedroom. The smile that emerged over her lips was slight, as a faraway look surfaced in her eyes. "My mother gave these to me on my sixteenth birthday," she informed me softly. "I've never taken them out of the box until now." She bit the inside of her lip. "Now's as good a time as any, right?" The small semblance of a chuckle that escaped her lips sounded more awkward than comforting. "Someday, they'll belong to you," she promised.

Someday was much closer than any of us even thought.

The very second my father emerged from their bathroom, her eyes lit up like Christmas lights. He looked so handsome, in his suit. Clean-shaven, with a smile and eyes that mirrored my mother's. The love between them was palpable. The looks I'd often catch them giving one another at any given time were hot enough to set a room on fire. It was the kind of love that I wanted to have, one day.

One day...

I wished for one moment that I were able to read her thoughts. Especially now, looking back, there were so many wistful, unfocused stares that I'd never really understood. She was my mother, but I never felt like I really knew her. As it turned out, I never really would.

"Are you ready to leave, Lindsey?"

Snapping out of her spell the instant my father spoke her name, she smiled at him and rose to her feet. "Of course, darling!" He leaned forward and kissed her forehead, and she blushed before her eyes flittered in my direction.

"You really don't have to stay home," my father spoke, before pulling me to him for a hug.

"I'll go next time," I promised absently.

"No you won't," he teased with a smile. "You never do."

"You're right," I agreed. "Stuffy parties have never been my thing," I bantered back with a smirk. "But you two have a good time, though!"

I should have gone.

Instead, I recall watching them pull out of the driveway in their sedan. Realizing that it was going to be a lonely night, I plopped into my father's plushy recliner and found a good radio station. I closed my eyes and started to sing. The next thing I knew, I was singing myself to sleep... and the phone was ringing.

I rubbed my eyes and reached over, grabbing the phone, turning the radio down.

"Oh, hi Hope!" I recognized the voice on the line as John Blackstock, one of my father's good friends. "Uh, aren't your parents coming, tonight?" He asked. "They said they were coming. Is your father there? Let me speak to him, would you please?"

Perplexed, I glanced at the clock. Had I really fallen asleep for nearly two hours? "They left almost two hours ago," I muttered, confused. "They should already be there."

"Well maybe they made a stop somewhere, or they're having car problems..." I was no longer listening to him. My heart was pounding now. When I hung up the phone, the feeling in the pit of my stomach was unsettling. My father wasn't late for anything, ever.

"Would you like anything to drink, Miss?"

Snapping back to reality, I glanced up at the flight attendant and smiled, shaking my head. "No. Thank you."

"Are you on your way home, or are you on your way to visit friends or family?" The elderly man who sat beside me looked at me with curious eyes, while I shifted in my seat.

I was far too nervous and anxious to really be interested in holding a conversation with anyone, but I swallowed it back. I was a bit lost for a response to his question. I mean, what could I say? I guess I was on my way home, yes. Family? Yes. Friends? I was unsure.

"I'm going to stay with some relatives for a while," I told him, forcing a friendly smile.

"Oh, well that's nice," he replied. "A change of scenery can't hurt. I'm just now returning from seeing relatives. Wore me out. I'm glad to be back."

I chuckled nervously, feeling worn out, myself.

"Are you Hope de Havilland?"

I glanced at the two state troopers standing just outside my front door. There was a lump in my throat as I stood there, holding the door open and afraid to move.

"There was an accident on Ellen Parkway, involving Lindsey and Jeremy Carter."

When I closed my eyes, it felt like my head was going to wobble off. I held my breath as they continued, confirming my worst fears had just become a reality. I clenched my teeth, willing myself not to fall apart, and knowing that I had to be strong, no matter what the outcome. Whatever they were about to tell me...

"I'm sorry, Miss, but it was fatal."

I buried my face in my hands, while they told me how a drunk driver had come down the road on the opposite side. The drunken driver crossed over the median, losing control of his car... and he collided with my parents, head-on. And according to what the policemen were telling me, my parents were killed instantly. After that, I only heard bits and pieces of what they said. I literally felt like myself falling apart, and as I approached the verge of hysterics, all they could do was look on, helplessly.

It hurt. It filled me with fear. It made my heart ache, and it also made me angry, and full of questions. Hadn't my parents seen this car coming? Couldn't they have swerved and avoided it? Where was this other person? What happened to he or she?

The worst part was learning that this other person was just suffering a few cuts and bruises, and aside from facing charges of manslaughter, he was alive and well. How was that even fair???

"This has to be a mistake," I whispered, trying to look calm, though I was shaking so bad that I had to lean against the frame of the door. "You must have made a mistake..."

That's when I was presented with a small clear bag of items, which he opened, and after walking just inside the doorway, he scattered on the small table just inside. I watched in disbelief as he removed my father's wallet, with his license, cards, some money, and pictures. The other trooper handed me my mother's small, dainty purse, and one of those damned diamond earrings that had never been taken out of their small box, in almost eighteen years. It was at this point that I completely fell apart. I couldn't think as they peppered me with questions, such as who I could stay with, or if there was anyone I could call. I had no one, now. I told them I could call the neighbors.

I didn't even have the neighbors' number.

And how I got from that point, and onto this plane, was still a mystery. I don't know how my long-lost grandmother and her husband found out about my parents' death. It all happened so fast. I received a phone call from Lawrence Van Steenburgh, offering his sympathy and bringing it to my attention that I had no one to turn to, now. How he knew that as well, I didn't know. He informed me that he was having my parents flown in, and buried in the family cemetery. No introductions. Never asking how I was doing. This man just swooped right in, before the bodies were even cold, and decided to take over.

"If your paternal grandparents were still alive, I'd consult with them, but since they are not, I will take it upon myself to bury your father, as well," he went on, over the phone. "I also insist that you come to live here at Van Steenburgh Manor from this point on. It's the least I can do for you in your time of need." Then, before I could say another word, he continued. "I understand how reluctant you must feel, being that you don't know myself, or my wife, but we are your family. Your best interests are here, and tomorrow there will be someone arriving to pick you up around noon. The arrangements have already been made, Hope. Your ticket is waiting at the airport."

Chapter 2

"Grandmother"

Clutching my small bag, I stepped off the plane and entered the lobby, looking around anxiously. I had no idea what I was looking for. Some person holding a sign, like you see in the movies? Was I supposed to go somewhere to wait? Was I supposed to be able to recognize my grandmother, and her husband? Would they recognize me?! I felt my heart pounding in my throat. I fidgeted with the small necklace I wore, and wondered what I was supposed to do. I went to baggage claims and picked up the two suitcases that now held my entire life, and then headed back toward the lobby area. Within a few moments, a handsome man with raven-black hair, bronzed skin, dark eyes, and a business suit approached me with a warm smile.

"You must be Hope," he greeted me, before motioning for the man following him to grab my suitcases. He took my hand within his own, and I marveled at how large his hands were. He was much taller than my father was, and his shoulders were broad. On his ring finger he wore a band with glittering diamonds, and there was not a single hair or piece of lint visible on his black, fitted suit. I looked up at him, and his eyes swept over me as his smile shone brightly. "It's wonderful to meet you, at last!" He then turned to acknowledge the classy woman that approached his side, who was looking at me with wide, surprised eyes. She was stunning; her hair was golden-blonde, cut to flatter her small round face, with eyes of bright blue—just like my mother's. She shared the same splendid, dainty figure as my mother, and immediately I noted how contradictory she was of the very image I always pictured when I thought of the word "*grandmother.*"

"Can you believe this, Vivien? She looks *just* like Lindsey did at her age! She's a spitting image of her!" The man exclaimed, unable to take his eyes off of me.

The woman narrowed her eyes at me after a moment, and scowled. "She's got dark eyes, dear. Lindsey didn't have dark eyes."

"Yes, but for everything else—she's perfect! Lindsey, all over again!"

She looked over me again, nodding. "I suppose you're right," she agreed, before quickly glancing around. "Now come along—we must be going on our way. I have appointments to keep, Lawrence. You know that."

He nodded, and then we were on our way.

"We will do everything in our power to make you at home, at Van Steenburgh Manor," he assured me, as we walked. My grandmother glanced back at me with a scrutinizing look through her narrowed eyes, and I forced a smile through my nervousness. I truly hoped they couldn't see me trembling, though I was doing it so badly I was sure they had already noticed. "Had your mother told you anything about the manor?"

I hesitated. "I've seen pictures," I spoke softly. "It looks beautiful."

My grandmother scowled, as if it were a sore subject with her. Lawrence didn't seem to notice her reaction. He opened the door to the black limo we approached, and he smiled with great pride. "It's magnificent, Hope. I'll tell you all about it once we get settled into the car. This is Charles, our driver," he introduced quickly, gesturing toward the tall wiry man with the bald patch at the back of his head. "You'll be seeing him around the house, also." Charles didn't even look up.

The second we were all settled in the car and on our way, Lawrence began chattering excitedly. "I realize that I haven't formally introduced myself yet, and I apologize. I'm Lawrence Anthony Van Steenburgh, and this is my wife— your grand-mother- Vivien."

"You may just call me Vivien," she spoke up, quickly. Then she smiled and gave me a light pat on the arm. "'Grandmother' makes me feel old. To call me 'Vivien' will suit me just fine," she cooed against my blank and overwhelmed stare.

"And," Lawrence continued, taking my attention back to him. "Just to avoid any confusion or misconceptions in the future, I think it's best to tell you right now that I'm not your biological grand-father. Lindsey was born from Vivien's first marriage."

"I already knew that," I piped up.

Now they both looked at me with surprise. "You do?"

I nodded. "Mom told me," I revealed to them. "It was one of the few things she had told me about her past." I narrowed my eyes at them both. "For some reason, she never liked to talk about her life at Van Steenburgh Manor, very much.

Lawrence cleared his throat, running his hand down the crease in his pant leg, and it was impossible to miss the uncomfortable glance he cast at his wife. She just quickly turned to stare out the window.

"Well, you wanted to know about Van Steenburgh Manor, correct?" he asked, taking it upon himself to just continue. "This house has been in the family for centuries—"

"One hundred-forty years, dear," Vivien interrupted sharply. "It hasn't quite been 'centuries', yet."

Ignoring her sarcasm, he proceeded. "The first son in each generation of Van Steenburghs takes it over and improves it in some sort of way."

Vivien snorted.

"You'll have plenty to do. There's an Olympic-sized pool outdoors, tennis courts, a private theater, and stables filled with horses for you to ride at your leisure. Or, if you like to read, our library has thousands of books—some dating back to the sixteenth century," went on. "We even have direct access to the Hudson River!" He boasted. "The house itself is planted on over thirty acres, with fields and fields of wildflowers and gardens. Would you believe that we hired a whole crew of gardeners last spring to plant fifty thousand flower bulbs?" I shook my head in awe. "One of Vivien's favorite things to do is sit out on the patio and eat her breakfast in the middle of the rose gardens. Why don't you tell her about it, my dear?"

She turned to me, her lips pursed. "One of my favorite things to do is sit on the patio and eat my breakfast in the middle of the rose gardens," she mocked, glancing back up at Lawrence with blatant annoyance before rolling her eyes and turning back to face the window.

At that point, I didn't really know what to think of my grandmother, and her husband. He appeared impervious to her indifference. She came across as if everything annoyed her. Meanwhile, I felt like he was trying to sell me his house...

"Oh! And you won't be alone, either," Lawrence rattled on. "My son Preston is coming home from college for a while. He's quite eager to meet you."

Son? He has a son? My mother never made any mention of him, nor would I have the time to ask, now!

"Alright Hope, we're coming upon Van Steenburgh Manor," Lawrence announced, his face brightening with the same excitement of a five year old getting the toy he'd been wanting. "Look out to your right, and wait for a break in the trees. That's when you'll see your first glimpse of your new home."

I did exactly as he asked—looking past Vivien—and I felt myself tremble with anticipation. We had driven past many big homes along the road we were taking. Very large estates, buried deep in the trees, down long winding drives. All along the way, Lawrence went on about this estate, or that estate. One belonged to an artist, one belonged to a President, and one belonged to a railroad tycoon. But then, I saw it! Van Steenburgh Manor! It looked like a beautiful stone palace perched on a hill out in the distance. It was gigantic, and I must admit, I was very impressed.

"Exceptional, isn't it?" He said it more as a statement, rather than a question. I was suddenly beyond overwhelmed.

And if I weren't impressed enough at first glimpse, when we actually pulled up the winding drive leading to the French Renaissance-inspired palace, it was enough to take my breath away! We passed through an extravagant pair of regal, iron gates, and we followed a long tree-lined driveway that led up to the front entrance. When I got out of the limo, all I could do was just stare up at it in awe. Charles got out to grab my bags, and Vivien went ahead inside, but all I could do was stand there, just gazing up at this magnificent palace. It was more beautiful than the pictures...

"Pardon?"

I whirled around and looked up at a confused Lawrence. My own look was blank.

"You said something," he prompted.

I honestly had no idea what I might've said. "I must've been talking to myself," I uttered sheepishly. "Don't mind me; I do it often. Mom always told me that it's a bad habit I need to break, before people started looking at me like I'm crazy."

He laughed. "Your mother *would* say that," he spoke with a glimmer of amusement in his eye. "I happen to talk to myself all the time, and I personally don't see anything wrong with it!"

He led me through the dramatic, heavy wooden doors, and my footsteps echoed throughout the foyer. There were floors of stone, Oriental rugs, and straight across the grand space was a set of French terrace doors. I tried to pay attention, but I was so taken by each and every detail adorning the luxurious space I was walking, that I was sure there was much I wasn't absorbing, as he explained where this-or-that was.. Beyond the French terrace doors was a ballroom. Off to the right, there was a huge formal dining area which Lawrence informed me was hardly ever used; with a fireplace that stood about fifteen feet high, and a long, cherry-stained table that I guessed had probably seen some grand affairs in its time. His office was here on the main floor as well, and so was the library—just beyond the staircase, and down the "gallery." It was exhausting trying to take it all in as he pointed and walked.

The grand staircase winded up and around to the second level, with dramatic banisters of mahogany wood. He was now telling me about an east wing, and something about a west wing, but I was just trying not to trip up the stairs behind him, and look like a total idiot.

"Here, on the second floor, are most of the suites," he explained. Wordlessly, I followed him down the hallway, and we passed by two doors before he opened one, leading me into a lavishly decorated suite complete with a sitting area, and a king-sized, four-poster bed. The furniture was stained a dark cherry color, which shone brilliantly in the sunlight, and everything was decorated in whites and various shades of purples. The room was three times bigger than the one I was used to, and looking straight ahead was a set of doors like the ones that led to the ballroom, with sheer white curtains hanging on each door. It seemed like an eternity as I stood there, taking a good look around, full of anxiety, and fearing I would take forever to learn my way around this gigantic house.

"This was your mother's bedroom," Lawrence spoke softly, snapping my attention and my gaze back onto him. His eyes glassed in the same fashion I'd seen my mother's do so many times before, when she was lost in her sea of memories. "When she and her mother moved in, she was fourteen. I wanted so much for her to like it here, and I had this whole room redecorated especially for her. Her favorite colors. Luxuries little girls only dream of..." Then he took a deep breath, and blinked, coming back to reality. "I hope you enjoy it." He walked across the room to the set of glass doors, and after unlocking them; he opened them and looked outside. "This balcony stretches across the entire wing," he informed me. "So you share this with all the suites on this side. You'll find that there is a wonderful view of the river, and the Catskill Mountains." His eyes explored mine for a brief moment. "Anyhow, I know you need to get settled in. You have a little while yet before dinner, so feel free to roam about the house, or the grounds, or really just do whatever you like. Though I warn you to not enter the woods just yet. I wouldn't want you getting lost. Wait at least until you have an afternoon to kill."

"Okay."

"I once had a child lost in those woods during a dinner party," he told me. "Had all the servants running about, and searching for him." He laughed, shaking his head. "Also, don't be afraid to talk to the servants. They certainly won't mind the company." *Servants.* Did they still call them that, these days? I nodded in acknowledgement, and he headed for the door. "There are a few outfits in your closet, already. Gowns, summer dresses, that sort of thing. If they fit, feel free to wear them if you like, but I do intend on taking you out to shop for a new wardrobe soon enough." He paused, looking at me with something in his eyes I simply couldn't recognize. "Welcome home," he spoke gently, his smile warm.

Then he simply turned and left the room, closing the door behind him.

I looked about the space I now stood in, and then slowly sat down onto the bed. My bed. The room faintly smelled of lemon—probably the cleaner that was used to polish the wooden fixtures. My father had always told me that the Lord works in mysterious ways. Mother always followed up on that by saying everything happens for a reason. As surreal as this felt, and as fresh as the loss of my parents was, I needed to be strong. I needed to look toward the future, and make the best of my situation. It seemed that now I had the world at my fingertips, and I was grateful that Lawrence welcomed me with open arms, and made me feel at home. It was obvious that Vivien was reluctant, but I was sure that in time, she would grow to need me, love me, want me, and see me as family. I was, after all, a part of her and the daughter that she valued so much.

Fate had indeed taken an ugly turn when it took my parents from me, but there had to have been a reason. *I was here for a reason.* I just needed to be patient, and understanding. And strong.

I stepped into my new bathroom and let my toes sink into one of its big white fluffy rugs. I ran my fingers along the marble countertops, and admired the large tub that inspired the sudden urge to fill it with hot, steamy water and bubbles. I then checked out the closet, and found that it was nearly full of clothes, already. Expensive gowns, cocktail dresses, summer dresses, and coats of fur, leather, wool... Upon closer inspection, I noticed that they were all about my size.

And they all appeared brand new, and didn't seem out of date, whatsoever.

I rubbed my eyes tiredly, heading for my suitcases, and I removed all of my own jeans, t-shirts, trendy dresses, shoes, etc., before placing them neatly on the shelves. I sat down at the vanity and fingered all the small bottles of perfume, wondering how many times my mother had done the same. This was a lot to take in. This room, this house, these people I was now expected to live with... Everything. I could literally feel my anxiety level elevating.

I still had some time before the sun went down, so I decided to go find the kitchen, and maybe have something light to snack on, before I journeyed the grounds. Downstairs I went, and I passed through the formal dining area before finally finding the kitchen. It was long, and bright—with windows all along the outer wall, between the counters full of food, and all the cabinets and shelves. An older-looking black man was humming as he worked busily, wearing a white apron that was stained with every color, and stirring some sort of custard. I froze for a second, wondering if I should even be in there, and he must have felt that someone was standing there watching him, because he turned slightly and glanced upward. Instantly, his eyes widened in delight, and he grinned from ear-to-ear.

"Sweet Jesus... girl—ya almost scared me to death! I thought I was seein' ghosts! If I didn't know betta, I'd think ya were your momma's incarnate. Ya must be Miss Hope!"

"Hello," I managed awkwardly. How in the world Lawrence and my grandmother found a country-speaking black man to work in their household was beyond me. Was this a kitchen, or did I walk through a time-warp!? It felt downright uncomfortable. But all I could do was force a smile.

"And sweet like ya momma, too," he exclaimed, forcing a real smile, as he put his spoon down, and stood to face me. "That smile takes me back in time, chile! The name's Redd. Redd Jacobs. I'm the chef 'round here. I'll make ya anythang ya like" he promised.

"Thank you," I accepted politely.

"Anytime. I remember how picky your momma was," he recalled. "So if ya anythang like her, I can expect the same. Are ya hungry now?" He asked in concern. "Made some fresh brownies this mornin'. Knew ya was comin'. Your momma always loved brownies, though she always worried 'bout spoilin' her figure," he said with a laugh. "She was only a kid, but she had the matured mind of a thirty year-old!"

I narrowed my eyes, looking at him with growing interest. "So you knew my mother well?"

He nodded, smiling as he picked up his spoon and continued stirring again. "Oh yes. She brightened up the house, soon as she got here. She'd come down every mornin' to say hello before she'd be on her way. Very sweet girl, she was."

"Do you know why she ran away from here, then?" He paused at the blunt question that spilled unapologetically from my lips, before I could even think to rein it in.

Then he shook his head and lowered his eyes back down to what he was making. "That's somethin' no one ever talks 'bout, Miss Hope. It's taboo. I advise that ya don' bring it up to Mist' Lawrence an' Miss Vivien right away, either."

I nodded thoughtfully, knowing full well that I hadn't intended to broach the subject with them, anyway. "I'll keep that in mind," I told him. "How long have you worked here?"

"My whole life," he answered, catching my look of surprise. "My momma grew up here, my mammy grew up here. My family has worked for the Van Steenburghs a long time." He sounded proud of that, but the idea of it made me queasy. "Why you look like that, chile?" He laughed at my apparently blatant discomfort. "It ain't like *that*," he spoke, inspiring a blush to wash over my cheeks. "I gets paid for what I do, 'round here. This ain't slavery days, no more."

My hands found my hips, and even through my own embarrassment that he was so obviously making light of, I could only cock my head at him and smile. "Okay, so if you've grown up here your whole life, why do you sound like a country boy just plucked off of a Georgia farm?"

His head rolled back on his shoulders, and the hearty laugh that roared from his belly was nothing but fun, for this middle-aged man with a lot of spirit. "I'm a product of my family," he answered, still chuckling. "Alabama, originally. Not Georgia. So've ya had the grand tour, yet?"

I couldn't wipe the disarmed smile from my face now, even if I wanted to. "Yes. Lawrence showed me around. I was just hoping to grab a quick bite to eat before I explore the grounds," I told him.

"Well go 'head, girl! There's some brownies over there, some cookies, cake, pies—ya do like that stuff, don'tcha?"

I nodded hungrily. "I love all that stuff, yes."

"Well help yourself," he invited.

I sat down on the counter top, and feasted on some freshly baked cookies, which were nothing like I'd ever tasted. I could almost feel my waistline expanding. I was in heaven! "Who else lives here?" I asked curiously, watching him grab an onion and begin chopping.

"We got Kate, who's Charles' wife. She's the headmaid 'round here. They's been here long as I can remember. Both of them lives in the slaves quarters—" he paused long enough to carefully watch my jaw drop, and then his laughter ensued. "Kidding! Just kidding," he insisted. "Really, I don't like to joke 'bout that kind of thang, but you make it too easy."

"Thanks. I feel pretty ignorant, right now," I confessed earnestly.

"Anyways, the servants quarters is that way." Still amused at my expense, he motioned back beyond the kitchen. "They comical together—quarrelin' the way they do, all the time. Don't let them scare ya with their bickerin'. Once, Kate got so mad she biffed him one, right in front of everyone at a dinner Mist' Lawrence was hosting!" He laughed, while I was having trouble just trying to envision anyone marrying that man who looked as if he might've been incapable of breaking a smile. "Then we got Preston," he said, making a face. "Heard that boy's comin' back here," he grumbled, his voice low. "He's quite the spoiled rich kid. Knows what he got, so he flaunts it to the world. What he needs to do is just stay in his fancy college, if ya ask me. But since ya didn't, I'll just keep my mouth shut."

I smiled amusedly. "He's that bad?"

"You'll see for yourself. Mist' Lawrence can't see, though. There are lot a-things Mist' Lawrence don't see, girl. I think he chooses not to see. And Preston is no exception."

"Okay but who is he?" I interrupted. "Is he... did my grandmother?" I was flustered by not even knowing what or how to ask. Luckily, Redd came to the rescue.

"He's Mist' Lawrence's adopted son. After he married Miss Vivien, she told him she didn't want no more chillren. Lindsey was a teenager when they got married, so she wasn't a baby no more. Lawrence was only twenty. He wanted a baby. He wanted a son. So he went out and got him one."

Lawrence was twenty, while my mother was fourteen?! "How old was Vivien at the time they got married?" This man was packed full of tidbits of information, and he definitely had my interest.

He laughed. "If I tell ya, ya gotta promise never to tell." He served me a look of warning. "Everyone round here gots a runnin' bet as to how old Miss Vivien really is. No one dares to ask her. But I know." I nodded eagerly, waiting for him to divulge this information that was such a ridiculously deep secret. "Miss Vivien was thirty-five."

That's right! My mother had mentioned her mother being fifteen years older than Lawrence. Still, I couldn't believe it, being that Vivien looked so much younger than him! Quick math in my head told me that Vivien was now fifty-four. Which placed Lawrence at thirty-nine. But never would I have guessed that my grandmother was that old!

"Don't look so surprised, girl!" Redd said amusedly. "Anyways, it was only two years later that ya momma ran away," he ended his story. Then suddenly, his eyes lit up. "Oh! Then there's Mist' Trent," he spoke with a smile. "I do hope ya get to meet him, Miss Hope. He's my favorite person in the world! Real good boy. Give ya the shirt offa his back, he would. Help ya with anythang."

"And who is he?" I shrugged. "Another house worker?"

The knife in Redd's hand continued to chop. "He's Kate an' Charles's boy. Actually, he ain't no boy, no more. He's twenty-one, now. Real smart, too. Graduated college when he was eighteen. Eighteen—kin ya believe it? His teachers were constantly advancing him through school. Heard he'd gone through elementary school in under two years. Very smart boy, he is. I reckon you'd call him a genius!"

Eighteen? He'd graduated college by eighteen? How!? At seventeen, I was going to be a senior in high school when it started back up, this fall. Whoever this Trent-person was, he intimidated me and I hadn't even met him, yet! As hard as I worked to make good grades, this guy made me feel like a dummy, already!

"An Italian boy, he is," Redd continued. "Takes afta his momma, Kate. Her parents came directly from Italy," he said, seeming to take pride in it, himself. "Drives the women crazy, he does. He never has steady girlfriends, though. The boy don't believe in love. I'm hopin' somebody might come along an' change his mind," he said, winking at me. My eyes as I felt myself blush. "Anyways, he travels the world. Says he tries to live anonymously. Free spirit. Makes his own money, doin' art and stuff."

I nodded, listening silently. It was apparent that Redd knew just about everything about everyone. I made a mental note that if I needed any extra information, I definitely knew who to go to.

" 'Course, I dunno where Mist' Trent is, now. Last I knew, he was in some place he call Naples."

"Florida?"

He shook his head. "Italy. But I sure do hope he comes back, Miss Hope, so ya kin meet 'em."

I smiled absently. "I hope so, too," I lied. "Anyway, thanks for the cookies, Redd."

I excused myself and exited the kitchen, passing back through the baronial dining room. Out of sheer curiosity, I stopped just outside the ballroom to peek inside. The doors were open now, and what I saw were seven extremely large bay windows spanning from floor-to-ceiling, forming a façade which curved outward, giving the ballroom a circular shape. The floor was a beautiful hardwood, and heavy burgundy-colored drapes hung about the enormous windows. Off to the right side of the room was a grand piano, and on the wall straight ahead was a fireplace that was even taller than the one in the dining area. From the dome ceiling, six chandeliers made of crystal sparkled like diamonds. Drinking it all in, I could almost hear music playing, and see people dressed in their finest gowns, waltzing around, sipping drinks, and mingling. It was simply beautiful.

"I'm surprised to see that you're still hanging around the house!"

I whirled around to find Lawrence approaching me from the grand foyer. "Just taking everything in," I replied humbly. "This place is just amazing."

"I thought for sure that you'd be outside, enjoying the fresh air and breathing in the scent of the flowers!"

"I was actually on my way outside," I admitted, "But I had to check out the ballroom first. How often do you use it?"

"A great many parties have been thrown in this room," he informed me proudly. "Since long before the Civil War, even. I even remember being a kid, sneaking down from my room every time my parents hosted a party in there. They would send me to bed, and yet I'd still want to sneak a peek, just to marvel at all the people dressed in their finest, just wishing I were a part of it. Vivien and I do throw parties in there quite often," he divulged. "We're always entertaining guests for this, or that. Vivien is quite the little hostess, and she's always organizing something. There's a function coming up in a week or so that we've been planning for a long time for associates of ours, so I can't fully pin that one on her. It'll be a good chance for you to meet everyone. Oh, and she always hosts a masquerade ball on New Year's Eve," he told me. "I'm sure you will love that. You women love disguises."

He walked me right over to the back door, and opened it for me, letting me know that dinner would be at five, before I stepped out. He apologized for not being able to show me around the gardens himself, but promised to do so later, if I desired. When he stepped back inside and closed the door, I found myself in a sea of roses, lilies, tulips, lilacs—and more! My senses were overwhelmed by all the fragrant flowers, and I marveled at their beauty as I crossed the stone patio. Beyond the patio was the pool, and I followed a stone path through the gardens lined with Greek statues and fountains.

It was such an incredible sight to behold.

Heading away from the gardens, and away from the house, the grounds turn to rolling hills of plush, green grass and wildflowers. The house itself was on a hill, up high, and when you gazed downward, you can see the river off in the distance, looming far and wide until it disappeared behind a thick forest of tall, dense trees. I followed the hills down, toward the river, and as I went along, I could hear it. Water crashing into rocks in the way that an ocean might. I followed its sound, until my feet landed on the sandy riverbank at the bottom of the property.

The river was nothing like the small, murky and dried-up rivers I was used to, back home. The water shimmered and danced beneath the sunlight, as its rays danced upon the water's surface. I glanced again to my right toward the thick, dark forest of trees to my right. I wouldn't dare go in there, but I was definitely intrigued by the idea that there might've been something in those woods.

When I had arrived back at the house, there was a woman sitting on the patio, by the pool. She was sipping on lemonade, and reading something she thought was funny. Based on description alone, I knew she had to have been the Italian maid Redd was talking about. She was stunning, with long black hair, and dark eyes lined heavily with thick lashes. She had a lovely olive complexion, and when she heard me coming, she glanced up, and her eyes grew wide, along with her smile. She jumped up, looking me over.

"You must be Hope!"

"Yes," I answered. "How are you?"

Her smile lit up her face. She was even prettier up close. "My name's Kate." She extended her hand to me. "It's a pleasure to finally meet you!"

She didn't look nearly old enough to have a twenty-one year old son. She didn't look a day over twenty, herself! I shook her hand, and her infectious smile found its way to my own face as I smiled back at her. I couldn't imagine what she would see in a man like Charles.

"You look just like your mother," she told me. "I bet you hear that a lot, don't you?"

I nodded. "Yes, thank you."

"I was so hurt when I heard what happened… She became like a sister to me, the couple years she lived here. She was just a few years younger than me, but I was so excited to have someone else around our – my – age." She paused at her own words, and even though I caught what she said, and figured she had to have only been referring to herself and Lawrence, I pretended not to notice. "I used to help her with her hair and makeup, for all the parties and things here at the house. She had such beautiful hair. Yours is just as beautiful," she added quickly, before sighing. "This must be so hard for you… losing her… How are you holding up?"

"Fine," I answered, trying to appear confident with my answer. "I'm taking it one day at a time."

"Well, if you ever need anyone to talk to, I'm here, honey. I know what it's like to lose someone. I lost my mother, too," she offered kindly.

"Thank you. And I'm sorry to hear that."

"You're gonna love it, here," she assured me brightly. "Isn't this the prettiest spot?"

I looked around, and nodded again. "It really is," I agreed.

"I've been here since I was a little girl, and still, there are times when this property will catch me off-guard and totally enchant me," she released breathlessly. Her eyes were lingering upon me now, sizing me up. "You look just like your mom did when she came to live here," she told me softly. Her long fingers reached out and took some of my hair between them. "I've had training which qualifies me to do manicures, hair styling, facials—you name any beauty ritual, and I can do it," she boasted. "Vivien paid for me to take courses. She decided that it would be perfect if she never had to leave the house anymore to get this stuff done. Then, after she had me do her nails one time, she decided that she didn't want me to work on her again. All that training has been a waste, since then." She bit the inside of her lip, and then smiled. "It's going to be fun to have another girl around here," she remarked brightly. "Are you on your way inside to see what 'Ole Jacobs is whipping us up for dinner, tonight? Have you met him, yet?"

"Redd?" She nodded. "Yeah, I met him just before."

She grabbed her magazine from the chair and began walking with me back inside. "Sometimes, while I'm working, I try to steer clear of him. Boy—he could talk my ear off!" She proclaimed jokingly. "Either that, or he's trying to force food down my throat."

It was that night when I learned that the dinner ritual at the manor was a formal affair. Every evening at five o'clock, Lawrence emerged to sit at the head of the table, and Vivien would stroll in to sit down about halfway through our meal. On this first night, Lawrence was asking me questions about myself, about school, about my parents. All the while, Vivien sat silently, and picked hastily at her food. Lawrence paid her no attention. When he finally decided to change the subject to something other than me, he turned it to Preston.

"He should be coming home soon," he announced brightly.

Vivien *and* Kate rolled their eyes, but Lawrence didn't seem to take notice of that, either. Charles, who sat beside his wife, glanced at me every so often, and I grew somewhat nervous under his watch. I tried my hardest to avoid looking at him. He gave me the creeps. Furthermore, I still couldn't understand for the life of me how he could convince someone as beautiful as Kate to marry him!

"And I must apologize, Hope, but Vivien and I will be leaving early tomorrow morning, and will be gone until late in the evening," Lawrence informed me. His tone was apologetic, and his eyes were pleading with me not to be mad at him. I wasn't mad. I certainly wasn't a child, after all. "It's just that we've already made the plans, and it's too late to back out. I really do hope that you understand."

"It's alright," I assured him. "I'll be fine."

Vivien immediately perked up, smiling for the first time all evening. "I told you! Didn't I tell you, Lawrence? I told you she wouldn't mind!"

He smiled gratefully, his eyes not leaving mine. "I thank you for being so understanding."

Feeling like my life had moved into the Twilight Zone, it was all I could do to hurry up and finish the food on my plate, while I could feel everyone's eyes periodically taking turns to study me. I hurriedly stood up to excuse myself, not two seconds after my plate was finished.. "Dinner was really good, thank you. But if it's alright, I'd like to go to my room and maybe go to bed early. So much to take in for one day," I smiled awkwardly.

Lawrence stood as well, just to say goodnight, and I awkwardly retreated from the dining room. Each stair that I climbed felt like a hurdle, to me. Until I thought about it, I didn't realize how much sleep I'd been deprived; I had hardly gotten a wink since my parents' death. Now my body was begging me for it, and I was more than willing to succumb. The plane ride, meeting my grandmother and her husband, the enchantment of Van Steenburgh Manor... not only was I physically exhausted, but I was emotionally drained, as well. I yawned as I ran my bathtub full of steamy water, and bubble bath that was scented of roses. The aroma took me back to the gardens I had just walked earlier, and I walked back to the closet to look for a robe. Funny how crisp and new the clothes in there looked...

Then again, there were many things at Van Steenburgh Manor that appeared frozen in time.

I grabbed a large fluffy terrycloth robe from the shelf, and then glanced over at the few long silk nightgowns hanging beside it. I ran my fingers along the sleek, blue material that almost matched the color of Vivien's eyes exactly. The chill of random, cold air that passed me by from somewhere caused my hand to immediately retract, and I removed myself from my closet with an odd sense of presence in the room with me that I could not place.

After I climbed into bed, I reached over to my night table, and opened the top of its two drawers. A small book of pictures was shoved towards the back of it, and I removed it to find that there were pictures of a little girl sitting on what must've been her father's lap. A split-second passed, before realizing it was my mother. And the man must've been my grandfather! I advanced through the pages, and my mother seemed to grow up right before my eyes. She stood with poise, and confidence, and she only grew more and more beautiful as time passed on. *This* was how she was raised. *This* was the kind of lifestyle that had molded and shaped her entire life.

And *this* was the place that made her run from it all.

I kept turning the pages, and somewhere between my grandfather disappearing from the pictures, and Lawrence entered them, there was something different about my mother. Her smiles were no longer genuine. In other pictures, her eyes almost looked...hollow. Then, after a while, even her phony smiles disappeared.

And oh... Vivien and Lawrence's wedding pictures. She looked like she belonged in a bridal magazine! Lawrence was positively handsome, and beside them was my mother, dressed in a simple pink gown. There were only a few pictures in the book after that, of my mother with a little boy. Those pictures were taken about the time she had run away. The little boy looked about three or four years old, I guessed. Preston, maybe? I had no clue. He had a mop of dark hair on his head, and a complexion like Kate's. Sure enough, the back of the picture read "Me and Trent." He was a cute kid.

I closed the picture book, and put it back into the drawer. Then I turned the lamp off, and not a moment after my head hit those fluffy pillows, I was out like a light.

Chapter 3

"Preston Van Steenburgh"

The next morning, I awoke completely refreshed! It was eleven by the time I finally showered, dressed, put on some make up, and headed downstairs. I remembered that Vivien and Lawrence were to be gone for the day. Which was more than fine, actually. It was the perfect opportunity for me to get acquainted with the grounds, and I intended to use it, as such. Besides, I was a big girl. I didn't need them here, anyway. Since the weather was so beautiful, I thought I would bring a book, find the river again, and spend my afternoon reading and napping under the sun.

The air was warm, with a cool breeze. The smell of flowers pervaded my nostrils and intoxicated me. I briefly contemplated the overgrown path that disappeared into the woods, wishing I were brave enough to tackle it on my own. But I would, another time. Instead I headed down the fields toward the river, and picked a grassy place under the sun that overlooked the water. We never had a view so pretty back home. It looked like something from a painting. The sky was bright blue, and the clouds were light and fluffy with hardly a break in the sunlight. The water sparkled, and the mountains in the distance were alive with color from the autumn trees. All along the other side of the river were mansions scattered about, lining the water. I must've been daydreaming awhile, because I was startled when I saw someone appear beside me, causing me to flinch where I sat.

I looked up to find a guy standing beside me casually, and gazing out at the river, himself.

"Olana is right over there," he said, nodding across the river, without even glancing down at me from behind his trendy, dark sunglasses. He just stood there, his hands shoved in his khaki pant-pockets.

"What?" I asked, wondering who he was.

"Olana," he repeated, now finally looking down at me. "Are you familiar with Frederick Church?"

"The painter?"

He shrugged, his golden blonde hair tousled by the breeze was falling over his forehead, and barely grazing his sunglasses. "Yeah, I guess. I don't know much about him, but my father likes him. That house, over there across the way, was his."

I nodded. "Oh."

He sat down on the grass beside me, and turned his gaze to me, again. "You must be Hope," he concluded.

"I get that a lot, lately," I joked. "Yes, I am. And you are...?"

"Preston Alexander Van Steenburgh," he announced, like he expected trumpets to sound at the mention of his name.

I raised my eyebrow. "You can say that all in one breath?"

He laughed. A short laugh. "That's good... You've got a sense of humor." If I had insulted him, which I thought I might have, it was gone in the next instant. "I like a sense of humor in a girl."

I caught myself staring at him blankly, before clearing my throat uncomfortably, and turning back to the river. "So when did you get in? I know that Lawrence and Vivien have been expecting you," I said, trying to fill the awkward silence.

"Late last night. I'm not sure if they even know I'm home, yet. They were already gone when I got up this morning. What are your plans for the day? I've got nothing planned, so maybe we could do something. Is there anything you'd like to do or see around here?"

"I'd like to see what's in those woods, actually," I confessed. "Lawrence advised me not to try it because I'd probably get lost, but after Redd told me there was something in there that would interest me, it was all over," I said with a laugh.

He frowned. "There's nothing to those woods," he pushed aside quickly. "Redd just needs to stay concerned with what's next for dinner," he snapped quickly.

My eyebrow lifted at him. "So, what's in that forest, then?" I challenged lightly.

"Trees," he answered.

I closed the book in my lap. "I guess I'll just check it out by myself," I responded nonchalantly.

"Fine," he caved, gruffly. "Let's get this over with then, shall we?"

I jumped up, and so did he. I didn't wait for him to lead; I marched towards the place where the overgrown path took us into the darkness of the woods, and he sped up his pace to keep close to my side. "Remember—you *did* say you know your way out of here," I reminded him as we entered it.

"Well, I didn't lie to you," he replied. "Have you met Trent, yet?"

I looked up at him and shook my head. "No, I haven't."

"I haven't seen him around, either. It's probably a good thing," he muttered. I didn't know what to say in response to that, so I quietly fell a step behind him, weaving in this direction, and that. He made a right, as I observed the quiet, peaceful nature that surrounded us.

Then my eyes caught it. Out in the distance, almost blending in with the trees. I paused, and then nearly jumped out of my skin when Preston grabbed my hand to pull me along with him. "This way," he prompted.

I took a step, but then stopped. "What's that? Over there?" He acted like he didn't see it, so I pointed, jerking my hand free from his. "That cabin," I pressed on.

"Huh. You're right. It's a cabin."

"Are you sure you and Vivien aren't related?" I rolled my eyes at his sarcasm, and followed my curiosity in the direction of this tiny, wooden structure.

"It's abandoned," Preston called after me. "Probably a fire hazard!"

"All the more reason to explore it," I called behind me, feeling like I had found some little treasure in the woods, that I couldn't wait to check out!

As I got closer, I saw there were two wooden steps, leading up to a wooden porch, and on either side of the door were windows, but inside looked very dark.

"I wonder if this was what Redd was talking about," I muttered in thought. The crunching of leaves behind me signified that Preston had just now caught up.

"Redd's a senile old man. My dad used to use this as his little hideaway," he explained. "I used to play there all the time when I was little. But no one's kept up with this place in forever, and we don't even know what kind of things are living in there." I took notice that there appeared to be freshly planted bushes on either side of the porch. If it were really abandoned, nobody would bother to plant anything there.

"Let's go inside," I suggested,

"C'mon," Preston pleaded softly. "It's just an old, beat-up cabin. Let's go back down to the river, instead."

"Where's your sense of adventure?" I teased lightly. Knowing that he wasn't going to give in, I promised myself that I would somehow remember how to get back there, and I silently followed him through the thick trees, until we found ourselves on a small trail, taking us to the river. All the while,

I was making plans on getting back to the cabin. Perhaps I would make it *my* hideaway, next.

We stopped at the same place, overlooking the water, and we both sat down, looking out at the pretty view. His eyes swung my way, studying me once again. "Feel better, now that you've gotten that out of your system?"

I turned semi-annoyed eyes upon him, and reopened my book. "Sure," I lied.

"It's just that I don't like being in those woods. I would much rather be out in the open, in the sun. You know, my father wasn't wrong about you being very pretty," he said, and I met his eyes with my own. Then I looked away. "So, do you have a boyfriend?"

I looked back at him quickly. "No," I answered. "I do not."

"Why not?"

I couldn't tell if he was trying to get to know me, or taking great joy in seeing me squirm. "Why do you ask?"

"Just wondering. Perhaps we can go out, sometime. I'm single, as well!" He smiled brightly.

"You're also my uncle. Has that not dawned on you?" I retorted.

"Au contraire! We are not related by blood. I was adopted!" He pointed out, obviously having fun with this.

I looked to him with a mixture of disgust and awe. "Well, would you sleep with your best friend's girlfriend?" He looked like he was prepared to argue that question, so I cut him off before he could even begin. "No. You wouldn't. Because that's wrong, and weird. And the same rule applies here." I punctuated my statement with a smile.

He looked thoughtful for a moment. "How does that correlate with this situation? You're not going out with my best friend, are you? Because, believe me—I'd break that rule."

"Would you really do that?" I asked.

"Maybe the question should be whether I already have, or not," he replied with a sly smile.

I rolled my eyes. "That, I don't want to know."

"You're difficult," he stated, grinning. "A challenge. Something I don't encounter very often, around here! Not with anyone who knows who I am, anyway."

I shook my head.

"Oh, come on," he reasoned. "You can't blame me for hitting on you, can you?"

I gave him a look. "Is that the line you feed to all of your victims?"

"Just the ones I deem worthy," he replied.

I looked down at my watch melodramatically, and began to stand up. "Well, I'm done, here," I announced, patting the grass off my pants. "It was nice to meet you, Mister Preston Alexander—," I paused, and inhaled deeply while he stood, well-aware of my mockery "—Van Steenburgh. But I regret to say that I do have to get away from you before I say something that will really get us off on the wrong foot, while there's still a chance you can redeem yourself!"

He reached out and grabbed my hand, not letting me go any further. "Wait a second, Hope. I apologize." He stepped closer to me, and I looked up at him cynically. "I didn't mean to offend you," he spoke, his voice low. I was frozen, not knowing what to say or do.

"It's alright," I accepted uncomfortably.

"Do you have any plans for this evening? Has my father got you bustled with things to do and places to see, yet?"

I shook my head. "No, I don't know..." I trailed off, glancing up at him. He had taken a step closer, and I felt really awkward and ill at ease.

"Perhaps we can go out, this evening," he suggested. I said nothing in response, and then he caught me by surprise, bringing his lips to mine quickly. I backed off immediately, startled and appalled by his audacity. He reached out again to grab my wrist, and I yanked my hand from his reach.

"Past the point of redemption now," I snapped at him. Disgusted, I turned and started away, my pace nearly a jog.

"Oh come off of it. We're not related!"

I shook my head, unable to believe my ears. I turned around to let him catch up to me. "What—so that makes what you just did okay? We may not share the same blood, but we're still 'family' now, don't you think?"

"I thought they didn't care about that much, down south where you came from," he sneered, his lips forming a ruthless smile.

My blood boiled at the sound of that, and before I knew it, I had reached out and slapped him hard across the face. Stunned, his jaw dropped, and I whirled back around to head towards the house, furious.

"You have no right to slap me!" He yelled.

"And you have no right to assume that I'm some easy, backwoods hillbilly girl!" I fired back.

"Hope, don't be such a baby!" He called after me. "You know you liked it! Besides, do you really think your little simple, country girl act is going to fly around here? It's not gonna happen! You should feel honored that I would even *want* to touch you!"

I shook my head, seething. "You need to come off of it, Preston. You're no prize!"

"That's what you think! I'm considered one of the town's most eligible bachelors!"

I whirled around to find him approaching fast. "Well if that's the case, I'd say that this town's in trouble!"

I was so angry that by the time I got back to the gardens, I could have screamed! I was thinking about tearing that golden mop of hair right out of his head when I nearly collided with Kate, who was stepping out onto the patio.

She shrieked, and I jumped, too. "Oh, honey, you startled me!" She said with a laugh, then taking notice of my distraught look. "What's the matter?"

"Hope! Get back here, dammit!" I heard Preston call from somewhere behind me.

"Oh, it's him," she muttered, looking past me. "I should have known."

She sat down in the reclining lawn chair, and I stood with my hands on my hips, facing Preston.

"Where do you get off acting like some righteous bitch?" He demanded, his eyes blazing with anger. "You don't even belong here. You're not one of us."

"You have your nerve saying that, Preston Van Steenburgh." I pronounced his last name with sarcasm dripping from my voice. "After all, just remember that I was born into this family. I wasn't adopted into it. I might even belong here more than you."

That hit home. It looked like his head was about to explode, and Kate's eyes grew wide before she hid her face behind the magazine she was reading. It wasn't too effective, however. Her eyes clearly displayed her amusement.

"You'd better not go telling my father any stories, Hope," he threatened. His eyes were filled with fury, as he waved his finger at me threateningly.

"I wouldn't dare dream of it, Preston," I told him in a mocking tone. "Unlike someone of your character, I don't go running to Daddy every time something doesn't go my way. Now just stay out of mine," I growled.

"You wouldn't even be here at all if your mother wasn't such a slut, running all about town until she got pregnant and was forced to leave here," he shot back.

I slapped him again, this time taking us both by surprise. I was shaking, now, and tears were threatening to spill over. "You didn't even know my mother," I hissed. He said nothing now, and both of his cheeks were bright and red. Wordlessly, he charged past me, and slammed the door to the house, behind him. I crumpled into the chair next to Kate, and held my head in my hands.

"That boy's been nothing but trouble ever since they brought him, here," Kate spoke softly. "You know, I used to say that he was just clumsy, but after a while of watching him—actually watching him closely—I realized that he wasn't clumsy." I looked up at her, and she brought her glass to her lips, and took a sip. "It was almost on a daily basis that vases would be broken, things would be knocked off the shelves. Hope, I had to go around and clean up after him constantly. But one day I decided that I was going to just kinda see what he was doing to make these messes. It wasn't that he was rambunctious. I literally saw him just take these things off the shelves, and throw them on the floor to shatter them into pieces!" She shook her head. "And every single time that you would ask him what happened, he would hide behind crocodile tears, and say it was an accident. Just like the time that Vivien's cat drowned in the pool."

My eyes widened. "Her... cat?"

She nodded, taking another sip of her drink. "Vivien was looking everywhere for that cat. It never went outside—ever. We all knew not to let the cat out. She spent all day looking for that cat, driving everyone up the wall, and then Charles found it outside. In the pool. He immediately called me out there to see for myself, and we couldn't figure out how it had gotten outside in the first place—let alone into the pool, where cats just won't go by themselves, anyway. That is, until we heard someone laugh, and I caught a glimpse of Preston hiding behind those bushes over there. He was seven, at the time."

I sighed. "So he's just looking for attention, then?"

"I don't know what he was looking for, Hope, but if it was attention he was seeking, it was attention he got. We were constantly questioning him as to what happened to this, or that. He profusely denied having anything to do with the cat, and of course, Lawrence sided with him. I know for a fact that Vivien blamed Preston—and rightfully so—and since that day, she hasn't said more than two words to Preston at a time. It's crazy.

"And it's not that he's stupid," she continued. "He really is intelligent. He makes excellent grades in school. Something's just not right up there," she said, pointing to her head. "From what I hear, he's near the top of his class, has lots of friends, does well in society, knows how to present himself—he just doesn't know how to act, here."

"Maybe he just knows that no matter what he does, he can get away with it," I offered. "If Lawrence always backs him up, taking his side. Maybe he just feels the need to keep testing that."

"You might be right."

"Trent popped in today to say hi while you an' what's-his-face was out roamin' 'round."

I was back in the kitchen again, looking for something to eat. "Askin' all sorts of questions 'bout ya, Miss Hope, he was. Askin' where ya was, an' stuff." Quite honestly, I didn't want to hear about it. "Whatcha lookin' like that for, Miss Hope? He's a good boy. Certainly betta than that thang ya was just out with."

"First off, I just want to clarify that I was not out with Preston," I corrected him adamantly. "He found me, then proceeded to make a nuisance of himself, and ultimately ticked me off and chased me back inside. I just wanted to get that off my chest so that you know," I told him as he laughed at my annoyance. "What time do you think Lawrence and Vivien will be back?" I asked.

He shrugged. "'Bout seven or eight, I reckon."

I nodded, thinking about that damned cabin again. But I had to make another stop, first. I headed to the door.

"Where ya goin'?"

"I want to visit my parents," I told him, exiting the kitchen, and heading down the back foyer. I had thought I caught a glimpse of the burial grounds when Preston and I were down by the river.

Back outdoors, I went. Through the flowers, which now gave me a headache. Straight ahead, over the fields, before cutting to my left. I figured that was where the family plot was.

I figured right.

I came to a gate, and surrounding the burial grounds was a small stone wall, maybe about 3 feet high, wrapping all the way around. Reluctantly, I pulled the gate open, and it creaked in protest. I saw where my parents were buried immediately, as the soil on the ground was fresh. Or at least, I was hoping that was them... For some reason, there were no headstones.

The other tombstones looked ancient. Time had aged them to the point where on many of them, you couldn't make out some of the dates of birth and death, or even the names. Not that I would know who these people are in the first place. It didn't matter. I walked back to where I presumed my parents were, and knelt down before them.

It seemed unreal that only a week before, I had seen them alive and well. It wasn't like I had any time to prepare for their departure. It wasn't like they had an illness, and that they knew they were going to die. It was just too sudden for me. I had no time to deal with it, just as I hadn't had sufficient time to mourn. Instead, they were gone in an instant, and I was left with no one. Panic and fear hit me like a ton of bricks where I knelt, as I recalled the events that took place, leading me to live with people whom my mother deemed horrible. I was brought to a place that she fled from years ago, for reasons so awful that she refused to talk about.

Had she ever stopped to think that I might have to be brought here? That one day, I would have to face these people, and possibly the same problems that forced her to leave? Why couldn't she have warned me about her mother, who quite honestly didn't seem to care that I was around? Why does her stepfather seem almost too good to be true? Preston couldn't have been a factor, if he was even around, yet. What could possibly have made her feel like it was hopeless, here? Was she just being selfish? Was it just because her mother and father split, that she felt bitter, and she left to punish her own mother?

These were things she would never tell me. The chance was gone. We would never be able to have another mother/daughter talk—about her past, or about anything. When I needed her the most, she wasn't able to help me. I was on my own, now.

And how strange it was that Lawrence and Vivien hadn't even hosted a funeral service for them. In fact, since I'd been here, they hadn't mentioned a word about it. They were buried the day before I had arrived at Van Steenburgh Manor, and not a word had been spoken about them. They were just... swept under the rug.

I would've given anything just to have my parents back, be back in my hometown, and act like this had never happened. But, of course, that was impossible.

Once it started getting dark, I headed back toward the house. I was tired and frustrated, and part of me didn't even care to wait for Lawrence and Vivien to come home, just to be polite and say hello.

I just wanted to be left alone.

Chapter 4

"Breaking and Entering"

All during the next week, Vivien spent her days planning for the social event that Lawrence mentioned was coming up. I found that her behavior during the first few days of my stay was unchanging. She made no effort to speak to me. Really, she made no effort to speak to anyone. She would never emerge from her room earlier than noon every day, unless she had an appointment at the spa, or brunch with a friend. Then, once she did surface, she would come downstairs smelling of sweet perfume—her make-up immaculate and not a hair out of place. She would announce to everyone and no one in particular her plans of either shopping, or her bridge club, or having tea with the mayor's wife, or whatever else she had to do that day that made her feel important. It quickly dawned on me that I may never truly know my grandmother—and it seemed that perhaps she preferred it that way. She did, however, pause one afternoon and manage to tell me that for her elaborate party, I would have to be dressed in my finest, and be on my best behavior.

When she asked if I had attended any classes on etiquette, I replied that I hadn't, and she scowled in disdain and said she'd have to see what she could do about that.

"I cannot have you opening your mouth around people, and acting stupid," she told me, causing me to bite my tongue for fear of saying something to disrespect her for her ignorant assumption. "Keep your mouth shut unless spoken to, and if you're in doubt about what to do at any point during the party, please pull me aside and ask," she said, thinking that she was actually helping me. "Just make sure you address me by 'Vivien'," she instructed with a painted smile. "I don't want to broadcast to everyone that I'm older than they might think. I put a lot of effort into projecting a very youthful, vibrant appearance."

Lawrence didn't seem to notice Preston's hateful stares directed my way, but then again, I think Redd was right. Lawrence didn't see a lot of things when it came to Preston. He only saw what he wanted to see. Even though Preston and I avoided each other like the plague after our initial introduction, Lawrence seemed so happy to have the both of us around that he was oblivious to the fact that we never spoke, and took great pains to stay as far away from one another as possible. During dinner, we would eat and only direct our talk to Lawrence. Vivien only picked at her food every evening. I supposed that was how she stayed as thin as she was. That, and she firmly believed that any kind of eating done in front of anyone else looked sloppy.

"Hope, you start from the outside and work your way in," she told me at the table during one dinner, pointing at the forks and spoons on each side of the plate. "You can't just randomly pick up whatever silverware looks good and start to use it, nor can you use the same fork for all dishes—it's just not sanitary!"

Not sanitary? It was all going to the same place, anyway. Either way, one fork or three forks were going to end up in my mouth. But I just sat and listened, allowing her to think that she was giving me pearls of wisdom. Inside, I found it all pretty ridiculous and petty.

Preston would go on to Lawrence forever at the dinner table, about his fancy law school, and all of the pretty, smart and popular girls he would take out. Then Lawrence would ask him if the money he supplied him with every month was enough, and then Preston would coyly get him to "up" his allowance. It wasn't totally the fact that Preston was so manipulative, but Lawrence seemed to have a big heart, as well. I knew that he would do the same for me. From the time I'd already been there, he was more than eager to make sure I was living comfortably. He made plans to take me out and buy me new clothes one afternoon, and go with me to pick out pretty new things for my room. Vivien never attended with us, but she did take the duty of arranging for me to have my hair done, and a facial with her cosmetician.

Overall though, my two guardians really didn't have too much time to spend with me. Lawrence made up for time lacked, with money. Money that I really didn't have any use for. Not that I really needed their attention, either. In fact, it wasn't really until the day of Vivien's gala that Lawrence took the time to invite me to his cluttered, dusty office for a 'private conversation,' he called it Up until that time, he and I really hadn't had much time to really talk, outside of the hurried "hellos", "goodbyes", "is everything going okay?" and "I'll see you laters". And I had gotten along in those days, just fine.

Now he sat behind his mahogany desk, and I took a seat in the chair before it. He clasped his hands and rested them on his desk, smiling pleasantly as he leaned forward.

"Well, you've been here for a little while, now. What do you think about the place? About living here?"

What, was this an evaluation? I smiled in response, not quite sure what to say. "This place is beautiful," I answered confidently. "Redd is wonderful. I love talking to him, and Kate's really nice, too."

"What about Preston?" He asked quickly, eyeing me closely.

"What about him?" I asked slowly.

"How are you two getting along?"

What could I say? That I disliked him and didn't want him within twenty feet of me? No, that's too blunt. "We really haven't had the chance to really get to know one another, yet," I answered carefully.

He nodded. "I want you to like him, Hope. It would mean so much to me for you two to become close. He is my adopted son, but I want nothing more than him to really be a part of this family, you know? But without further ado, I brought you in here so that I could go ahead and lay down a few rules, Hope," he started, sitting back in his chair, unclasping his hands, and folding them across his chest. "Like I stated earlier, you've had some time to adjust to your surroundings. I think that if we are to be successful guardians to you, we must have our expectations out in the open, so you can adhere to them without any questions. Understood?" I nodded. "Good. First, and foremost, we must always be completely honest with one another." He leaned forward again. "There is nothing I cannot stand more than a liar, Hope. If I catch you in a lie, all privileges will be taken away until I see that I can trust you, again. Lying goes hand in hand with cowardice, and I also hate cowards.

"Always be on your best behavior. Vivien has brought it to my attention that you're lacking in the etiquette department. Now, I realize tonight's party has come upon us too soon to possibly be able to squeeze some instruction in, but I expect you to exercise your best judgment until you begin school. We are having some of the most important, wealthy people in this area over this evening, and it's important that you do not embarrass us in any way. No chewing with your mouth open, don't interrupt people when they're in the middle of conversation, and I don't necessarily believe that you should only speak when spoken to, but I strongly believe that you shouldn't speak unless you have something truly intelligent to say. Do you understand that, as well?" I nodded.

"Furthermore," he continued, his voice softening, and his gaze leaving me, and instead focusing downward, to his desk. "Don't bother Vivien. She doesn't need added pressures to her already complicated life."

My heart sank. Sure, I got that Vivien didn't really care much about anyone, or anything in the house. It was easy to see. But hearing it? It felt like a slap in the face. "I see," I uttered weakly.

Lawrence's eyes glanced at me, and then flicked away. "She needs time," he spoke gently. "You coming here seemed to open old wounds, regarding your mother leaving us. Granted, you aren't her, but you look enough like her, and in a lot of ways, you're her all over again. She just doesn't want to get hurt."

"It's unfair for her to just assume I'm going to do the same things my mother did to upset her," I piped in. "I'm her grand-daughter, and she doesn't even acknowledge me when I'm in the same room as her, and if she does, it's to be rude."

"Well, you don't understand Vivien. My wife is like an ostrich, who would much rather bury her head in the sand and pretend that everything is fine, and that problems don't exist."

"Yes, you're right. She'd much rather pretend that I don't exist, and she's doing a good job."

He sighed, and stood up. "Give her time, Hope. She might surprise us both, and come around. If it means anything to you, having you here has already brightened up this house, and given it life that it hasn't seen in a long time. I thank you for that."

I couldn't help but to smile at his compliment. He seemed sincere. I stood up, as well. "Thank you."

"Sure. Now, go do whatever you girls do, to get ready for the party, tonight," he spoke with a wink. "I know it takes you ladies forever, that's for sure!"

Having no idea what to really expect, I nodded in acknowledgement and turned to leave. I retreated upstairs, and to my closet I went. Good lord, what was I supposed to wear?! Red, blue, black, long, short— every dress was different! I was at a loss, until I heard someone knock on the door, behind me. I turned, and Kate stood in the doorway, grinning.

"Lawrence asked me to check on you." She stepped inside and closed the door behind her. "But I told him you'd be fine. After all, you're a girl, and we were born to get all dressed up and pretty, right?"

I shook my head, flustered. "I have no idea what to wear. In fact, I've never done anything like this, and I have no idea where to even begin!"

She smiled. "There's nothing to it." She headed into my closet, bypassing the three gowns I held in my hands, and seconds later she emerged with a pretty dress with a few different shades of dark blue. It had a strap on one side, and the other shoulder was strapless. "Try this one on."

I handed her the other gowns, and took the dress from her hands, disappearing into the bathroom. I unzipped it, stepped into it, and pulled it up, admiring the beautiful subtle pattern on the fluid material. It was classy but stylish at the same time. But—

"Shoes!" I panicked, coming out of the bathroom, looking at her helplessly.

She stood there for a moment, eyeing me up and down, and she nodded in approval. "That dress flatters you. But you're right. Shoes." She disappeared back into the closet, and emerged with some black heels. "These will do just fine. Try them on and see if they will fit."

In the next few hours, she managed to transform me into magazine material, as well as getting herself ready, as well. She chose a simple, slender, strapless black gown that hugged her body, and went to the floor. While I was bathing, she set her hair in big rollers, and once I was done, she had already finished her make-up. It didn't take much to make her beautiful. She curled my hair with a large curling iron, and then swept it up with some sparkling barrettes, until it was loosely piled on my head, with some tendrils hanging down to frame my face. She plucked a few stray hairs in my eyebrows, and then applied my make-up quickly, but to perfection. My eyes were dark and smoky, and my lips were flushed with a rosy pink. I felt like a million dollars, and even I had to admit—I looked it.

"Lawrence has me afraid that I'm going to do or say something stupid." I told her nervously, before filling her in on what he'd said to me, earlier.

She made a face and waved it off. "Honey, don't think for one minute that any of those people are better than you," she told me. "Anytime you start to feel inferior, just picture those people, sitting on the commode, with their pants around their ankles." She winked at me. "Because trust me, they're regular people, just like you and me."

I couldn't help but to laugh at her. She was raw, but honest—and true. I thanked her a hundred times for being a help to get me ready, and once we were both done, we walked downstairs together. I could already hear the commotion. I asked her if we were late, and she told me that if anything, making a late entrance was a good thing, as long as it were a fashionable one. I heard soft music coming from the ballroom, and I heard Lawrence's thunderous laugh. Kate left me at the bottom of the staircase so she could go into the kitchen to see if Redd needed any last minute help. I had intended on going with her, but she laughed and told me to quit being nervous, and to get over to the party. Vivien was standing in the doorway of the ballroom, with Lawrence standing behind her. They were talking to another couple who apparently had just arrived, and were on their way in. Lawrence and the man, who looked a lot older than he, shook hands. Vivien leaned in to speak into the woman's ear, and they both giggled before Vivien caught sight of someone else that she must've wanted to talk to, and she fluttered off.

She was a portrait of perfection, in her black gown. Her golden hair was in a sleek chignon and from her ears dangled very heavy looking diamonds. Lawrence was dressed black also, and I had to admit— they made a splendid-looking couple. As Vivien had wandered away, he glanced over and spotted me standing reluctantly at the bottom of the stairs. Immediately, he gestured for me to come to him, so I did, and he took my hands in his own to get a good look at me.

"You are positively ravishing!" He exclaimed. "Ordinarily, my wife is the belle of the ball, but I think tonight you give her a run for her money!"

I smiled, feeling slightly self-conscious. "Thank you, Lawrence. I'm just hoping I don't make myself look like an idiot, tonight."

"Well, just try not to talk about subjects you are ignorant on," he offered simply. I looked up at him blankly, and wanted to tell him that I probably wouldn't have anything in common with any of the people here tonight, anyway. I really wanted to just run back upstairs and not come out of my room for the rest of the night! "Now, stop looking so frightened, and come with me," he invited, holding out his arm for me to put my arm through. I did, and we entered the ballroom.

The sparkling lights hanging from the ceiling took my breath away. There must have been at least thirty couples there already dressed to the nines, laughing, talking, and mingling... We stopped at a small group of men, and Lawrence broke his own rule of interrupting.

"Good evening, gentlemen!" he cut in, grinning at them, while they turned and smiled, greeting Lawrence. "I'd like to introduce you to Hope. She's staying here with us. Hope, these are a few of my colleagues." He went on, introducing them by name, and each of them took my hand. I smiled graciously, speaking slowly and deliberately. They seemed relatively harmless. Perhaps Kate was right.

"Well where are you from?" One of them asked. "Will you be here long?"

"I'm from—"

"She's from down south," Lawrence interjected. "She's a relative of Vivien's. Her family needed help, so we have decided to take her in, full time." He made it sound like a job.

"Distant relative? They look a lot alike, Lawrence. It's uncanny, really. Does her entire family look alike?" This drew laughter from the other men. I felt my face redden.

"Well, I do agree they look alike, and for that I cannot complain. I have a house with two of the world's most beautiful women," he boasted proudly.

Inside, I was seething. Wasn't it bad enough that Vivien had denied me any rights of calling her "Grandmother?" And my family didn't need "help." They were *dead*!

And honestly, when it came down to it, these people really weren't my family, either. Not if they could so readily deny me.

"Excuse me, Lawrence. I need some water," I told him, removing my arm from his. I'm not even sure if he heard me, since he hardly acknowledged me, except for a brief nod, before he jumped back into the conversation.

"It was nice meeting you, Hope," one of the men called to me as I started away.

Likewise.

I went over to the bar to grab a glass of water, and I spotted Kate across the room. She looked like she may have been bickering with Charles, who stood close to her, looking quite miserable. People were still pouring into the room, and upon glancing around I then spotted Preston. He did, in fact, look quite handsome. He ran his fingers through his thick, golden hair, and he was flirting with one of the few other younger women attending tonight's affair. Unlike his father's formal attire, Preston only wore black slacks, with a pressed button-up that brought out the blue of his eyes. His smile was charming enough that for a moment, I forgot how irritated he turned out to be. Until he looked up, and his eyes caught mine. His expression was as cold as ice, and it locked with mine until I looked away in disgust.

"Oh please, Gavin. If you had any real artistic bone in your body, you'd appreciate fine artists such as Escher. The man was a genius!"

I paused to listen.

"Alright, well what about Kandinsky?" I heard a man challenge, somewhere behind me. "Was he not a pioneer of modern abstract art?" Finally, a conversation that I could identify with.

"You said it, Brent. *Abstract.*" These men didn't sound too old, though I wasn't going to turn around just yet. "It's not the same as surrealism."

"Dali was the king of surrealistic art," another spoke up. Dali also happened to be my favorite artist.

"Well, technically, he was kicked out of the Surrealist Group."

"Because Andre Breton 'expelled' him from the group in 1934, but he is still regarded as one of the most prominent surrealists out there."

"Yes, definitely," another agreed. "I admire all of his work up until his religious pieces, really."

"Oh, what was the name of that one with you know, all the clocks? Do you know which one I'm talking about?"

If ever I was to find my "niche" tonight, it was now or never. " 'The Persistence of Memory'," I interjected, turning around to face a group of approximately seven men, ranging from maybe twenty to thirty, whose eyes were all now curiously fixed upon me.

"Yes, but isn't there another piece involving timepieces, as well?"

I looked up at the handsome stranger who acknowledged me. His eyes were dark, pools of black ink, and they settled on mine with intensity. For a brief moment I forgot what it was he had asked. "There is, but it's only one clock. 'Clock Explosion.' The one he's referring to, with the many clocks, is the one I mentioned first."

I found it hard not to stare at this beautiful man standing there staring at me. His lips were full, and they were pulled up in one corner as if he were poised to smile. A dimple played in and out of his cheek. His hair such a dark brown, almost black, and it was pulled back into a slick ponytail at the start of his neck. He was tall, with broad shoulders. His nose was straight and narrow, and his features were nothing short of perfect. He had an olive complexion, and when he smiled, he revealed a set of straight, sparkling white teeth.

"Well, wasn't he kind of strange? He was the guy with the funny mustache, right?" I turned and nodded to the gentleman on my left.

"Yes, he was the one with the mustache," I confirmed.

"Alright, well this is interesting," another jumped in, eyeing me. "I take it you are a fan of Dali?"

I nodded. "Very much, so. He's one of my favorites."

"Alright, well then how do you feel about pieces such as the one with the girl who's being sodomized?" He cocked his head to the side, and raised one of his eyebrows. I glanced around to the rest of the group, and they eyed me, as well.

"I'm not offended by it, if that's what you're asking," I denied. "He had painted that specifically for someone," I told them.

"Okay, well what about the other paintings, crudely depicted with genitalia and other hints of sexual activity?"

"Well, Dali used to pride himself on being the greatest painter of the female posterior," I countered. "Now, I'll remind you that not all of Dali's work have sexual overtones, but his suggestive pieces are indeed erotic, in my opinion as well as many others."

I glanced over at the handsome stranger again, who just seemed to be watching on, silently. His eyes never left mine, and inevitably I felt myself start to blush.

That's when Preston stepped up behind me, and grabbed my arm. I gave him a perplexed look and gently tried to free my arm, but he wouldn't let me.

"Come with me."

I shook my head, looking up at him like he was ridiculous. "No thanks, Preston"

His grip on my arm tightened. "My father asked me to dance with you," he told me through clenched teeth.

"Well tell him no, then," I retorted.

"Look, I don't want this either, but he's over there watching us right now, and I think he'd be greatly disappointed if we didn't." I glanced past him, and sure enough, Lawrence was on the other side of the room, smiling our way, and waiting.

I swallowed hard, and allowed him to awkwardly lead me away without even excusing myself from the group of men. I couldn't help but to roll my eyes as Preston took my hand, and then without warning, he pulled me close to him, so that our bodies were tight together. Furious, I tried to take a step back from him, but his hand was firm on my lower back, and he held me to him. When I looked up at him, he had a wicked smile on his lips.

"It's not so bad, is it?" He asked sarcastically.

"How long do we have to do this?" I demanded.

"Hell, I don't know. As long as it takes to make my father happy, I suppose. Look at him. He thinks we're enjoying ourselves." He stared down at me, his eyes full of trouble. "You know, my father has it in his mind that you and I should get together."

"You're *not* serious."

"Oh, but I am. Believe me, I can tell you right now that it's not going to happen, but I'd still like to take you for a test drive," he said with a chuckle.

"Your key will never make it to my ignition, Preston," I snidely retorted, taking a step backward.

He pulled me right back to him, even harder. "I usually get what I want, when I want it," he smiled casually. "You'll get used to that. If I decide that I want you, I can have you, too. You might prove to be a challenge, but in the end, it'll happen." He shrugged. "That's just the way it works."

"You're ridiculous, Preston."

"It's a shame you feel that way, Hope. You excite me!" He pulled me to him harder, and I gasped, before jerking away from him, leaving him to stand there, smirking. I glanced back over in the direction of the group of men I had been talking to. The good-looking stranger's eyes were still upon me. I couldn't even look back.

Angry and annoyed, I decided that my short stint at this party was now over. I was positive no one would miss me. So Lawrence had it in his head that Preston and I should become an item? I wasn't sure I believed it, coming out of Preston's mouth. But if it were true? Hell if I had any real clue as to what was going on in anybody's head that lived under that vast roof.

I stole out of the ballroom and out the back foyer, into the cool evening air. It was dark now, and the lights scattered about the gardens dimly lit the pathways on the grounds. I just started walking. I didn't care where to, at that point. I just knew I didn't want to be there. Van Steenburgh Manor was absolutely the most enchanting place I'd ever laid my eyes on... but it certainly wasn't "home."

Before I knew it, I had landed directly on course for the woods, and I had no desire to turn back. Perhaps I could get lost in that intimidating mass of forest and never come back out. No, surely it couldn't be that hard, but something inside of me was calling me a fool to accept its challenge by myself.

But, of course, I was too stubborn to turn around and go back.

It wasn't long before I regretted that decision. The cloudy skies erased any hopes that the moonlight would provide enough light to guide me along. I tried to retrace my steps, but I couldn't remember! Trees, trees, and more trees... I stopped and briefly wondered whether I should just walk the straight line back in the direction of which I came, and I was just about to do that, when out of nowhere, a break in the clouds afforded the moonlight to shine down.

I was maybe ten yards from that small, wooden cabin.

The only sounds I heard were the twigs breaking with each step, amidst the incessant chirps of crickets. Then finally I was there, stepping up the small wooden steps, up to the door. I hesitated a moment before turning the doorknob, and then I pushed it open, slowly. Before I stepped inside, I fumbled on the wall for a light switch, and quickly turned it on. Good, at least there was electricity.

I stepped inside and closed the door behind me, shivering from the cold. The light switch turned on a small lamp on a nearby table, and though the tiny light was indistinct, I could plainly see that the living room was fully furnished. There was a bookcase to my left that caught my eye, and upon taking a closer look, I noted books ranging from astrophysics, to art, to Greek mythology. I was immediately impressed by the wide spectrum of different topics. It was quite a collection! The hardwood floors creaked lightly under my every footstep. The living area had a cozy-looking couch in front of the fireplace, and there was an oriental rug sprawled before it. Off to the side of that was an easel, though it was empty. No canvas. No finished work lying around. Actually, there was nothing on the walls at all. No television or radio, either. I walked over to a desk, and there was leather bound notebook sitting on top of it. I ran my fingers over it, but decided not to open it. Moreover, my fingers left no marks. No dust. Clean.

Everything was clean. Too clean for a place that had been abandoned.

I ventured out to the quaint kitchen with a little table set in the middle of the white, tiled floor. The only décor that graced the table was a single, white pillar candle atop a silver saucer. Melted wax dripped and dried down its sides, and it was halfway gone.

Yes, someone definitely used this place—if not for living here, then just as a hideaway. I knew it. It must've been Lawrence. What a great place to escape Vivien, and just be alone. I left the kitchen and walked down a short hallway, past a clean, pristine bathroom. Just past that, at the end of the hallway, was the bedroom that was furnished with beautiful oak furniture—a single nightstand, dresser, and a four posted, king-sized bed. An antique silver pitcher sitting on a matching tray. It was filled with water, and there were two glasses sitting on the tray to accompany it. I found it both unusual and charming. I'd never known anyone to keep things like that next to their bed.

It was every bit as cozy as I had imagined it being, that day I stood in the woods with Preston, just wanting nothing more than to run up to the tiny place and check it out. Was it coincidence that I felt like I had been there before—in my dreams, perhaps? At any rate, as I kept discovering small hints of life, I now wondered if someone actually lived here. One of the groundskeepers, perhaps? There were far too many "small details" here for someone to use this place as an occasional retreat. I just knew I had to get out of there before its inhabitant returned and shot me on the spot for trespassing.

I headed back out into the living room. Only, as luck would have it, just as I was walking out from the hallway, the door opened, and someone stepped inside. My heart skipped a beat, as panic swept over me... Then I realized—it was the same handsome stranger I discussed art with from the party!

I stood frozen, not knowing what to do as he shut the door behind himself. He hadn't spotted me yet; poised in the area coming from the hallway into the living room. He loosened his tie and then he paused, glancing at the lamp that was already turned on. No, it wasn't on when he left the house—I could almost hear his thoughts. He stiffened, and I knew... I knew he now saw me from the corner of his eye, and for a moment we both just... stood, unmoving. I studied him, wondering what he was going to do, or say. His dark hair, which held hints of copper from the lighting, was still pulled back, and let loose a tendril that hung down in his face. I was paralyzed with panic. What was I supposed to do? Should I run? Apologize?

Then suddenly, he stood straight, and walked into the kitchen— his pace slow and purposeful. A breath held in my lungs as I stood, watching him pull a glass from a cabinet overhead to fill it with water from the sink. His back was towards me, when he raised the glass to his lips. And then, leaving me completely perplexed, he casually removed his jacket, draped it over one of the four chairs at his kitchen table, and then continued to unravel his attire! I was completely bewildered! *I knew he had seen me!*

Now I had to say something. I stepped forward, just as he removed his tie from his neck completely. I swallowed hard, and then cleared my throat. He never looked back up at me.

"I'm sorry, I didn't know that anyone lived here," I apologized sincerely, hoping that my feeble explanation would suffice.

"Well, now you do."

My breath was caught. His tone was husky, and cold. I guess I should have been grateful that he hadn't shot me. Instead, I meekly asked, "Who are you?" I watched him toss his tie over his jacket, and then proceeded to unbutton the sleeves on his black dress shirt. He began rolling them up, and I was offended by his ignoring me. "Who are you?" I repeated, a little more impatiently.

"I don't see what difference it makes to you."

I raised my eyebrow at him, and then shook my head. "Well you don't have to be rude about it."

"You didn't have to let yourself into my house either, but you did."

I nodded. Okay, he had me with that one. I blushed, feeling like an idiot. "You were at the main house just a little while ago."

"You're very observant."

I was now very tired of his biting answers, but I just wasn't ready to leave, yet. "Do you work at the manor?"

"How did you find your way here, anyhow?"

I felt like banging my head against a wall. "It wasn't easy. I got lost in the woods, and then I finally found my way, here." I explained.

"Right, so the first time you enter the woods, you take a few wrong turns and then you magically wind up at my doorstep, and let yourself in, totally disregarding my privacy? Tell me, Hope, haven't you been here, before?"

"You know my name?" I paused, and then glared at him, lifting my chin defiantly. "What difference does it make if I've been here before, or not?" I retorted.

"Perhaps the same difference it makes to you, who I am," he replied, meeting my eyes with his. A sensuous smile played in and out on his lips.

"I haven't been here, before," I denied adamantly.

"You have, with your buddy Preston. I saw you two. Why are you wasting my time?"

"Well if you saw us, then why are you even asking me?" I was growing more increasingly frustrated with every word. "He just showed me through the woods, and I don't even see why it matters! This is just ridiculous," I exclaimed, clutching my purse in my hand, and heading toward the door.

"Oh come, now. Catch you in a lie, and you're ready to storm out. It's no big deal, really," he said with a chuckle. He came out from behind the kitchen counter, and I paused at the door. "Trent."

"Excuse me?" I glared at him, confused.

"You inquired about my name. Trenton Anthony Forrestor at your service." He took a quick bow. It was obvious he was mocking me, but now I was intrigued.

"You are?" I asked skeptically. This was Redd's favorite person? Kate and Charles' son?

"I try not to lie about such important things as my identity."

I felt the heat rush to my face again. "Right..."

"And of course I know who you are," he continued, walking past me to take a seat on the couch. I remained standing, but took my hand from the doorknob. "Hope Lindsey de Havilland. I must compliment you on your name—not only because your middle name belonged to your mother, who was most wonderful, but also because Hope is such a beautiful name. Quite inspiring, I think." He grinned at me, making himself twice as appealing as I already found him. "I know Redd's been spouting off at the mouth about me to you. What exactly has he been saying?"

I shrugged, and stepped away from the door. "Redd likes to talk about you a lot," I told him.

"He's quite a character."

"He raves about how intelligent you are," I answered. "Of course, I consider someone who graduated from college by eighteen more than just 'intelligent'. I call it 'genius'."

"I'm glad to see that someone thinks my intelligence is actually worth something. It's not worth much to me—I never use any of it. It's my so-called creativity that gets me by. You don't need much intelligence to be an artist. I also dabble in the stock market. You don't have to be Doogie Howser to do that, either."

"I'm sorry you feel that way. I would give anything to be as smart as you are," I told him.

He swung his eyes my way. "Don't wish to be any different. Honestly, it was Hell going through my school years. The girls thought I was 'cute', because I was so much younger, but the boys resented me for making them appear obtuse and foolish. I couldn't win."

"You've already won, if you ask me. There aren't many who can brag about accomplishing half the things you've done, in such little time."

He chuckled. "Anyone can splatter paint on a canvas, Hope. If you visit a mental institution, there are people there with only half a working brain that can make the same visions come to life as I can. If I could take some of this knowledge you speak so highly of and give it to you, I would—believe me."

"Why do you live out here, in the woods?" I asked him. "Why don't you live in the huge house, with everyone else?"

"I live here because I'm in my own little world. I come and go as I please, and for the most part I'm alone, except for the few people who can actually find their way here, and waste my time."

"That's the second time you've implied that I'm wasting your time. I'll go ahead and leave," I announced, actually hoping he would stop me. "I wouldn't want to *waste* anymore of your oh-so-precious time," I pronounced dramatically.

"Oh come, now," he prodded. "You've gotten what you wanted, haven't you? I'm harmless." His eyes were studying me, watching me very closely. I didn't dare move, as his eyes seemed to drink me in from head-to-toe—until he realized himself that he was staring, and abruptly turned away.

"Why is it that Preston was so adamant about me staying away from here?" My questions were endless.

He turned to deliver me the most wickedly charming grin I'd ever seen, quite taking my breath away. "Preston likes to think that I steal his women," he answered smugly. "He's actually accused me of doing so, many times."

"Do you?"

"Of course not," he answered, appearing offended. "I never try to bother myself with anyone—let alone schoolgirls! It's *them* who come looking for me, 'getting lost in the woods' and landing on my doorstep. Those such as yourself, who suddenly find themselves stranded here, and ask me silly questions." He said this very matter-of-factly, and now it was my turn to be offended.

"First off—I am not one of Preston's women, thank you very much! Second—I didn't go *looking* for you, or anyone in particular! And there you go again, with the time-wasting references! Forget I even came here, and I'm going to forget I ever saw you," I raged, throwing the door open and storming out into the cold, dark air. I slammed it behind me, and stomped straight back into the woods. What is it with everyone around here? Didn't anyone know how to be civil? Putting aside that it was me who intruded; he could have at least shown me a little hospitality, right?

I managed to get back through the woods relatively easily, and before I even entered the house, I could still hear the people inside, laughing, talking. I slipped back in through the back door, and went into the kitchen, to find Redd.

"Well, chile! Ya done fixed yoursef up like one of those models in the magazines!" He grinned at me. "Ya look mighty fine, Miss Hope!"

I smiled back at him. "Thank you, Redd."

"Enjoying yourself in there?"

I hesitated, wondering if I should say anything about meeting Trent. "Yes, I guess it's okay," I told him vaguely. "It's certainly different."

"Ya get used to 'em," he assured me. "After a while, it ain't nuthin." Great, I can't wait.

I left the kitchen, and headed back to the ballroom. I wasn't intending on going back in there, but I guess I just wanted to see it again, for myself. From the outside, it looked magical. Inside, I had found, was a whole different story.

"Where have you been?" I whirled around and found Lawrence standing behind me. His eyes hinted at anger, and he looked tense. "I have scoured this entire house looking for you."

"I—I was in the kitchen," I stammered, wondering why he was so mad.

"No you weren't, because I checked in the kitchen. You've been missing for at least an hour!"

I started to sweat. "Well I needed some fresh air, I'm sorry. I'm just overwhelmed—"

"Do not disappear without letting me know where you are going, first," he warned. "And remember—I hate liars, Hope."

"I'm sorry—"

"You're excused," he dismissed with a wave of his hand. "You're free to go to your room, if you like."

I stood there gaping at him while he walked back into the ballroom. What in the world had gotten into him?! Surely he couldn't have been that mad because I had left his party! An hour? I had been gone longer than that, so apparently he didn't miss me too much.

I marched back upstairs, and headed towards my bedroom. As I turned the corner to go down the hall, I was just in time to see Preston entering his suite, with the young woman I'd seen him eyeballing earlier. She was giggling; her hands were all over him, responding to his kisses, and neither of them noticed me before they disappeared into his room. I disappeared into my suite, locked the door behind me, and threw my shoes across the bedroom floor.

Everyone in this house had a chip on their shoulder.

Chapter 5

"Drowning in Sorrow"

The next afternoon, I went downstairs to find Preston on the back patio. He turned when he heard me come out, and smirked at me immediately.

"I hope my guest and I didn't keep you up, last night."

I glared at him. "No, Preston. To be quite honest, I didn't hear a thing."

He shrugged. "She was just a little loud, so I figured I'd apologize."

"I really don't care to hear about your sexual exploits," I told him. "Keep the details to yourself."

"I heard you ran off last night," he said, eyeballing me. "Where did you run off to?

I shook my head. "Nowhere. Who told you that?"

"My father."

"He was really looking for me?"

"Like a madman, actually. Asked me if I'd seen you. I told him I hadn't since we had that amazing, romantic waltz." His tone was dripping with sarcasm.

"Did he even say why he was looking for me?"

He shrugged again. "Nope. Did you take on a lover? Surely you didn't pass me up for someone else, Hope. No one else there was even worthy."

"Not that it's any of your business, but no—there was no 'lover', and if I were to take one on, it would not be you," I snapped, turning around to go back inside. So much for a quiet afternoon of reading.

When I went back inside, I caught Lawrence emerging from the hallway to his office, and I considered running back the other way, but he saw me, so it was too late.

"Hope, if you'll follow me, I'd like to discuss something with you, quickly." He gestured for me to follow him, and disappeared back down the hall, to his office.

I swallowed hard, and followed him in there, filled with dread. I expected to be berated again for disappearing the night before, and he shut the door behind me, motioning for me to have a seat. I did so, and he sat behind his desk, clasping his hands before him, and resting them on his desk.

"First off, I'd like to congratulate you on last night," he told me, looking pleased. "Apparently you dazzled some people with your knowledge on art. When I caught wind of how impressed they were, I had to remember to pass that along." I thought he was going to say something next about my unexpected disappearance, but he chose not to. "I'm honored that I get to introduce you to the social world, Hope. I can see that you will have no trouble fitting in. Your mother fit in perfectly, as well. She could win a crowd over with her wit and intellect in a matter of minutes. You and she are a lot alike," he complimented.

"Thank you," I accepted softly.

"I brought you in here for two reasons," he began. "The first one is that I want you to stay away from the cabin in the woods. Trent is much too old for you, and I caught you and him exchanging curious glances at the party. I'm not going to say it again." I felt myself blushing, and I was perplexed as to why he made it seem so important as to why I stay away from him. Was he aware that I was there last night? Did Trent tattle on me, telling Lawrence to keep tighter rein on me so that I wouldn't find myself on his doorstep anymore to "waste his time?"

"I find him fascinating," I muttered.

"Yes, you and every other female," he interjected. "Just stay away from there. And the second reason I brought you here, is because I've enrolled you into school," he announced with a pleasant smile. "Springcrest—one of the finest private schools in the northeast. Your mother went there while she was here, and did extremely well. There's normally a waiting list miles long, but I happen to know the dean of the school, and he pulled a few strings. You start this semester. I just need to have you take a few exams so they know which classes to place you in."

I smiled, pretending to be thrilled, while on the inside, I was screaming. Of course, a private school. Someone, please show me a place to hang myself now...

"I went ahead and promised to bring you in tomorrow morning, bright and early. Originally, I had a meeting, and Vivien said you should be fine to go by yourself if Charles drove you, but I wouldn't hear of it. I wanted to take you, myself. So I cancelled my meeting." He smiled, and for some reason, I think he expected me to appreciate his sacrifice. To an extent, I did. I didn't want to go by myself!

"Now, although I won't push you, I would strongly advise you to join some sort of extracurricular activities there," he continued. "Not only will it involve you more in the school, but it will help you win scholarships, so you can go on to bigger, better things. I realize that you are interested in arts, and theater, and they have a magnificent drama program there. Their performances always get rave reviews."

I snapped to attention, narrowing my eyes at him. "How did you know I was into theater?" I asked. I had never mentioned it.

"Looking over your past school files," he answered, without blinking. "Anyhow," he stood up. "I expect you to be ready to go around nine in the morning." He reached for his jacket and put it on, opening the door and looking at me expectantly. As if in a fog, I rose from my chair, and left the office. For some reason, I wanted to cry.

"Chile, why ya look so glum?"

I forced a smile, entering the kitchen. "No reason, Redd." I took a brownie from the tray on the counter.

"Trent popped in to say hi early this mornin'," he told me, slipping me a sly look. "He said he saw ya last night, at the party. Askin' all sorts of questions 'bout ya, Miss Hope, he was. Seems mighty fond of ya."

I wasn't going to tell him that I thought Trent was almost as awful and rude as Preston. Instead, I remained silent.

"So what'd ya think of my boy?" He was grinning from ear to ear.

I labored another smile. "He seems very intelligent," I managed.

"He raved 'bout how pretty ya are," he rambled on. "Says ya look exactly how he remembered ya momma."

I felt myself blushing, and I remembered his beautiful face in my mind. His dark eyes, and well-defined jaw-line. His face looked like it was hand sculpted by God, Himself. Never had I seen such a beautiful man. So he thought I was pretty, but didn't want me around. How perfect was that?!

Redd laughed. "Now, there ain't no need for ya to be embarrassed 'bout it. He's a good boy."

I nodded, forcing a smile at the happy old man. "I'm sure he is," I told him, grabbing another brownie before leaving the kitchen. Why would he bother to ask about me, anyhow? He chased me out of his place, mocked me, and told me several times that I was wasting his time. All of the men in this house were impossible to truly understand.

I decided to go to the library, and I was intending to pick out another book to take down by the river and read, when I heard hushed voices coming from Lawrence's study. The door was cracked open slightly, and I paused outside to see Vivien sitting on the edge of Lawrence's desk. He was sitting behind it.

"Darling, truly I do intend on spending time with her, but you know my schedule is so hectic," she told him, her voice low. Her lips were pouty, and his look was stern.

"She thinks you don't like her, and quite honestly, I don't blame her. After all, you've hardly said two words to her since she's been here."

"Oh, Lawrence," she scowled. "She has everything her little heart could possibly desire. She's not lacking in any department."

"Well at least try to make some effort to make her feel like you want her here, even if you don't," he ordered, standing up and buttoning his jacket. Her hand reached up and caressed the side of his face, and he paused to look down at her, his eyes softening.

"I will, darling. I will," she cooed, standing up. "You know, you and I need to take a trip somewhere. Alone," she added. "You know, to get away from everything here, the distractions, and all the hassles. Maybe a cruise to the Mediterranean," she suggested, giving him a soft kiss on the lips.

He looked like he was under a spell, and he nodded. "I'll check on that," he promised.

How manipulative she was... But now I saw what I was to Vivien. A distraction. A hassle. He shouldn't have to tell her to spend time with me. I was her grand-daughter. She should want to do that all on her own!

I hurried away from the door, fuming. I was beginning to understand in short time why my mother left. Perhaps her mother didn't even want to spend time with her. All Vivien seemed to care about was herself!

I quickly ducked into the library, and moments later, Vivien emerged with her purse. I don't even think she noticed me in there. Then I heard the echo of the front door shutting. She was gone. Lawrence materialized shortly after, and he poked his head in, grinning.

"There's some books on Dali on that shelf over there," he directed me, pointing across the room. "I'll be back later this evening. Don't wait up." He winked, and then he was gone.

I blankly stared at where he had been standing. *Dali.* Did nothing escape him? Did he know absolutely everything that came out of my mouth? I reasoned that whoever regaled him of the conversation I partook in the night before not only expressed how impressed they were at my knowledge, but probably indulged him with the details of what we spoke of.

I saw that Preston was no longer out back, so I decided to try sitting out there again with book in hand, taking a seat next to the pool. Were things going to get better? Was I just being ungrateful? Sure, Vivien was right. I had every material possession I could possibly ask for. Whatever I didn't already have, they could provide for me.

Somehow, that just wasn't enough.

I looked up towards the sky, and it was comforting to think that my parents were watching from up above. I missed them more than anything, but I had to stop crying. I was done pitying myself. I knew that they wouldn't want that, anyhow. I had to start learning how to fend for myself. How to live without them, and on my own. Truly, I was on my own, now. Lawrence seemed to be watching over me, but Vivien wasn't any sort of valid parental figure. Lawrence apparently checked up on my whereabouts. He was the only one I'd have to watch out for.

I heard the door open behind me, and I turned to see Preston step out. Our eyes met, and I rolled mine, turning back to face the pool. I just wasn't in the mood, today.

"You know, this is my house, too," he pointed out, catching my blatant annoyance.

"Preston don't start, please."

"Well, you see that I didn't roll my eyes when I saw you out here," he continued. "I find that entirely unnecessary."

I shook my head.

"You've had a chip on your shoulder ever since you got here," he remarked.

I turned to him with eyes so wide they could've popped out of my head. "Me?!"

"You need to lighten up."

I huffed and turned my attention back down to my book. "Look, if your parents died, you might be a little upset, too, Preston."

"You've been playing that card since you got here, Hopeless," he called me, taunting me. "You need to get over it, already. Your parents are dead, and you can't bring them back. Quit dwelling on it and feeling sorry for yourself."

This was the remark that brought tears to my eyes. "I'm trying to get over it," I uttered, refusing not to cry. "In fact, I thought I was doing just fine up until now."

"Well you need to try harder," he muttered, putting his sunglasses on, and approaching me. "You just have to make the best of the situations at hand."

I glared at him through watery eyes. "Thank you. You ought to go into psychology."

"Actually I was thinking about it," he replied nonchalantly. "In fact, Hope, I'll even do you this favor—giving you sessions for free. You need them, and I would love to help!"

"Are you a jerk to everyone?" I shot at him.

"Oh, you're right. Well, I should probably step back to create some space before you slap me a few more times," he retorted.

I stood up. "This is silly," I murmured, wiping the tears away that had started to spill from my eyes. "I don't need this."

"No, I guess you don't. So go ahead—run and hide. Like mother, like daughter."

I looked at him, shaking my head. "What do you have against my mother?" I demanded.

"Don't worry about it. This is when you go ahead and get all offended, turn around, and then stomp off," he said with a shrug.

I was sick of it. Sick of him! My head was swimming with my rage, and efore I knew it, I reached out and shoved him—sending him stumbling backward. He lost his balance, and in less than a second, he fell into the deep end of the pool. "Now I'll go ahead and stomp off, okay?" I threw my hands up in the air at him, and then turned on my heels. He was splashing, and I knew he was furious, so I had every intention to get out of there quickly. I knew slapping him was pushing it, even though it was a reflex, but pushing him into the pool might've actually taken it too far. When I reached the door, the splashing sounded more frantic, however, and a red flag went off in my head. I turned, and I didn't see Preston at first. Then I saw his head bobbing in and out of the water. The look on his face was panic, and his arms were flailing in every direction.

That's when it hit me. *He didn't know how to swim!*

Without hesitation, I kicked my sandals off and ran to the pool, jumping in. I raced over to him, and tried to get a hold on him, but he fought me at first. I tried to get my arm around him again as he struggled, but he battled against me, pushing me away. The idiot! I had to help him, because he certainly wasn't getting out on his own! By tugging at his clothes, and dragging him a few inches at a time when he would give me the chance to get a hold of him, I finally got him to the side of the pool. As soon as he grabbed the side, he pulled himself up and climbed out. He was visibly shaken, and neither of us said a word. I felt really bad. I shouldn't have pushed him...

"Preston—"

"Don't talk to me," he snapped brokenly. He wouldn't look at me, and his voice trembled as he shook. "Leave me alone."

I climbed out of the pool, and then reached out to touch his arm, to get his attention. I still couldn't catch his gaze to apologize sincerely for what I'd just done. He would only look down, his hair dripping down his face. He pulled away from me quickly, and backed away, towards the door.

"But Preston, please," I begged him. "I didn't mean to—"

"I don't care, Hope. I won't bother you again," he vowed, before disappearing into the house. I felt so bad. I really did overdo it, this time. I took it way too far, and I felt ashamed of myself. Damn, why did he have to push my buttons? Why did he bring out such anger in me?!

I collapsed into a chair, and bowed my head into my hands. I deserved whatever revenge he was going to take on me, this time. I had never anticipated the possibility of him not knowing how to swim. I just felt absolutely horrible, and rightfully so. Somehow, I just kept making things harder on myself.

I retreated upstairs, and within minutes, I stripped my wet, uncomfortable clothes off of me and settled myself in warm water. I closed my eyes, and my thoughts drifted from what happened earlier with Preston, to Lawrence and Vivien's conversation. Her words kept echoing in my mind. *We need to get away from everything here, the distractions, all the hassles...* She had no desire to get to know me. I could no longer even kid myself. Then there was the cabin, and Trent. His eyes haunted me—black as midnight, they were so intense. As coarse as he was towards me, I still couldn't get him out of my mind.

Once I got out of my bath, I wrapped myself in my robe and entered my bedroom. It was dark now, and on my way over to my vanity I saw from the corner of my eye something out on the balcony. It was Preston, and I paused to watch him before I flicked the lamp on. He was just standing there, leaning against the railing and looking out. His hair dried in a tousle, and he had changed into a pair of loose-fitting jeans, a t-shirt, and a flannel over top of that, which was left unbuttoned and blowing gently in the breeze. The sight of him was quite humbling. He merely stood, gazing out into the darkness. I debated on whether or not to go out to him, and try once again to apologize, but decided against it. If anything, he was probably still too embarrassed to face me. Putting myself in his shoes, I would've felt the same way.

I sat down at my vanity, and turned the lamp on. It cast a light glow out on the balcony and glancing up, I saw that he noticed it as well. He stood straight, and I held my breath while he turned and stepped back into his suite. I wondered what he was thinking. Surely if he didn't hate me before today, he hated me now. Of course, I didn't know why I cared, really. He'd been nothing but crude and mean to me since we met. But I still couldn't help but to feel bad.

I got into bed, and my eyelids practically thanked me when I closed them for the night. I dreaded the morning, knowing I had to rise early and get ready to be acquainted with my new school. The thought of attending a new school was nerve-wracking enough, but a private school full of wealthy kids frightened me ten times as much!

I was just about asleep, when the sound of piano music echoed through my head. I really didn't pay attention to it, at first. I thought it was a figment of my imagination. I closed my eyes again and turned over, and it only seemed to get louder. I looked at the clock. It was just after midnight. I really had fallen asleep. And where was that music coming from?

I rolled over, thinking that it was probably Preston playing music in his suite. It sounded beautiful, but really, it was just not the time to have a radio on. Then it dawned on me—Preston wouldn't listen to music like that. I'd seen a few of his CD's lying around, and classical music wasn't part of his collection. No, this music was coming from below—downstairs. The ballroom, perhaps?

I rose from bed, and grabbed the matching robe to my long black silk gown. I wrapped it around me, and opened the door to my bedroom, stepping out into the hallway. As soon as I had opened my door, the music was a little louder. I passed by Preston's door just to make sure. No, it wasn't coming from in there. Not a sound was coming from inside Preston's bedroom.

I went to the top of the stairs and looked down. One of the doors to the ballroom was cracked open slightly, and light was seeping out. The music was a slow, haunting melody. It sent a chill up my spine. I tiptoed down the stairs, cautious as to not make a sound, and then I quietly crept over to the door. I pushed it open carefully, so it wouldn't squeak, and there was a small fire going, in the fireplace. My breath caught when I saw Trent seated at the piano.

His eyes were closed, his head bowed down. He radiated such a strong sense of masculinity, that just being in the same vicinity as him gave me this strange feeling of longing... A reaction more concentrated than I'd never felt around any man, before. His hands floated over the ivory keys, and the sheer sight of him mesmerized me. His hair hung loosely this time, falling gently over his shoulders. The fire cast a reddish glow on his thick, dark hair. He wore a white button-up shirt, and his sleeves were rolled up halfway. The unshaven shadow on his face made him dangerous-looking, and my fingers impulsively begged me to touch him. My breath caught in my throat as I leaned against the frame of the door, falling into some sort of trance that his fingers inspired as they played. He was beautiful, and it seemed his talents were endless. All I could do was continue to watch him, as he sent me into a deep reverie. The fire crackled behind him, and he didn't even notice that I stood there. He didn't notice anything at all—even he seemed to be in another world.

He played and played, heightening into one climax after another... I'd never heard anything like it. I wondered how other things this man was good at. He seemed limitless. I envied him, for that.

And God help me—I had never wanted anything so badly in my life, as I wanted him in that instant.

"Good evening, milady."

I snapped back to attention and as my eyes began to refocus, I noticed that the music was no longer playing. A heat swept over my body, and I just looked at him, embarrassed. "That was beautiful," I remarked sincerely.

"You were falling asleep," he countered softly, through those perfect lips.

"No... not sleeping," I denied.

"Did I wake you?"

"No," I denied quickly, raking a hand self-consciously through my hair.

"You must be a night-owl, then."

"I can be. Why did you stop?"

"Playing?" I nodded. "The piece was done."

"I've never heard someone play like that. Don't your fingers get tired?"

He chuckle was light. "My fingers never tire." His eyes swung my way, and whether or not he meant to be suggestive was unclear, but I felt my entire body heat up. "Did you like it?"

I just stared at him blankly. "Like what?"

He laughed softly, and stood up. "You can just tell me it was horrible. I don't play all too often, anymore," he said apologetically. "I'm beyond rusty."

"No! It was perfect," I assured him, getting my head back in order. "I was just kind of lost, in a daydream or something," I told him. "I had no idea a piano could sound so beautiful."

"You've been deprived," he quipped, picking up his jacket and slinging it over his shoulder. "You will definitely need to catch one of the symphonies now that you're here." Then he stood there and eyed me for a long moment. I was suddenly aware of the gown I was wearing, underneath a matching, and equally flimsy robe. No doubt, I was underdressed. I gave the robe a subtle tug to make sure it was wrapped around me securely, and I looked back at him. "Since you're here, I want to apologize for upsetting you, last night," he spoke low, his eyes locking with mine.

I shook my head and looked away. "Don't. I shouldn't have been there."

"No, you shouldn't have," he agreed. "But—," he glanced at me, and a small smile played over his sensuous lips, "—to your defense, you were curious, and I cannot fault you for that. I must only learn to keep my doors locked while I'm away."

I sighed. "Well, I apologize, as well," I told him quickly glancing at him. He was still watching me closely.

"That said, I should let you go," he announced, stepping towards me. "It's obvious I *did* wake you, and it's late, so I don't intend on keeping you one moment longer." He didn't know that inside I was screaming for him to keep me as long as he wanted to.

But, I nodded in agreement anyway, and took a step backward. "Yes, of course. Goodnight," I wished him, just before turning my back to him and heading across the foyer.

"Goodnight, Hope."

I didn't turn back, but I know his eyes were glued to me, all the way until I disappeared up the stairs. I felt his eyes watching me. Call me crazy, but I even willed for it. And it wasn't until I was out of his sight that I stopped and listened, until sure enough – that's when this man who thrilled me on so many different levels commenced his footsteps, and moments later, the terrace doors opened and then shut behind him. So, he was curious about me, after all? I considered this one small, slight victory.

I quickly shut myself behind the door of my suite; leaning against it for a moment, and closing my eyes. I almost pinched myself to see if what had just taken place was real, but if it wasn't, I didn't want to know. All I knew was that I'd never felt such an insane attraction to any of the guys I'd ever dated back home. This was the kind of chemistry I had only read about in novels. And I heard Lawrence's words echo with warning, in my head. Stay away from Trent. Finally, one thing about Van Steenburgh Manor that excited me, and I was ordered to squash it.

All I could do, was just crawl back into bed, and drift away curiously to sleep...

Chapter 6

"Springcrest"

Morning snuck up on me way too quickly, I decided, as I got up and proceeded to get ready for "school". Lawrence knocked on my door to make sure I was already up, and he was pleasantly surprised when I answered the door already dressed. I hoped I successfully masked my anxiety, but my stomach was in knots as I plastered a smile over my face and assured him I would be downstairs in five minutes. I agonized over everything, from my hair to the minimal make-up I applied. I had settled on a pair of khaki pants and a white button up shirt, but despite how covered up and "safe" my outfit was, I still stared at my reflection with uncertainty for what felt like an eternity, after Lawrence checked on me.

"Are we ready?" He smiled pleasantly when I met him at the front door.

I nodded, swallowing the lump in my throat. "Yes." *As ready as I'd ever be.*

The ride was about an hour, and I might've enjoyed it more, had I not been so anxious to get this over with. Our car crossed the Kingston Bridge, over the river that stretched so far and wide. The sunlight danced upon its surface making the water sparkle like a sea of diamonds, and I wished I was back on that grassy knoll I loved so much, watching the water instead of inside that long, black car. The sky was bright and blue. The mountains loomed ahead of us, alive with color.

Funny, how one minute I was wishing time would speed up, for me to turn eighteen and get on with my life. Then, the next minute I was wishing to be safely back at the manor, where I felt more like an unwanted guest, than a family member.

Finally, the driver turned onto a road that came to rather large, wrought-iron gates that opened, allowing us to pass through. Huge, thick trees that must've been hundreds of years old lined the way, before the car slowed to a stop in front of one of the most beautiful campuses I'd ever seen.

I followed Lawrence up the walkway, unable to pry my eyes from the cathedral-styled building that loomed over us. There were several more buildings sprawled out around us, linked together by concrete paths and decorated with thousands of flowers. Girls were walking around with boxes and bags, and everyone looked like they were moving in for the school year. Parents were helping, and dads were doting on their daughters as everyone wore the same look of excitement mixed with anticipation. It looked like a scene from a movie. It looked like perfection.

It looked intimidating.

"Well hello, Lawrence! You look well," said a woman who greeted us just as we stepped inside. She looked to be about Lawrence's age, wearing a fitted gray suit with pinstripes. Her dark brown hair was gracefully pulled back into a bun, with shiny black "chopsticks" holding it together. Her eyes were twinkling at him in such a way that it gave me the impression they knew one another well.

"And you look breathtaking, Elena. As usual." Their knowing smirks told me all I needed to know. I pretended not to notice. Instead I was looking up, at the three stories above me, with girls bustling up and down the corridors, gossiping about whatever, or giggling about something funny. I attracted several curious glances, but for the most part, no one really paid that much attention. It took Elena a few more minutes of flirting with my handsome escort before she even acknowledged me.

Her eyes scanned me, and with a nod of approval she smiled at me warmly. "Welcome to Springcrest." I smiled nervously, and she beckoned for us to follow her into her office. "I'm Miss Winfield." I was in awe of this school that had been around nearly as long as the Van Steenburghs, before I'd even sat down. There were plaques and signs everywhere denoting historic tidbits of information about the school in which I was now enrolled. "I've already placed you in your classes and produced for you a schedule that you will follow," she handed the paper to Lawrence, and then sat down behind her desk while he scanned it over. "I decided her courses based on transcripts from your past schooling," she once again addressed Lawrence, as if I were no longer in the room. "The school she came from is pretty parallel to our curriculum, so in all actuality, you really didn't have to make the trip here, after all." She delivered him a mischievous smirk, and he winked back at her.

"I never do mind catching up with old friends," he bantered back. "Besides, it doesn't hurt for her to visit campus before she arrives here full-time. It'll give her a moment to breathe it all in, and acclimate."

"Absolutely," she agreed smoothly, allowing her eyes to linger over his face for a moment before remembering I was sitting right there. "I took notice that you were very active in English courses such as journalism, creative writing, et cetera, so I catered to that. I also noted that you were very active in theater, and took the liberty of enrolling you in the drama program. We offer some of the best programs in the country, Hope. I hope you like them. If you have any problems regarding the classes assigned to you, feel free to report back to me or your counselor, Miss Hayden." She put on her glasses and thumbed through a stack of papers sitting before her, while I sat frozen. "You are welcome to walk around and familiarize yourself with the grounds ahead of time to cut back on the anxiety of trying to find your next class." She flashed me a gentle smile, looking over her glasses. "This school is old, dating back to the late 1700's. Originally, this very building was a church. The other buildings were added on at a later time. What is also unique is that there is a passageway underground which links every building. The girls usually use it when the weather is cold, or rainy." She handed another paper to Lawrence. "Now, Astoria Hall houses the dormitories, along with the dining areas." *Dormitories... Right...* "You must be in no later than eight every evening, and there are room checks, so be advised. Breakfast is served at seven every morning. Nothing fancy, but enough to get you going in the morning, so you're not dragging to class. Our discipline program works on a points system. For each rule that is broken, you're served with a demerit. The amount of points taken off depends on the severity of the rule broken. For being late to class, you will be penalized with five points. For cheating on a test, you would be penalized with twenty five points. You start with a hundred points, and at the end of each grading period your discipline grade will be factored in with your other grades. So, overall what I'm trying to say is that your discipline grade could make you, or break you." Every little move I made would be scrutinized, and basically, I was to be ruled with an iron fist. No wrong moves whatsoever. Not only did I have to worry about making the grades for my classes, but I also had to worry about looking at someone the wrong way. No sweat, right? I never was much of a troublemaker.

"Dress code is simple. White button up blouses, and black or khaki pants—much like the ensemble you are wearing right now," she pointed out. "That is perfect."

Lawrence even smiled at this, and I could almost hear his thoughts praising me on my decision to wear what I had on. "If you decide to wear a skirt, it must come no higher than the top of your knee. Some of the girls around here dare to see how much they can get away with, but I assure you that they are reprimanded."

My nerves were twisted into knots, and after she went through the rest of the rules and my life seemed more and more confined, she took us to Astoria Hall, to show me to my new dorm room. I would be picked up from school at five o'clock sharp every Friday afternoon, and would be driven back on Sunday night, or Monday morning—whichever was more conducive to Lawrence's schedule. Surprisingly, I had a dorm room all to myself. I wasn't expecting that, at all. The room was just big enough for a single bed, and a chest of drawers. The closet was just big enough to hang maybe two jackets and a put a few pairs of shoes. The bathroom had just enough space for a toilet and a standing shower stall. A small porcelain sink protruded from the tiled wall, and a small mirror hung above it. But at that moment, I was grateful. The size of the room didn't matter a bit. The fact that I didn't have the added burden of meeting and getting to know a roommate is what relieved me.

"All of the rooms have a single lock on the door, of which you have a key. The headmistress of the house has a skeleton key, which she can use for any door in the dorm, and that is what she uses when she does her room checks. You see, we do want you to have your privacy, but at the same time, we don't permit any indecent behavior. We also do not permit any hoarding of food in any of the rooms. Eating is only to be done in the dining halls. We have enough to worry about around here without having to worry about our girls inviting the likes of roaches or any kind of bugs into the dorms.

"Also, we require that your rooms are kept tidy at all times. Have you ever heard the saying 'A place for everything and everything in its place'? That is what we command of our students. You see, Hope," she said, turning to me. "We not only teach our girls an education, but also a way of life. We not only wish to bestow a gift of higher learning, but to take with them a keen sense on how to survive on their own. Whether you realize it now or not, what you learn here will last you a lifetime. That is how we have earned such respect here at Springcrest, and you will find that any college of your choice will jump to have you."

At that point, I wasn't thinking of college, or even of the future at all. The only thing that kept me standing there, and not screaming and running in the other direction was that my mother had been able to pull all of this off. If she did it, then I had to conjure up the courage to, as well. I felt overwhelmed as Miss Winfield congratulated me on my arrival, and then I felt alone sitting in that long black limousine that took Lawrence and I back across the river that now danced mockingly under the sunlight, in spite of how dreary I felt. Not a single word was exchanged between Lawrence and I during the entire ride back to Van Steenburgh Manor. I just stared out the window, and he thumbed through the morning's newspaper.

The positive side to all of this was that at least I knew what I was walking into now, when I returned to Springcrest for the first day of school Monday morning.

Of course, this prompted over the next few days what Lawrence eagerly called "school shopping". He took me around to some of the finest boutiques and equipped me with every school supply imaginable, as well as clothes enough to suit an army! Khakis, black slacks, and white button up shirts piled up in my hands, and each time, the saleswomen would come and insist on holding them for me, or starting me a dressing room.

It was something Vivien should've wanted to do with me.

By Saturday night I had everything from every day wear, to school attire, to evening gowns to accompany my new look. I literally felt like a completely different person. I liked it, actually. Funny how a little pampering can make a girl feel like a million dollars. When Preston first caught sight of my new bouncy hairdo, my sun-kissed skin, and my smart clothes, an eyebrow lifted just enough to let me know he was impressed, even while he still said nothing. As soon as he made eye contact with me, he quickly turned the other way, and I sighed inwardly. He was still mad about the incident at the pool. And he had every right to be.

While I was still immensely nervous about attending a new school in a matter of less than forty-eight hours, at least I had a newfound sense of confidence. Perhaps Lawrence had sensed I needed that in the first place, when he arranged this day of shopping and pampering. Or he had some idea what I was in for. I was soon to find out, either way.

Monday morning landed me trembling nervously in my dorm room. Lawrence dropped me off himself the night before, insisting on helping me with my suitcases, and making sure that I was settled in before he left. Everyone else on campus had already moved in over the weekend, and now I felt like the last one to show up to a dinner party. During times like this, when I was rattled, I preferred being alone to deal with everything on my own, but I wouldn't dare tell him to go away. It wasn't until he left that I was able to relax a little. In neighboring rooms, I could hear girls giggling, and every once in a while I could hear little details of someone's exciting story through the thin walls. I was just as curious about them as they were of me—the "*new girl*". I knew my time was fast approaching, to meet them and encounter their evaluating stares. Was I going to be accepted? Did I really care?

Kind of, but not really. I had one year to go, before graduating. I just needed to keep my eye on the prize, and keep my nose clean.

Fortunately, school never came hard to me. I wasn't half the genius Trent was, but on the other hand, I never really had to study too hard to pass. Until that moment, Trent hadn't passed through my mind at all. It had been almost a week since I'd seen him that night in the ballroom. Or had it all been just a dream?

I didn't have time to think about him. I had twenty minutes to find my class. English class in Olana Hall. Olana—no doubt named after Frederick Church's estate. For a fleeting moment, I thought of Preston.

I threw the door open to the classroom just as the bell began to sound. All eyes turned and fixed themselves on me as I held my breath and made it to the first available seat farthest from the front. There were not quite twenty girls seated already, and a rather pretty younger woman with pale blonde hair swept back from her face stood at the front of the classroom, dressed in a black skirt and jacket, and wearing an amused smile on her lips.

"You made it just in time, Miss de Havilland," she greeted me pleasantly. "I'm glad you found it here, alright." I managed a smile, aware that everyone's scrutinizing eyes were upon me. "I'm Miss Alexander, and it's a pleasure to have you here. Why don't you step up to the front, here, and introduce yourself," she invited. "It's customary that I ask all new students do so, and it allows us to get to know you."

My eyes widened, and I stared at her for a long moment before resting my book bag on the floor by my desk. Obviously I had no choice. It's a good thing I didn't get stage fright.

"My name is Hope," I began, first addressing Miss Alexander, and then briefly catching the eyes of each girl in the classroom. Then I paused for a moment, not really knowing what else to say. I had never been one to readily and openly talk about myself.

"What are your hobbies? Do you have any interests?" Miss Alexander prompted, prolonging my torture.

I shifted awkwardly on my feet. "Reading is one of my favorite things to do when I have a little time to myself, and I was really into theater back home..." I stopped and looked at her. She still had a million questions written all over her face. The rest of the girls just stared at me.

"Well, what brought you here? Did your family move here?"

Without thinking, I blurted, "My parents died." Realizing what I had just said, I added, "So I moved here, to stay with remaining family."

Now looking uncomfortable, Miss Alexander lowered her eyes from my gaze, and stood up from behind her desk. "Yes, the Van Steenburghs. Very good people," she said softly. "Thank you, Hope. You may take your seat."

The rest of the classes went something to that effect, only this time I already had it rehearsed, what to say and what not to say. I was careful not to divulge too much personal information. I vaguely revealed just enough to satisfy each teacher's curiosity, and allow me to take my seat, at last. *"My name is Hope, and I love reading and theater. I grew up in the south, but came to live with relatives recently and I'm excited to be here!"* It became the perfect, vague response that seemed to satisfy everyone.

When lunchtime arrived, I entered the dining hall and stood in line to be served. Chicken, greens and potatoes weren't high among my favorite meals, but I politely accepted what was given to me and looked around for an available seat. No one really made an effort to talk to me yet, and that was fine by me. Upon noticing that there weren't any empty tables, I opted for the outdoors instead and took a seat in the courtyard. Few others did the same, so it was quiet for the most part. I sat my plateful of food down beside me, and took out my homework assignments. Might as well get them done and over with early, right?

"How come you're not inside, eating?"

It took me a second before I realized someone was standing right in front of me. I guess I'd been lost reading the chapter of my history book we were threatened a quiz on the next morning. I looked up, and a pair of green eyes surrounded by fair skin and strawberry hair stood in front of me. She was smiling warmly, and I smiled back and shrugged. "There wasn't really any free place to sit inside," I replied.

She glanced behind her toward the dining hall and then nodded. I recognized her from my drama class. Third period. "Mind if I sit here?" She asked brightly.

Not really in the mood for any company, I wasn't going to be rude to her, so I quickly marked the page in my book and closed it. I made room for her to sit beside me, and she set her book bag down before she sat, crossing her legs and running her fingers through her long hair.

"The girls around here really aren't that friendly towards you, are they?" It was more a statement than a question. In fact, when I caught the wry smile upon her lips, I realized it wasn't a question at all.

I shrugged. "They just stare," I told her nonchalantly. "But I guess that's normal for every 'new girl' on her first day, right?"

She looked amused. "My name is Jackie. I was in your last class."

"I'm Hope."

"I know."

I looked at her. Clearly, there was something on the tip of her tongue that she wanted to say, but wasn't. We simply stared at each other, and I guess once she determined that we were on common ground, and that it was safe, she lowered her voice and went on.

"Everyone around here is whispering about you," she started. "Nothing bad, really. They just don't know what to think. Mostly everyone around here is of 'blue-blood,' and that's something that really matters to most of the weirdos around here. Their lineage dates back to the earliest Dutch settlers, so for generations and generations our families have all known each other. You see what I'm saying?" I stared at her with a lifted eyebrow, and she continued. "I don't know. The Van Steenburghs have always been somewhat of a mystery. They're the wealthiest people in the area, yet no one really knows much about them. Some people are just intimidated. So if some of the girls around here act indifferent, just know that it's envy. There's not a girl around here that likes to be outdone. And if one thinks that she will be outdone, out comes the claws." She smirked again, and then picked up the textbook I had set aside. "Anyhow, I'm not telling you this to scare you, or anything. If anything, I can tell that you are new to all of this, and if there's any comfort, I've been in your shoes. I was introduced to this life when I was twelve, when I was adopted into the Hammacher family. I'm not quite sure what walk of life you came from prior to this, but I'm sure it was a lot better and far more sophisticated than an orphanage, and believe me—if I was able to handle it, I know you can, too." An orphanage? Well, just that statement alone earned my respect.

I contemplated her, while she thumbed through my book. "My parents died recently," I confided, deciding that it was only fair. "After that, the long-lost family I never knew came calling, and immediately insisted on taking me in." I caught her square in the eye, as if I were desperately looking for some sort of understanding, and maybe it was my imagination, but she seemed to identify with me, connect with me. She was right—there was a common ground between us. "I'd never even met them before." My voice had gone soft. Suddenly, every feeling I had been suppressing for the last few weeks was trying so hard to surface itself. I kept my composure. "So here I am," I sighed. "And you're right—I didn't come from anything like an orphanage, but it's a hell of a lot different here, than it was back home. And to be honest, my mother never even told me anything about the people I'm staying with, so her silence is my obstacle to hurdle."

"What's the rest of your schedule look like?" she asked, handing me my book back, and attempting to brighten the mood of our conversation. I ran down the list of my remaining classes, and she and I stood up, getting ready to begin the rest of our day. "Why don't we meet back here after school, and maybe go get some coffee in town?" she suggested.

"I'd like that," I replied. Looks like I made a friend after all.

Chapter 7

"Not so Pure and Innocent"

Jackie did become my first friend at that school, and over my first week at Springcrest, she quickly became who I spent most of my time there, with. A kindred spirit, she and I always seemed to be on the same page, and we had many of the same interests and hobbies.

When I mentioned to Lawrence over one of his many phone calls to check on me whom Jackie was, he instantly approved, saying that the Hammachers were very prominent people, and they had good family roots. Turned out, he went to school with Jackie's adopted father. And as promised, Friday evening Lawrence picked me up from school, and asked a million questions about how school was going, and how I liked it. I didn't let on that I knew he had already made a habit of calling my school and talking to the teachers personally about how I was adjusting. I just indulged him, telling him what he wanted to hear, pretending that he didn't already know. I grew accustomed to the fact that Lawrence would always poke his nose into any and all aspects of my life. I had no privacy, but at the same time, I also had nothing to hide. So I tried not to let it bother me.

On the car ride home, he informed me that he and Vivien would again be going out of town, and wouldn't be returning until the middle of the week. I had to pretend I was disappointed by this, but I really wasn't. Vivien still didn't have anything to do with me unless she had to, and that was hardly ever. It no longer hurt that the only grandmother I'd ever known preferred the company of herself to others. "Not to worry though. You won't be lonely—Preston will be home over the weekend," he assured me. No, he still hadn't caught on that Preston and I weren't the best of friends. Or if he had, he just decided to overlook it.

Not five minutes after we passed through the dramatic entrance of the glorious Van Steenburgh Manor, I retreated upstairs to lock myself inside my bedroom suite. I closed my eyes, drew my knees close to my chest, and rested my head upon them. I shut out the ornate room that was now mine. I wasn't distracted by the enchanting mountains peeking in at me from beyond those terrace doors. I just simply needed a few minutes to allow my head to spin. How crazy it felt, that I had just returned home to a mansion, after being away all week at a boarding school. Literally, I was plucked from one world, and thrown into another, at full speed ahead when my parents died. All I'd been running on since the second I arrived at the airport and boarded a plane to come here was confusion and adrenaline. And after having come here, I was torn between missing the mother I had known all my life, and resenting her for feeling like I never really knew her at all.

Going from *this*, to a modest, three-bedroom home in the suburbs? Really?? Going from being pampered all of her life, to going to a small salon around the corner to get her hair done every six weeks? Refusing to speak of her childhood, or her teenage years? Acting like that point in time had never existed?

But it didn't feel so lost on me. Comforting, maybe, that my mother had stayed in this very room, where I was now. Sure, I had jitters and some apprehension about this new school that I was going to – a completely different experience from the schools I had attended back home, but... my mother went to that school. Call it weird, but walking through those buildings, and down those very same hallways... it almost felt... familiar.

My eyes were still squeezed shut, and I was literally willing my mother's spirit to come to me and see me through everything I was going to experience, here. School, elegant dinner affairs, trying to come off as polished, like I've been living this way all my life... it was all new to me.

I caught a glimpse as I had headed for the stairs, of everyone buzzing around the ballroom with preparations for Vivien and Lawrence's upcoming dinner party taking place the following weekend. A crew of people that they must've hired busily cleaned the crystal chandeliers, glass wall fixtures, and all of the vast windows facing outside. A flush of heat warmed my body, in anticipation of another event where I was going to face some of the area's most prestigious people. Lawrence's colleagues. Vivien's socialite friends. I never imagined so much preparation went behind these lavish get-togethers. My guess was that Vivien didn't really know how much went into them, either. To her, all that was involved was barking out orders to maids and house-workers, and then retreating to her parlor with a dirty martini.

Not even remotely delusional at all, right?

I took a deep breath and finally lifted my head. I wished I were able to have one more conversation with my mother. I'd have gladly given my soul just for another fifteen minutes with her. Fifteen open minutes, where she would've honestly answered every question I had for her. I wiped away some stray tears that had fallen without my even noticing them. Of course, my wishes weren't realistic. Neither of them. My mother, who I'd always seen as a pillar of strength, and someone who I had aspired to be, would forever remain a mystery.

By Saturday afternoon, my legal guardians were already gone, so I decided to fill my time outside, walking through the gardens. The air was brisk, and the sky was overcast, but I went ahead down to the river, and sat in my favorite spot, on the grassy knoll. My eyes gravitated toward the thick patch of trees where I knew Trent's cabin was, and I wondered what he was doing. I couldn't help it. Call me a glutton for punishment, but I had to see him.

I made my way into the trees, heading to the direction I knew the cabin was at, and within fifteen minutes, I was there. Suddenly shy, I tip-toed up the steps to his porch, and had the urge to run back the other way. What was I afraid of? Was I still intimidated by him?

Like a dummy, I went straight for the doorknob and nearly kicked myself for it. I felt myself blushing, and then stopped to hear soft music playing from inside. I leaned in, and it was something of the classical variety. Was this guy for real? He really was like some character from a fairy-tale.

Poised to knock, I hesitated for a moment, but continued anyway. I heard nothing else aside from the music at first, so I waited, and knocked again. This time I heard some rustling, so I knew he heard. But still I waited. He wasn't answering. Did he have company, perhaps? Oh, really—what was I even doing there? I didn't have a clue what to even say to him if he *did* answer the door! Feeling stupid, I turned away, and headed for the steps. I was just about all the way down, when the door opened behind me. I whirled back around to see him standing there, holding the door open.

And wearing nothing but a towel.

This was like a scene straight out of a sordid soap opera. A white towel was swathed about his hips, and his skin was still damp from his shower. His hair was soaked, and hanging to frame his face. He had a tattoo of some tribal design winding down the thick bicep of his left arm, which only added to his sexiness. Suddenly aware that he was amused by my reaction, I felt the heat rush to my face. His eyes were alight with mischief.

"Where are you running off to, milady?

Blank, I stammered "I was going home."

"But, you're *here*," he pointed out smoothly. "What brings you?"

He was playing with me. "I don't know," I conceded. "Lawrence and Vivien are gone, and I just... ended up here," I rambled, making myself look an even bigger fool. Why couldn't I have been gone by the time he opened the door?

"Is Preston not there to keep you company? Surely he would much oblige keeping a beautiful woman company."

"Preston and I aren't speaking," I replied, trying not to pay attention to his chest, his thick arms, and his abs. It should've been a sin for a man to be so beautiful.

"Well, I suppose you would probably like to be invited inside." He tossed a look behind his back, which gave me a stunning visual of the muscle in his shoulder blades, and then he opened the door wider to invite me in. "Please allow me to take a few moments to dress myself more appropriately," he said as I walked inside, past him. At that point, I couldn't determine whether I had suddenly become feverish, or if the cabin itself were burning up. "I'll only be a minute. Make yourself at home. Are you hungry? Help yourself to anything you like," he offered before disappearing into the bathroom. I took my jacket off, and sat down on the couch. He had the drapes all drawn, and the only lighting in the room was from the fire he had going. It was so warm, and so cozy. I stared all around me, and then I wondered how many women had sat on that couch before me. How many did he invite to his cabin—willingly, and sit with them... maybe hold their hand... stroke their cheek... Ugh, I needed to put myself in check. I didn't even know this guy, and this full-blown crush I had on him was downright ridiculous.

"I apologize for keeping you waiting," he spoke upon his reemergence. I couldn't decide half of the time whether he was dripping with sarcasm or if he was just overly polite. He hadn't been gone for more than two minutes. He was wearing a pair of black drawstring pants and a white t-shirt. Even dressed casually he was a sight to behold. His hair had been towel dried, and fell comfortably about his face. The light from the fire cast a glow over his golden skin, and it made a wonderful contrast against the white of his shirt. He was remarkable. For a moment, I couldn't speak. "You aren't hungry, are you?"

I shook my head. "No, I'm actually not."

"I can make you something," he offered. "It's no problem."

"No, thank you, but I'm fine," I insisted.

"Suit yourself, then." He left the kitchen area, and then walked into the living area. He went to the chair seated by the fireplace, and picked up a book, marking it before he closed it and set it aside. "So why did you come?"

His question caught me by surprise. I thought we already went through this. "I told you, there's no one at the main house." I eyed him for a moment, and he simply stared back. "Would you like me to leave?"

He abruptly stood up. "Nah. If I didn't want any company, I wouldn't have invited you inside." He again headed out toward the kitchen, and took two champagne glasses from a cabinet. "Would you like a glass of wine?"

"Wine?"

"Yes, wine. Why the chaste look on your face?"

"Chaste?"

"Yes, chaste. Meaning, pure, innocent." That amused, mischievous look was back on his face.

"I didn't know that I was!"

"Well, would you?"

"No, thank you. I would not. The last thing I need is Lawrence finding out I've been drinking," I muttered. Even though my mother had allowed me to enjoy a glass of wine with during dinner, I could definitely see Lawrence frowning upon it.

He laughed, displaying those perfect, white teeth. "It wouldn't be the drinking that Lawrence would disapprove of," he said with a wink. "But alright. And just for the record, I can assure you that I wouldn't dare try to inebriate you and take advantage of you," he vowed. His eyes took on an impish glow.

"I wish you wouldn't speak to me like I'm a child." I eyed him coldly. "Maybe you wouldn't have invited me in here if you didn't want any company, but at the same time, don't invite me in here just to belittle me." I sighed and then rose to my feet. "I came here thinking I might actually get some decent conversation," I continued, grabbing my coat. "But you're actually no better than Preston, or Lawrence, or even Vivien. Hell, even the workers around the house act like they want to talk to me. Perhaps I should go bother them, instead." I slipped my arms into my coat. "I'm sorry for intruding. Now *you* can rest assured that I won't be back to take advantage—of your time, that is!"

He didn't allow me opportunity to flee. In seconds he'd made his way from the kitchen to me, and he put himself between the door and me. Startled, I stared up at him, and he while he gently put one hand on my shoulder, I couldn't focus on anything other than the warmth of his other hand that closed over mine that was now frozen on the doorknob. His eyes were dark and burning into mine. A breath I had gasped inward in surprise at his stealthy interference now expelled from my lungs as if he had sucked it out of me, himself. For once, it was he that seemed speechless. But me? I couldn't do anything but feel his touch on my hand, and the rise of temperature in my body as I felt he was staring right into my soul.

"I'm sorry," he apologized sincerely, as I just continued to stare up at him. His eyes lowered and I could feel them raking over my nose, my cheeks, and my lips. I couldn't move. I was paralyzed under his gaze, and his hand was still holding mine, over the doorknob. My heart was now pounding so loud that I would've bet money that he could hear it, too. He smelled so good that it was making my mouth water. He inspired a million thoughts that were now racing in my head—I just had to keep myself in order. "It's thundering," he whispered. "Did you hear that?"

"Then I'd better get back to the house before the storm gets too bad," I replied softly, turning my eyes from and giving the doorknob a twist beneath his hand.

"Damn it, woman— are you always so hard-headed?" He swiftly tugged my hand from the doorknob, and stubbornly I jerked my hand free from him before going for it again. He let out a chuckle at my determination, and his hand went firmly up against the door, making it impossible for me to open. For me, this was a battle of will. I wasn't going to be his doormat. I wasn't going to allow him to make me feel ridiculous. Although, that was exactly what this was turning into. This feeble attempt for me to leave, when I never wanted to, in the first place.

He was quite amused by my attempts to get away. In all honesty, I was flattered that he was preventing me from leaving this time, even though I wasn't about to let him know that. So I kept trying to get away, knowing full well that he was ten times stronger than I was. All the while, he was fighting not to laugh, as he was having too good of a time with this. "If you would just let me apologize—"

"I don't want your apology," I fiercely denied him. I was engaged in full-on brat-mode, by this point. "Why do you want to apologize, anyway? You're only going to make fun of me again, fifteen minutes from now, so save it."

"I can't help it if you have no sense of humor," he countered innocently. This only fueled my mock fight.

"That's fine—keep me here as long as you please. You'll get tired of this eventually, and then I'll leave and you won't have to be worried that I'll ever come back," I gloated. He was still laughing, and it actually took me some effort to not chuckle, myself. But he took it one step further – whether he realized I wasn't truly mad, or not—and he reached out for me, causing me to lose my footing on his rug.

Forever the klutz, I slipped, taking us both down onto the hardwood floor.

I landed hard on my elbow and howled in pain. He scrambled to me instantly, and it hurt so bad that I was curled up in a ball, my eyes tightly shut. Immediately, he took fault.

"Hope. Hope, *look at me*. Let me see it." His voice held a hint of panic, and I was too embarrassed to give in and let him take a look at it. What made me feel more of an idiot was that I knew I'd be fine—I hadn't broken anything. It just hurt something awful!

"Hope, please—will you look at me? I'm so sorry—I didn't mean for this to happen. I suppose I should have let you go, if that's what you had really wanted." He sighed and I felt him make himself more comfortable on the floor, beside me. His fingers found themselves in my hair, and my entire body tingled so that I forgot the pain in my elbow. I thought I had murmured that I was fine, but perhaps the words never did actually come out. He stroked my hair for a moment before I lazily opened my eyes and exhaled a dreamy sigh.

That's when I saw the smirk playing about his lips. Still, he looked amused! "Ugh," I muttered. "Really? I could have been seriously hurt!" The nerve of him! So, he knew at this point that I was being a big baby.

He won, again.

I sat up, grimacing more for my pride than my elbow. "Now, not only is visiting you emotionally draining, but physically tiresome as well," I quipped, causing him to roar with laughter.

"Would you like that glass of wine, now?"

I glared at him. "You're as incorrigible as Preston."

"That hurt, milady."

"Yes, I'll take that glass of wine."

His laughter roared as he stood up, and he extended his hands to me. I grabbed them, and he pulled me back to my feet swiftly. I accepted my defeat. I sank back into the couch, and let my eyes follow him as he poured himself a glass of wine, and then one for me. He returned, this time sitting next to me on the couch, and he handed a glass to me. "What do you say we call a truce?" He asked, presenting his glass to me.

"Fine," I agreed, raising my glass to his. "Truce. Until next time. I'm going to start training at the gym, for you."

"That sounds like a challenge!" He looked visibly impressed.

"I'll get you next time," I vowed.

"You're on!" The clank of our glasses finalized it. For a moment, both of us were silent. Now that we had nothing smart to say, would we not have anything to say, at all?

"You've completed your first week of school. How do you like Springcrest?"

I sipped the wine, blanching at its strength, and managed a nod. "It's fine. At first the thought of going there terrified me, but it's not as bad as I anticipated. There's certainly more to do there, than there is here. I have never had red wine before. This is actually not that good."

His laughter roared. "Sorry, I figured being a part of this family meant that you were probably already a seasoned drinker."

"I'm only seventeen," I reiterated.

"We get started early around here," he quipped.

"So did you have to go to a school like mine, too?"

"I went to school at Springcrest's gender counterpart—Pleasant Valley Academy. It wasn't entirely unexciting. One of the boys' favorite pastimes was stealing down the hill and trying to spy on the girls of Springcrest. I remember a few even got expelled after being warned several times to stay off their campus. I admit, I stole down there a few times, myself, but I wasn't totally preoccupied with it, like others were. I was more focused on making good grades and getting out of there." Yes, I could picture Trent's charming self pulling such stunts, and having his way with the girls of Springcrest. I didn't want to, but I could. "I can get you something else, if you like," he graciously offered. "I apologize for not taking into account that you haven't been here long enough to become a wino like the rest of us," he cracked with a smirk.

"I'm not going to be picky," I muttered before taking another sip.

"Lawrence and Vivien love their alcohol. I think once Preston and I were in our teens, they were serving it to us at dinner with our meals. I guess they have to put up with one another somehow, right?"

"During that last party, between talking art and getting yanked away by Preston, I was being offered drinks of all kinds, left and right," I recalled, staring down to the red liquid in the glass I now held.

"I'm pretty certain they gave us wine in sippy-cups when we were babies, just to knock us out." His statement made me laugh, but the wink he punctuated it with made my face hot.

"My father... he used to joke about that," I sighed, glancing around about my surroundings... bookshelves stocked full of volumes, the warmly-lit kitchen. Everything had something on it. "He used to say that I would never be able to fall asleep unless he would pick me up and rest me on his chest as a baby. But then he'd throw in there with this mischievous look in his eye that he would slip some vodka into my bottle when my mother wasn't looking, to make me go to sleep fast," I let my eyes rest on his mantle, where miscellaneous knick-knacks rested. "Is all that stuff yours?"

He took a look around, shaking his head. "Most of the books are mine, but much of everything else was already here when I moved out here."

"What did you know about my mom?" I asked him.

Obviously, my question caught him by surprise. "I was a child when she lived here," he replied, scratching his head thoughtfully. "Forgive me if I cannot recall much, but I was maybe three years old when she came here." I nodded, and he took a breath and continued. "I'd only seen Vivien a few times before Lawrence married her, and she really had no patience with children, so I knew enough to steer clear of her," he went on softly. "I remember my parents mentioning in conversation that she had a daughter, but I never really thought much of it. I didn't see her until the day of the wedding. The whole affair was such an enormous ordeal. They turned the grounds here into a bewitching array of flowers and lace. There were so many people here, or at least it seemed that way to me, and because there was so much to do they kept my parents busy the entire day. I met your mother when—from what I was guessing— she was put in charge of looking after me, that day. Come to think of it, perhaps they were trying to keep her out of the way, and keep me out of the way at the same time. I remember her being very pretty, and she was very sweet to me. I was very shy of people I didn't know, but I know I took to her very easily. And then I became very excited that she was going to be staying with us, and not too long after that, every morning when I arose from bed, I would go looking for her. She was always up before me, and usually I'd find her sitting out in the gardens."

I sat, listening as he stared into the fire and spoke. Every word he spoke created a moving picture in my head, of that beautiful little boy in the picture book I found in my bedroom, and my mother as a teenager. "What else?"

His dark eyes flicked briefly in my direction, and then he took a moment to think some more. "I remember that she was very patient with me—for a child of my age could be quite trying at times. I was constantly badgering her with questions such as what this was, or that was. And she spent a lot of time watching me over the summer she came to live with us, so it saddened me when she went away for school. I felt as if I'd lost a friend, but on the weekends she would spend as much time with me as I demanded of her. I have to admit, I had quite a crush on your mother," he confided, smiling coyly. "She was enchanting, with her long dark hair and blue eyes. Her smile lit up every room. You look exactly the way I remember her."

I might've been jealous of his childhood crush, until he followed it up with flattery. His eyes then caught and held mine once again, but I broke our gaze. I still had one more thing left to ask him. "Why did she leave here?"

He shook his head. "I don't know," he answered earnestly. "One day she was here, the next day she was not. Again, I was but a child, but I did sense that something was wrong, even if I couldn't comprehend what. It wasn't that she stopped sitting with me and indulging me, for she hadn't. She did become slightly distant, though. All I know was that I got up one morning and ran out to the gardens to look for her, and it was raining. She wasn't there, and when I found my mother, she was gathered along with everyone else, in the front foyer. Vivien was crying, and Lawrence asked that everyone look for her. She left without a note, or even a goodbye."

"You still have no idea why? No one has mentioned anything since?" I asked.

He shook his head and took another sip from his glass. "After her departure, Vivien demanded that Lindsey's name never be brought up again. Not by anyone, and especially not in her presence. It was almost as if she wanted to go on pretending that Lindsey never even existed. Lawrence did everything possible to see that all of us honored her request. And so life began without her, and Lawrence poured all his attention into Preston."

"Preston was my mother's replacement," I muttered.

"Perhaps, in a sense. But Lawrence wanted a son, and he tried everything he could to get Vivien to have a child with him. She wouldn't. I think even if your mother had stayed, Preston's transformation into the spawn of Satan would have been inevitable," he told me, finishing his glass of wine. "I'm sorry I can't help you more. I wish I had the answers that you're seeking."

"No, it's alright," I dismissed, feeling frustrated. "Apparently I'm not meant to know the real reasons why she fled Van Steenburgh Manor. She, herself, wouldn't tell me, and no one else seems to know. Maybe it's best this way."

"Would you like another glass of wine?"

I looked down, and hadn't even realized I'd consumed the rest of it. The glass just sat empty in my hands. I stared at it, and Trent stood up, removing the glass from my hands before retreating to the kitchen.

"Well, for such an imponderable situation, all you can do is let matters rest," he suggested, returning seconds later with a full glass of wine for us both. "For all one knows, it may not even have anything to do with this house. Maybe she simply missed her father."

"I don't think that was the case," I muttered. "If it were that simple, there wouldn't have been such shadows over her face just to bring this place up. There is more to it."

"Well, we could continue to speculate, or we could let it be. Don't drive yourself crazy over a mystery that may never be solved," he advised. My eyes lingered on his full lips for a long moment, and then to his eyes, that stared down at me

I glanced down at my glass of wine, which was already half-empty again, and then sighed before standing up. "I should probably go," I told him. "The thunder is getting closer and closer by the second, and it's getting late. I appreciate you inviting me in, Trent... and for making me stay."

"The pleasure is all mine," he said, rising as well. I expected him to follow by telling me that I would be welcome to come by anytime, but the invite was never brought up. Disappointed, I continued for the door and said goodnight.

Chapter 8

"Starting Over"

Preston was out on the balcony, the following morning. I eyed him all the way across my bedroom, before I disappeared into the bathroom to clean up and get dressed. I needed to figure out what I was going to say to him. Enough time had passed, and we had spent days in silence around one another at the house, now. It was time to make amends.

He was still out there when I came out of the bathroom. Having come up with no real plan of what to say, I threw open the door leading to the terrace, and stepped out. He was propped against the railing, looking out at the beautiful view sprawled out before us. There was a slight breeze that was tousling his golden hair, and he looked at peace. Relaxed. The smell of wood burning from somewhere nearby lent a rather wintry feeling in addition to the gray skies. I think I half-expected him to run the other way when I opened the door to come out, so when he didn't, I thought that was a good sign.

"Preston," I spoke gently, approaching his side. "I never should have done what I did… It was childish and wrong, and I really am sorry."

His blue eyes continued to stare out, while I took the opportunity to study his face. His boyish good looks were appealing, when he was humble. When he wasn't being arrogant and snide, Preston was actually very handsome. Now, I watched as he drew a deep breath inward, before responding to me.

"You see those mountains over there?" He nodded toward the distance, and I turned my perplexed stare in the direction he was addressing. "When we were little, Trent told me that once upon a time, a giant walked through the valley during a long journey, and he was so tired that he laid down in that very spot, and slept for so long that he turned to stone. Said he turned into those mountains." He chuckled at himself, and I turned to eye him closely. "It seems so ridiculous now, but I believed him, because even then, we weren't that much different in age, but he seemed to know everything…" He paused, narrowing his eyes as he looked off into the distance. "Anyway, it's just funny, because if you look very closely, those mountains do look like the shape of a giant man who had laid down on his back with his knees bent toward the skies." It was then that he turned my way, and his eyes met mine. They begged for me to understand him, and I was trying to. I wanted to. Then he flicked them away, looking back out. "Growing up, I always felt like I was in a race… a race with time, and a race with Trent. It was a race I was always losing. He was always so much better than me at everything, and while he was constantly being praised for his brains, I was always frowned upon because I was nothing in comparison. That sort of thing really can mess up a little kid, you know? In the beginning, I tried and tried to keep up with him, but after a while I just gave up. I had no chance…" He went quiet, but I decided to say nothing. If anything, I wanted him to go on and say more—say all that he could to make me understand him. "I… apologize, too," he spoke, turning back toward me. "For everything. Especially for the things I said about your mother. I didn't know her, and even if I did, I still wouldn't have had the right to say what I said. So, I'm sorry for that," he said.

"It's okay," I accepted.

That day, Preston and I got off to a fresh start. I would finally get to know the real him, and it was kicked off with a bout of raw honesty. At the point when he admitted that he was beat down as a child by always being compared to Trent, I saw plain-as-day that he was nothing at all like the pompous jerk he'd portrayed himself to be when we first met. Deep down, I think all he ever really wanted around the house was for someone to understand him. But since no one had ever taken the time to do so, acting arrogant and bratty was the only way he knew of to get himself noticed.

And after that day, our newfound understanding of each other actually turned into a wonderful friendship. My phone began to light up on a regular basis, with text message banter that would incite a smirk, before my fingers tapped and sent a witty response. Jackie teased me constantly, asking me what was really going on between us, and despite my insistence, she never really seemed to believe me when I told her Preston and I were just friends.

"Oh come on," she prodded. "I've never seen him for myself, but I've heard from several other girls that he's hot," she taunted light-heartedly. "So... is he?"

I laughed. "Cut it out. It's not like that."

"Well then what's up with that Trent guy? I've heard about those two. You've got the town—no, make that two of the state's—supposed hottest and eligible bachelors living right under your nose. Sink your hooks into one of them, and then come back and tell me all about it," she teased as we took a seat at our normal lunch table. "Are you going to try out for a part in Romeo and Juliet?" she asked, mercifully changing the subject.

"Of course I am," I replied. "I've played Juliet so many times I could do it in my sleep!"

She gave me a weird look. "Juliet?"

I narrowed my eyes at her. "Yeah, why? You don't think I make a good Juliet?"

She rolled her eyes. "No, it's not that. Have you talked to Mr. Peck about it, at all?"

"Actually, yes," I replied. "He thinks it would be a good idea for me to try for the part. He thinks I definitely have what it takes."

"Yeah, well good luck," she muttered. "Amanda Cox has been 'Juliet' for the last three years."

I looked at her strangely. "Amanda?"

Amanda Cox was the principal's daughter. She had already rubbed me the wrong way the first day I attended Springcrest when I'd entered that very same lunchroom, and she stopped me as I passed by her table. "Aren't you that girl who's living at the Van Steenburgh house?" I stopped to confirm her question while she smirked up at me. "So I'm sure you know Trent Forrestor, then. He's a *very*—" putting heavy emphasis on the word *very*, "—good friend of mine," she purred. "You tell him that Amanda said hello and wants him to give her a call whenever he's free," she said, twisting her long blonde hair with almost an inch of dark roots within her fingers.

"Yes, *that* Amanda. She wins the part every year by default," Jackie said disgustedly. "It's sickening. You cannot imagine how horrible she is... You'd have to see it for yourself. She can't act to save her ass."

"Well, hopefully I won't have to see it," I told her confidently. "I plan on auditioning tomorrow after school, *and* winning the part."

"You definitely have my vote," she said. "Actually, last year no one even bothered to audition for the part other than her, because they figured there was no point. How sad is that?"

Well, not this time. This was a part I was destined to play, and I knew how to play it well. Mr. Peck, our theatre instructor had confidence in me that I could definitely get the part. All he had to do was persuade the other two instructors to vote in my favor as well, instead of Amanda just because of who she was, or who her father was.

Of course, when Amanda caught wind of me auditioning for 'her' part, it wasn't a pretty sight. It wasn't until the next day—the day of the audition—that she stormed up to me in the hallway after classes, backed by three of her ditzy friends, and proceeded to try and get in my face.

"You might as well just back out of the auditions, because the part is going to me," she stated, both hands on her hips.

Keeping calm and composed, I looked back at her with a smile. "Maybe so, but I'm still going to try for it."

"You're not going to get it," she declared confidently. "What makes you think a newcomer like you could come and just take what's mine?" she snarled. "You aren't anybody special—just some orphan without a home that came to mooch off her relatives," she said, giggling at her own joke.

I rolled my eyes. "Mature. Anyway, if the part is already yours, then you have no need to worry. Let me waste my time then and audition. What's it to you?"

She leaned in closer, and I could see all the make-up caked on her face. "Because I don't like the fact that you're trying to take what's mine," she hissed.

"If the part was already yours, then they wouldn't be conducting auditions to begin with." I retorted tensely. "I'll see you after school, Amanda. At the auditions. Good luck, by the way." I edged around her and her little entourage, with Jackie right behind me. Amanda's nerve enraged me, but I think what bothered me even more was the suggestion that Trent would even give her the time of day! Sadly, I didn't know Trent as well as I'd have liked to, but I wanted to believe that he wouldn't have anything to do with a snotty little wench like Amanda—even at his most desperate time.

"I am not a fan of hers," I grumbled as Jackie and I made our way to the auditorium.

"Join the club, honey," she replied, patting my back. "It's going to be okay. Save all this emotion for your audition," she encouraged, opening the door for us to step inside.

There were many people in there already—most were people that were going to audition, and some people were there as friends to lend their support. I thought nothing of it, until I was heading to the front of the auditorium, and saw a small group of people standing there talking.

One of which was Preston.

Surprised, I approached him, and he beamed a smile my way, happy to see me. "What are you doing here?" I asked, giving him a hug.

"I wanted to come by and wish you luck," he offered.

"You drove all the way here from college?" I was in awe.

And he was flattered by the surprise upon my face. "I thought you might need someone to root you on, in this snake pit." He nodded towards the group of girls standing around Amanda.

He stayed throughout my entire audition. Jackie was undoubtedly right when it came to Amanda. When she got up on that stage, Juliet never looked so bad! How anyone could sit through one of her performances was beyond me. Jackie sat beside me and had to stifle her laughter several times as Amanda stuttered and fumbled through several of her lines. One would think that having played this part for three consecutive years now, she would have it down. Even Preston was wincing, and he admittedly had no interest in Shakespeare to begin with, except that I was hopefully going to be a part of it.

When it was my turn, I took a deep breath, and what little nervousness I had was gone by the time I began my first line. I never faltered. Never wavered. I flawlessly recited my lines, and the rest of the world disappeared when I became Juliet. Both Jackie and Preston rose to their feet in applause, at the conclusion of my performance. Mr. Peck seemed very pleased as well, as his eyes were alight with a smile of approval dancing about his lips.

When Preston saw us back to the dorms, Jackie went ahead without me and I stayed behind to thank Preston for coming out to see me audition. "I just really hope I got it," I thought out loud.

"You did," he assured me. "They'd be crazy not to give it to you. I mean, you do remember how she butchered her lines, right?" he asked with a chuckle.

I smiled and nodded. "Yeah… but, thank you for coming. It means a lot to me. You didn't have to drive all this way."

"I wanted to," he insisted. "As soon as you told me you were going to do this, I'd already decided that I was coming out."

"Okay. Well, I guess I better go before I get yelled at for being out past eight," I told him, rolling my eyes with a smile, before taking a step back from his noticeably fond gaze.

The next afternoon as Jackie and I made our way through classes, we looked for the results posted on the bulletin board outside of the theatre classroom, and sure enough, there they were. I was both surprised—and not surprised—by what I saw on that list, and Jackie stood beside me, doing an excited dance when she saw the same thing. For a moment I was stunned—I won! I got the part! It took a moment to register, but that small victory was enough to make me the happiest I had been, since coming to Van Steenburgh Manor!

From that day on, Amanda glared at me every time she saw me. It didn't bother me at all—she wasn't anyone to me. Never was. Preston was so excited for me that he was sweet enough to send an enormous, overflowing bouquet of flowers to my class the next day to congratulate me, which was both flattering and embarrassing. I finally felt like I was becoming comfortable in my new surroundings. Or that, perhaps, I might've actually belonged there. I had things to fill my time, and now rehearsals would take up two more hours of my days, after school. Not to mention that each teacher liked to pile you up with homework each night, which usually kept me up later than I would have liked to admit.

I rather liked not having too much time to myself to think, anymore.

"Oh, oh oh!" Jackie exclaimed, catching up to me during lunch. "The dance next Friday," she began, talking fast like she always does anytime she got extremely excited about something. "All the guys from Pleasant Valley are going to be there," she continued, bouncing around and looking at me. "We have to go!!!"

I looked at her like she was crazy. "Oh Jackie, no... Besides—our first performance is that following Monday night. I need to stay home and relax," I denied her. "You can go if you want to."

She started to pout, and looked genuinely heartbroken. "Oh, Hope, come on! Please? Don't you realize how desperate I'll feel if I go in there by myself?" I shook my head, not budging. "Please?" She continued to beg. "Hey, all you have to do is show up with me. Just show up! That's all! Then, once we're in the door, you can ditch me if you want. Just, *please* come with me so I don't go alone!"

By this time I was laughing at her. "You're something else, Jackie. I absolutely detest these things. I never even went to them, back home. But I'll go. I'll go just for you," I promised her before she squealed in delight and hugged me.

"Thank you so much!" She cried. "I need me a boyfriend," she said, leaning in toward me, talking under her breath, causing both of us to laugh again.

"Well, I hope we can find you one so you don't have to drag me to anymore crappy dances, then."

"Oh stop, Miss Serious—who knows, you just might have a good time, yourself!" she threatened.

Chapter 9

"Playing With Fire"

When Lawrence brought me home Friday night, Preston hadn't arrived yet. He'd told me earlier in the week that he might be coming in on Saturday, so I then counted on having the evening to myself.

Lawrence headed left after we walked in, no doubt heading directly down the hall to his office, and my footsteps echoed throughout the foyer as I made my way to the stairs. I hesitated for a moment—half-startled to see Vivien standing across the way. She turned her head slightly to give me a sideways look, and I came to a full stop. Should I say something? Would she? But I couldn't find any words. Apparently, neither could she. Instead, she simply turned her head away to stare back outside. I continued on my way upstairs.

Lawrence had informed me that he and Vivien had dinner plans. They always had plans. Dinner plans, trips, anything to get them out of that house, and away from me.

Though, this time he invited me to come along, and I was sure he only did so because he knew I wouldn't take him up on the offer. I declined and said that I was too tired from the goings-on from the week. He showed a lot of interest in my schooling, and always asked me how everything was, and what was new, but when I told him when my first performance was, he didn't even mention attending.

Nothing surprised me, anymore. Though, I did originally expect that he would go just to make a social appearance and at least seem like a caring parental figure. I guess I was wrong.

It seemed like ages since I'd last seen Trent, not counting how many times he invaded my dreams. So, not a moment after Lawrence and Vivien left for dinner, I stole out of the house and headed for those woods under the moonlight.

As I approached the cozy, stone hideaway, it looked dark inside. I wondered if he was even home, but before I could even reach the door, it opened, and he stood there holding two glasses of wine.

"Good evening," he greeted me with a wide, white grin, stepping back to allow me inside. Bewildered, I entered his home, looking around to see whom the other glass might've been for.

"Are you... expecting someone?" I prodded, eyeing the second glass in his hand, and peering down the hall to see if someone was in the bathroom.

"Just you," he replied nonchalantly, offering me the second glass.

"Me?" I was confused. "Are you a mind-reader? You had no idea I was coming."

"But I did," he countered, taking a seat back on his plush couch. "I was pouring a glass of wine for myself when I saw you coming out of the woods." He pointed to the window that clearly would've given him direct line of sight to me approaching his cabin. "Aware that you don't usually come out here to converse with the trees, I assumed you were coming here and poured a glass for you, as well. Take a seat, make yourself comfortable," he invited.

I took my coat off, and took notice of the atmosphere surrounding me. A fire burned and crackled in the fireplace, and light from a dozen or so votive candles danced all about the room, and through the kitchen. They provided the only lighting in the cabin, and they cast a warm ambiance that wrapped itself cozily around met. Instead of taking a seat beside him, I sat on the floor, and propped myself against the side of his armchair next to the fire. For a moment, I just sat and bathed in its warmth. It was comforting and relaxing. At that particular moment in time, all was right in the world.

"What brings you this evening?"

"Stimulating conversation," I replied deftly. His black hair was damp, and it was apparent that he hadn't shaved, as the dim lighting highlighted his five o'clock shadow. He looked stunning, beyond words. His eyes were studying me right back, and if he were trying to read me, I was afraid he would be disappointed. It was on the tip of my tongue to ask him if I needed a specific reason to come see him, but I was afraid he'd say yes. After I realized that I was staring back at him, I self-consciously broke the hold he had over me, and directed my attention toward the fire. Wine probably wasn't the best idea. Neither was coming here. I needed to keep my wits about me, even when I didn't really want to.

When it came to Trent, I was always going to be in over my head.

He was above me in so many different ways, and he was so much like the fire I was gazing into. I knew that if I played with it, I'd get hurt, but it was such an exciting idea... "Are you up to it?" I broke the silence, snapping us both back to reality.

"Well, I don't mind the company," he admitted. "Previously, I'd decided to throw myself into my work tonight, but once I sat down to do so, I found that I had no motivation what-so-ever," he disclosed. I glanced back up at him, and his eyes were still fixed on me. "How is school?"

I shrugged, wishing he wouldn't even bring it up. It just reminded me of the difference of age between us. It took away from the fantasy that played out in my head. It brought me back to reality—and the reality was that I would never have a chance with him. Ever. "It's school," I muttered, blinking back my thoughts to just enjoy the moment. "For the most part, it's just like any other school, except that the people are more hoity-toity than I'm used to," I confided. "I just have to keep reminding myself that they're not really any better..." I trailed off, then deciding not to let them ruin my evening. "However," I began on a lighter note, "I got the part of Juliet in our upcoming play," I boasted with a smile. "So that made my day."

He smiled with a nod of approval. "Very good," he praised, taking a sip of his wine. "I may have to catch one of those performances once they begin."

"You should," I encouraged him, noticing that he had started a painting that was now resting on his easel. I casually stood up to investigate. "You'll never see a better Juliet," I bragged. "I even beat out your little girlfriend in the process."

He looked baffled. "My girlfriend?"

The canvas was a good size. The silhouette of a woman was drawn by light, airy strokes of black. "Yes. Or at least, that's what she made it out to be."

He frowned. "Who are you speaking of?"

"You don't know?" I asked coyly, tilting my head slightly at the curves of the woman's body on the canvas.

"Surely I would know if I had a girlfriend, don't you think?"

"Well then you must know who I'm talking about," I concluded, masking my slight jealousy as best I could. Maybe subconsciously, that which I had become fixated upon was my driving motivation for seeing him, this time.

"But I don't," he countered through narrowed eyes, curiously following my every move.

"Amanda Cox," I announced brightly. "And she would be sorely disappointed if she heard you say that," I sputtered at him. "By the way, she asked me to have you call her at your earliest convenience."

He raised an eyebrow at me, and then chuckled, tossing back the rest of his wine. "Ah... Amanda. She's nothing. I'm sure she said that just to rattle you."

"Rattle me? Why would that rattle me? It didn't rattle me at all," I lied, as his eyes narrowed even more at my odd behavior. "Besides, she seemed very sincere," I added brightly.

"Are you going to drink that?" He pointed at my glass as he stood up. I hadn't even touched my wine, yet, but when he said that, I took a long sip of it. Perhaps Van Steenburgh Manor, along with its inhabitants, were to make a wino of me, yet.

He proceeded to the kitchen with his empty glass, and refilled it before heading back to his seat. "Amanda attended a dinner of Lawrence's a few months back. She probably could have had any of the schmucks at the affair, but for some reason decided she wanted to sink her bloodthirsty claws into me," he explained. "However, she didn't succeed. She even tried every little schoolgirl act she could to try and beguile me. At the end of the night, she stuck her number in my jacket, and that was it."

I shrugged. "That's it? She saw you at a party and gave you her number, and nothing else happened?"

"She followed me from conversation to conversation, and I thought she sounded very immature and foolish. I thought she seemed more to be Preston's type," he went on, eyeing me.

I was just about to defend Preston against the remark Trent made, but I bit my tongue. "Well, she certainly made it seem a lot different, that's all," I said softly, drinking some more wine.

"I can assure you, it was nothing," he asserted. "Would you like a resume of the other women I've spoken to?" I snapped my eyes to his, and he was clearly amused. "I'm kidding," he gently went on. "Don't look so disgruntled. How about you? Have you found anyone that you've taken a liking to?"

I wanted to tell him that I *had* found someone. Someone so exciting that they took my breath away at a glance. Someone far worldlier than any of the guys at Pleasant Valley Academy could ever hope to be, and more intelligent than anyone I'd ever known. Someone whose face looked like it was carved from a Greek statue, and whose eyes could see right through me, and deep into my soul. But I couldn't. I just shook my head without response. "There's a dance next Friday that my friend Jackie asked me to attend with her," I told him. "She's looking forward to meeting the guys from Pleasant Valley."

"Ah, yes. Those things... I'm so fortunate to be done with all that," he said, leaning back further into his couch. "I don't miss those days at all. It's nothing but a bunch of arrogant guys trying to score an equally arrogant, spoiled rich girl that thinks that she's God's gift to the world."

"Well I'll stick out like a sore thumb, then," I retorted.

"Yes, you most certainly will," he agreed. Then, upon eyeing me for a long moment, he added, "Or maybe not. Now that you're living at the manor, you're most likely the envy of every money-hungry schoolgirl-and-boy alike."

I shook my head, allowing my eyes to scan the room again. None of that mattered to me. I just wanted to hurry up and be done with it all. "Maybe I'm ungrateful, but I'd rather be back in my hometown, going to school with the rest of us low-lives."

"This life takes a lot of getting used to, indeed. You'll acclimate." His tone was assuring. I wasn't so sure...

"So is that why you're single? Because you think that all the women you meet are money-hungry wenches?" I asked boldly.

Taken aback, he raised his eyebrow. "What makes you think I'm single?" he countered.

"The fact that you're always here. By yourself." I answered blandly.

"Valid point you have, there." He brought his glass to his lips and downed the remainder of his wine. "I'm single because I choose to be."

"Of course," I said cynically. "And I'm sure that has nothing to do with your point of view."

"It has little to do with it," he debated. "I just haven't found anyone who has compelled me to commit to them. Once I do, I'll no longer be single. It's that simple."

"What are you looking for, then?" I quizzed him. "You must meet lots of people, doing what you do, and living here. And you claim to have never met someone who catches your eye?"

"I never said they didn't catch my eye. They just haven't kept my attention."

"So you get bored quickly?"

"Never had a chance to get bored. I haven't found anyone worth my while to allow them to capture my attention." He loved this, as his eyes danced with mischief. His lips were slightly curled into a menacing smile.

"So, you're unattainable," I concluded.

"Not unattainable. Just hard to please, if you will."

"High standards?"

"You could say that."

I nodded, deep in thought. "Have you ever been in love?"

He scoffed. "I don't believe such an emotion exists."

It was my turn to be taken aback. "No? Why not?"

"I believe in lust. I believe in passion. I believe in respect, and companionship. I've felt and experienced all those things. But I don't believe in some magical feeling that will someday capture me and render me giddy, and ultimately become someone's doormat. If true love existed, do you think there would be so many divorces? I don't believe so." He shrugged nonchalantly. "People fall into lust, mistake it for love, get married, and once the fun and passion dies down, they want to walk away. Nope. Not for me, but thank you."

"What a strange way of thinking!" I chuckled at him and shook my head, as he now looked surprised by my mixture of annoyance and amusement. "Love is not just that," I argued. "It's a deep respect two people have for one another, and the common ground they stand on. It's the hard work they put into making a relationship, and all the feelings they have for one another. It's not *just* the lust and excitement. It's wanting to make someone happy, and that person wanting to make *you* happy. Your take on it just sounds... lost," I chastised regally, before taking another sip.

"Well, if I ever feel that way, I'll be sure to let you know," he poked.

"And I suppose your views on marriage are just as skewed?"

"I'm not the marrying kind," he retorted. "I prefer to come and leave as I please, without having to answer any questions, such as 'Where are you going?' or 'When will you be back?'"

I shook my head in frustration. "That's not what marriage is about—"

"Yes, I know. It's about love, and respect, and everything else you mentioned," he said with a grin. "We are too young to even think about that." Even still, he continued to look thoughtful for a moment, eyeing my closely before he once again turned to his wine. "As it stands, I think I'm too independent to take on a wife. I couldn't handle having to consult someone else on every decision I make," he said, drinking the last of his wine.

"Sounds to me like you're trying to talk yourself into believing that," I countered with a smirk.

He addressed my bold statement with a look that resembled defeat. Wordlessly, he got up and put his empty glass on the kitchen counter, before strolling back in my direction. Only, he didn't take his seat on the couch, this time. Instead he joined me on the floor, in front of the fire.

He turned to face me; his face was maybe a foot from mine. Him suddenly being so close to me made me acutely aware of every inch of my body, in proximity to his. My eyes grazed over the smooth, flawless skin of his face, down to the stubble on his upper lip and chin. It was a habit of mine to stare at him, but I couldn't think of a better hobby... He was breathtaking.

And when his eyes turned to mine, I could swear I felt them reaching in to touch every one of my deepest thoughts, before they slid gracefully down over my nose. They those dark pools of black ink flanked by equally dark eyelashes had the nerve of settling upon my lips that silently begged to feel the softness of his mouth against them. Again they dared to lower themselves, following the line of my collarbone before dipping down to the swell of my breasts.

They lingered there just long enough for me to take notice of my heart beating wildly in my chest, before he swallowed hard and broke the gaze that left me swooning.

"Why *do* you come here?" His voice was low and husky enough to make my ears tingle. I could barely detect the scent of wine on his breath, and that, accompanied by being so close to him, intoxicated me more than any amount of wine.

"I don't know," I answered again, my voice small. "I feel like I'm drawn to this place," I told him, looking around at everything. "Everything about being here feels good... It feels right... It's just hard to explain..."

"I have nothing to offer you, Hope. I want you to remember that," he rasped, gently but firmly. His statement caught me by surprise, and I felt my face get hot. His face was only inches from mine, and my heart dropped with disappointment that made me feel like such a child. I knew what I wanted, but I was too timid to seize it. He was so sophisticated that he made me feel awkward, immature, lacking... If he only knew that he need not offer anything— just what he was, was enough. "You come here, and I feel like there's something that you're looking for. Something I can't help you with."

I couldn't look him in the eye. I knew he was right. I wanted something that I couldn't have, and I didn't like to be reminded of that. "I don't know what I'm looking for," I uttered sadly. "But I guess you're right. Whatever it is, it's not here."

He was quiet for a long moment, studying my face again before he spoke a startling confession that made my heart jump in my chest. "I was attracted to you from the moment I saw you at Lawrence's party," he confessed, barely above a whisper. His breath on my neck was making me dizzy with longing, as his roaming eyes embarked on what had to have been an accidental mission to seduce me. "I tried to disregard it, but then there you were, *here* when I came back. It caught me completely off guard." I still sat, frozen, unable to speak. Not wanting to break the spell of this moment. This stunning, romantic admittance that whatever this was that had been welling up inside of me wasn't just one-sided. "I was consumed by the sight of you at the party, but seeing you here made it personal... And, nowadays when I play the piano in the ballroom, Lawrence usually ignores it. Vivien sleeps so barricaded by masks and blankets that there's no way one could wake her. Preston avoids me like the plague. But that one night you came down, I sat down before that piano with the explicit hope that if it reached you, you'd come down. You did."

I finally brought myself to look at him at this point, and now he was staring off, his eyes unfocused. I had no idea what was bringing this sudden honesty out of him, but I didn't want it to stop. I opened my mouth to speak, but nothing came out. He didn't even notice. He was so close that I could've easily closed the gap of space between us, had I made a move. And I might have, if he hadn't continued to speak.

"I knew you were standing in that doorway before I even saw you," he recalled with the slight upward twitch of his beautiful lips. "Every note I played was an apology for being coarse to you, that night." As he spoke, my heart drank in his words as eagerly as my memory. "It's strange to me how I hardly know you, but I feel as if I've known you all my life," he continued with a flick of his eyes that connected with mine. "At first, I equated it to the fact that I was close to your mother early on in my childhood, but even idea that was short-lived." His hand reached up and cupped my face. I closed my hand over his, and I was growing dizzy with anticipation while my heart continued to pound. I willed for him to kiss me. I wanted it. But instead, he continued to speak.

"So, I can definitely relate to your feeling of being drawn here, and feeling like you've been before. But... You and me? We can't do this. It's unfair. You deserve so much more—much more than I could offer you." He released his hand from my face, and from my grip.

I snapped to attention, and stared back at him, bewildered. "Wait, what!?" I jerked my face free from his hands, feeling like every single thing he said before that was nullified. "What makes you think that you couldn't make me happy? Do you realize that I've had nothing but you on my mind ever since the night of that party?"

"You heard what I said, earlier! What could I possibly offer you? I'm not what someone like you needs. I can't think beyond tomorrow, let alone consider someone else's feelings in everything I do." He was quick to his feet, and before I knew it, he was far away from me in an instant. In the kitchen. Propped against the counter. Putting distance... I knew I was in over my head. His words hit me like a blow to the stomach! "Do you know how many women I've been with, who have tried to change my ways?" He asked, reading my mind. "I've never found one yet who has inspired me to keep her around."

"You act as if a commitment is a job," I sputtered bitterly.

"Isn't it?" He asked. "After all, you must work to keep it together, correct? It's a constant tug-of-war with emotions, problems, and it is a *job*. One that you cannot just walk away from. Suddenly, there are a person's emotions at stake. No," he concluded. "I'd rather just keep things simple."

"When the right one comes along, she'll change that," I barked at him.

"And who would that be?" He asked. "You?" He grinned maliciously, and it only served to infuriate me even more. If it were possible to read minds, he could, and it wasn't working to my advantage.

"No, of course not," I countered. "Because you would definitely need a woman who could put up with your cocky attitude and oppressive behavior!"

"Oh stop. I'm not a tyrant, milady. I'm simply being honest with you. If you would prefer that I lie to you and tell you that my head is lost somewhere up in the clouds and I believe I'll find true love someday, then I will."

"One minute ago you were telling me how much you wanted me, and now you're on the complete opposite side of the spectrum," I observed. "Tell me the logic in that."

"Perhaps there is none," he simply answered. There was a silence that followed, and the only sound was of the rain pounding the roof of the cabin in large sheets of rain. We were now engaged in a stare down. His dark eyes bore into mine from across the room, and I sat unmoving for what felt like ages. I couldn't read him.

"I should go," I said abruptly, standing up. He started for the door after me, and wordlessly watched me as I put my coat on. "Thank you for the company," I said curtly.

"I thank you, as well," he said sincerely.

All I could do was clench my teeth and reach for the door, but he beat me to it. Opening it to let me out, I now just wanted to punch him in the face...

"Until next time."

I wanted to tell him there wouldn't be a "next time," but instead I simply walked past him, and down the steps of his cabin, into the wet dirt and leaves. When the door closed behind me, it was everything I could do to keep myself from releasing the tears of frustration that now stung at my eyes.

How two people could want one another and deny each other at the same time was beyond me. I decided as soon as I left the cabin that night, that I wouldn't return. Why torture myself with the idea that I wanted someone who would never indulge me? And it was someone who wanted me in return, nevertheless. I just didn't understand, and I was done trying to understand. I was in over my head anyway. I had to stop playing with that fire before I actually did end up getting burnt.

Chapter 10

"Preston's Angel"

Right or wrong, I decided to pour all of my attention into Preston, after that night. Preston was all too eager for my attention, and since I had no one else clamoring for it, he won by default. We spent most of our free time at the manor just hanging around the house, or out in the gardens. I never told him anything that transpired between Trent and I. As far as he was concerned, we'd never even formally met. As far as I was concerned at this point, we hadn't.

And I did everything I could to think as little about Trent as possible. Being around Preston helped that quite a bit. All of the workers around the house were quite visibly surprised by the sudden change of heart between he and I, and that we were speaking to each other by choice, let alone enjoying it. And since he and I started spending time together on a regular basis, dare I even go so far as to say he even began acting nicer to everyone around the house? I decided that I would let everyone at the house believe what they wanted to about Preston, but I could actually say I knew him better than they did. He was opening up to me, and I saw him for who he actually was. The real Preston was sweet and attentive, not crude and obnoxious. And I didn't miss the bad side of him one bit.

I could also report that things between Lawrence and Vivien and I were unchanging, as time wore on. When they were in town, whoever was there at the house at that time was required to promptly appear in the dining room at 5pm for dinner, and it never failed to feel like the longest forty-five minutes of my day.

"Hope has a banquet at her school, coming up," I shoveled a forkful of potatoes in my mouth, giving Lawrence a brief glance as he addressed Vivien one evening. "Perhaps tomorrow morning Charles can take the both of you into the city to shop for a dress for her, and whatever else you ladies might need."

Vivien's eyebrow lifted, and she very slowly, deliberately finished the tiny bite of food she'd carefully placed in her mouth. "I'm very busy this weekend," she answered firmly. "We have so many things coming up. You know that."

Lawrence returned his gaze to the newspaper which sat beside his plate. "Just a suggestion, dear. If you have other things to do, that's fine. Perhaps Kate can take her."

"I'm sure I already have something suitable in my closet," I spoke up, just wanting the conversation to pass and be done with. "If I don't, Jackie and I will go somewhere during the week and look around after class."

Lawrence gave me a thoughtful look, and then nodded. "I will transfer a little extra into your account this week," he offered with a smile. "If you need anything else, don't hesitate to call."

All I needed was some normalcy, which obviously didn't exist in this house. I cast Vivien a brief look of disgust, and then returned to my plate. She could stay consumed with whatever it was she imagined kept her busy, as far as I was concerned. My feelings weren't hurt, anymore.

As usual, outside of our "mock" family dinners, Lawrence and Vivien made themselves scarce until it was time to take me to school, Monday morning. That's when Lawrence appeared; smiling as I came downstairs with my bag, ready to go.

"There's my princess," he announced, suddenly making me feel as if I were five years old again. "Are you ready?"

I nodded. "Yes, I think so."

Vivien appeared behind him, holding her cup of morning coffee, and she was eyeing me up and down. "Do you try to look that frumpy for school, or did you just get up late and you were in a rush?" she asked.

Looking down, I glanced over my outfit. It was the same thing I always wore. "I got up on time," I replied meekly.

"You need to quit slouching," she ordered, stepping closer. "You carry yourself like you've been raised in a trailer," she chastised. "Pull your shoulders back," she snapped. "Like mine. See?"

I resented her criticism, but did as she asked, before looking to Lawrence, desperately just wanting to get out of there. If she wasn't griping at me about my posture, she was griping at me because I ate too fast, or too much, or didn't use "proper enough" English. I just tried not to pay attention to her.

And life at Springcrest. What could I really say about it? It was more often than not a welcome escape from the dysfunctional atmosphere at Van Steenburgh Manor. Hell, I remembered being a little girl, and anytime my mother became upset at me for doing whatever I did to misbehave, she would threaten to send me "to boarding school" if I didn't stop with the nonsense. As I sat in my room, reflecting, the remembrance of it brought a bittersweet smile to my face.

It wasn't so bad. I had friends here. I had a place to get away from Vivien's glares, or Lawrence pretending to give a damn about anything going on in my life. As far as I was concerned, school had more semblance of a "family life" for me than the enormous house I now called "home."

I sighed as I gazed out of the small window, from my bed, out into the rain. Even when it was dreary out, the grounds were still beautiful. I wondered how often my mother had sat on her bed, in her dorm, gazing out onto the campus grounds and pondering her life. What ultimately drove her away from her home, and away from a lonely little boy who adored her and relied on her to be there? Was it her resentment towards Lawrence? Did she really miss her father that much? Did her mother's negligence finally get the best of her?

Hope of ever finding answers to my questions kept slipping further and further away. I'd probably never know. It was now simply up to me to either take advantage of every avenue this kind of life could provide me…. Or let it drive me completely insane.

I was even beginning to like the advantages of having money, and never having to ask "How much?" I even started to resemble the rest of the girls at my school now, with sun-kissed skin, silky hair with touches of color, trendy clothes, and best of all—people were impressed when they asked where I came from, and who was I staying with. I was even impressed when Jackie presented me with a copy of the city newspaper, which featured a picture of me on the esteemed *Society Page;* announcing that I'd been selected to be the next Juliet in the upcoming play.

And I certainly got satisfaction when further down the page it mentioned how I beat out Amanda for the part.

All week long, I was buried in rehearsals until late in the evenings. When finally I would make it back to my dorm room, Preston would normally call or text, to see how everything was going. Sometimes I could hear a party in the background, and sometimes he was alone in his own dorm room. Other times, he'd be driving to or from somewhere, getting some take-out food, or coming from a movie with his friends. But he'd always call like clockwork, and it kind of made me feel important that no matter what he was doing, or who he was with, he called me like I was someone of importance.

"I'll be coming home early this Friday," he hinted over the phone, one evening. "I can come pick you up instead of Lawrence, if you want," he offered.

I sighed into the phone. "Yeah, well that would be nice, except for that Jackie is forcing me to go to some dance here, Friday night," I told him. "I'm really not looking forward to it. She just wants me to go with her so that she doesn't have to go alone."

"Well, that sucks for me. But you'd better be careful, because those Pleasant Valley guys haven't seen a girl in ages, and they might paw you to death," he cracked.

"I know," I agreed with a laugh. "How much can I pay you to be my date, so they'll think I'm off limits?" I teased.

"No need to pay me," he replied quickly. "I'd do it for free."

"Yeah right," I countered in amusement. "Just what every college guy wants—to hang around with a bunch of high school kids."

"Actually, this probably sounds bad, but a few of my buddies are dating girls from that school, and they'll probably be there, too," he admitted.

"What!? You bunch of cradle-robbers," I joked, causing him to laugh into the other end of the phone line. "Anyhow, I'm just not looking forward to this night, at all."

"Well, if you ask me nicely, I'll go with you as your date."

I laughed, grateful that he couldn't see me blushing. "Oh, do I have to ask you nicely?"

"Yes. You have to say, 'Preston, will you be my date this Friday night?'"

"You're out of your mind," I told him, cracking up.

"What time should I be there?"

I was silent for a moment, stunned more by the fact that I was excited about the prospect of having him there. "Seven," I answered, surprising myself. "And... thank you,

Preston. At least I know I won't be standing in a corner by myself."

"And," he added mischievously, "My date will be the hottest girl there!"

As expected, with rehearsals, homework, and Jackie going on and on about the dance, the rest of the week flew by. Mid-week, I was somewhat worried when my theater instructor asked to see me after my classes were done, and when I arrived to his classroom at the end of the day, my head was spinning with the endless possibilities of what he might have to say.

"Have a seat," he beckoned, pushing his glasses to the top of his nose, and eyeballing me. "How are you? How are you adjusting here?"

"Fine, I think," I answered with uncertainty. "It is definitely a change, but...one I think I have met head-on, if I do say so myself."

"Oh yes, no doubt," he agreed. "But where do you see yourself going from here?"

His question surprised me. I suppose up to this point, I really hadn't thought about it. I never even had the time to think about it.

"Envision this school as a stepping stone." He leaned forward. "Where is the next step for you?"

I shook my head. "I don't know, sir. All I've ever wanted to do was act. Be on a stage. Get to Broadway. Make this a career."

"Well what avenues are you looking at to get there?"

I was becoming flustered. "I don't know!"

He sat back and sighed. "You are incredibly talented. Just from these rehearsals alone, I'm floored to see how these performances go off. I've looked over your past school records and I know you've been doing this for all of your junior and high school years. Frankly, I can't wait to see what else you're capable of!"

Friday after classes, while Jackie and I hid away in my dorm room, I told her about my meeting with my theater instructor while we get readied for this school shindig. Jackie had picked out a gorgeous A-line gown in a deep plum color that she was eagerly changing into. Within minutes, she had her hair pinned up in a sleek chignon, and applied some light make-up to her pale skin. She made it look so easy. Meanwhile, I wished Kate were around to work her magic on me.

"He wants me to broaden my range," I rattled on to her. "I'm all for that, but he's setting me up with a voice coach. To sing onstage." She didn't seem to understand my plight. "By myself."

"What's the big deal?" she paused to look at me like I was crazy.

"I've never had to sing on stage… by myself. I've had to sing with a group. Like, choir-style. But he's talking about me going for the role of Christine in Phantom of the Opera."

"I didn't know our school did that play." She was now concentrating on her mascara.

"They don't. It's the community theater he wants me to try for."

She turned around, wide-eyed. "You better go for that, Hope. Do you know how good that would look on your applications for colleges? They like stuff like that."

I didn't want to talk about it anymore. I needed to get ready for this thing I was coerced into. I chose a long white gown that I thought looked wintry enough to pass for our winter-themed dance. It was a simple, long one-shouldered gown. It had an underlining that went the length of the dress, and then a chiffon overlay, which flowed down and had minimal sparkly rhinestones on it that reminded me of snowflakes. I chose a pair of silver heels to wear with it, and when I emerged from the bathroom, Jackie nodded her head in approval, and gave me thumbs up. "I love that dress!" She exclaimed. "I just wish I had a body like yours to fill it out!"

"Hey now, you're doing alright for yourself, too," I assured her. "That dress looks fantastic on you!"

"What do you want me to do with your hair?" She asked. I didn't know. I told her I'd leave that up to her.

Before we walked out of my room, I took a last look at my reflection, and I saw my mother, on the night that she left with my father, never to return home. It was uncanny. I almost had to look past that thought, in order just to see myself in that mirror. Jackie did a terrific job on my hair, twisting pieces and pinning them back. My eyes were dark and smoky, and I wore a pale pink on my lips. Now it was time to go meet Preston downstairs.

The dance was across campus, in Century Hall; a building that was erected specifically for dances and other social functions held at the school, instead of holding them in the cafeteria, or the auditoriums like I was used to, back home. I realized that people in this part of the country took their social affairs seriously. Everyone that had money and history had their own salons and ballrooms, here. Even the schools. Jackie and I arrived just outside our building, but we were a bit early, and there was no sign of Preston, yet. Girls were already on their way into the party, and I saw many guys arriving as well, via limos, or expensive cars. It wasn't long before I saw Preston's little silver Mercedes convertible pull up, and he parked in the nearby lot. Jackie teasingly elbowed me when she saw him pull up, and I found myself nervous and antsy by his arrival.

I watched him as he opened his car door to get out. He was dressed in his black suit, and it flattered his slender frame really well. He instantly looked around, and when he caught sight of me, he paused for one palpable moment. After that, he began his approach with eyes that never left me, and once he got to us, Jackie started teasing him immediately.

"Hey, you're late!"

"No I'm not, I'm on time—you're just early," he retorted lightly, briefly flicking his eyes away from me, to her.

"Whatever, you're fired. We're ditching you for some guys who will be more on time," she kept on, smiling mercilessly.

"Go ahead and try to find anyone better than me—I'll bet you couldn't," he insisted with a sizzling smile. "I'm the best there is."

"Preston, no one loves you more than you love yourself," she bantered as we made our way to the dance hall.

"You're probably right," he agreed with a wink. Then he smiled down at me, and offered me his arm. It was a chivalrous move that caused a flutter in my heart. Unable to stifle my smile even if I wanted to, I slipped my arm through his and began to walk to the entrance of the party.

There were probably already about a hundred or so people in attendance already, and there were still many entering behind us. The hall looked fabulous, and I was quite impressed. We made our 'grand entrance', and it took no time at all for Jackie to find an admirer, who immediately took her attention away from Preston and I. I watched her as she walked off with the good-looking guy who undoubtedly must've come from Pleasant Valley Academy, and as she went, she turned and gave me a thumbs-up signal.

"Looks like we're not needed, anymore," Preston quipped, grinning. "That was short-lived."

"I know," I muttered. "Okay, so, now what?"

"Would you like to dance?" He asked, taking my hand.

"Are you kidding? After the last time we danced?" I cracked, gently trying to pull my hand away.

He laughed. "Come on, let me make that up to you, then," he offered.

Feigning reluctance, I followed his lead out to the dance floor, and we joined several others who were dancing to the slow, dreamy melody provided by the hired DJ for tonight's ordeal. Preston then slipped his arm around my waist, rested his hand on the small of my back, and his other hand held mine. Something in me awakened, and it stirred something within me that made me suddenly "aware"... Aware of him, of myself, and of the way I felt being held against him. We were both quiet for a long moment; I think just taking each other in.

"This is definitely a lot different than the last time we danced," I murmured softly.

His breath tickled my ear, further driving home exactly how close to one another we actually were. "You're never going to let me live that one down, are you?"

I shook my head. "Nope," I replied with a sheepish smile.

"Okay, well why didn't you dance with me then, like you are now?" He countered.

"Because I despised you then, understandably."

"Understandably. It was exciting though, dancing with you," he complimented between us. "There were a lot of eyes on us. On you..."

I didn't quite know what to say to that. I was flattered, but speechless.

"So when is your first performance?"

"Next Wednesday," I answered him. Frankly, I was grateful he had picke another topic, altogether. "We'll have one performance every night until Friday. Then it picks up the following week, and we will have our last performance that Friday night."

"I'll plan to be at every one."

I laughed. "Yeah right—no one loves Shakespeare that much," I quipped.

"You're right," he agreed. "But being that I'm your biggest fan, it's something I want to do. I'll be in the front row, center."

I smiled up into his handsome face. "Well then, suit yourself. But don't let me catch you falling asleep in that chair," I warned, causing him to laugh.

"Are you thirsty? Can I get you anything to drink?" he asked.

"No," I replied. "But thank you." Surely there was no wine at this event...

"No problem," he assured me, eyeing me for a moment. "You look beautiful tonight, by the way."

My eyes caught his, and I felt myself blush, quickly looking away. "Thank you, Preston. That's sweet of you to say."

"I mean it," he insisted. "When I got out of my car earlier, I had to do a double take. Then I realized—that's my date for the night. *My* date!" He had the most charming smile upon his face, before his look softened. "You look like an angel tonight."

I felt compelled to pull him closer to me. Grateful just to be adored, my arms went up about his neck, while his other arm dropped to my waist. "If you keep complimenting me like that, I might have to keep you around," I threatened.

He let out a low chuckle, while his blue eyes dipped downward between us. "Promises, promises."

"Well, trust me—you wouldn't want that," I purred. "Then you might have to attend more of these functions with me, and shower me with more compliments."

"I don't know if I could do that on a regular basis," he said, pretending to look panicked.

"Well, we could always go back to you acting like a pompous jerk," I offered.

"And you could go back to slapping me around, and trying to drown me," he countered with a mischievous grin.

My jaw dropped, causing him to laugh. "I can't believe you just said that!"

"You're violent!"

"Oh, and I suppose you never said a mean word to me?"

"Never."

"Right," I said, shaking my head and laughing.

"You're very beautiful when you're angry," he taunted, as his bright blue eyes sparkled with mischief.

"Oh, am I? You ought to know," I told him.

"I'm an expert. I've seen it enough times."

"Only because you know how to bring the best out in me, Preston," I joked.

He expelled a deep breath. "Well, I'm glad we've put that behind us," he said with light-hearted sarcasm. "Never thought I'd say this, but you mean a great deal to me, Hope."

I smiled in response. "Thank you again for coming here tonight."

"I'd do anything you ask of me," he promised. "No questions asked." Then he spotted Jackie, off somewhere behind me. "She's quite the social butterfly, isn't she?"

I smirked back at him. "Yeah, well she claims she hasn't had a boyfriend since last summer, so I think she's trying to make up for lost time," I joked.

At that point, we heard some commotion toward the front of the hall, and Preston and I both turned to look as we continued to dance. I was surprised to see Amanda coming in, dressed in an ensemble that looked like Mrs. Claus-meets-Fredericks of Hollywood—a tight, strapless red number with white fluff around the top, and a slit that went all the way up her thigh. She came in looking slightly disheveled, as did her date, which Preston immediately identified as one of the football players from his college.

"I believe she's been to a few of those things that my father and Vivien throw at the manor," Preston recognized. "My father represented her father after he was charged with driving while being intoxicated," he revealed to me. "Of course, my father got him off, but he's still a drunken bastard who hasn't learned his lesson, from what I hear." He paused to study Amanda as she made her way inside, and then commented, "It looks like his daughter may not be too far behind him..."

She did appear as if maybe she had a drink or two before she came. There was a bit of a stumble in her walk, and it wasn't because of her stiletto heels. And try as I might to ignore her presence that had now taken over the attention of everyone in her path, it wasn't long before she caught sight of me...

"Well, look who's here!" Amanda exclaimed, approaching us. Preston and I both turned, and she stopped a few feet away from us, flask in hand, and a smirk on her face. "Don't *you* look like the belle of the ball," she spat. "Don't you know it's not appropriate to wear white after Labor Day?"

I felt my back stiffen, and my face grew hot with anger as people around us stopped to look. It was all I could do just to maintain a look of calm. "You know, I was just thinking to myself when I saw you come in, Amanda... I wondered why girls who comes from so much money and 'class' would wear something so cheap and tasteless." She narrowed her eyes at me. "And what better person to ask! So... why *did* you choose that outfit, Amanda?"

The smile that washed over her face was chilling. "You know what? I have a solution to your problem," she declared. She then stepped forward, and before I even knew what was happening, and before I even had a chance to respond, she tossed her date's cup of red punch at me, effectively splattering the entire front of my gown, and shocking me where I stood.

Preston intervened at this point, putting himself in front of me.

"What the hell do you think you're doing?" Preston demanded angrily, as Amanda's date took her aside and got in Preston's face.

"It's not your problem," he told Preston defiantly.

Rage flared in Preston's eyes. "Yes, it *is* my problem—you better put your bitch in check!"

"Guys stop!" I cried, trying to brush off the punch from my dress, which of course was not going to work. The next thing I knew, Amanda's date swung at Preston, and Preston clocked him in the eye. In no time, they had both disappeared into a swarm of a crowd, comprised of cheerleaders for either side, or teachers pushing students aside to try and intervene. This was now an issue. This was something bigger than a verbal altercation.

This was a mess

Jackie pulled me out of there altogether, until we were out in the parking lot. "Are you okay?" The look on her face was dumbfounded, and her eyes trailed down over the red stain on my dress. "What a bitch… I can't believe she threw this at you," she muttered, dabbing at my dress with some tissues she took from her clutch. "We'll get this cleaned, if we wash it right away it shouldn't stain—"

I never heard the last of Jackie's statement.

Chapter 11

"Nowhere Else to Go"

Oh, my head hurt… I felt so groggy, and when I tried to open my eyes, they were so hazy and unfocused that I groaned. I tried to move, but couldn't. My entire body ached! If a person could survive after being hit by an eighteen-wheeler, I was sure that this was what it would feel like. When my eyes finally focused, I was staring up at a ceiling. My ceiling? The room was dimly lit, and I saw a lamp off to my side… Was I at home, at the manor? I was so confused. I didn't remember going there… the last thing I remembered was… the dance. The dance, of course. Then Amanda. And Preston… Instant panic coursed through me—what happened to Preston? And how did I get here? Why was I so sore? I had no recollection of what happened, and I think I whimpered because in an instant, Preston was at my side.

"Hey," he said, taking my hand. My eyes focused on him, and he looked worn, tired, and his furrowed brow assured me of his worry. "You're alright, Hope. You're home now."

"How did I get here?" My words fell meekly from my lips. My tongue felt thick and swollen. "Why do I feel so strange?"

He sighed and continued to hold my hand. "Do you remember anything?"

It took everything I had in me to answer him. I felt so awful... "I remember the dance, and I remember Amanda... and the drink... then you... Jackie pulled me outside, but I don't know what happened after that," I told him, wanting to cry because my head hurt so badly.

"I didn't see it, but Jackie said Amanda attacked you from behind, and struck you. You twisted your ankle before you fell, and hit your head on the curb," he explained, caressing my face with his free hand.

"What about you? Are you okay?" I asked. "Oh God, Preston, I'm so sorry," I told him, spotting a nasty scratch below his eye. "I'm so sorry—"

"Shhh... you have no reason to apologize... I'm just glad you're okay."

"Am I?" I asked skeptically. "I hurt so badly..."

"The doctor gave you some painkillers so you wouldn't feel your ankle, or your head," he told me. "You're probably feeling that."

"Doctor? I went to the doctor?" I was still trying to drink it all in. I couldn't believe what I was hearing!

"Yup. The ambulance took you."

"Ambulance? Oh my..."

"But you're going to be fine," Preston assured me.

"What time is it?" I asked meekly.

"Just after three."

"In the morning?" I asked with surprise.

"Yes," he answered softly.

"Oh Preston, you don't have to stay here with me—you need your sleep," I told him, feeling incredibly guilty.

"No, I'm going to stay right here," he promised. "Just in case you need anything."

"What about Jackie?" I asked groggily.

"I gave Jackie a ride back to her house, after we left the hospital," he gently explained.

"What happened to you?" I asked. "You didn't get in trouble, did you?"

"No," he assured me. "Don't worry about anything, okay?"

I felt so guilty for involving Preston in all of this. I reached up, and touched his face, and he caught my hand between his, holding it there while he stared down at me in concern. "I should have been with you to prevent this from happening," he spoke hoarsely.

"No," I argued. "You had no idea—I had no idea," I told him. "Amanda is the worst kind of person..."

"You should try to get back to sleep," he gently urged. "You need it."

"Where's Lawrence?" I asked. "What did he have to say?"

"Nothing really," Preston said. "He just stepped in and insisted we bring you home tonight, rather than wait and let you spend the night in the hospital. When we got here, he made sure you got up here safely, and then he disappeared for the night."

"Are you going to be in trouble for fighting?" I asked, worried.

"Not if he knows I was defending you," Preston assured me. "Get some sleep, Hope."

That didn't sound like such a bad idea, and in no time, I drifted off, clinging tight to Preston's hand. A million times I dreamt the same dream, over and over. I heard the same haunting melody, and watched his long fingers gliding over the keys of a piano. He was playing... playing for me. Shadowed by the glow of a fire burning brightly behind him, I saw his silhouette. So heavenly. And then I was dancing. I thought I was dancing with Preston at first, but when I looked up, it was Trent's face I saw, and those intense eyes were staring right into my soul.

And then he was be gone, and suddenly I'd be all alone.

Even in my cruel mind, I couldn't even have what I longed for.

When I finally opened my eyes for good, I was more aware of my surroundings. The sun was bright throughout my suite, and it was almost noon, already. I reached out for Preston, but his chair was empty. Figuring that he probably went to his own room after he got too tired to sit, I decided that I wanted to get out of bed, and clean up. All was well until I swung my legs over the bed and I attempted to stand. It was then that I felt a most excruciating pain in my foot that shot up from my ankle. Crying out, I collapsed back down on the bed immediately, and wondered what the hell had happened to me, the night before. That's when I saw the crutches propped up against the door—at least fifteen feet from where I was sitting. But before I could make an attempt to get across the room to them, my door opened. It was Lawrence.

"Ah, I see that you're up," he commented brightly. "How are you feeling?"

"Sore," I admitted. "Where's Preston?"

"I'm not sure," he answered. "I haven't seen him. Anyhow, the doctor tells me that you need to stay off your foot for several days. I've already made arrangements to keep you from school, and Jackie will be bringing your assignments," he informed me.

"I can't stay out of school," I stated. "I have to be at rehearsals—our first performance is Wednesday."

"Your health is more important," he insisted. "I will keep you out as long as I deem necessary."

I shook my head, looking at him with pleading eyes. "Please, Lawrence—this play is extremely important to me," I begged. "I'll be fine!"

"I'm sorry, but—"

"Okay, how about I stay home Monday, and Tuesday," I bargained. "And I'll stay completely off my foot. Then, Wednesday, if I still can't walk on it, I'll stay home," I promised, praying that he'd agree.

He pondered it for a moment, and then looking at me, he sighed. "Fine," he conceded, obviously more as a way to pacify me. "Anyhow, here are your crutches." He picked them up from where they were propped against the wall, and brought them bedside. "Don't attempt the stairs by yourself, you hear me? Call for one of us to help you." Then, before he opened the door to walk out, he turned to add, "By the way... Fighting is unacceptable, Hope. I'll not tolerate any more of that behavior."

I narrowed my eyes at him. "Perhaps you should be telling that to the person who started the fight," I said smartly.

He released the doorknob, and approached me, his jaw squared in annoyance. "I'm telling *you*, Hope. I'm responsible for *you*. No one else."

"I wasn't even fighting," I defended myself. "Amanda Cox has had it in for me for a while, and she walked right up to me and threw her drink—"

"Enough," he snarled. "Like I said before, I will not tolerate any more of that behavior," he warned. "You are living under *my* roof, and you will adhere to *my* rules!"

"But you're not even listening—"

"I don't have to listen to you," he retorted. "Every move you make reflects upon our name, you understand that?"

I shook my head. My mind was reeling! "I didn't do anything wrong!"

"Make sure you keep it that way then." His eyes were unforgiving. "Because you have nowhere else to go," he made sure to point out, before throwing the door open and slamming it behind himself.

I slouched over, putting my head in my hands. He couldn't possibly threaten to send me away simply because of

what happened last night! I DIDN'T DO ANYTHING WRONG!!!
If anything, *I* was the victim! I didn't even throw a punch—
and I was attacked from behind without being able to defend
myself!

I looked out toward the balcony, hoping to see Preston
standing out there. I wanted to thank him for standing up for
me the night before, and then also for watching over me
through the night. He wasn't out there. Surely, he had
retreated to his room to get some sleep, after the night we
endured.

I finally managed to stand up, and used the crutches to
get me into the bathroom. I washed up my face, which still
had light traces of make-up from the night before. My hair
was matted from hairspray and other product that Jackie
used to put it all up. I looked like a mess, but I felt even
worse. Lawrence's outburst bothered me considerably, but I
wasn't going to let his threats get to me. What was he going
to do—throw me out? Fine. I'd been through enough to last
me a lifetime, lately, and if he did throw me out, I'd be able to
manage.

Eager to see Preston, I quickly dressed and then
cautiously opened the door to peer out into the hallway. I felt
ridiculous—was Lawrence really going to get mad if he
caught me trying to go down the stairs by myself? His words
from the day before echoed in my head, as I hobbled my way
to Preston's bedroom door. I heard no noise coming from
inside, but I knocked anyway. No sign of him. Ignoring
Lawrence's orders about taking on the stairs myself, I fared
quite well, using the banister as a source of support, to make
my way down by myself. Everything was quiet. There was no
sign of any of the house workers, no sign of Lawrence and
Vivien.

I just wish I knew where Preston had gone, and why I
had such a strange sense of worry settle into my stomach.

His car was gone from the driveway, and I had no calls
or messages from him. Bewildered, I tried to call and then I
left a message, asking him to call me back and wondering

where he was, before confusedly shoving my phone into my back pocket.

Kate appeared from the direction of the kitchen, and she sighed at the sight of me maneuvering my crutches to get around. "Dear, do you need any help with anything?"

I shot her a crooked smile. "Nah, I'll manage. Have you seen Preston at all? He just up-and-left in the middle of the night."

She half-frowned at the mention of him, and then shrugged. "He left right around sunrise with his bag, but didn't say anything. Of course." "Have you seen Preston at all?"

"His bag? That he brings home from school?" What the hell happened!?

She nodded. "I didn't ask any questions." Then she narrowed her eyes at me. "By the way, what happened between you two? I thought you hated one another?"

"We did," I muttered softly. But not anymore. So what made him just up-and-leave? Did Lawrence come in while I was asleep and rail him, the way he did to me when I woke up? I frowned and felt my head begin to pound. I may have sounded a tad obsessive, but considering the circumstances, Preston's abrupt departure seemed a bit uncharacteristic...

"You need to stay off that ankle," she ordered sternly. "Last I checked, Juliet never needed crutches."

A chuckle rose up from my unsettled stomach, and I shot her an impish smile. "I'll have that covered," I assured her. "Don't worry about that."

"Yeah, well it's not me you have to convince," she pointed out. Then she nodded down the hallway where Lawrence's office was. "It's that one. Maybe he knows where Preston rushed off to, so early," she hinted, before starting her way towards the dining room. "I'll bring you up some of Redd's delicious brownies as soon as they come out of that oven," she promised with a wink, before heading out of my sight.

Lawrence. I stood there for a moment, staring down the gallery where the library was, just after his home office. Should I even bother? I was still miffed by our confrontation the day before. How he could possibly find me at fault for what happened was beyond me. It was unreasonable. It was unfair.

Still, I made my way down to his office, and I gently knocked on his door. I didn't care if he was going to be mean to me. I only had one question for him.

"Come in," he called out, and then I opened the door to go inside. He was sitting at his desk, and when he saw me, he looked up and smiled brightly. "Hello! How is your ankle feeling?" His tone was perfectly pleasant. Was this the same person who exploded at me the day before, and stomped out?

"It's fine," I answered. "Have you talked to Preston?"

"Yes, I have," he answered. "Why do you ask?"

"Because I find it weird that he left so early and now he won't take my phone calls," I told him. "Did he say where he was going?"

"He went back to school. He said he had a few things to work on for class," he answered nonchalantly, while rummaging through some of the papers sitting before him.

I was utterly confused. "Okay..."

His eyebrow lifted up at me, and then he stopped rustling through the papers to lean forward and address my concerns. "Is there something else you'd like to discuss, Hope?"

Was there? It seemed, from the look upon his face, that he thought there might've been. *Something else to discuss...* Like what, though? I said nothing for a moment. "I just wanted to make sure he knew how much I appreciated him standing up for me," I answered him.

I turned to leave, and just as I approached the door, he asked, "When I speak to him next, would you like me to ask him to call you?"

I paused, then answered, "No. That's alright—I'll keep trying him. Thank you."

Chapter 12

"Resolution"

Sunday came and went, with no word from Preston. I couldn't shake the weird feeling that something had happened. Intuition, perhaps. It would've been squashed, had he just replied back to any of the numerous text messages or voicemails I had left him, curiously wondering why he disappeared. Monday, I would've just rather been back to school, instead of laying around the house because Lawrence somehow thought keeping me out of school would help me more than letting me hobble to-and-from all my classes. Nope, instead I wandered from room-to-room in the house every few hours for a change of scenery, and desperately trying to keep my mind occupied. Tuesday I was grateful that Jackie came by with all of my assignments that would keep me caught up through Wednesday. Thank goodness for teachers who loved homework, at a time when I craved some busywork.

"Amanda's trying to spread it through school that since you're hurt, you won't be able to perform, and the part

150

is hers again," Jackie told me. "She's such a witch. But I talked to Mr. Peck today, and he told her no such thing," she assured me.

"I already talked to him," I told her. "This morning. I called the school, and they connected me to his office. Luckily, he has a lot of faith in me."

"Yes, that's what he told me," she said. "Have you gotten a hold of Preston yet?"

I shook my head. "No. Apparently, he's talked to Lawrence several times, but he hasn't called me back." I frowned. "I don't know what's wrong, but I suspect I'll see him when Lawrence hosts his little dinner party this Saturday night." Or, that's what I was hoping, anyway.

"Yeah, my parents mentioned coming," she spoke.

"Well you should come, too," I told her. "Then you can keep me company."

"Instead of staying home and missing the tension? I'll definitely be here," she promised with a wink. "But I've got to go for now. Text me later?"

"I will. Thanks for bringing me my work," I called to her as she left.

"Hey it's no problem. Just get yourself back to class," she ordered, pointing at my ankle.

And then she was gone.

By Wednesday, I could walk without the crutches, but I was still limping. Determined, I acted like my foot wasn't bothering me when I entered Lawrence's office. I showed him that I was walking fine, and sweetly asked him if he would drive me back to campus. He watched me closely as I walked around, looking for any sign of pain. Thank goodness for ibuprofen and acting skills, because he had no choice but to say yes, now.

I was anxious to return back to school. Partly so that I could get ready for the opening performance of Romeo and Juliet, but mostly because I wanted to prove to everyone that

Amanda hadn't "beaten me up" like she'd been going around saying.

A few of my classmates asked me what "really" happened the night of the dance, and I told them exactly what happened. Amanda threw her drink at me, and then Preston stepped in, sticking up for me. I went outside, where I proceeded to try and wipe my dress off, and Amanda did attack me. From behind. Like a coward.

When I saw Amanda coming through the halls, she first scowled at me. I didn't think she expected to see me back so soon—and just in time for the opening performance. I think it was part of her plan all along to put me out of commission, so that I wouldn't be able to perform at all, leaving her to take over, as she was labeled my "understudy" after the results of the audition were posted. But I wasn't going to give her that satisfaction. The part was mine.

The rest of the day, she walked by me, giving me a menacing look. I just held my head up high, stood straight, and looked straight ahead as I passed her. I wasn't going to give her another reason to attack me, just yet. Let me get through my performances. Then we could continue our battle, as soon as I knew she wasn't going to do anything that would jeopardize my presentation as Juliet.

Our final rehearsal, just hours before our first event, came and went without any problems. Everything was running smoothly, everyone knew their places, and I felt like I hadn't missed a thing while I was home for those few days. We received report that our night's performance was now sold-out, and I was confident that we would do well.

Everyone was bustling with excitement as we got into our costumes, and applied our make-up. There was a definite nervous energy floating around, but I worked well under pressure. We all huddled into a group, and said a small prayer before going onstage, and soon, it was all happening.

It all went off without a hitch, and at the end, we received a standing ovation. It felt so good to be on that stage, and just as I expected, it didn't take me long to lose my nervousness, and I got lost in a world all my own. There wasn't an audience; there wasn't "Lawrence" or "Vivien". I was Juliet, and I was tragically lost in a world of love, angst, and misery.

But I couldn't help noticing that looking through that front row, Preston wasn't there.

With that in mind, when I got back to my dorm room, I decided to give up. Obviously, he didn't want to talk to me, and he wasn't going to tell me why. He went from hot to cold overnight, and I wasn't sure if he resented me for getting into that fight, or what. I wasn't going to try, anymore. If he was mad at me, I at least deserved an explanation. But whatever.

The next two days' performances were perfect. Most of the cast members decided to all go out in a group Friday night to celebrate our success, but I was planning to just go ahead and go home, as scheduled. When we parted ways, Jackie hugged me goodbye and promised that she'd be at the manor early the next day to get ready for the dinner party with me. Good, because I felt like I needed some sort of ally there to keep me from getting bored all evening, anyway.

Although, after spending a few hours at home by myself, I realized that I would've probably been better off going out with the theatre group, and enjoying myself out on the town. I know that what made me pass on going out was the faint bit of hope that Preston might've been home for me to confront him, and see why he'd been avoiding me. But once I was home, and I was fueled by my anger for passing up a good time on his account, I decided that if I did see Preston at the gala the following night, he'd get the same cold treatment as Trent would. I wasn't planning to glance in either of their directions even once.

By the next afternoon, I'd already had my ensemble picked out. When Lawrence had taken me out shopping for fall and winter clothes, he encouraged me to pick out a wide variety of apparel, and I wasn't lacking in any type of attire. I settled upon a silver two-piece dress that made even Lawrence gawk with admiration when I emerged from the dressing room to take a look at myself. The matte satin corset top had black lace peeking up out of the top of it, and embroidery in subtle blues, and lilac. My favorite detail was that it laced up in the back, for the true "corset look", and it made me feel more like a vixen than a clumsy teenage girl. The matching pencil skirt ended at my knees, and it hugged every generous curve of my body. I opted for the highest, pointiest heels that I had, and then I donned a black, beaded choker around my neck. Jackie came in just as I'd finished dressing, and her eyes widened.

"Wow, that's quite an outfit," she complimented, looking me up and down. "That's almost on the verge of scandalous, don't you think?"

I smirked at her. "What better way to ignore the men in my life, than to look gorgeous while doing so?"

"You little harlot," she teased. "Definitely a bit risqué, but I think I'm more concerned about you walking around in those heels."

Quite honestly, so was I. "No sweat." I shrugged, giving myself one last look in the full-length mirror. "Did you see Preston's car outside?" I asked her.

She laughed. "What's it matter, if you're just going to ignore him?" She met my scowl with a smirk. "*No*, I did not."

"Maybe it was parked out back," I reasoned, turning to get a side-view.

"Or, maybe you're just obsessed."

I whipped my head around to face her. "No, I'm not. Just concerned."

"Whatever, Hope. I think you care more about him than you'd like to admit." I hated how she was smiling like she knew all the answers.

"We're friends, that's it," I insisted. "Or, *were*, anyway."

Jackie unzipped her garment bag and took out a breathtaking crinkled-silk dress of rich, wine-based hues ranging from maroon at the top, to a dusty rose, and then at the bottom, a deep pink. Its spaghetti straps were adorned with thin rhinestones, which glittered in the light, and it went down in a V-shape. Once she put it on, I realized that it, too, was a form-fitting dress that hugged her soft curves and took the chance to brand her a "harlot" as well.

"Yeah, well, I can't sit back and let you get all the looks," she cracked.

Tonight, I did want to be noticed. My eyes were painted a sultry, dark color—heavily lined, with black, plush lashes. I splashed a subtle apricot blush on my cheeks, and then kept my lips a pale, pink hue. Just the way Kate applied my make-up for the first party I went to.

Jackie wore her hair in dark auburn ringlets cascading halfway down her back, but I opted for long, sleek and straight locks. I thought I was done and ready to go, until Lawrence knocked on my door.

"May I come in?" He asked, cracking the door open slightly.

"Yes," I obliged. "Come in."

He stepped inside, and smiled warmly at Jackie. "Good evening, Mr. Van Steenburgh," she greeted him.

"Jackie, always a pleasure," he acknowledged her, removing a long box from his jacket and walking towards me. "Hope, I brought something for you," he said, handing me the black velvet box.

I glanced up at him quizzically, but said nothing while I held the box, and opened it up. I gasped at the sight of what was inside—a beautiful white gold tennis bracelet, with diamonds sparkling in the light!

"I bought it for you to wear tonight," he told me, stepping forward to remove it from its box. Impressed by this random generosity, I extended my wrist, and he fastened it on me. I couldn't take my eyes from it!

"Thank you," I uttered breathlessly. "Lawrence, it's beautiful!"

"You're quite welcome," he assured me. "You both look beautiful tonight. I'll see you downstairs, alright?" And, just like that, he turned to retreat. Stunned, I watched as he simply closed the door behind him, and then I looked at Jackie wordlessly.

"Look at the size of each of those rocks," she murmured as she looked over my new accessory. "That's gotta be at *least* three carats," she observed.

Up until that point, I didn't know a thing about carats, but to hear her say that must've meant it was a big deal. I had to admit it was the most beautiful piece of jewelry I had ever been given. Maybe Lawrence gave it to me to make up for his behavior as of late. Maybe he was trying to buy my admiration... I didn't know. And I wasn't going to ask. He baffled me, and I was done exhausting myself trying to figure him out.

Cocktail hour had just started, and Lawrence had hired a pianist specifically to play during this time. My heart skipped a beat as we neared the top of the stairs and heard the music playing faintly. It took me back to a time not too long ago where I was doing this very thing in the middle of the night, to the sound of similar music.

We made our grand entrance, and as usual, Vivien was making her rounds. There was already a roomful of people, and long tables were set up in a U-shape to the far end of the room in front of the fireplace, with what must have been around seventy chairs surrounding the outside of the tables. White linen tablecloths covered the tables, and there were several large five-branch candelabras used as centerpieces, with black magic roses and other holiday flowers cascading from the middle of the lit tapered candles. Richly colored sugared fruits were arranged neatly in crystal bowls that were scattered throughout the tables—plums, grapes, apples, and pears, among a few of them. It was quite enchanting. It was elaborate. It was borderling over-the-top.

It was one hundred percent Van Steenburgh-esque.

My breath caught when I saw Trent standing at the bar. He was talking to two other men, over glasses of wine— no doubt Trent's favorite; the Italian born wine that stocked his cabinet in the cabin. He looked breathtaking, in a double-breasted black jacket and sleek black trousers. A flattering black and white striped necktie peeked out at the top of his jacket. I thought he looked like some mobster out of one of those mafia movies. Very suave and sophisticated. His hair was pulled back, and he was clean-shaven.

And then there was the attractive blonde that walked up, and hugged herself to his side for a second, before she gazed up at him with adoring eyes. At that precise moment, jealousy shot through my veins, and I felt like an idiot for the way my heart now pounded with rage. As if I radiated my emotion across the room, he looked my way, and I turned quickly. "Trent," I whispered through clenched teeth to Jackie.

"Where?" She asked, trying not to make it look obvious as she glanced off behind me.

"At the bar. With a *date*," I spat hatefully.

She raised one eyebrow and then turned her back to him. "He *is* good-looking," she agreed enthusiastically. I rolled my eyes. "That chick is *with* him?" I turned to look again, and sure enough, Trent was holding a conversation with Charles, who was tending the bar, and the blonde kept putting her hand on his arm, and talking to him. I wanted to scream.

"Oh well. Let her have him," I mumbled. I turned my back to him also, and as I faced the door, who else would walk in at that very second but Preston! He was dressed in a similar suit to Trent's except no necktie. It looked like he'd brought two of his college guy-friends, and I turned away quickly before he could see me.

"There's Preston," Jackie pointed out quietly. "Well, well. He also brought someone."

"Two someones," I corrected her. "This party sucks, all of a sudden..."

"Oh stop," she laughed. "It's fun, remember? I'm here," she quipped, nudging me. "C'mon, let's get you over there and out of sight of your delicious love triangle," she prompted.

We made our way over to the other side of the room, where Lawrence was entertaining a group of men and their wives. One of them spotted me, and beckoned for me to come over to them.

"Hope, you look lovely tonight," said the rotund, older man whose face I remembered from the first party, but whose name failed me. "Will you regale us with more talk about art tonight?" He asked. "Surely you can bring a much more interesting light to the subject than a group of stuffy old men," he said light-heartedly.

I smiled graciously. "Of course I will, so long as it's a subject I'm not ignorant on," I said, briefly catching Lawrence's eyes. I don't even think he caught my sarcasm.

I cast a nonchalant look in the general direction Trent had been. He was no longer there.

"Well, my Hope is starring in Springcrest and Pleasant Valley Academy's production of Romeo and Juliet," Lawrence boasted. "So perhaps theatre would be more of her caliber."

"Ah, yes! I saw that," the man exclaimed. "My wife attended Springcrest and still loves to be present for all of their productions," he explained. "You were wonderful—the best I've seen yet!"

It was ironic that later on, I would find out that he was Amanda's uncle.

"Well, thank you," I accepted. "That's awfully kind of you." At that point, I noticed Preston off to the side of him, and his eyes met with mine. Though my initial plan was to avoid making contact with him at all, that evening, I couldn't bring myself to look away. There was something in his eyes that I couldn't quite figure out. He looked solemn for a moment. Even after he broke eye contact with me and looked away, mine still remained upon him. My feelings were hurt, and my mind was clouded.

Not two seconds after Jackie and I approached the bar to get something—anything—that might perhaps calm my nerves at this point, Preston's two friends walked up beside us. After Jackie asked Charles for a couple of waters, I just stood there eyeballing the glasses of wine. Charles definitely caught me, and I pondered whether or not he would tattle on me if I grabbed one. Trent's words about the manor turning everyone into drunks replayed in my head to evoke a small smile over my face, and as the bottles of water were pushed across the bar counter to us, one of Preston's friends had decided to strike up a conversation with my flirty, outgoing accomplice.

"Don't I know you?" he asked her.

She turned to look at him, and narrowed her eyes in thought. "I'm not sure. Where do you think you know me from?"

"Didn't you attend Springcrest?" He asked.

"I still do," she replied.

"Okay," he said, nodding as he placed her in his recollection. "I remember you. I graduated from Pleasant Valley last year."

"Oh! Okay, well that's cool," she said.

"Can I get you something else, Miss?" I glanced back across the bar, and Charles was eyeing me as if he could read my mind. I hesitated, but his eyes suggestively dipped down to the array of glasses sprawled out, filled with wine, and ready for the taking. "It's an open bar, you know."

"I know," I replied coolly. This wiry old man was either baiting me, or taking pity. I couldn't yet decide.

"Would you feel better if I turned away for a moment?"

Now he was mocking me, but I wasn't about to argue. I left the bottle of water on the counter, and plucked a glass of white wine that was up for grabs. Jackie was now entertaining Preston's friend.

"You don't mess around with your drinks," said the guy at my left—who was silent up until this point—as I eagerly drank down half of my wine like it was water. "Most people sip on wine, not guzzle it." I turned to face my critic, and he was quite good-looking as well. He was tall and slender, with short, black spikey hair, and hazel eyes.

"I don't mess around, period," I countered with a tight smile, tossing back the rest of the liquid, and boldly meeting Charles's smug gaze as I set the empty glass back on the bar counter.

"You attend Springcrest also?"

I evaluated him once more, and figured if he were to serve any purpose to me this evening, his time was now. So I smiled prettily up at Preston's good-looking friend and brushed my dark hair back from my face. "I do," I confirmed with a nod.

He nodded. "Very cool. I graduated from Pleasant Valley two years ago," he informed me. "I'm so glad to be out of that place!"

"I can definitely relate to that sentiment," I cracked, briefly glancing about the room. Lawrence was on one side of the room, entertaining. Vivien was on the other side. Was this what happiness looked like? My parents were always glued to one another's sides, during any kind of functions. Laughing, smiling, touching, sharing flirty glances. Not really surprised, I glanced back up at this guy who I now caught checking me out. He did have a nice smile

"A lot of the Springcrest girls come out to attend the parties at our college on the weekends. You should come out, sometime," he invited eagerly.

"Maybe I will," I flirted back.

"C'mon, we have to go sit down," Jackie urged, taking my arm. Lawrence just announced that dinner's ready to be served."

Following the herd of people who, like sheep, filed to the tables to figure out where they all wanted to be, I snatched a chair and Jackie took the one beside me. She was still talking to Preston's other friend, who took the other seat beside her.

And Preston's other friend took the spare seat on the other side of me.

I pretended not to be smug that his friends ditched him for us, but if not for the new guy who was preoccupied with me, I would've sat there feeling like a third wheel during dinner, as Jackie talked nonstop to her new friend whose name I caught was Chad. I didn't know the guy's name sitting to my left, and I didn't care to ask. I knew I wouldn't give him the time of day again, but I knew that if I wanted to get a reaction tonight, he could definitely help make that happen. And whether he had planned it, or if he got stuck with that being the only seat left, Preston sat down directly across the way from me, on that other side of the "U"-shaped table. Close enough to shoot darts at me through his eyes if he so wanted, but just far enough to be out of earshot from anything we were saying on our side. I could talk about the War of 1812, but as long as I looked like I was enjoying myself, that's all that mattered.

My stomach flip-flopped at the sight of Trent taking a seat further down from Preston. The blonde that had attached herself to him earlier took the seat beside him, and I recognized a brief look of blatant annoyance on his face that almost caused me to laugh out loud. Maybe he sensed my amusement. Maybe my smirk drew his attention, because his eyes met mine and locked to wipe all semblance of mischief from my face, entirely. His date was still talking. She had no clue that he wasn't even listening. Those dark eyes of his, even with the span of space between us, felt like they were still able to see straight through me...

There was no doubt that I still felt for him what I did from the beginning. There was still that magnetism, and longing. I wanted him, and I was utterly disappointed by it. Unable to take it anymore, I forced myself to look away.

"This is quite an amazing place," my handsome friend commented, stirring me from my thoughts. Back to reality. Back to where Trent was a jerk, and Preston just didn't want to speak to me. "My folks' house isn't anything quite so spectacular. What about yours?"

At that point, I realized that he had no idea who I was. Apparently, he hadn't been informed about me, and Preston didn't point me out when they came in. That's fine, because when I caught the next look on Preston's face, it was obvious he wished he had!

"I'd have to say the same," I agreed. "I've never seen a place so spectacular," I said with a smile.

"You'll definitely have to come party at the college some weekend," he repeated. "You'd have a blast!" At that moment, he looked across the table and spotted Preston. He gave him a nod, and didn't even notice that it wasn't returned by Preston. Preston was seething.

"I just might do that," I returned, as our meals were placed before us. "So what brings you here tonight?" I asked him, keeping the conversation going.

"I'm here with a friend," he replied. "His folks live here, the lucky bastard. What about you?"

"I'm here with a friend as well," I replied quickly.

"Your friend right over there?" He asked, meaning Jackie.

"Yes," I replied. It wasn't exactly lying. After all, I was here with Jackie.

"That's cool. This food is delicious!" He exclaimed.

"Yeah the cook is wonderful," I slipped, hoping he wouldn't catch on, but to no avail.

"You know the cook?" he asked.

"No. I mean, well, yes, kinda," I sputtered. "I've attended parties here before, and had the food," I explained. "It's always been good," I saved myself.

We continued to make conversation, and I could feel Trent's eyes fixed upon me. The few times I glanced Trent's way, he was staring without even attempting to stop, once I'd catch him. He looked tense, even as he gave the blonde beside him short, snappy answers to appease whatever she was asking him. And then there was Preston, sitting solemnly between two other couples, while his friends entertained Jackie and I. As soon as his plate was set before him, he didn't look up from it, even once.

Quite the awkward little triangle, we had going on.

Once people began finishing their food, the next act of entertainment brought in by our gracious hosts began to play some light music. People began getting up to mingle, and soon there were couples dancing off their dinner, while Kate and other hired sets of hands stepped in to clear away plates. After Chad asked Jackie to dance, my new friend did the same. This is what rich people did. They liked to play dress up, they liked to remind others how much money they had, through lavish get-togethers.

And they liked to dance.

I let him lead me to the middle of the dance floor, and he took me into his arms. He told me a story of how his mother had made him take ballroom dance lessons when he was a teenager, and this would be the first time outside of prom that he'd be able to take advantage of them. He was charming, and I might've truly given him a chance if my mind weren't somewhere else. I had enough troubles with the opposite sex already on my hands, and I didn't particularly feel like adding another. And as if on cue, just moments after we took to the dance floor, I looked up to notice Preston approaching us. He curtly asked if he could cut in, and then my charming friend graciously stepped back, and excused himself to the bar.

I stood uncomfortably for a moment, and Preston stepped toward me. "Dance with me?" His blue eyes dipped down to mine, and his voice was low and husky.

I narrowed my eyes at him, but didn't utter a response. I just solemnly allowed him to close the gap of space between us and take my hand into his, while his other rested at my hip. It was hard not to feel awkward, but my eyes lifted to implore his. What was this???

He expelled one long, tortured breath before his hand roamed to the small of my back and pull me even closer, still. "I'm sorry." His warm whisper caressed my ear, and made my neck tingle. It took me back to the night that started this whole mess. At school. His hands, exactly where he had them, causing my mind to wander and wonder.

"Why were you avoiding me, Preston?" My own voice came out a shaky whisper, before I inhaled the scent of his cologne. "It really sucked, being ignored..."

"I know, and I'm so sorry for that, Hope. I really am," he apologized, pulling back slightly to look me square in the eye.

"So? Why?" I shrugged up at him. "Why couldn't you return my phone calls? What made you leave and not want to speak to me again?"

He shook his head, and he looked away before attempting to pull me closer. "It's not important," he swept aside softly. "I'd just rather forget about it, and pretend it didn't happen."

I stopped moving with him and took a step backward, dropping my hands from him. "Don't you think I deserve an explanation?" My look challenged him, while I just wanted one simple answer. "It hurt, Preston. I at least deserve to know why."

His shoulders dropped, and he suddenly looked as if he wished to be anywhere but there. Having any conversation except for this one. "It's not important," he insisted. "It's really stupid, actually. I'd really rather forget—"

"I know you would," I cut in. "But it's important to me."

He shook his head. "Fine," he gave in, stepping forward once more. I allowed him to take me back into his arms, and tried to ignore the goose-bumps that now covered my flesh. "But I'm begging for you to understand," he pleaded quietly between us. I nodded, urging him to go on. "That night, after we got you home from the hospital. I was more worried about your welfare than I've ever worried in my life, Hope. And I wouldn't have wanted to be anywhere other than sitting by your side, all night. So, you were asleep, and I was drifting in and out of sleep, until you started talking in your sleep..." he trailed off, breaking eye contact with me, and looking beyond my shoulder. "I thought maybe you might've needed something, so I tried talking to you, but you were too out of it. You were calling out for someone," he said, brokenly. "All night long, saying his name over and over. You just kept calling out for Trent."

I felt my eyes nearly burst out of my head! Trent?! What the hell was I doing, calling for him in my sleep?! "Oh, Preston," I told him, wincing in embarassment. "I don't know why I did that," I muttered sheepishly.

"I know it seems like nothing, but it stung," he admitted. "I couldn't sit there and listen to it. So I left," he muttered, before his eyes flicked upward, over my head. I knew just who they were looking for. "Is there... something going on between the two of you?"

The reluctance in his question made me feel so awful. "No," I answered honestly. "There isn't. I have no idea why I called out to him, Preston. Honest," I vowed, looking up at him now with pleading eyes.

A slow, small smile of relief formed over his lips. "I'd rather just forget about it, to be honest."

"I'm sorry, Preston." I literally couldn't stop wincing.

"It's alright. Like I said—I don't want to waste another thought on it," he pushed aside. "I've acted stupid all week, and I apologize. Every time my phone rang and it was you, I wanted to answer, but I just couldn't," he told me, his eyes raking over my face. I glanced over his shoulder, and caught sight of Trent, who was eyeballing me again. His sensuously shaped lips were shut together tight, and his jaw was squared and tense. There was a pensive look about him as he studied Preston and I dancing together.

Then he simply turned away.

"You've outdone yourself tonight, by the way." I pushed Trent out of my head once more to glance upward into Preston's bright eyes. "You look great—beyond words," he complimented.

"Thank you," I accepted politely. "I noticed that you're dressed impeccably, also!"

He offered me a crooked smile. "I've missed you this week," he made sure to tell me.

"I missed you, too. Even though I hadn't heard from you, I still looked at the first row Wednesday night, hoping you'd be there," I confessed. "And Thursday. And Friday..."

"I was there."

I looked up at him, perplexed. "No—I looked for you. I didn't see you."

"Because I wasn't sitting in the front row," he answered with a smirk. "I was a few rows back. I had to be there, even if I didn't want you to know I was there," he disclosed.

I smiled up at him, and startled myself as I wrapped both of my arms about his neck. "That means a lot to me," I told him, unable to hide my surprise. "Thank you."

"But you'd better believe I'm going to use my front-row seats for the rest of the performances," he said with a wink, causing me to laugh. "You were great," he said. "The best Juliet I've seen!"

"Right," I said skeptically. "And I know how many Shakespeare plays you've sat through."

"Well, that just makes my decision that much easier," he cracked.

I laughed. "Whatever."

Jackie was dancing with Preston's friend Chad. The guy who had sat by my side at dinner now moved on to the blonde that Trent had at some point managed to break free from, and now he was nowhere in sight.

And then it started. "So, what exactly was my buddy saying to you?"

I met Preston's unabashedly jealous eyes, and then shrugged playfully. "Nothing about you," I taunted with a sly smile.

"He sat just a little too close to you," he observed, displaying his apparent jealousy, which I found profoundly flattering.

"*You* could've sat closer," I fired back with a wink.

"Oh? I'll keep that in mind for next time. Did he touch you at all?" His questions were ruthless, but I couldn't wipe the smugness from my face.

"Not anywhere that I wanted him to stop," I continued, all the while keeping a smile on my face.

"You're killing me, here. Certainly you don't find him more attractive than me," he fished playfully.

"You're both easy on the eyes," I countered.

"Did he ask you out?"

"He asked me several times to go to some of the weekend college parties," I admitted. "I told him I'd think about it." It was fun to watch him battling the green-eyed monster!

"But you wouldn't, would you?"

"I don't know. Maybe."

"Please don't."

"Why not?"

He paused, holding me a little closer. "Because I don't like the thought of you being involved in what goes on there."

"You don't think I could handle myself?" I asked.

"It's not that..."

I laughed, letting him off the hook. "Chances are that I wouldn't go anywhere with him, anyway," I told him. "I don't even know him, and my parents taught me never to talk to strangers."

"I know him, and you don't need to," he insisted.

"Are you this pushy with all your friends?" I teased.

"Only the ones I care about."

I smiled up at him, and suddenly felt very aware of myself. Enough so, that I felt myself blushing in his arms.

"Would you like something to drink?" he asked. "I think I'm going to get something."

"Yes, I think I would," I told him. "I'll take a glass of—" I stopped, and quickly changed my mind, "—just get me whatever you're having," I told him, releasing him and stepping back.

"Okay," he said, not thinking twice about my change of mind. "I'll be back in a few."

I spotted Jackie and Chad standing off to the side, and I intended to walk over and say hello.

Until Trent startled me by gently taking my arm to stop me. Subtly, and very discreetly, he caused my breath to catch in my throat as he passed. Jackie paused to look in time for him to whisper, "Meet me at my place at midnight," into my ear. And just as his warmth of his hand dropped from my arm, my breath released from my lungs. Frozen where I stood, I didn't even have a chance to respond to him. He wouldn't have even heard me, if I had. He had moved on, that fast.

I caught Jackie's curious look, and then I watched her tell Chad she'd be right back. My head was fuzzy, as I stood alone in the middle of the floor, wondering what the hell just happened.

And how Trent so easily high-jacked my mood.

"What was that about?" Jackie cast a glance in the direction Trent disappeared into.

"He told me to meet him at his place. At midnight," I told her, perplexed.

"Dramatic, much? I wonder why." She looked down at her watch. "It's eleven now."

"I don't even know if I should go," I muttered.

"Well, you have an hour to decide," she told me. "I know I'm a bit curious as to why he wants to see you, myself," she admitted, raising her eyebrow quizzically. If I needed any small push to persuade me to go, it was going to be that.

"Do me a favor," I asked of her. "Give me some sort of signal when it's ten 'til."

"Will do," she said. "And I'll expect full details tomorrow," she sternly informed me. "I'm glad to see you and Preston are back to normal," she observed. "What was his deal?"

"You don't want to know," I told her, rolling my eyes. "But it was my fault."

"What? What did you do that you were so unaware of?" she asked quickly, keeping her voice down.

"Apparently when I came home from the hospital Friday night, I was calling for Trent in my sleep," I gravely explained, causing her to cringe. "Anyhow, Preston heard it, and he was apparently pretty hurt by it."

"I would've been too. He adores you—it was probably a low blow."

"Here you go," Preston walked up and handed me my glass, as Jackie's statement bounced around the forefront of my mind.

I smiled, taking the glass from him. "Thank you," I accepted.

Jackie excused herself after giving Preston a hard time and reaching up to tousle his hair to get a rise out of him. The party was beginning to thin out, and my anxiety level was on the rise. By the time I had finished my drink, I had twenty minutes to decide whether or not I was going to slip away to find out what Trent now wanted to get off of his chest. As Preston led me past the bar, Charles's scrutinizing eyes caught me swiping one more glass of wine to add to the others I had downed, over the course of the evening. He still wanted to dance. Rather, I suspect all Preston really craved, more than anything, was an excuse to be close to me. No, I wasn't stupid. I was fully aware that his crush on me was full-blown.

It was just easier to play it off, than to meet it head-on.

"I'd never danced with anyone before, prior to coming here," I confessed with a crooked smile that was absorbed by his thirsty eyes. "We never had fancy dinner parties where I grew up."

"Eh, once you've been to one, you've been to 'em all," he cast aside, as his gaze roamed over my face.

"I love this song, though," I said softly. "It was a favorite of my mother's. She used to play it while she was getting dressed and putting her make-up on, to go out."

He didn't say anything. He didn't have to. He was content just to watch me get lost and glassy-eyed, as I recalled the night she left the house and didn't come home. At the time, her ritual had seemed so ordinary. Now, it was frozen in time, and moments like this had a way of bringing her back to life. This song. This place. It was once her home for a short while, before she ran from it. How many times she had been listening to this same song, where I now stood... Was this where she first heard it? When he leaned in, his lips were so close to my ear that I could hear his breath. I felt him against my neck. If not for him, I might not have returned from the time warp I had hurdled myself into. It was such an intimate moment between he and I. For a moment, only we existed in that ballroom.

But all good things must come to an end. Even at spellbinding Van Steenburgh Manor.

"Hey, Hope?" Jackie cut in, breaking our spell. "It's time."

Snapping to attention, I realized what she meant. But Preston didn't. "Time? Time for what?"

"Well," Jackie faltered. "I asked her to do something with me, and then told her I'd let her know when I needed her," she made up, making effort to look convincing.

"What are you going to do?"

"Preston, have I ever told you that you ask too many questions?" She tossed him a tight smile and took me by the arm. "I promise, you'll survive just fine without her for a little bit," she poked at him with a wink.

He was about to protest, but I had to hurry. "It's okay," I assured him. "I'll catch up with you later," I promised, realizing that he still had a hold of my hand. Giving his a light squeeze of assurance, I slipped mine from his grasp. His eyes followed Jackie and I all the way out of the ballroom, until she saw me out the backdoors onto the terrace.

"I'll talk to you later," I spoke nervously.

"Sure you will. Go find out what the other lover-boy wants," she urged with a chuckle. "Seriously, you've created quite the pickle of a situation for yourself," she pointed out as I tip-toed over the stone terrace. "I'll be waiting for the details!"

Avoiding the light from the ballroom that spilled over the lawn, I hurried over the field to the path that led into darkness. I wasn't sure which had me shivering more; the cold air, or my nerves. Either way, I was shaking like a leaf, and unaware what to expect as I entered the woods. The light of the moon guided me on my way, and I paused at the end of the woods. It was completely dark among the trees, and there was only a light glow coming from the cabin. I cautiously approached the small porch, and I was startled when as I got to the top step, the door opened ahead of me.

He'd been waiting for me.

I could hardly breathe at the sight of him. He stood with a bottle of wine in one hand, and an empty glass dangling in the other. He was disheveled—tendrils of his hair had now fallen about his face, and though he'd shed his jacket and necktie, he still wore his slacks and his white dress shirt, which was unbuttoned a few notches. His eyes were hidden by shadows, and he took a step backward to allow me just enough room to come inside.

He looked like danger, personified. I was filled with a mixture of thrill and hesitation. Inside, I could see a fire raging angrily in the fireplace, crackling and spitting embers. It set the perfect tone. To the left, a candle was lit on the kitchen countertop, and another one on the small end-table behind him was flickering from the wind coming in from the door.

As I slipped past him to enter the cabin, the scent of his cologne intoxicated me. I felt the heat coming off of his body. He shut the door behind me, with some force behind it. He locked it, and standing there, I was briefly overcome by a touch of fear. His look was menacing. Serious. Intimidating. Inebriated. And without saying a word, he set the empty glass down and lifted the bottle to his mouth. My heart was pounding in my chest, and my defiant eyes were greedily glued to the man who did nothing but ignore me all evening.

Smugly, he thrust the bottle outward to me, and I took half a step back. "No? Not in the mood for wine, now?" His tone was combative. Taunting. Goading me into a response, and I knew I was in over my head.

"No thanks," I managed in a shaky voice.

"Why not?" Now it was his turn to look defiant. "Sure, it isn't the chardonnay that Preston served you earlier, but I find that it serves its purpose quite well," he taunted, setting the bottle down on the counter.

"You're drunk," I observed in disgust. "Why am I here?"

"Hardly, milady," he snarled. "It takes more than a glass or two of wine to have any effect on me," he declared, stalking towards me. My step backward in defense left me pressed against the door, and took the opportunity to press his hand to it, just inches from my face, and lean his weight against his arm. He towered over me, and I was surrounded by his heat. My breath held in my lungs, and it was all I could do to just look up at him timidly. "Look at you," he marveled, as his lips curled upward in a malicious smile. "Eyes wide and innocent. Quite a sight you are," he growled. He leaned in and his nose caressed a tantalizing trail up my neck, making me dizzy. "You smell delicious," he commented, catching my eyes before he stepped back again and dropped his hand from the door. A low, noxious chuckle rumbled upward from his insides, before retrieving his bottle of wine from the counter and taking down a generous drink from it. "At least you're on time," he observed. "Twelve o'clock—on the dot." My heart was pounding, but I remained silent. Even if I had a response, I don't think I could've uttered the words. My head was reeling! "My, but you played quite the vixen tonight, Miss de Havilland," he commented dramatically. "You played that role almost as well as you played Juliet," he said, catching my attention. Had he made the effort to see one of my performances? "You strutted in looking confident in your skin-tight dress, and your eyes painted black. Quite amusing," he mocked, accompanied another vicious-sounding chuckle. "Did you get the reaction you sought after?"

"I wasn't looking for any kind of reaction," I countered weakly. This man was about to eat me alive...

"Weren't you?" He stalked closer to me. "You went through all the effort of finding the perfect ensemble to make you so striking that you intoxicate the minds of every male in that room, and then flaunted yourself to lengths which drove Preston wild with jealousy—for nothing?" He was like a panther circling its prey...

My defiance straightened my back and afforded me the courage to glare back at him. "What does any of this have to do with you?" I snapped crossly. "Is that why you asked me to come here? Because if I had any inclination of being invited here just so you could mock me, I wouldn't have shown up!"

"Then why *did* you come?" The growl of his words was surpassed by one swift movement that once again pinned me between himself and the damned door! Breathless and wide-eyed, my head was spinning. My pulse raced throughout my body that now shivered against the heat pouring off of his body, closing around me like a winter jacket.

Frightened, nervous, excited—all five of my senses were overwhelmed by him. I shook my head, and flicked eyes that were annoyed by my own body betraying me up at him tensely. "I'm here because you invited me," I seethed.

His nostrils flared as his hand dropped from beside me, once more. "You drive me insane," he ranted, backing away again. "I simply don't understand!" Several feet away now, he stood and threw his hands up in the air in defeat. "You're a woman, and a little girl, all at once! You're innocent, and you're beguiling! You're the devil, and an angel—it's infuriating!" He shook his head, and then ran his hands through his hair in frustration. "I've never met anyone like you," he growled. "Your eyes—they haunt me every night in my dreams. They keep me up at night!" He paced madly where he stood, and then flung his wild stare back at me. "And then I see you, tonight, and you are the very image of beauty," he boiled. "I couldn't take my eyes off of you! I can't take them off of you now!" Every word he spoke sent me on a roller coaster that I knew he was in control of. My heart soared, before reminding itself that he was about to pull the plug. Nothing that he said would amount to anything that I had hoped for. This meeting would just end up like the last time we were in this very space. My hands found my hips, as I panted before him with a stare that burned as equally into him as his was, to me. "There is something that connects us," he went on, in a tone that was much softer, now. "Something that draws us to each other, and for the life of me, I can't put my finger on what it is." He swiped the bottle of wine up from the counter, and drank the last of it. His eyes were so intense that they seemed to penetrate my mind. "You know why you came here. It's the same reason I asked you to come."

I didn't have time for games. I didn't have the patience for games. It was late, my nerves were now shot, and all that was left was the indignant look I stared back at him with. "What, your date wasn't interested in coming back here with you?"

I stiffened while he stalked towards me, to stop just inches from where my feet were firmly planted. He set the empty wine bottle down on the small table beside me, and the candle flickered from the motion. He dared to take one step closer. I refused to move, or back down. I expected his next words would be caustic. Though I was growing tired of arguing, I was ready for it. One more step he took put us just about toe-to-toe. His hands reached upward between us, until his hands took my face between them with a touch as light as a feather. "What is it about you," he muttered so softly, "that drives me to madness?" My breath caught, and held, and my eyes fluttered before lifting upward to search his. Downward his hands slid, dropping from my face, to slide down my neck, and over my collarbones. A small moan escaped between my lips, and all I could do was wait. Wait for him to wake up. Wait for him to change his mind. Wait, and enjoy, how good it felt to be touched by him, before he would drop the bomb on me that *this wasn't what he wanted.* "I haven't had a full night of sleep since I first saw you," he uttered, his voice raspy now. "And watching you, tonight... with whoever that guy was, who sat with you during dinner... And then dancing with Preston..." He leaned in, and I felt his lips next to my ear. "I've never wanted to be Preston so badly in my life," he whispered, making me so light-headed that I leaned back against the door for support.

I couldn't catch my breath! And I think he knew that, in the way my chest heaved up and down with every quick breath I took. His fingers continued to roam, over my collarbones, and down my shoulders, until I dared to catch one of them into my own. My fingers were so tiny as they twined between his, and they were warm—so warm that they set every part of me that he touched on fire. I brought the palm of his hand to my lips, and I caught his eyes that were so dazed now instinctively shut as I kissed the inside of his hand. Feeling empowered by the effect I was visibly having over him, in addition to not being turned away, I slowly and deliberately pressed my lips to the inside of his wrist. Every schoolgirl crush I'd ever had. Every date I ever went on. Each of the few boyfriends I'd had prior to this... Not even the summation of every romantic experience I ever had could possibly come close to this very explosive moment in time.

But he wasn't about to let me have an ounce of control, or reprieve. In an instant, he untangled his hand from mine, and his arm went around my waist, pulling me close against him. Then he brought me down with him, onto the couch. In front of the fire that blazed as erratically as what was brewing between he and I. "Tell me that you want this as much as I do," he whispered into my ear before his lips kissed my cheek. "I want to hear it from you."

"You know I do," I whispered, my hands eagerly reaching up to unbutton the remaining buttons on his shirt.

"I knew it since the first second I saw you," I conveyed, under the weight of his body that held me firmly against the couch..

When his mouth touched mine, I might as well have been shocked with a jolt of electricity. I melted under his touch that was gentle but eager at the same time. I couldn't get enough of him—touching him, feeling him, tasting him, the scent of him... When his tongue coaxed its way into my mouth, my hands took the liberty of roaming over every tight and toned inch of flesh over his chest and arms. Each inch we dared to travel only seemed to heighten the excitement of our endeavor. Our mouths continued to explore. His kiss became hungrier. The strength in his hands demonstrated his urgency. I wanted it. All of it. Neither one of us wasn't going to be happy at this point, until we owned each other totally and completely, and this was only just the beginning...

His lips moved from my mouth to my cheek, and the arm that encircled my waist pulled me even harder against him, yet. He groaned as he buried his face in my hair, and his lips burned a hot trail on my neck, making me feel faint from dizziness. "I know you do," he murmured softly. "I knew you wanted me from the night I found you here, in this very spot." His lips found mine again, and I again succumbed to his delving kisses. "But this," he spoke, bringing me back to reality, "is not our time."

The small flame from the candle danced, casting its warm glow over Trent's face as my eyes quickly focused again. Of course it wasn't our time. I had to reach up and caress his cheek just to make sure this was all real, and that I wasn't dreaming, as usual. But no, this wasn't a dream. Not this time. It might've just come to a screeching halt, but it was still far better than any dream, and I never wanted it to end.

But once again, I was shut down.

He pulled the afghan from over the side of the couch down over us. Those beautiful dark eyes looked down at me, but I couldn't read them. "I'm four years older than you are."

I couldn't hide my annoyance. "I know that."

"Then surely you understand the implications."

"So this is just about my age?"

"Let's not get ahead of ourselves, milady," he climbed over me and stood up, leaving me bewildered on the couch. His shirtless form was being devoured by my hungry eyes, but my irritation still burned. "You're only questioning sleeping together. This is so much bigger than that." I didn't even know how to respond to that. All I could do was watch him pour himself a glass of whiskey.

"What, you're worried about going to jail?" I blurted out.

His look was earnest. "Perhaps."

"I turn eighteen in a few months," I blurted with a scowl. "Besides, seventeen is the age of consent, here."

The smirk that emerged over his face was wicked. "I see you've already given this some thought," he teased gently. I sat up and straightened my dress, ignoring his joke and causing him to expel one long, frustrated sigh. "Look, it's not *you* I'm concerned with." He gave his glass a light shake, and then took a hefty sip. "It's complicated. We are far out in the woods, and we might be hidden by a woods, but we aren't altogether invisible."

I shook my head. "Seriously.... Who even knows that we speak to one another?"

"For the record, it was quite difficult to get up off of that couch, and move away from you. That was no easy feat."

"Well, it won't get you tossed in jail, either," I retorted bitterly.

He chuckled, and his eyes looked mischievous. "Please. What's the rush? And, just so you know, I'm not just interested in what's in your pants."

My eyes swung back up to his. "No?"

"No."

I sighed, turning an absent stare into the fire. "Well, this is an interesting spin on things."

He looked serious again. He set his empty glass on the counter, and thoughtfully twirled it beneath his hand. "I don't want you to stop coming here."

"I won't." I promised softly. "Just...come back over here."

He did as I requested, and I pulled him down to me, back onto the couch. On top of me. *Fine, don't sleep with me. But I have to have you close. As close as possible.* So I kissed him. Lightly at first. Then hard. I wanted to engrave the taste of his lips into my memory. I could've kissed him all night.

Or forever.

"Are you sorry? For coming here tonight?"

"Sorry?" I lifted my eyebrows at him. "No," I denied confidently. How could I be sorry for something I've wanted so badly, and for so long?

"There are only two weeks until Christmas," he reminded me. "A week after that will be Vivien's New Year's Eve masquerade ball. It's going to become extremely hectic around the house, with all the affairs they'll be hosting, and the ones you'll be required to attend," he mentioned. "Just do your best not to drive me insane with jealousy," he pleaded with a smile.

Tickled, I looked over at him with a smile. "So you *were* jealous?"

"You couldn't tell? I thought it was blatantly obvious," he retorted, as a smile curled his lush lips. I couldn't help but to smile with satisfaction. "It's almost two," he told me softly. "Will anyone know that you're missing?"

I didn't care if I never went back to the main house ever again, but at the same time, I didn't want someone to find out where I was, and then ruin everything before it even started. "I should go back," I told him dreadfully. "I wish I didn't have to."

"Will you take my coat?" he asked. "The temperature has dropped considerably."

I refused. "Just in case anyone should see me slip back in, the last thing I'd want them to be able to confirm is that I was with you," I told him. "Besides, they think I was with Jackie all evening."

His look clearly conveyed that he didn't want me to leave. I hated having to. But he walked me to the door and then kissed me sweetly before I stepped out. Then his eyes followed me into the darkness.

Life was certainly unfair.

Chapter 13

"Kingston's Royalty"

I wasn't able to breathe until I was sure I was safe from getting caught coming back inside. I undressed and got into bed, but I didn't feel tired in the least bit. All I could do was lay there and think about what had just taken place. I recalled every kiss, every touch, every feeling that washed over me, and kept replaying it all over and over. Trent admitted that I pervaded his every thought and dream. Was he lying in his bed at the very same moment, thinking the very same thoughts as I was? I had to wonder.

I felt robbed of the joys of waking up snuggled next to him, or feeling his warmth against me through the night. But it was enough to know that what had been welling up inside of me, since my arrival at the manor, was inside of him, as well.

I awoke after the few hours of sleep I got, feeling rested. I bounced out of bed, jumped in the bath, and then dressed, thinking I was yet again in the clear. Everything was perfect, up until I looked out on the balcony.

Preston was standing out there, and as soon as I saw him, I felt like I'd been hit with a ton of bricks... All of the warmth, all of the excitement—it all disappeared in the blink of an eye. I felt a wave of guilt wash over me that was worse than any other emotion I'd ever experienced. I felt like somehow I had betrayed him, and then the thought crossed through my conscience-stricken mind that maybe he knew where I was at last night, instead of with Jackie. If he knew, he'd be surely hurt... But while I felt guilty, I knew that I had no real reason to feel that way. Preston and I weren't in any type of relationship. We were friends. I needed to relax. Guilt? I had no reason to feel it.

The wind whipped through my hair, the second I stepped out onto the terrace. My intent was to go sit down by the river, and just take some time to drink in the beauty that surrounded me while I reflected on everything that had happened in the last twenty-four hours. The sky was gray and dull. It was cold, sure, but the temperature didn't seem to faze me. I traipsed down to the riverbanks, and took the same seat I had the first day I arrived here. Winter turned the grass brown, and the trees bare, and I hadn't really noticed how different everything looked until that moment.

"Hey there!" I turned, and with the grass crunching beneath his feet, Preston's smile greeted me as he approached. "I didn't even know you were up, yet."

"I just got up," I confessed with a tiny smile. "I realized that I haven't been down here in forever, and something in me just wanted to come and just sit."

"I know what you mean," he agreed. "So," he started, with a glint of mischief in his blue eyes. "My buddy was asking about you after you left the party."

I chuckled, and had totally forgotten about Preston's friend until that point. "Oh, really? What about?"

"It doesn't matter, does it?" he taunted.

Suddenly, I was completely disarmed by his playfulness. I shrugged at him nonchalantly, playing along with his game. "That's okay. You don't have to tell me what he said. I gave him my number, so when he calls me later I'll just ask," I poked.

"No you didn't," he protested in disbelief.

I looked at him. "Are you sure?"

"Did you?!"

"It doesn't matter," I answered, smiling devilishly. "Does it?"

"You hate me," he said, dropping down beside me on the ground. "Or else you wouldn't torture me constantly."

I laughed, nudging his shoulder. "He doesn't have my number. He's not even my type. Did I miss anything last night?"

He shook his head. "Nah."

"These extravagant parties are definitely an experience," I mused. "Not really sure if I find it enjoyable."

"I don't see why you wouldn't. You're usually the main attraction."

I narrowed my eyes at him. "Meaning?"

He shrugged. "Everyone's always asking who that gorgeous girl is who came outta nowhere," he answered. "They all talk about how you and Vivien look so much alike, and their closest friends remark about how you could be their late daughter Lindsey all over again."

"Pfft," I scoffed bitterly. "Vivien avoids any and all questions about me," I muttered. "One of these at one of these stupid parties and yell at the top of my lungs that I'm Vivien's granddaughter so that they all know," I threatened. "I don't see what the big deal is!"

"Well, I guess if you've had as much cosmetic surgery as Vivien has to look like she's still thirty years-old, you'd want to play the part too," he pointed out. "Besides, I wouldn't want to claim to be related to her anyway. To be adopted into her home is enough, but to be related by blood? No thanks," he muttered.

"Hey now, don't forget that I really am related to her by blood," I reminded him with a laugh. "And yes, sometimes it is as bad as you imagine it to be!"

"Oh yeah, sorry," he said with a wink. "Anyhow, do you want me to take you back to school in the morning?" He asked. "It's on my way."

"No it's not," I denied, laughing. "Preston, my school is forty-five minutes *out* of your way," I pointed out.

"I know, but I don't mind the detour," he countered, laughing also.

"Whatever, Preston," I waved aside, giving in. "It's your gas you're wasting!"

And so he did drive me to school in the morning, which Lawrence seemed to take great joy in. He dropped me off, and Jackie was there waiting for me. We only had five minutes before class began, and that wasn't nearly enough time to go over everything, so she made me promise to meet her after classes in the dinner hall. She did manage to tell me that she and Chad had exchanged numbers before she left that night, and they then made a date to go out yesterday. That, I was happy about. But I was also eager to tell her my news.

"So sorry I'm late!" Jackie hurriedly sat down in the chair across from me, putting a plate of pasta down onto the table. "Miss Lillius gave me a B on the report I turned in to her last week, and I'm sorry, but I was certain that paper was A-worthy. Key word, 'was.' As she explained to me all the ways that it wasn't, I couldn't stop imagining reaching across her desk and choking her. But anyways, what's going on? How was your day?"

I couldn't help but to laugh at her. Hair tousled, nearly breathless. "You didn't have to run clear across campus," I teased her. "I've only been sitting here five minutes, maybe."

"Eh, I was hungry," she smiled. "And curious, considering this is the first real time we've had together since this weekend. So what happened after you left the shindig the other night and met Trent?"

"Oh," I sat straight up and then coyly shifted my eyes downward to the remains of my salad. "Not much, really."

"Not buying it," she narrowed her eyes, which I avoided looking into. "Hope. *Hope!*" My eyes widened as she caught them with her imploring gaze. "What are you doing? Really? You're not going to tell me what happened!?"

I sighed heavily. "Nothing serious. We kissed. I kissed him. Maybe he kissed me first," I confessed airily, as if it were nothing. "But I kissed him back. And it was beyond perfect, Jackie. He is just –"

"Preston," she interrupted me, immediately causing me to frown. "You know he's going to be crushed. That boy is in love with you. I don't care what you say."

"There isn't even any need to tell him," I hushed my voice, aware that people nearby were close enough to hear now. Like I needed any more rumors running around.

"How is he not going to know?"

"I thought you would be more supportive than this," I argued quietly. Now I was just pleading with her to try and understand.

She scratched her head and sat back, slightly. "Hope, I am supportive. I've got your back. But I mean, it's like you're leading a double-life on the weekends. You steal away and see Trent, and I get that— he is really one of the hottest guys I've ever laid eyes on. And the way he looks at you is a tell-all in itself. So yeah, I get that. But you're leading Preston on –"

"Whoa," I interrupted her. "Stop right there." I quickly glanced around us, and became more mindful again of my tone. "I absolutely do not lead him on."

"You guys flirt, Hope. A lot. He looks at you with those blue puppy-dog eyes, and he just adores you. Tells you you're beautiful, pretty, hot, whatever, and then you wink and smile and flirt, and it's just not right. One or the other. You can't have both."

We just sat silent for a moment, and I think I was just stunned by the reality of what she had just aired out. She was right. I didn't want to admit it to myself, but... she had a point. I sat back in my chair, and nervously picked up my fork and toyed with a piece of lettuce. She wordlessly shoved a forkful of pasta in her mouth. "You're right," I admitted.

"I'm sorry," she muttered.

"Don't be."

She leaned forward again. "I mean, you're my best friend. And I'm glad you're my best friend. We tell each other everything. I don't want you to ever think you can't tell me everything. I just never expected to really like Preston as a person, and see him as a good friend."

"He is a good friend," I agreed.

"Yes. He is. So that's why I just feel like... I don't know, like maybe this whole thing isn't going to end well, and that I hate the thought of him being hurt."

I didn't like the idea of Preston being hurt either. In fact, instantly, I felt guilt again. Had it really not dawned on me up until that point, that what I was doing, was leading me right down that path with him? "What do I do?" I asked meekly.

"I can't answer that for ya," she answered. "I'm not trying to beat you up over this. I promise. Just think about things, and make sure that what you're doing is what you want to do, or intend to do. Be more mindful of your actions, and your words. Regardless, I'm not going to rat you out, or not be your friend anymore. You've got me, always. You are my sister," she managed a light smile. "Whatever you do, I will be behind you, and I'm not going to judge you. Just do what comes naturally."

"I thought I was doing what comes naturally," I smiled sadly down at my plate.

She laughed. "Well, if having the town's two hottest boys as your boyfriends is what comes naturally, well then honey you better keep riding that train," she cracked with a smirk.

"My home life is quite the mess," I shook my head, finding some amusement in it all. "I wonder if my mother and father are looking down at me, wondering what the hell I'm doing."

"Nah," she said, taking another bite. "Just get through the rest of this year, and then we'll get the heck outta this town, and take this show on to college."

"College," I said thoughtfully. "I need to get through the auditions for 'Phantom of the Opera,' first."

"You're going to be an amazing Christine," she assured me confidently. "Your home life alone has prepared you plenty for that role."

I went back to my room that night alone. Jackie said she had some homework to finish, and that was fine, but this evening, being alone with my thoughts was a little unsettling. Had I been consciously trying to plant that seed with Preston? I had no doubt that at this very point in time, if he had learned that Trent and I had started something, Preston would be crushed. But even I didn't know where things would end up with Trent. So why bother telling him? Why get him upset? Why change anything from how it was, right then?

Before I knew it, Wednesday was here, and not only was I preparing for auditions, but we had another performance every night until Friday. Preston was front row, center—just as he'd promised—for each of the three performances, and on Friday he brought Chad along, which delighted Jackie to pieces. We were finally done with the play, and everything went so perfectly. Preston and Chad wanted to go out and celebrate which sounded good to Jackie and I, and we had them give us a half an hour to clean up and change into something really cute before we hit the town.

Preston and I rode in his car, and Chad and Jackie followed us. Preston promised me a good time, and told me that he was going to take us into town, where all the places that he used to frequent were.

"Used to?" I asked. "Why don't you go anymore?"

He shrugged. "Well, I stopped once you came to live here," he said. "You were much more interesting than clubs," he reasoned. "Even when you hated me."

"So where are we going, exactly?" I asked.

"To some of the best bars and clubs this town has to offer," he replied with a killer grin.

"And how are we supposed to get into these clubs and bars if we're under age?" I pursued, intrigued.

"I know people," he replied. "They let me in all the time—they know me."

"And me?" I asked skeptically. "Won't they just turn me away at the door?"

"It's a different world around here, Hope," he explained. "You're going to be shown what it's like to be treated like royalty tonight!"

The part of town we were now driving through had tons of people around walking around, strips of bars and clubs up and down both sides of the street—nothing like what we had back home where I was from. Music blared from each place, and people were even dancing outside as they waited in lines to enter these places. People drove up and down the strip in souped-up, flashy cars, and people sat outside at little café tables just people-watching. Before I knew it, Preston pulled up to a curb, and someone was at my door, opening it for me. I got out, and Preston did the same, shaking hands with a guy who then took his keys and told him it was good to see him again before he got into Preston's car and took off in it.

"Who was that?" I asked, pointing at his car as Jackie and Chad pulled up behind me, getting the same treatment.

"Valet," he said casually, putting his arm around my shoulders, smiling. "Let's go."

"Hey man, where've you been!?" A big, burly guy dressed in black addressed Preston, smiling as we approached him. The music coming from inside was loud, and it looked dark and smoky beyond the door.

"It's good to see you again," Preston shouted at him over the music, shaking his hand, and the guy gave us clearance to just walk in despite the long line that waited to our right, eyeing us curiously. I did feel like someone important as our group strolled in, getting nods and hellos from bartenders, bouncers and just random people. There was a long bar with people packing all the seats, and the dance floor was on my right with different colored lights, and a live DJ playing hip-hop music.

Watching Preston interact with everyone from doormen, valets, bartenders, patrons— it was constant. And exhausting. He seemed to know everyone, and they would all light up at the mere sight of him. Yet another sign that Preston surely couldn't be as horrible as people around the manor make him out to be. Or even what I had thought in the beginning.

"This place is packed!" Jackie exclaimed over the loud thumping of the music, and the crowd hovered at the bar around us.

"Have you ever been here before?" I asked Jackie in her ear.

"No—I didn't even know I could get in here until now!" she exclaimed, laughing excitedly. "This is pretty crazy!"

"Hey Jack," Preston called, leading me up to the bar with his arm still around my shoulder. The bartender looked up, and then grinned.

"Long time, no see, man!" He greeted him. "The usual?"

"Yeah," Preston answered. "And whatever they're having," Preston added.

"What can I get you, pretty lady?" he asked me.

Looking around, I decided to try something new. "Give me a shot of something," I told him. "Your choice."

"Me too," Jackie interjected. "I guess we'll get shit-faced together," she said with a grin.

He winked. "I like your style. Shots are quick, and to the point. Nothing like that sissy-shit that Preston drinks— you have to drink ten bottles just to get a buzz on," he cracked, causing Preston to laugh.

"If you like your tips, you'd better shut it!" Preston threatened.

The bartender winked at Jackie and I, handing us our tiny glasses. Preston grabbed his beer, and Chad got the same thing. Immediately, I went for mine, taking it all in, and swallowing it in one gulp. "Crap!" Jackie cried, not about to let me out-do her. She downed hers as well, and we slammed our glasses back onto the bar, satisfied with ourselves.

"Now that's a real woman," one of the guys sitting at the bar called out to me. "But how well can you hold your liquor?"

"Better than you can," Jackie called back, grinning.

"Wanna bet?"

"Bring it on," she invited.

"Bartender, three more shots, please!" The guy ordered, smiling. "Let's see what they've got!"

Preston came up behind me, and he and Chad were amused by Jackie's and my blatant attempt to get drunk, and he was just in time to see us both down our second shot in five minutes. "You're going to get sick," Preston commented. "C'mon, let's go dance!"

"No way!" Jackie denied. "This guy thinks he can drink more than us, and look at him—what are you, a buck-thirty?" she teased the slender guy who was probably around Preston's age. "I could bench press you, buddy!"

My laughter roared over Jackie's trash-talking. "Bartender, honey, we'll take another round!" I called out, getting his attention.

"Preston!" I heard a voice call out behind me as my new friend Jack handed out another three drinks to Jackie, the guy challenging us, and myself. On the count of three we all downed our third shot, and the guy wussed out, saying he had to drive home.

"See?" Jackie taunted. "I told you—what'd I tell you? You're a lightweight, buddy! Take your butt over to Chucky Cheese's with the rest of the kiddos!"

"Oh my God, it's so great to see you again!" I heard the same voice behind me, and I turned around to see a petite redhead throw her arms around Preston's neck, hugging on him. I noticed that he looked really surprised to see her, and also a bit uncomfortable, which showed when his eyes flicked back and forth nervously from her to me. I raised an eyebrow quizzically, but decided to leave him alone, grabbing Jackie and leading her to where everyone was dancing out on the floor, followed by Chad.

I started feeling pretty good. Warm and fuzzy. I started moving to the music, and just let go. Jackie and I danced with each other, and Chad danced with us as well. But I wanted another drink before too long, and Jackie asked me to bring her one as well.

"There you are!" Preston shouted, approaching me. "I didn't know where you went!"

"Yeah well don't let me keep you from anything," I told him passively, grabbing two more shots.

"That was nothing," he dismissed, ordering another beer for himself. "Besides, I haven't seen her in forever."

"Yeah, I got that much," I told him with a sarcastic smile.

"We dated back in high school," he shouted over the music.

"Whatever," I waved aside, eyeballing him as I downed another drink and set the empty glass on the counter. I started feeling a bit giddy from the buzz, and at that point, the redhead popped back up again. I could tell by the way she was making eyes at Preston while she ordered her drink that she was interested in more than just chatting about old times, and I grabbed Jackie's drink in one hand, and wrapped my arm around Preston's neck. "Let's dance," I told him devilishly, glancing over at the redhead defiantly before pushing him out to the dance floor.

I picked up where I'd left off before I went to the bar, and I quickly discovered that slow dancing wasn't the only kind of dancing Preston was good at. I teased him, rubbed up against him as we danced, and he returned the favor as we partied on the dance floor. I liked this. I liked being able to let loose and have fun. I liked being treated like someone important, just for being out with Preston. I was flattered by how Preston was watching me move as we kept daring to tease each other a bit further. If not for Jackie grabbing my hand to drag me away, I wasn't sure how far it would've gone, in the middle of the dance floor madness. She wanted another drink. I thought it was best that I stop, while I was ahead. This was fun, but we were already teetering on the border of *too much.*

"Look at them," Jackie pointed up, to a few girls who had gotten up on the bar and started to dance. "How trashy are they!? We'd look so much better up there!"

I'm not sure exactly how I got up there. I am not even positive I was in my right mind when I did so. But I do have a slight recollection of climbing up onto that bar, and joining those other girls dancing, and the boys cat-calling us all the while. *Too much* was no longer a concern of mine.

Between the alcohol, and the high we felt getting all that attention, Jackie and I were screwed in terms of morals, and surpassing the point of no return. We began doing mock strip-teases, unbuttoning our shirts a button or so while we danced, and gyrating against each other on the bar. Preston and Chad were waving dollar bills at us. We were taking the bills from their hands, sticking them down our shirts and shoving them partway into our jeans. When I noticed a few girls casting interested glances at Preston, I sat down on the bar, and beckoned Preston to come towards me. I dared to put my arms around his neck so that he could lift me off the bar. He set me down, and I grabbed Jackie's shot that she had not yet taken, before handing it to him with a wicked smile. His level of intrigue was clouded by the carnal look that had long-since taken over his eyes. This night was already going down in history, I was certain. We checked any and all good sense at the curb, along with his car, and this alcohol was starting to become a problem, in terms of making bad decisions over the course of this evening.

I grabbed the saltshaker and handed it to him, unbuttoning my shirt one more button and exposing quite a bit more flesh than I had any business revealing. Taking my cue, he "licked, poured, slammed, and sucked"— another phrase I'd become acquainted with, over this evening—and I could tell that he didn't want to stop just there, either. His eyes were burning, and I knew he wanted me.

This was *not* me. This was *not* anything I had ever done, before. This was *not* the way I acted in public, and I already knew as the guys were tabbing us out that the chances of this ever being repeated were next-to-none. Blame it on making mistakes, and growing up. Blame it on bad judgment. Blame it on Jackie's fired-up persona that was infectious, and made me feel alive and free. Blame it on whatever you want, but I did have a good time, and—at that particular moment—I was glad it happened..

"Let's get out of here," Chad hollered over the music. "I want to go see if there's anything else goin' on, anywhere else!" I suddenly wasn't so sure I would last anywhere else.

I grabbed Preston's hand, and we filed out of the club behind Chad and Jackie. The cold night air was a little sobering, but not enough so. We were all flying high as kites, and we walked down the sidewalk—my arm interlocked with Jackie's, and Preston's arm possessively went around my shoulder. Chad had to reach out and grab Jackie around the waist, because at the rate she was going, it wouldn't be long before she stumbled and fell.

"Who needs healthy livers?" Jackie called out. "I don't!"

"You are drunk," I told her, stuttering over my own words.

"Look who's talking," she slurred. "Oh oh oh!!! I want a tattoo!" Jackie's eyes lit up as we passed by a tattoo parlor.

"You've never talked about getting a tattoo," I told her. "That's a bad idea..." *And squinting doesn't help you see better when you're drunk. Noted...*

"So? I want one anyway," she said, stopping in the middle of the sidewalk.

"Okay, so what are you saying?" Preston asked her. "Are you saying you really want to stop and get one? Now?"

She smiled and nodded, and then let out an embarrassingly loud hiccup, causing her to laugh hysterically. "Noooooo I want one!" she protested as Chad guided her along past the parlor. "I do!"

"Bad idea," I muttered while we walked. "No."

"Ugh, I'm starting to not feel so well," Jackie moaned. "I don't think dancing on that bar agreed with me!"

"I don't think those last twelve shots agreed with you," Chad quipped, picking his date up into his arms.

"Who's the lightweight now, Jackie?" Preston teased, laughing.

"Oh, be quiet," she mumbled, wrapping her arms around Chad's neck. "I think I'm going to be sick..."

"I'd better get her home," Chad decided, taking a deep breath. "Pray to the Puke Gods for me that she doesn't hurl everything up all over my car," Chad joked after saying goodnight.

"So what do you want to do?" Preston asked me once we were all alone. "Have you had enough bar dancing for now?"

I managed a laugh. "For now," I echoed. "Maybe I'll have to ask Lawrence to install a pole in my room," I cracked.

"I'd like to see that," he laughed as we turned back around to give the valet his ticket for his car.

"I had fun tonight, Preston," I told him while we waited for his car to be brought around. "You were right about the 'being treated like royalty' thing."

"I know," he said as we watched his car pull up in front of us. The valet got out and came around to open my door for me. "It's great, isn't it?"

The ride home flew right by, undoubtedly because I fell in and out of consciousness the whole time, and it was after one when we pulled up to the manor. We snuck inside to make sure we came in undetected, and then snickered all the way up the stairs and down the hall to our suites. "I don't want to go to sleep yet," I pouted. "I was having too much fun!"

He laughed. "Well, you can come in here if you want," he invited, opening the door to his suite. I obliged by hurrying in there past him, and I flicked the light switch on to find that his suite was exactly like mine, only decorated for a man's taste. Everything was darkly colored, from the plush, black leather sofa and chairs in his sitting area, to his oversized bed set with dark navy comforters, blankets and pillows.

"This is the first time I've been in here," I mused aloud.

He nodded. "It is. Does it feel weird?"

I shook my head, sitting down. "No," I answered. My eyes panned the room, drinking it in.

"You're quiet," he observed, unbuttoning his shirt and tossing it over his armchair. "Don't throw up on my bed," he teased with a look of warning.

"I'm not going to get sick," I denied with a small laugh and a roll of my eyes. "I might be fuzzy, but one thing I've learned here so far is that I can hold my liquor." I flopped back onto his bed, and stared up at the ceiling. "Maybe I'm just tired," I muttered with a sigh.

"Do you want to talk about your bout with the green-eyed monster earlier?" He tossed one smug, lingering look behind himself before stepping into his bathroom.

I sat up and glared in his direction. "Excuse me?"

"No, excuse *you*!" He poked his head out of the bathroom, still smirking. I felt the blood rush to my face. "You got so riled up when Carmen—"

"—oh, is *that* her name?" I interrupted sarcastically.

"That *is* her name." He was trying not to laugh, as he found me profoundly amusing. "Why don't you tell me how you really feel?"

"I feel like you're antagonizing me, and making stuff up," I retorted, flopping back down onto my back.

He came out of the bathroom wearing a loose, white t-shirt and a pair khaki-colored, linen pants. He approached his bed and lay beside me, turned toward the ceiling, like myself. "Don't puke on my sheets," he warned again.

"Yeah? Why don't you re-enact that little strip-tease you did on the bar?" he requested, flicking those sky-blue eyes in my direction. "That was pretty hot."

"Oh you thought so?" I asked, glancing at him.

"The jealousy thing was hotter."

"You really are delusional," I muttered, staring back up at the ceiling.

"Well then I'll settle for the strip-tease. You can even use me as your mock-pole!"

"You're gonna have to pay me a lot more than just single dollar bills to see that again," I cracked.

"Name your price."

I rubbed my eyes, as he laughed at my reddening face. "I've had enough of you," I teased him. "I'm going to bed. Goodnight, Preston."

"Goodnight, Hope."

Chapter 14

"Hopes and Dreams"

    The next morning, I might as well have just been dead. I felt so lethargic, and my head was killing me—no doubt from all the booze the night before! The one thing I could say for myself was that I was at least able to remember everything.. Well, and I didn't vomit. I got out of bed and went in search of some aspirin, which thankfully I found in the bathroom cabinet. I grabbed the glass from the sink and filled it with water before tossing back a few of the small pills. What time was it, anyway?

    All I knew was that I had to make myself look presentable by the time I was to go and secretly meet Trent that evening. But I had plenty of time for that.

    I washed last night's smoke and grime off of me in what felt like the best shower of my life, and then proceeded to dress and put some light make-up on. Fortunately, the aspirin was already kicking in, and what had become the first hangover of my life was quickly diminishing.

I went down the stairs and heard commotion coming from the hallway that led to Lawrence's office and the library. All of the drapes that lined the walls were pulled open to reveal the stunning outer wall of nothing but windows, and I paused to admire how much lovelier the hall looked when all the drapes were drawn! There was a man up high on a ladder, and it looked like he was cleaning the ceiling. It was then that Lawrence emerged from his office, stepping around the man on the ladder and looking somewhat annoyed, before he approached me staring curiously at what was going on.

"Good morning." Lawrence greeted me with a sardonic smile. "Or, I hope it's a good one for you—mine's not going so well." As if on cue, Vivien appeared from beyond the doors to Lawrence's office being followed by two men. She was barking orders, and pointing at the floors. Lawrence cast an agitated glance behind him. "You see, sometimes I fail to remember that this is Vivien's house, and I'm just living here," he said sarcastically.

"What's going on?" I asked him nosily. "What's that guy doing up there with the ceiling?"

"He's some painter that Vivien heard of at one of her little teas, or bridge games," he explained. "She absolutely insists he's the next 'big thing'," he said dramatically. "Now she's got this asinine idea about re-doing the entire gallery, there. He's painting one of his 'masterpieces' on the ceiling, and she rambled on about brightening the entire corridor up by taking down the drapes and tearing up the floors. I happened to like that area just the way it was," he griped. "It was dark, it was masculine—and now it's going to be turned into another one of her feminine, pastel debaucheries! But hey, it's a good thing I caught you. Could I get a moment with you in my office please?"

I wordlessly followed behind him, and sat down before his desk. He closed the door behind me, and then took a seat as well.

"I received word today that you achieved a partial scholarship to some college for performing arts?"

My heart swelled with pride and excitement. "Did I?"

"Why didn't you tell me?" His stone-cold demeanor was unchanging. And it wiped the smile off my face. "That you were applying to colleges already?"

He was not happy. And this was strange to me. "Well," I drawled slowly, "I just started, really. My theater instructor has been helping me with looking at schools, and—"

"Why acting college? What use does that really have in the real world, Hope? Why not finance? Why not law? Why something that thousands of people try for and fail at, all the time?"

"This is what I love to do," I offered meekly. "This is all I've ever dreamed of doing..."

"No one takes actors seriously," he pressed on. "I fully supported you when you became active in the theater department at Springcrest. I understood that being on a stage is something young girls love. It's a good hobby to keep you busy, and active, and make friends. Or enemies, in your case." I frowned at the mere mention of what happened with Amanda. "But it's not a career, Hope. It's a fantasy world."

I swallowed hard. A fantasy world... I had no idea what it was, that he wanted me to say. I was at a loss. The minuscule scholarship that my teacher who believed in me had fought for me to get, meant nothing to the person whose job it was to look after me. I was now fidgeting with my hands, in my lap. I felt like a five year-old. And I wasn't sure what any of this even meant.

"You turn eighteen soon, and technically you will be able to do whatever you please," he continued, his tone more calm and soft. "I would love nothing more than for you to remain here, and continue your schooling after you graduate. I would also be willing to foot the bill for your entire college education, but you would have to pick a career that you would absolutely succeed at, and gain respect for."

I was dumbfounded by his offer. "I've never wanted to do anything but act," I blurted crossly. "I don't really know what it is you expect me to do, aside from going to school for something else altogether that I probably don't even care about!"

"You make excellent grades in your math and science classes – what about a chemical engineer? A doctor? A nurse, even?"

"I have zero interest in any of those fields, or anything pertaining to math or science," I spouted, feeling attacked. "The only thing outside of theater that I have any interest in is writing, and I mean, I could go into journalism—"

"Journalists are tacky," he waved aside. "Another field that you wouldn't be taken seriously in. Apparently, you like to argue – lawyers do that for a living." His suggestion was sarcastic, but valid. I glared at him. He shrugged. "I'm just saying, Hope. Hell, if you became a lawyer, and a damned good one, I would make you a partner at my firm, no questions asked. I would leave the business to you, to carry on."

"Preston is going after that," I reminded him tensely. "That's *his* dream."

"Preston will go onto bigger and better things," he retorted. "He won't remain here. He's destined for the city. Any city. He, too, will make a damned good lawyer, but it won't be my business he takes on."

"What makes you think I'd want it?" I countered boldly.

His look was surprised. "Why wouldn't you?"

"Because acting is what I want to do," I reiterated pointedly, shaking my head and shifting in my chair. "If you don't want to support me in my dream, and doing what I want to do, then I accept that," I told him. "I'll accept my scholarship, and I will even keep applying in hopes of getting a full scholarship, but I will go to school for what I love, and I will support myself as best I can while doing so."

"I will cut you off from your allowance once you graduate." His threat was delivered in a sweet, cunning voice. As if the promise of money would deter me.

"If that's how it's going to be, then so be it."

He looked defeated, now. "Hope. Think about it. Think about things. Major in something—anything else, that would be worthwhile. Minor in theater, if you want. But don't waste your time on a school for performing arts. Do something with your wit, and intellect that will gain you a lifetime of staunch supporters, and colleagues. Go to a university. There is so much more to experience, there!"

His eyes were pleading with me to just give it some thought. He was very adamant, and suddenly it was sad to me how important it was, to people like him, for acceptance in society. I'd never cared about it my entire life, and I couldn't imagine caring so much about what people thought of me, as he did. I nodded, giving him some false sense of hope that I would actually give the entire exchange any thought. But as soon as I headed straight for the door, it was the furthest thing from my mind.

He followed me out, and then paused briefly in the doorway to call out to me, "And one word of advice my dear—when you move into a man's home, don't take away the one spot in the entire house that makes him the most comfortable." He cast a look down to where his wife was still giving orders to people around the foyer, and with that, he stalked off in the other direction, muttering to himself. I had to admit, though—I was with Vivien on this one. I thought the corridor looked so much better now that it was being brightened up.

And if I thought my morning hadn't been oppressive enough, Vivien and a table of friends were set up in the back foyer, cackling like hens, and it was too late to avoid them.

"Goodness," a woman shot up out of her chair at the sight of me, and Vivien's eyes followed. "Vivien, who might this be?"

She stood up also, and made her way around the table, after the lady who was on her way over to me with wide eyes. "That's Hope, my dear."

The woman stopped before me, and looked me over in wonder. "My, my – aren't you a beautiful young woman!" She turned to Vivien, confused. "She looks just like—"

"She's Lindsay's daughter," Vivien quickly cut her off. It was at that point that the other three women who had been left sitting at the table, curiously wandered over to us. Vivien was suddenly aware that she had an audience with a ton of questions on the tips of their tongues. "Hope was born not long after Lindsey left us," she added with a solemn face.

"You never told any of us that you had a grand-daughter!"

"Well, why would I?" Vivien countered. "I thought I would never see my beloved daughter again. I didn't even know she'd had a daughter, or what kind of life she'd led after she left us. Left me." She wiped at something in the corner of her eye, and it was nearly impossible for me to not laugh at her pathetic act of being sad and heartbroken. Give me a break... "When Lawrence and I got the phone call that my Lindsey had been in an accident recently, it broke my heart all over again, but I insisted right away that she come here to live with us." Fortunately, I didn't inherit my acting skills from my grandmother. For me, her performance was transparent. Her friends, however, seemed to be buying into it.

"Honey, how sad," one of them put their arm around her.

"It is." Vivien sniffled, and my eye roll was blatant, though unnoticed. "Every time I look at her, it just reminds me..."

"You poor dear," said another. "I cannot even imagine!"

I forced a small smile, and excused myself to leave the conversation. Screw Vivien. Her "reminders" were few and far between, considering how little we interacted.

I had to get out of there. I fled out the back doors into the gardens, and headed straight down that walkway to the plots where my parents rested. Good God in Heaven, sometimes I could've sworn I was being punished for things I hadn't even done, yet.

This broken household was a drain on me. These people had more secrets that I could count. They had more personalities amongst them than I could possibly keep up with. But I, too, had undergone a transformation after arriving at Van Steenburgh Manor. I knelt down onto the ground, where only a short while ago had been dirt; was now covered over with grass. My entire life had been bred out of secrets until the very moment I set foot in that gigantic palace. I instantly had to get used to a family that I'd never even met before. And if my life didn't encompass the famous term "rags-to-riches," I didn't know what did.

Tears fell onto my hands, which were pressed to the ground. Even though there was no emotional foundation at the manor for me to thrive on, I couldn't say that my life here was entirely bad, though. I had Trent, who thrilled me more than any person in my life ever had. I had Preston, who despite our rocky start had become an invaluable friend. There was Jackie, who was my closest girlfriend, and knew all my secrets, and I felt came from a similar walk of life as I did. We were both orphans to an extent. Me, more so now than her.

I was receiving recognition at Springcrest for my acting, which meant so much to me. It was my passion. My greatest joy—outside of stealing away to see Trent. My performances were featured in the local newspapers. My instructor was my biggest supporter—and when he had caught me by the arm after class and handed me his own personal letter of recommendation, and then finally the news that he had helped me gain the first scholarship towards reaching my dreams, I was so very excited and grateful.

I had also gained respect simply out of living where I lived, and being related to who I was related to. My possibilities were endless. With, or without Lawrence's support, I had to go full-steam ahead.

Being at my parents' gravesite didn't give me the satisfaction I had hoped. It felt empty. I felt more alone than ever. I just felt sad. I just had to get myself together.

Chapter 15

"Black, White, and Read All Over"

I was startled in the morning by someone angrily storming into my suite and ripping the covers straight off of me! I bolted upward in fright, and there Lawrence stood before me, with a menacing look that rivaled Trent's. The gasp I sucked inward now held stubbornly in my lungs, and I stared back at him with wide, frantic eyes. I'd never seen Lawrence this incensed, and suddenly my mind was racing to figure out what had inspired it, as I sat paralyzed by fear.

"I don't know who you think you are," he fumed loudly. "But while you are living under my roof, you will live under my rules!" He slapped the newspaper he held in his hand down in front of me. I looked, and it was the "Society Page." I then saw what he was so angry about. I was staring straight down at a picture of me and Jackie, from our night out on the town with Preston and Chad. At the bar. Me standing upon it.

A shot that documented me naughtily unbuttoning my shirt, with a sea of guys surrounding me.

And dollar bills being waved in the air.

"Don't act like you're shocked," Lawrence snapped. "This behavior is intolerable! How the hell do you explain this?" he demanded.

"I—we—it wasn't what it looks like," I stammered, not knowing what to say. "I wasn't actually—"

"Oh?" His tone began to drip with sarcasm. "Did the photographer just ask you to get up on the bar and pretend to strip so he could get a picture, then?"

"I never *saw* any photographer!"

"*Anyone with a goddamn cell phone is a photographer, you idiot!*"

"I wasn't stripping," I screamed back at him.

"You will not behave like this anymore, do you understand?" His voice bellowed, as Kate hurriedly appeared in my doorway to see what all the fuss was about. "I will throw you out of my house so fast you won't even know it happened until you were out on the street with your suitcase," he threatened. "Everything you do reflects back on this house, Hope. Every move you make reflects on us. On me! I have clients who read this paper—what do I tell them? Should I tell them that I'm an excellent lawyer that can win their case easily, yet I can't even contain a teenager living in my household?"

"Lawrence!" Kate rushed in, and her eyes and tone were frantic. She reached for his arm, but he was so infuriated that he jerked it away from her. "Calm down!"

"It was all in fun!" I scrambled to my feet, eyeing him angrily. "What—is no one in this house allowed to have fun? Are we all to just sit around here like stuffy fools, staring at the walls? I had no idea that picture was even taken—"

"You *ever* disrespect me once more by shouting at me and I'll make sure you never see the light of day again," he raged, backing me up against the wall. "Do you understand me?"

I looked back at him defiantly, but said nothing.

Kate had covered her mouth with her hands, watching on in horror, but now she dared to reach forward once more to try and talk some sense into Lawrence. "Please," she coaxed softly. "Darling, calm down—"

"*This is not the way a young woman should act,*" he rampaged, before charging forward to point one long, slender forefinger in my face. "From this point on, every time you leave this house to go anywhere, you will report to me first, so I will know exactly where you're going," he hissed, before backing away from me, and leaving the copy of the paper behind. "I mean it, Hope. I don't want to hear anything like this happening again," he warned, exiting the room, and slamming the door behind him.

Kate lingered for just a moment, and when I dared to look up at her, I saw that her eyes had focused on the newspaper photo sitting in front of me. I saw her look of disappointment. I felt my heartache intensify, as the groan that crawled up my throat followed her exit from my bedroom, with my door closing softly behind her.

My head dropped into my hands, and I felt horrible. That person in that photo wasn't me. It wasn't something I did on a regular basis.

But it was something captured in a photo, to be published all through town for everyone to see, and I know exactly what it looked like. I knew I had more sense than to get naked on a bar in some club.

I had no one to be mad at, but myself.

I nearly jumped out of my skin when I heard a knock come from behind me. I saw the silhouette of someone through the curtains of my terrace doors. I went over there and opened them, and it was Preston. He looked at me with concern.

"I heard yelling in here," he said, peeking inside. "What was that all about?"

I opened the door wider, allowing him to step inside. "It was your father," I replied tearfully. "Our night out on Friday made the papers."

He looked confused. "What do you mean?"

"This," I told him, picking up the paper Lawrence had left behind, and handing it to him. "Did you know someone was in there taking pictures?"

He first looked surprised as he perused the article. Then his surprise turned to amusement as he looked over the picture. "That's a pretty good shot."

"Yeah, well Lawrence didn't think so. He stormed in here and blew up at me threatening to kick me out," I told him. "*That* was the yelling. I tried to tell him it wasn't what that picture makes it look like, but he didn't want to hear me out."

"I'm offended," Preston said, dropping the paper back onto my nightstand. "They only mentioned me once in this article!"

"Well if it's any consolation, that's the back of your head right there, waving the dollar bill at me," I told him, pointing at the picture.

"That's not even a good shot of me!"

"I'm glad you find all of this amusing," I snapped at him, taking a seat back down upon my bed. My heart was still racing from my confrontation with Lawrence. "If your father kicks me out, I'll have nowhere else to go," I muttered.

"He's not going to kick you out," Preston denied, sitting beside me. "Relax! He gets angry over things like this. He's stopped getting angry with me over the things I've done that have made it into that stupid paper. I've been branded the town's 'bad boy' probably a million times in that very same paper, and none of the things I've done are half as bad as the way they tell it," he reasoned. "As long as I know I'm alright, then I don't care what they say."

I looked at him and nodded appreciatively. "Too bad your father doesn't see things the same way."

"You just have to understand… to the wealthy socialites in this town, being put on that stupid page is either a blessing or a curse. If you make it in there for something good, you call all your friends—who also read that page religiously—and you brag about it. If it's a curse, then you get a bunch of calls from your friends, who've seen the dumb article, and want to rub it in your face," he explained. "I've never even bothered to read that paper, except when my father used to bring it to me to show what stupid picture they've put in there and an article they wrote to blow the whole thing out of proportion. Don't let it bother you," he told me.

"Let's just not talk about it," I suggested softly. "I think I'm going to just hide in my room until tomorrow when I have to go back to school, so I don't have to face Lawrence."

"You won't have to do all of that," Preston told me. "He and Vivien probably already left."

"For where?" I asked.

"Out to visit with some of Vivien's friends, I think. I heard all the yelling going on in here, and after I heard your door slam, I peeked out into the hallway and heard my father going down the stairs. Vivien was telling him to hurry up because she was going to go wait in the car. They'll be gone for the rest of the day," he assured me.

Preston left, so he could shower and get dressed. I had another idea entirely, after learning that Lawrence was going to be gone for the day. Seizing what seemed to be a perfect opportunity, I immediately set myself into motion.

I quickly went into the bathroom, pulling my hair up into a ponytail, and after cleaning up and dressing, I slipped out of my room.. I very quietly crept down the stairs, and made sure no one spotted me as I turned right—down the hallway that was half-way torn up from Vivien's workers. Undetected, I tiptoed into the dark, cherry-stained office that was Lawrence's, and I closed the door behind me, slowly twisting the lock to make sure no one would disturb me.

There was no other way. Not if I wanted to see for myself whether Lawrence had anything which would open my eyes and give me a glimpse into the world my mother left behind.

It was dark in there—as it always was—but I didn't dare turn on any lights, or open the dark, heavy drapes. I sat at his desk, in the same chair he always sat in, and I took a flashlight out of my pocket that I'd brought down my bedroom.

I rummaged through the drawers on the left side first, and found nothing except for files he kept of his clients. Everything from traffic tickets to burglary, extortion to murder—you name it, he defended it. And he always won. I couldn't help but wonder how many sick people were walking around town because of his capabilities.

There was nothing in the right hand side of his desk either, so I headed to the filing cabinets to the side of the office now, to see if I could find anything there. Clients, clients, clients... I couldn't find anything that remotely looked like it had anything to do with me, or my mother.

I sat back, about ready to give up, except now I was staring at a door. Not the door to exit the office, but another door, that I never really paid attention to before. I stood and walked over to it, turning the knob slowly. It was a closet. I felt around inside for a switch, and when I found it, I closed the door behind me and flicked the light on.

I was surrounded by filing cabinets.

They were dusty, and dirty, and upon opening several of the drawers, I discovered that some of these files were twenty and thirty years old! I looked around, wondering if this were a lost cause, but something odd caught my eye, and made me stop. The filing cabinet in the very back corner had fingerprints on it, through the dust. Obvious that someone frequently went into that cabinet, I walked over to it, careful not to put my fingerprints on there as well, and pulled it open using the very tips of my fingers.

I hit the jackpot!

I took out a file - a thick manila folder which was appropriately named "Lindsey" - and opened it up. It had my father's information in there as well—driver's license numbers, social security information, addresses for what looked like the place he lived while he was here, and then every place they stayed along the way up until they bought our house. Copies of receipts from places where they bought furniture, home appliances, all sorts of unnecessary information. Things that no one would ordinarily care about. Unless they were a control freak. So Lawrence had known where my mother was, all along. I wasn't really surprised, considering how much he knew about every move I made. There were also numerous VHS tapes with no labels in the cabinet as well, behind various DVDs in dated cases, and though Lawrence did have a VCR and small TV in his office, I wasn't about to take the chance of playing them and getting caught by Kate, or anyone else walking by and hearing something. I think it was more than obvious what was on them anyway.

Nothing in there hinted at why she ran away from the manor, so I slid her file back into its place in the drawer, and right behind her slot was a file with "Hope" written on it. I took it out, and my heart pounded as I found copies of every report card I'd received since I began Kindergarten! Every class schedule, every class agenda, all of my teachers' names, and—the kicker—pictures of me! Pictures of me when I was newly born, pictures of me on my first day of school, pictures of me learning how to ride my bike, and pictures that were taken for school... I felt my face get hot, realizing that I'd been watched for my entire life, and a million thoughts were swirling through my mind so fast that I couldn't catch onto one of them long enough to get a grip on what I was feeling at that time... I flipped a picture over, and saw that the date that the picture was taken was written on there, along with a little description of the picture "learning to ride bike". My mother's handwriting... I flipped the rest of them over to find the same things on every one—the dates and descriptions "1st grade class picture", "2 months old", etc.

I put the pictures down and continued flipping through my folder. I found letters—letters that my mother had written to Lawrence. The first one was dated a month after my birthday, and in it she wrote that I had been born, and I was perfect, with ten tiny fingers and ten tiny toes… She told him that she agreed to send him updates on me and how I was, and what progress I made as long as he promised to stay away from us. Apparently, he must've agreed, which was how he continued to receive my pictures. The rest of the letters were similar—short, and to the point. They revealed nothing about anything, except how I was doing.

But it wasn't until I saw the copy of my birth certificate that I fully understood the complete picture. It had my name, and my birth date, and my mother's name, but where my father's name should've been was… was Lawrence's! It stated that *Lawrence Anthony Van Steenburgh* was my father, clear as day, right in front of me! The letters, the pictures, the running away from home… it all fit together, now!

I sat down on the floor, and held the birth certificate for a long time, just staring at it. *Maybe it was false.* Maybe Lawrence had it typed up for whatever sick reason! How could I let him know what I found, without letting him know that I'd been snooping in his office? I had to confront him to find out if it were true!

In a daze, I somehow managed to put everything back in my file, and I put it all back in the drawer, in the same place I took it from. I didn't know what I was going to do from that point—all I knew was that I needed to get out of there fast. My heart was in my throat, when I grabbed my flashlight, turned off the light, and left the skeletons that were hidden in Lawrence's closet. I put my ear to the door to see if I could hear anyone walking in the gallery. I heard nothing, so I slowly unlocked the door, and turned the knob. The coast was clear—until I stepped out into the gallery and heard Preston's voice coming from the foyer.

"Have you seen Hope at all?" I heard him ask.

"No, not yet. Is she not upstairs in her suite?" Kate asked him.

"No. Well, I knocked, and she didn't answer," he replied. "I'll just look around some more."

I darted down the gallery and disappeared into the library. I ran up the spiral staircase which took me to the second level of books, and then I played dumb when Preston entered the library, looking around.

"Hey you!" I greeted him breathlessly.

He looked upward, and then grinned. "You know, I have been looking everywhere for you!" he announced. "I checked in here but didn't even see you!"

I laughed nervously. "Well, you probably didn't think to look all the way up here," I called down to him, quickly grabbing a random book from one of the shelves to make it look legit before I ran down the stairs.

"Did you find what you were looking for?" He eyed the book in my hand. It was some random book that was undoubtedly outdated, as the many layers of dust on its cover would suggest.

"Oh yeah—took me awhile, but I finally found it," I told him with a winning smile.

"You feel like brushing up on your history, or something?" he cracked.

I was confused until I glanced down at my book, titled The War of 1812, and then I nodded. "Well, my history class is covering it, and I just wanted to read up more on it and maybe get ahead," I lied. Horribly. I couldn't help but to cringe at my desperate attempt.

"I guess," he muttered, eyeing me strangely. "Are you alright?"

I nodded—perhaps a bit too quickly. "Yes," I lied again. "I'm fine."

"Well you're acting weird," he observed. "And you look like you've seen a ghost."

"Oh, well it's probably from running up and down those stairs," I excused. "Anyway, what were you looking for me, for?"

"I wanted to know if you wanted to go into town and get a bite to eat," he said. "Are you up for it?"

I wasn't. "Why don't you go on without me, Preston. Besides, I'm not supposed to leave this house now, without Lawrence knowing exactly where I am, and he's not even here," I excused.

"Well if he's not here, he won't find out," he replied with a shrug.

"Yeah, I've been down that road before. It might show up in that stupid paper," I said sarcastically. "I could do something wrong like knock over my drink and make tomorrow's news."

He laughed. "C'mon, let me take you out," he pleaded. "I don't want to go eat alone."

"You have friends," I countered, managing a smile. "Can't you call them?"

"The question shouldn't be if I 'can', or not. It should be if I 'want to', or not."

I was in no mood for company, but he simply wasn't going to take no for an answer. Lunch with him was only half-way distracting, but the movie just afforded me the chance to tune everything out and then relive the discovery I made earlier in the day. The discovery which made me rethink everything about my life, prior to arriving at Van Steenburgh Manor. I kept dissecting the information I read over and over again, and still didn't want to believe it. My mother ran away because she was pregnant with Lawrence's child. *Me.* I am Lawrence's daughter. Did Vivien know? Was that why she resented me? *Was it because her own husband preferred her young daughter over herself?*

I brushed back tears that I cried for the man I believed had been my father for my whole life, up until now. Tears for the man who taught me to read. He taught me to drive. He loved me so much that I wondered if he even had a clue that I wasn't his own flesh and blood. I ached for him, and for the likelihood that my mother deceived him, too. For she had deceived me. And I felt robbed, for it. Would she have ever told me the truth?

There were so many questions I needed to ask, but didn't know when, or how. I decided that somehow, I needed to suppress my anger, and all of my questions, until the right time arrived for everything to come out into the open. Unfortunately, patience wasn't one of my virtues, and I knew it would be tough. But it had to be done.

Chapter 16

"Winter Break"

I paused in the hallway to look at the painting to my left. I'd never really paid attention to the artwork hung all throughout the manor, but the stunning, vibrant scenic piece of what looked like the Hudson Valley right outside the property caught my eye this time. Or, rather, the small TAF in the bottom, right-hand corner stopped me in my tracks. What a perfect example of what Lawrence was asking for. Here Trent was, effortlessly trading stocks by day for a "job", and income... and then doing what he loved, which was painting, at his leisure.

Did Lawrence really buy into that? I guess he didn't have to. I shook my head and kept walking. Trent's "career" in stocks was nothing more than one or two day-trips during the week, into the city, to meet with people and have lunch. He only had a few clients that he worked with, investing their money, looking after their accounts, moving funds around, etc. But other than that, he mainly toyed with his own money; investing it to let it grow. Hell, he made it sound like stocks were his hobby, and art was his main career. He made a good amount of money painting for people – murals in their home, similar to the ones he'd painted in the manor, and selling his pieces.

When I reached the bottom of the stairs, Lawrence was already waiting to take me to school. I didn't say a word to him, and he made no effort to start a conversation with me. He was still mad about the stupid newspaper. I, however, had much bigger reason to be angry.

After he dropped me off, a wave of relief washed over me to be out of that car, and away from anywhere he would be for at least the next five days. When Jackie asked me what was wrong, I avoided telling her anything. I didn't want anyone to know. I was armed with some powerful ammunition, but on one hand, I was too ashamed to let anyone know that my sixteen-year-old mother had slept with her young stepfather, and conceived me.

On the other hand, I would've liked to let the world know how awful of a man Lawrence really was.

"Hope, seriously—you look like you're carrying the weight of the world on your shoulders," Jackie told me after classes, Monday afternoon. "What is wrong with you?"

"Nothing," I answered, trying to smile convincingly.

"That's a load of crap. What is it? Is there something wrong with you and Trent?"

I shook my head. "I'm fine, Jackie."

"Did he tell you that you guys couldn't see each other anymore?"

I looked at her, begging for her to drop it. "It has nothing to do with Trent," I assured her. "I just don't want to talk about anything."

She grew more concerned. "Hope... you know you can talk to me."

"I just...need to process a few things."

She eyed me for a long moment, and then nodded. "Okay," she agreed. "I won't ask you again, but I do want you to know that you can talk to me about it whenever you're ready to," she told me.

I nodded. "I know. Thank you, Jackie." I thanked her mostly for dropping the subject.

I no longer cared that Christmas was right around the corner, now. I didn't care about upcoming dinner parties, or the stupid plans for a masquerade that Vivien was preoccupied with, above all else. I didn't care about anything Lawrence had to say, about anything. I didn't care to converse with any resident of that house at all, period. I just didn't care.

I take that back. I really did care. I cared too much. I was royally upset by the realization that my mother tricked me into believing that someone else was my biological father. I would always see him as the man who raised me, but why the Hell lie about it?! Why not just tell me your story, and be open about it?

I was extremely aggravated by the sight of Vivien. Every time I saw her, I just couldn't help but to roll my eyes. As far as I could tell, she was mostly to blame for everything that transpired in my mother's life, which had in turn spiraled down into mine.

Mr. Peck provided me with a very important tool to channel everything I was feeling, and going through. Petrified as I was at the idea of what a voice coach would signify to me, I gave it my all and downright surprised myself. The only singing solo I'd ever done prior to that, was singing in the shower, or the few times I had driven by myself, shortly before coming to live at the manor. But I gained confidence. And I threw myself into readying for the audition in the town's theater production of "Phantom of the Opera."

"*Feel* the music. *Be* that character," he coached me, after class one day in the auditorium, amongst a handful of other students he mentored on his own time. "I selected you all because you have talent that exceeds any high school production, guys. *You guys*," he pointed out at all of us. "You all have what it takes to move forward. Be inspired. *Get* inspired. Pour every ounce of yourself into this. Don't 'act' like the character you are portraying, folks. *Be* that character."

I'd seen the movie a million times. "Phantom of the Opera" was my absolute favorite musical production. I knew the soundtrack front-to-back. Would I be able to pull off Christine, the female lead character's angelic voice? I practiced. And practiced. A million times the voice coach stopped me. Started me. Interrupted me again. Had me back-track. Fast-forwarded me. I was encouraged. Discouraged. On the verge of tears from frustration. Ready to give up. Then fired back up again.

When audition day arrived, I felt as ready as I'd ever be. Lawrence didn't know. Preston didn't know. Jackie didn't know. Not even Trent knew that I was doing this. I needed no outside distraction. No extra eyes on me—in case I did fail miserably. The only other people I knew there were the few other students that had been in this with me, and then Mr. Peck for moral support.

Once my name was called, I went up to the stage, before a panel of four strangers, whose faces were just barely visible in the lighting. We were given two scenes to memorize, and I had them down. The first scene was easy. The second scene mandated full use of my vocal range. I pushed my doubt into the back of my head. I channeled my vocal coach, and the firm instruction she barked at me all week long. And I nailed it. God help me, I nailed it.

I stuck around to see how everyone else did. I really had some stiff competition. But I needed that part. I needed a reason to be excited. I needed something to really look forward to. Something to lose myself in. We were all told that we would be contacted within the week, or we could stop by the theater to see if results from the audition were posted.

Hours seemed like days passing by, and I continued to live in a fog. I would go on to dwell on what I learned, until I confronted Lawrence. I had no idea when that time would come, but I was going to wait patiently. In the meantime, my sole reprieve was the joy I felt when I hiked into town after school to read the posted letter on the front entrance with audition results. I got it. I got the part of Christine.

Winter Break had arrived, and I faced returning to Van Steenburgh Manor for three full weeks. Three weeks of awkwardness, tension, and dinner parties. When I arrived home, the house in the process of being decorated, and Preston was already there to tell me I missed the frenzied committee of people who had breezed through the house to complete their task of transforming Van Steenburgh Manor into a Winter Wonderland.

As if Lawrence anticipated any inconvenience beforehand, my "Christmas present" had come early – he had my mother's car delivered to the manor from wherever it had been, and had it cleaned up for me to drive myself to and from school on my own. It was about time. Perfect timing, if I were going to fully pull off flying under the radar, going to rehearsals and performances. But at the same time, it was all so very bittersweet.

The first time I sat in my mother's white Mercedes sedan, I could've sworn I'd gotten a whiff of her perfume. I checked the back of my seat to see if any stray hairs had remained. I checked the glove compartment for any sort of personal items. Handwritten anythings, receipts, I didn't care. Nothing. It was her car... but it was completely wiped clean of her.

That voice that had become so used to begging for just one more chance to see her, and talk to her, faded into the distance. My heart felt heavy. The car started like a champ, though. It was the first real token of any sense of freedom I had at the manor. Would he take it back from me if he knew I was using it to go support a passion of mine that he didn't believe in?

Would he even notice?

I missed dinner that first evening of my return home, in lieu of my very first performance at the community theater. It was the first time that I missed a dinner with Lawrence and my grandmother. I knew if Preston came home, he would instantly begin wondering where I was.

The second I walked into the theater, excitement ignited my bones. The auditorium was alive with people putting finishing touches on the scenery onstage. When I went backstage, there was a healthy frantic mixture of nerves and excitement. I was ready. I was born for this.

The very first second I walked out on that stage, Jackie's smile was all I saw. And it was all I needed before Hope was lost. I became Christine—the singing protégé of the opera house's dark Phantom—and I identified with how divided she must've felt, torn between a mysterious longing and loyalty to a man who remained hidden in the shadows, and then her highly-regarded, adoring, handsome suitor.

When the audience of people stood up to applaud at the closing of our performance, a wave of satisfaction unlike any other, swept over me. This was what it was all about. This was exactly what I lived for. Screw Lawrence – this was it for me.

I changed, gathered my belongings, said goodbye to my incredible cast-mates, and then went to my car – only to find a single red rose set neatly on the windshield. I picked it up, and it had a small ribbon tied around the stem. A significant gesture, given the circumstances. I smiled at the irony, but wondered who left it. A brief glance around the parking lot as I got into my car gave me no clues.

When I got back to the mansion, it was almost eleven. I expected no one to be up, but I walked in to laughter and all kinds of noises straight back into the foyer. I curiously headed in that direction to see what was going on. The commotion was coming from the ballroom, and I walked in to see Kate and Charles arranging dozens of assorted sized boxes around and beneath the enormous Christmas tree, which was now half-decorated. The boxes were wrapped with all different colored papers, and lavish bows. Kate grinned as she saw me enter, and I was in awe at how many boxes they were setting about.

"Do you need any help?" I asked, picking up a box from the pile, and realizing that it wasn't empty.

"No, you're not supposed to touch these until Christmas," she said with a wink, taking the box from my hands.

"These aren't empty?" I asked, straining to see a tag that protruded from beneath the box's fluffy lavender bow as she put it under the tree with the others.

"Of course not!" She scoffed as Lawrence bounded into the room with another armful of gifts. "Why would they be empty?"

"I thought maybe they were just for decoration," I muttered, watching Lawrence happily stride over to us, setting the boxes down.

"Beautiful," he remarked with a broad smile of approval. His dark eyes were sparkling. He looked excited and handsome. It was... almost charming. "It's starting to feel like Christmas in here," he beamed.

"What a beautiful tree," I marveled softly, just standing back and drinking it in.

"Isn't it?" Lawrence piped up, the smile still plastered about his face. "The tree is my favorite part of decorating," he spoke, arranging the boxes beneath it neatly.

"Every year I always looked forward to going out and buying a tree with my parents, and then we'd stay up all night until it was completely done." I stared wistfully upward. "But we never had a tree this big."

"This was your mother's favorite time of year." Lawrence's smile faded, and I found myself wondering exactly what he was recalling, when his eyes landed on me. "Having you here is a wonderful reminder of how it used to be to have her around." His words fell on deaf ears. Not only could I not stand to hear him speak about my mom, but it now just served as an unnecessary reminder that none of us would ever be graced with her presence at Christmas, ever again.

Kate paused, and I swear she was reading my thoughts. "We will do our best to make your first Christmas without your parents as nice as it can be," she promised with sympathetic eyes. "Just remember that they are up there smiling down at you. They will be here in spirit."

Maybe. I had my doubts that even after death, my mother would have any desire to revisit Van Steenburgh Manor.

"And I see you've started without me, Mother—how kind of you," a voice spoke as I heard someone enter the ballroom. I perked up at the sound of Trent's voice, and as he approached his mother and I, smiling broadly, my heart melted at the mere sight of him. He was breathtaking, as always. "Lawrence," he smiled and extended his hand to shake Lawrence's, and whatever brief spell he'd been under, thinking back about my mom, had been broken at the sight of Trent. He grabbed Trent's hand and pulled him in for a solid hug.

"Honey, I told you to hurry over here," she said before Trent turned and pulled her in for a hug. "I wasn't going to wait up all night for you!" She turned to me. "He knows it's tradition that we decorate the tree together every year," she shook her head as he kissed the top of her head and freed her.

"One that I see doesn't mean all too much to my beautiful mother, seeing as how she's apparently started without me," Trent joked turning his gaze to me. "Good evening," he greeted me. "I see my mother at least waits for *you* to help her decorate. She must like you more!"

"Oh stop," she chastised him, laughing. "She happened to actually show up at the right time. And I already told you—I *wasn't going to wait all night* for you!"

"And I see now that you were serious," he teased. It was obvious that he wanted to say something to me; I could see it in his eyes, and written all over his face. But he let it go for now, and just continued to study me with a light in his eyes.

"Lawrence!" All of us stopped in our tracks and turned around to where Vivien appeared in her long nightgown. "All of this racket... It's far too late an hour to keep this up!"

He exhaled and frowned. "Did we wake you, dear?"

"When are you coming to bed?" Her hands came to rest impatiently upon her hips. "I just keep tossing and turning."

"I'll be up in a few minutes," he promised her. "We are just about done." No we weren't.

She scowled and disappeared from sight, and I watched Lawrence look like the wind had just been sucked from his sails. He set another box beneath the tree before giving Trent another light squeeze, and then surprising me with a similar hug. "You weren't at dinner tonight," he recalled thoughtfully. "Did you return home from school late?"

I nodded. A twinge of guilt conflicted me. "I'm sorry," I apologized softly.

"No worries. Just missed you at dinner is all." He smiled down at me in such a way that I felt inclined to believe him... "I looked forward to catching up with you about school as of late. Tomorrow, then." He gave one more squeeze and then headed out. "Try to keep it down guys," he ordered lightly. "The Queen has spoken." He winked before disappearing from our sight, and my gaze lingered into the darkness, behind him. I was so confused by how I felt.

"How have you been, Hope?" My heart skipped as Trent broke my thoughts, and I turned to see him removing his coat to get more comfortable, before draping it across the piano.

"I've been good," I answered. My eyes settled upon his ravishing smile. "And yourself?"

"Wonderful."

"Okay I think there's some more tinsel that your father pulled down from the attic, so I'm going to go look for it," Kate called to us, staring at the tree thoughtfully. "I'm going to go check."

Trent watched his mother exit the ballroom, and his dark eyes fixed upon me. "Welcome home." He dared to put his arms around me, and I nervously looked around him to see if his mother was still in eye/ear-shot. "Shall I look forward to you sneaking away to see me later?"

"Am I invited?" I shot a flirty gaze upward into his handsome face.

"Have I ever had a choice before?" He chuckled at my look of offense. "I've been in need of some stimulating conversation," he pressed on, before stealing a kiss that caused my head to spin.

"Found it!" Kate announced, hurrying back in. She glanced at us and for a faint second I thought I might've detected some suspicion washing over her face. Quickly convincing myself that I was paranoid, I still looked away from her and created some distance between myself and Trent, who was now picking up some random ornaments to hang.

"So, how do we decorate the top of the tree?" I asked, trying to spark a conversation. "Ladders? Hang from the chandeliers on ropes and throw ornaments at it in hopes they'll catch?"

Kate laughed. "Lawrence has people come in and decorate the rest of it," she informed me. "Every year we insist that we can do it if he just brings us a ladder, but he wants to hear nothing of it," she explained. "It's so silly... hiring people to decorate your Christmas tree. But it's the same people that come in to decorate the rest of the house as well."

"Which reminds me," Trent spoke, "I came here earlier today to leave a file in Lawrence's office, and there were a slew of workers working just down the hall from there? What's all of that about?"

"Vivien hired a crew to tear up the hallway down there," Kate told him under her breath. "Re-doing the floors and painting everything. Lawrence has been ranting that he hasn't been able to think straight since they've started making a racket all day long."

"This is one of the many, many times I'm glad to live out there, by myself," he commented, reaching up to hang the ornaments above Kate's and my reach.

"Well I don't see why she didn't ask you to do the painting. A mural along that wall would look fantastic," Kate said just low enough for Trent and I to hear. "I mean, she knows you paint..."

"It doesn't matter," he dismissed. "Anything I could've done wouldn't have been good enough for her, anyhow," he pointed out. "I'd just rather not be involved.

I went out of my way to avoid looking at Trent, to not arouse any more curiosity from Kate, but Trent didn't make any effort. I constantly caught him eyeing me, and even smirking at times because he knew I was blatantly avoiding looking at him. Kate rattled on about this or that, and occasionally she would catch our sly glances, but she never acknowledged them. It was nearly one in the morning when we were done with our portion of the tree. I excused myself to retreat to my room, and Trent's eyes followed me out of the room as he hugged his mother goodnight.

I crept out the back door and the moonlight lit a path for me through the darkness. It was cold, but that wasn't the reason I was shaking. When I exited the woods, Trent was already waiting at the door, leaning against the frame as he casually ate an apple.

He greeted me, taking the last bite from his apple. "Long time, no see."

"Funny," I cracked, passing him up to enter the warm cabin. As always, a fire greeted me from the fireplace. A book laid open on the couch. Two glasses of wine sat on the coffee table. "Were you in the middle of something?" I asked him, removing my coat and setting it on the armchair.

"Of course not," he replied, shutting the door and then tossing his apple core into the trash. "Would you like a drink?"

"Yes, please." I sat on the couch, and he removed a glass from the coffee table to extend to me. I looked to see what he was reading, but it wasn't in English. "What is this?" I asked.

"I'm brushing up on my Italian," he said, gently removing the book from my hands before closing it and setting it aside.

"For what?"

"Because I intend to visit there again very soon," he replied, taking a seat beside me on the blanket.

"You've been there before?" I asked, interested.

"Two years ago almost," he answered. "It's amazing there," he said. "I didn't want to come home—and I probably wouldn't have if I didn't have business to tend to," he admitted, pulling me close so that I could lean back into him. "Was my mother still fidgeting with the tree when you left?"

"No, she'd already gone to bed," I answered, enjoying the warmth of the fire—and the warmth of Trent's body.

"She asked me about you, after you walked out," he said, causing me to look up at him in surprise.

"Did she? What did she say?" I asked.

His grin was playful. "She asked me what all the funny looks were about. She said we looked like we were hiding something," he said. "She's a smart woman."

"What did you tell her?"

"I ignored her. Until she asked a few more times."

"She kept asking?" My eyes widened up at him.

"When she continued to ask me again if there was something going on between you and me, I told her that she'd find out all the details as soon as she received a wedding announcement—and only then," he recounted.

"Well, I'm sure she appreciated that," I muttered, curling up beside him.

He laughed. "I'm not worried about my mother," he assured me, wrapping his arms around me a little tighter. "So, are you any closer to finding out any more about why your mother left here?"

"No," I lied. "I've given up," I waved aside. "No one is going to tell me the truth… I've resigned myself to the idea that I'll never know. And I'm okay with that." Looking back, I could only wish that were the case.

"That's no way to be," he scorned softly. "Don't you have any detective abilities? Any access to keys such as photo albums, or any kind of files? If I wanted to find out why my mother fled from that house, I'd do everything in my power to do so. What about Lawrence's office? There must be something in there!"

I whipped my head around at him defensively. "If Lawrence ever caught me in his office—"

"How would he? Naturally you don't go in there to snoop when he's sitting at his desk working, Hope," he chastised softly. I was quiet for a moment. "Look, I'm certainly not telling you to do anything you don't want to do, by any means. I'm just letting you know that you have options, that's all."

I picked up my glass of wine and took a sip of it. "I don't know if I even want to know," I told him bitterly. "Maybe I'm better off not knowing." If only there was an erase option…

"Suit yourself," he gave in, getting up. "It's entirely your decision." He bent forward, placing his lips on my neck, for a long, lingering moment, before he took a seat on the stool before his easel.

"When are you going to go back to Italy?" I asked him.

He picked up his brush. "I'm not sure, yet. Why do you ask?"

"Take me with you," I requested.

"You would love it," he spoke, taking a stroke down the canvas. "There is so much to see. I love Capri; though it's a little touristy. It's a wonderful place. Inspiring. I stayed at a hotel which looked over the cliff into the water, and it was breathtaking," he recalled. "And the Vatican is truly inspiring. I could tell you all about it, but words cannot compare to how phenomenal it really is to witness, firsthand. But it will be hard for me to pick up the women if I'm there with one," he teased, making me scowl.

"That's alright— I've heard nothing but good things about handsome Italian men," I came back swiftly. "I'm sure there's someone over there who would love to keep me company."

"I'm quite positive that there is," he agreed with a lifted eyebrow. "However, I'm confident that none of them will be as witty and intelligent as I am."

"That's something I'll just have to judge for myself."

I enjoyed just sitting there with him, away from everything, and everyone else. Being with Trent was like being in a whole other world altogether. It was a world where I could let my guard down, and not have to worry about anything outside of that cozy cabin. A world where I found warmth, and now happiness. Intellect, mystery, emotion, beauty, and brutal honesty. The honesty part was the most welcomed.

"You got quiet," he remarked, rousing me from my own thoughts. "You know I was just kidding about the women."

"You better be," I told him with a look of warning that I couldn't quite pull off successfully. "Nah, I was just thinking about how much I like to come here," I confessed. "You know, I feel as if there's some dark cloud hanging over that house, sometimes," I told him. "And I feel like there are secrets in every corner. It's like everyone in that house is hiding something. It makes everything so surreal."

"Another reason why I prefer to stay out here," he agreed. "And it's not just your imagination. There are secrets all over that house. Secrets and dirty laundry that will never be aired out. As soon as I turned seventeen, I begged Lawrence to let me have this cabin. Well, I didn't have to 'beg', really," he corrected. "I dropped a few hints to him, and then after no response, I just came right out and asked him. I feel that I only got a 'yes' simply because he wasn't prepared to say 'no'."

"Do you ever see yourself leaving here?" I asked him.

He cocked his head to the side, and narrowed his eyes at his work. "I'm sure, in time," he replied thoughtfully. "But right now, no. Lawrence asked that I remain here and continue overseeing his fortune, and in return I have a place to live for free. I can come and go as I please. My parents are here. I grew up here. Why?" He turned to look at me quizzically. "Are you in a hurry to leave this place?"

It was a complicated question. There were a few aspects of living at Van Steenburgh Manor that I would greatly miss. Him being the biggest one. Preston. Kate. The history of the property. But with recent developments...information I'd found out and didn't know what to do with... Lawrence making it clear that I either live my life his way, or get out... I felt like my days there were now numbered. "Maybe," I finally answered.

"So, you'd just leave everything here and take off?"

"With you, I would," I answered quickly. "Yes."

"Why?"

"Why not?" I answered. Now he was quiet. I watched him wordlessly for a moment. Concentrating on his work. His dark eyes shadowed. "What made you change your mind about me, Trent?" I asked.

"Change my mind? How do you mean?"

"I mean, going from how we started out, to *this*. Something changed your mind—what was it?"

He was thoughtful for a moment. "The fact that I had no rational explanations anymore as to why I had to keep being an ass to you, when I really didn't want to be one in the first place. I had no more excuses to tell myself. Every time I saw you, it made things ten times harder to deny you. Every affair we attended together made it all the more difficult not to just... watch you, and admire you. The more I observed you, the more fascinated I became," he answered tenderly. "I saw other men want you, and every time I saw one of them approach you I became envious. I highly enjoy every second I spend with you."

He studied my face, and from across the room I watched his dark, pensive eyes rake over my nose, my cheeks, and my lips. The glow from the fire danced about his face.

"Are you hungry at all?" he asked me, bring me out of my daze.

"A little," I admitted.

"Would you like me to make you something?"

His eagerness to please me evoked a smile that crawled over my face. "No, you don't have to go through all that trouble," I answered. "It's so late anyhow."

"I'm famished," he stated. "I'm going to make something for myself, but if you're hungry, I'll prepare you something as well."

Well, since he put it that way... "Okay," I agreed. "What are we having?"

He got up and proceeded to the refrigerator. "Eggs," he declared. "I'm in the mood for some breakfast."

"You need a Christmas tree in here," I told him, looking around.

He laughed. "What for? So I can sit here and give myself presents on Christmas morning?"

"I love Christmas," I spoke. "It's my favorite time of year."

"I know it is."

"Have you done your shopping yet?" I asked him.

"What for?"

"Christmas gifts," I answered.

"No," he replied.

"Me neither," I muttered softly. I just didn't have it in me this year."

"What's on your list?" he implored curiously.

"Do people still make those?" I laughed. "Nothing. I don't want anything. Don't you get me anything, either," I warned.

"Bah humbug!" He teased with a grin. "Lucky for you, I don't Christmas shop, anyway!"

Chapter 17

"Secrets of My Own"

Waking up the following morning in my own bed was a dose of reality, after another few stolen moments in Trent's cabin, before the most delicious session of tantalizing kisses that neither one of us wanted to end, and then ultimately sneaking back in the house. My schedule was fuller now than I cared for it to be. I had several performances before Christmas for "Phantom," and I wasn't sure how I was going to keep that to myself when I would be disappearing so much. Keeping Lawrence from knowing was just saving myself from another argument.

I was just going downstairs when Preston also emerged from his room. "There's the face I've been looking forward to seeing!" He smiled. "Sorry, I was going to call you last night when arrived, to see if you wanted to go out with a couple buddies and I."

"Oh, really?" I looked at him, perplexed.

234

"Yeah, but we just couldn't get a plan together, and it was all last-minute, and well—you weren't even home yet anyway," he waved aside. His behavior was unusually weird.

"No big deal," I assured him, positive that the look on my face was equally as weird. "I had some things to do and didn't get home until late, anyway."

"What are we going to get into, tonight?" His face brightened up.

"Tonight?" I echoed. "I have plans with Jackie."

"Me and a couple of buddies want to go catch a movie and maybe go shoot some pool, You guys should join us."

"Nah, you need your guy time, so you can sit around and do those repulsive things that guys do," I said with a wink.

"Well what do you plan to do?"

I shrugged and tossed him a devilish smirk. "Stuff that girls do," I tossed back airily. "Talking about nails, and hair, and makeup." I took a step back from him, and he continued eyeing me with those pretty blue eyes of his.

"Alright then," he accepted reluctantly. "Well, I have to go out and run a few errands," he said, putting on his coat. "So unless I finish them early and I have a chance to come back home, I guess I won't see you until tomorrow," he told me with a sheepish smile of his own. It made me wonder what exactly he had up his sleeve, but the second he disappeared out the front door, suffice it to say that he exited my mind, also.

"Hope!" Vivien seemed to appear out of thin air as soon as I reached the bottom of the staircase. "Have you already started considering what you will wear for the masquerade ball on New Year's Eve?" She raised an eyebrow at me.

Is that really all she had to worry about? "It's not even Christmas yet," I replied blandly.

"You act as if you have all the time in the world," she scoffed. "This is a huge ordeal that everyone looks forward to for the entire holiday season. I advise you get something in order," she demanded before sauntering off.

I was fully aware that as she walked away from me, the look I gave that lingered upon her clearly conveyed how ridiculous I thought our entire exchange had been. If Vivien was short on patience with me, my level of impatience was now beginning to rival hers. I shook my head and stalked off in the opposite direction, vowing not to give her another thought, until the day of her stupid party when I would then open up my closet and decide what to wear, on the fly. Glancing at the time, I had a little while before I needed to sneak away. I knew exactly where I wanted to go.

But Trent was not home, much to my chagrin. What a different feel the cabin had, when he was absent... The air was completely still, all around me. It was so quiet that I could hear the birds chirping outside, off in the woods. The usually exciting space was lifeless and devoid of warmth. With each step I took, the floor creaking beneath my feet was reminiscent of the very first time I ever stepped foot into that cabin...

I strolled past the fireplace to glance out the window, into the woods. Trees and trees forever, it seemed. I paused to listen just for a moment, before deciding I had just imagined I heard a noise. But no, he wasn't back yet, from wherever he went.

My eyes stopped on the unfinished painting that rested upon his easel. What had been, just a silhouette outlined in black strokes, was now actually a view of a woman, standing next to a window, looking out. Her hair was pinned up. She was wearing some sultry dress that conformed to her body, and she had no real detail other than her eyes, painted thoughtfully as they stared out into whatever she saw, out that window. She looked like she had an interesting story to tell.

Disappointed, I went on my way to meet Jackie in town, at the theater. I was positive she had no idea how much I valued her, and our friendship. I loved seeing her, for she was the only real sense of normalcy I had in my world, now. She was my balance into the real world. Without her, I might've already driven myself completely insane.

"You still don't know who is behind the mysterious rose-on-the-windshield?" She eyed me curiously, and I shook my head. "I'm going to leave the performance and hover in the parking lot to wait and see who does it," she laughed.

"Maybe I don't want to know," I muttered, laughing along with her.

"It could be a secret admirer!"

"Right, and I really have room for another boy in my life," I argued.

"I'm sure you could squeeze another one in there." She winked. "Well, I want to know who's doing it, even if you don't. Have you even bothered to ask Trent or Preston?"

"Neither of them even knows," I revealed, causing her eyes to widen. "I just... I don't know. I can't even say at this point that it's because I'm afraid either of them will say anything to Lawrence, because I'm positive I can trust both of them. And I don't even care anymore if Lawrence finds out. I just don't. Let him." I sighed. "Now it's just become more of... I need something outside of that house that is just mine." I shook my head. "Lawrence has known my every move since I've gotten here. He knows everything that goes on at school. He thinks my passion for acting is a waste of time, and meanwhile, I feel like for the first time since coming here, I finally have something that only I control."

She frowned at me, but I didn't want her pity. "I get that. But why wouldn't you want Preston and Trent there? I mean, obviously not 'together', but either of them to even know, or offer moral support? This is something to be proud of. Something I think both of them would be hurt to not know about, being how close you are to them."

Her words stuck with me throughout getting ready to go on stage. Of course I agreed with her. And upon leaving that night, I grabbed that single rose from my windshield yet again, and drove home with the radio muted. Just reveling in my own thoughts. The only one thing that was certain to me was that I was addicted to Trent. I always longed to be near him. My fingers craved the feel of his skin.

And he was focused on my age. Preoccupied with morals. Moreover, it was blaringly obvious that he was still battling with the idea of actually caring for someone, after making such a fuss about it not being a priority.

Whatever. His inner struggles with "feelings" and "emotions" always took a backseat anytime I was in his presence. And that was enough for me. Since I came to live at the manor, he is what made my world go around.

But I realized I was becoming emotionally withdrawn, at the main house. In spinning my own web of lies peppered with truths, I was distancing myself from everyone around me. I had resorted to snooping. Snooping led to finding out information I wasn't meant to find. Information I kept silent about, and avoided processing. I felt like a mess. Conflicted. Confused. Sullen.

I went to Trent immediately after returning home from the theater, and my double-life. Leaving one double-life to head to another... But what better a way to escape from every unsettling feeling at the manor! There were three missed calls on my cell phone from Preston, and I knew I would have to come clean to him, at some point. I'd have to come clean to the both of them. But for now, I was preoccupied with the excitement and anticipation that washed over me as I approached Trent's doorstep. Nothing else mattered, the second I opened up that door.

Instantly, my eyes darted from Trent, who was seated with a book in his hand and a smirk upon his lovely face, to the tree glittering with lights beside the fireplace!!! "You brought in a Christmas tree!?" I quickly shut the door behind myself and tossed my coat aside to take a closer look.

"You look so astonished. Of course I brought in a tree. For you. You wanted one." He rose from where he sat, and had every right to look as proud of himself as he did, right now.

I was beyond floored, knowing that he had somehow made all of this happen over the course of time I had been at the theater. "I'm impressed," I acknowledged, as I reached out to touch one of the glass ornaments clinging gracefully to a branch before my eyes.

"It actually didn't take much time," he replied, snapping his book shut and setting it aside. "Every store around town looks like it's puked up Christmas, so I didn't have to go far to pick up a tree, and ornaments, and such."

"I love it." I grinned at him, feeling nothing short of flattered. "Thank you."

"You're welcome." He wrapped one of those strong arm saround me from behind and kissed the top of my head. "Like I could even tell you 'No'," he said, causing me to laugh softly.

He was still wearing black slacks and a tie over his white dress shirt. The matching suit coat was draped over the arm of the couch. I knew he had told me he needed to meet some clients in the city for dinner. I also felt it was a perfect opportunity to give him the gift I had picked up for him. I reached into my coat pocket and pulled out the box. "I saw this and thought of you immediately," I handed it to him.

He raised an eyebrow at me. "I didn't know we were exchanging Christmas gifts."

I looked up at him slyly. "I know, but that tree is gift enough. Here, just take it."

He reluctantly took the small box into his hands and gave the ribbon a light tug to unravel it. A few more hesitant looks were tossed my way, and then a very impressed gaze washed over his beautiful face when he caught sight of the watch. "How did you afford something like this? It's stunning."

"I have a little saved up," I revealed modestly.

He removed the watch from its casing and inspected it closely. "Definitely the nicest gift I've ever been given," he admired.

"I noticed yours was broken and hadn't moved in months. Every well-dressed man is completed by a classy, timeless watch."

"That sounded like it came straight off of an advertisement," he teased.

"Maybe I've found my true calling," I flirted.

"Impressive indeed," he uttered softly, placing the watch neatly back in its box. "Well I suppose I should give you *your* gifts, now."

"I didn't know we were exchanging gifts," I teased him, taking a seat on the couch, in the warm glow of the Christmas lights from the tree. I watched as he began to reach down around the backside of the tree, but I stopped him in his tracks. "You know what? Whatever it is you have for me, I'd just much rather wait until Christmas," I interrupted him, provoking a slightly confused stare. "It'll give me something to look forward to that day, that's all."

"Something other than the overwhelming amount of gifts that are already waiting for you to open at the house?" he laughed. "Did you pay attention to how many gifts were under that tree?"

Chuckling, I nodded. "I did. But Lawrence's gifts are meaningless," I reasoned. "I can tell you right now they didn't spend a second buying anything, themselves," I guaranteed bitterly. "And whatever they have, and whatever strings are attached to it all... I don't want it."

"Fair enough. These can wait, then."

I was so grateful for his effort to make me happy with a tree. It probably meant more to me than he intended it to. I don't know. I felt overly-sensitive about everything anymore. Foregoing the couch, I took a seat beside it on the floor, before the fire that was crackling. Just staring up at the lights reflecting off the ornaments, and the smell of pine... it was all enough to evoke a sigh from me.

How did I become this lucky?

"How was your day?"

I didn't want to talk about my day. "It was fine," I answered, forcing a smile. "How was your business dinner?"

"Same as it's ever been." He loosened his tie, and headed into the kitchen. "Sometimes it takes an evening of ass-kissing to remind myself why I have very few clients in the first place," he thought aloud.

As he removed a glass from the kitchen cabinet, the sleeves of his shirt stretched slightly to conform to his biceps. "I'm sure it wasn't all bad." I curled my feet up beneath me and rested my back against the arm of the couch.

"Perhaps it wasn't. But it certainly wasn't as glamorous as it probably is in your head," he teased with a sly smile.

"Maybe not," I agreed. "But I admire you for what you do. All of it. Doing what you really love, and making it your primary focus. Treating this – your actual clients, and your 'real job' as the part-time thing. You're very fortunate."

He narrowed his dark eyes, handing me my drink before taking a seat right beside me on the rug. "You've clearly got something on your mind."

I exhaled deeply. "I've never *not* been supported in what I love to do. *Never.* My parents always encouraged me. They attended my performances all through school. They never told me my aspirations of being an actress were silly, or stupid."

"But Lawrence has?" It was definitely more of a statement than a question. My eyes met his, and I nodded. "You have to understand that Lawrence doesn't have a single, creative bone in his body." He took a drink of his whiskey. "He's never painted a picture. Never done a play. He rarely listens to music. The only movies or symphonies or operas he's ever seen or attended have been due to obligation by Vivien. He doesn't appreciate the arts. The man can't even assemble a coordinating outfit – Vivien just tells him what to wear," he cracked, causing us both to laugh. "He's a robot, Hope. Don't let him bring you down."

"Easy for you to say... You don't have to deal with him," I sighed, sipping the wine he'd graciously poured for me. "This is good – what is this?"

"A new Riesling I found that I thought you might like."

"It's good." I nodded down at my glass. "I got the part of Christine in the local theater production of 'Phantom,'" I chose to throw in there innocuously.

"I know."

My head whipped around to face him. "How do you know?!"

"I read the papers. They tend to mention things like that in the Arts section. Funny, but I don't recall you telling me you were going for the part."

His look was inquisitive. I shook my head and looked down. "I didn't want to jinx myself, so I didn't tell anyone."

"I see. Well, I guess I can't fault you for that."

Now I really felt bad. "I'm sorry," I apologized, meeting his offended stare.

"Don't worry about it. I'm just surprised you wouldn't be proud of something like that."

"But I was proud."

"You should've mentioned it."

"I know."

He stared at me for a good long minute. His look was serious. His beautifully-shaped lips twitched thoughtfully. "So, your birthday."

Random, much? "What of it?"

"Don't make any plans," he ordered casually, turning his gaze toward the fire. "In fact, tell everyone you're spending the weekend with Jackie. Tell them whatever you wish. Just make sure you're free."

"You aren't going to tell me why?"

He shook his head, his eyes unmoving from the fire which made his eyes glow. "No."

"Not even a hint?" I coaxed.

The smile he served me was deliciously mischievous. "You'll be with me. That's the only hint you're getting. Oh, and pack a bag."

"Sorry, sir, but I'm going to need a little more than that. Packing for where? Hot? Cold? Nice? Casual?" My interest was now definitely piqued.

"One very nice outfit. Casual the rest of the time."

"What's the nice outfit for?"

"I'm going to enjoy my wine, now."

Ha! My eyes lingered upon him in amusement as he stretched his arm out, behind me and gave me a squeeze. My heart skipped a beat, anticipating whatever it was that Trent had planned for us over my birthday weekend. Now I had something else to look forward to.

"Hopefully this extracurricular activity I'm devoting my spare time to will get me more than just a partial scholarship beyond Springcrest," I mused aloud, staring back up at the tree.

"What's your back-up plan?"

"That's a Lawrence question, if I ever heard one."

"Ouch."

I raised an eyebrow at him. "I don't have a back-up plan. All or nothing. Acting is what I want to do, and I'm going to leave myself no room for failure."

His smile widened into a grin, and he chuckled with approval. "I'll drink to that."

Chapter 18

"Christmas Eve Dinner"

Five performances successfully made it under my belt, and the production was now wrapped. Five red roses with ribbons lain across my windshield. Five standing ovations, and five nights where I was allowed to get lost in somebody else, in another time altogether and accomplish something I had never before attempted, prior to this.

Success was in the details. The singing lessons that trained me to sound like an angel, as my voice echoed off all four theater walls. It was in keeping Lawrence out of it, and having no one to plant any doubt that this could actually be my future. I dodged Preston all five nights... It wasn't even that difficult. He had plans mostly every night, and we seemed to miss each other every time we were coming and going. As long as he knew I was with Jackie, he didn't ask any more questions.

And Trent made it out to my final performance, sitting front row and center. I was glad he came. Seeing his beautiful face there to support me was enough to make my heart flutter, all throughout the performance.

But it also made me feel bad for keeping Preston out of the loop.

I still had no idea who was behind the roses...

Along with my comfort in leading this parallel life, something within me relaxed a bit; no longer fearing that anyone would find out about me stealing away to see Trent. Everyone in that house was oblivious. As long as I stayed out of trouble, stayed out of the newspaper, and out of Vivien's way, no one really cared what I did. They had their heads so far up in the clouds that they didn't have time to notice me anyway.

Fine by me.

Christmas Eve was the first time they really cared about making sure everyone was all together for a meal, where there wasn't a party involved, or having people over for a stupid gala. Kate, Charles, Redd, Preston, Lawrence, Vivien and myself had just taken seats at the formal dining room table, when my eyes lit up to see Trent enter the room to join us also. His lips curled upward at me in a smirk when he saw me seated between Preston and Lawrence, and I had wished he'd said something earlier so that I would've made sure to leave a seat next to myself open.

Preston's eyes flicked from Trent to me, immediately upon Trent's entrance, and I already took notice of Preston's discomfort. It was a given, any time they were in the same room.

"Potatoes?" Preston offered, ready to scoop some from the bowl he held, onto my plate. I shook my head, and he passed that dish along, taking another one and taking the initiative of scooping some grilled asparagus from the next bowl, onto my plate. He knew I liked it. He also never minded serving me at dinner. I never even felt weird about it. I thought it was sweet. Charming.

Until now. *Now that Trent's eyes followed Preston's doting on me very closely.*

It made me uncomfortable. Next was the chicken. Then he carved me a piece of ham.

"You don't have to do that," I uttered softly. He barely noticed. He was now reaching for the condiments. "I can get it," I insisted politely. Trent's eyes were curiously burning a hole into me. I pretended that Preston was a bother, but I didn't have the heart to outright demand that he stop serving me.

"Trent," Lawrence piped up, reaching across the table to hand him one of the bowls making its rounds around the table. Trent's eyes lazily swung Lawrence's way and he thanked him before his eyes flicked back to me, and then downward to spoon out some food. "How are you? Any plans to travel anytime soon?"

"Thinking about it," Trent replied.

"Vivien and I were just discussing a possible trip to Ireland soon." Lawrence turned and smiled at Vivien. "We found a castle that was recently renovated into a hotel, and it looks positively breathtaking."

"I'm sure it is." Trent's eyes flicked back at me. "I'm thinking Italy again. Spain, perhaps. We shall see."

"I can't imagine any castle in Ireland being more breathtaking than the palace we live in here," Kate interjected with a charming smile. "Plus, I always hate it when you leave the country." She swung her pretty eyes at her son. "I always worry when you're so far away!"

"There are many places more breathtaking than *this*." Vivien didn't even look up from her plate. "If you ever had the opportunity to leave the country, you'd agree."

Kate ignored her biting remark, and continued to address her son. "I just hate having someone I love so much so far away, that's all. What if something happened to you? It would take forever to get to you over there."

"Forever, as in a fourteen-hour flight," Vivien smiled tightly. "Kate, you are so amusing sometimes."

Kate's pretty smile diminished, and I thought I saw her look at Lawrence for help, but Lawrence didn't acknowledge either of them.

"Some people are happy with their lives at home, and having their loved ones around," Trent piped up, his dark eyes staring straight into Vivien. "Nothing wrong with that at all, any more than it is for people to want to see more of the world."

I shoveled a forkful of food into my mouth, and Preston did the same. "Awkward," he muttered to me under his breath. I couldn't help but smile. This was the weird rich family I'd read about in books, or seen depicted in movies. To be sitting at a table with them was beyond awkward right now.

"Is this normal holiday dinner stuff?" I asked him under my breath.

He tried to stifle a laugh, but wasn't entirely successful. "Yes." Trent's eyes were on us again. "Dad!" Preston looked up and caught Lawrence's attention. "I've been meaning to talk to you about some of the classes I'm taking, and some of the things I'm kind of confused about regarding law. I need to make sure you're available sometime before I return to school."

Lawrence nodded enthusiastically. "Of course," he agreed. "Hope? Have you heard anything back from some of the other universities you've applied to?" I shook my head. "I talked to some of my colleagues at Stanford. They were very helpful when it came time for Preston to go to college, and they have extended the same help for you. We should talk."

I didn't want to talk. "Okay," I agreed absently, staring back down at my food.

"I thought you were going to go to the one you got the scholarship to," Preston looked at me in confusion. *Now was not the time.* This dinner was already weird enough.

"She needs to go to a reputable university," Lawrence chimed in. "And obtain a career that will lead her down a definite path, with a guaranteed income."

"Soon she will be eighteen and free to do whatever she wants," Vivien snapped at her husband. "Once she leaves here, you will have to let her do what she pleases."

"I'm looking out for her best interests," Lawrence snapped back at her, causing the rest of us to pause. "She doesn't *have* to leave here as soon as she turns eighteen, or graduates. She can remain here and go to school. She can stay as long as she likes, actually."

"If she wants to waste her time by going to some acting school and waiting tables in hopes that someone will 'discover her', let her," Vivien glared at him and defiantly took her next bite of food.

"I like it how everyone expects me to fail," I spoke up. I was irked. No, I was irritated! I shook my head, stabbing at another bite of food. "Lawrence tells me what I'm doing is a waste of time. Vivien's got me waiting tables. So what!?" My voice was progressively getting louder. "Who cares if I'm not rich? Who cares if I do have to wait tables between roles? I'm doing what I love—"

"*Love* doesn't pay your bills, sweetheart." Vivien smirked at me. "You're delusional if you think that there aren't hundreds of thousands of pretty little girls out there with the same dream as you. Do you really want to compete for the rest of your life with girls that keep getting younger, while *you* age and aren't looked at as the next big thing anymore?"

"I just want to do what I love," I answered back fiercely. "If I don't end up in a huge place like Van Steenburgh Manor when I grow old, at least I grew old doing something I loved."

"She's actually really good," Preston shrugged, coming to my defense. "She walked right into Springcrest, being the new girl, and completely took over that drama class. She nailed Juliet, there. She told me she's going for the role of Alice in the 'Alice in Wonderland' production this semester. She's good. You should both take the time to go see her."

"I'm sure she is," Lawrence looked down at his place. "But I want her to secure a profitable career, is all. Like you. You're going into law—"

"Nothing in life is guaranteed," Preston interrupted Lawrence, taking his father by surprise. "I could go into law, and be a terrible lawyer. There's a possibility that I may not even be able to pass my BAR exam—"

"You would just keep taking it until you did pass," Lawrence interjected firmly.

"My point is, stop setting her up for failure before she even gets out there and gives it an honest try," Preston argued, clearly taking up for me, and aggravated by his father.

"It's okay, Preston," I spoke up softly. "He doesn't approve of my ambitions, and it's okay. Really." I shook my head and just wanted the whole topic to go away.

"Just another happy family dinner!" Vivien sat there with a satisfied smirk. "If there's nothing else this household is good at, we can at least embrace how dysfunctional we are."

"I'll drink to that." Trent raised his glass. My eyebrow rose at him.

"Seriously though, Hope." My grandmother eyed me with a glare. "Beauty is fleeting. Once you get older, what will you have to cling to? Make something of yourself *now*. Act on the side, if you must carry out your little girl dreams. But don't rely solely on that. It's not practical."

I clenched my teeth for a moment. Trent was observing closely. I was partly miffed that he never even spoke up in my defense. I couldn't bite my tongue any longer. "Who here has any right to talk about reality, or practicality?" I pushed my chair back from the table. "Living in this... house... this *castle*! That's not very practical! I haven't even seen half the rooms in this place—how practical is it to have so much unused space? You have '*things*' just to say you have them!" Lawrence and Vivien were both staring at me with nostrils flared, eyebrows raised, and eyes narrowing. "You want to talk about beauty being fleeting?" I addressed Vivien.

"When clearly *you've* exhausted every cosmetic and medical option out there to hold onto your youth! *You* have the problem with getting old—not me!" I turned to Lawrence. "I'm sorry that you don't support what I want to do. I'm sorry that you think I'm unrealistic, but it's my life, and I'm going to do what I want with it!" I then stood up. "And dysfunctional? Oh yeah—there is a *ton* of that, here. I'm seventeen and I'm served wine every night at dinner. No other kid I've grown up with gets dressed up like it's prom every couple of weeks, to attend balls and fancy dinners. I grew up with a mom, and a dad, and now I'm thrown into a home with two guardians who are never around and don't care about anything but themselves, unless they think I'm doing something that might reflect badly on them." I paused and realized I was shaking in anger. I stood up. "I definitely see why my mother felt like she had to run," I turned hateful eyes on Lawrence, and I swear he felt like he understood exactly what I meant. "Excuse me."

I turned and left the room, and I heard Vivien say "You're going to let her talk to us like that?"

Lawrence told her calmly to just let me go, which was more than fine; I didn't want them to stop me.

Preston called after me and left the table immediately after I did. I was mad that Trent made as little effort to come after me as he did to stand up for me. Screw him, too! Apparently he was too caught up in our little charade! Maybe I just didn't mean anything to him, really, either. Maybe it was all in my head.

Maybe I really was just another stupid girl who came stumbling upon his cabin in the woods, and nothing more.

"Dysfunctional" was my reality.

"Hope," Preston's hand caught mine in an instant, and he stopped me at the bottom of the staircase. "Let's get out of here," he beckoned softly, giving me a light tug and leading us toward the front door.

"Where to?" I asked him once we hit the cold air, outside. "It's Christmas Eve. Nothing is even open!"

"Just a drive," he replied calmly, opening the passenger side door for me. "Just some time to clear your head."

So I got into his car. We left the grounds of Van Steenburgh Manor, and he just let the radio do the talking, for the longest while. The second we exited those huge iron gates, relief washed over me. Temporary relief. I didn't know what was going to happen once I returned home. I had clearly disrespected the two people who were taking care of me, and panic was making my heart race. Preston told me not to worry about it. Preston assured me that his similar conversations with his adoptive parents led to nothing more than scorn later on. "I wanted to be a lawyer, though," he explained, focused on the road. "From the second I was cognizant enough to know what my father did and stood for, and that this was the foundation for this empire that he and his family had built...I wanted to be him. I aspired to do what he did. So, your hesitance is new to him. Appease him sometimes, and it will get you a long way."

I felt it was hopeless, but I appreciated Preston's words. Preston's candor. Preston caring. I thanked him from saving me from locking myself in my room the rest of the night. Being out, seeing people's homes and yards glittering with Christmas lights... it really lifted my spirits back up and reminded me of being a kid and doing the same thing with my parents. It reminded me how much I really loved Christmas.

It just wasn't the same this year.

I couldn't stifle my disappointment in Trent. When we returned back to the manor, late, it was now Christmas, and the clocks had just finished chiming in the foyer. The house was dark. I paused just inside the front entrance, wondering what wrath I was going to have to face with Lawrence. My father. I shook my head, trying to shake that confusing thought out of my body.

"You wanna come to my room and hang out?" Preston reached out.

"No," I answered. "I need to get some sleep, but thank you," I tried to smile. "Thank you for taking me out tonight. It helped a lot. I needed that."

"You're welcome. If you need anything else, I'm just one door down." His blue eyes held mine for a long moment, and then he watched me walk upstairs and disappear from his vision.

Walking down that long hallway to my room, I felt defeated. I took a look back down the hall and pondered actually taking Preston up on his offer to hang out with him in his room, but he never came up behind me. I entered my suite, closed the door behind me, and then locked the world completely out.

Or not.

"How was your date?" My eyes tried to adjust to the darkness, but I fumbled along the wall to quickly find the light switch. Trent was sitting in the armchair next to my bed. In the dark. *Waiting*.

"Why are you sitting in the dark?" My tone was perturbed, even though I hadn't meant to come off that way. I mean, I was definitely irritated at him... And hurt. Why mask it? "How long have you been in here?"

"Long enough," he replied. His hair was pulled back. He was still in the same slacks and aqua blue dress shirt he'd shown up to dinner in. His skin was bathed in a golden glow from the small lamp I had turned on. Those eyes as dark as wells of black ink were fixed on me intensely. He looked exciting and dangerous all at once.

He continued to eye me now, just as he did all through dinner. I strolled past him to pull the drapes of the doors leading to the terrace shut. If Preston went out there, he'd have a clear view of my room.

"Dinner was... interesting," he remarked. I couldn't yet read his tone, but it didn't sit well with me. I nodded, and sat down on the pastel-colored sofa adjacent to him. "Never a dull moment at this house."

I continued to say nothing. He was here for a reason, and though I was curious as to what that was, I couldn't get past my own feelings to ask him, yet. His eyes never flitted away from me. Not once. But I avoided making contact with his completely.

"You and Preston looked like the picture of perfection." He cracked his knuckles, and I think I rolled my eyes. I know I did, on the inside. "Am I missing something here?"

"Are you?" I snapped in annoyance, unable to keep myself from glaring at him defiantly.

"Well, well—you are related to your grandmother, after all," he bit back, causing my eyes to widen. I jumped to my feet, completely floored by his insult, and he rose to his just as quickly.

I froze, and he circled me with that same, dangerous air about him that he had that one night, in his cabin. My breaths came quick as I anticipated an argument. "You came here to give me hell about Preston?" I seethed. "After what took place down there—"

"Yes, what *did* take place?" His eyes were burning with jealousy that for once, didn't make me feel like I had the upper hand. No, this was much darker, and ominous.

"Keep it down," I hissed through clenched teeth. "It's late, and you *certainly* don't want anyone to know that you're here with me," I narrowed my eyes crossly.

"Your sarcasm is uncalled for." His voice lowered to a growl. "But not to worry—I won't make it known to your boyfriend that I'm in his territory."

"Say what you will about Preston, but at least he came to my defense earlier, which is more than what I could say for you!" I blurted out, feeling a lump in my throat. Of all people right now, feeling betrayed by him was what stung like hell.

"What could I say?!" he shook his head madly, his eyes filled with all kinds of emotion. "Defend you?! They aren't even aware that we speak to one another! What did you want from me?!"

"Nothing!" I turned away from him so he couldn't see the tears that had so quickly formed in irritation and frustration, fall from my eyes. "Nothing," I whispered, at a loss. "I don't want anything."

He leapt up from the chair and paced tensely along my bed. "Looks like he did a fantastic job of coming to your aid anyway," he muttered. "Don't think I wouldn't have, if things were different," he added pointedly.

"But they're not," I replied bitterly. "It is what it is..."

"How long have you been living this double life!?"

"What double life!?" I threw my hands up in the air. "What do you even mean?!"

"You. And Preston. I come in, and you're sitting next to one another. Smiling and laughing together. You looked like the cat that got caught in the fish tank—"

"Don't go there," I warned, pointing a finger angrily. "Don't, Trent."

"No?" He paced in front of the door quickly. Crazily. He might've been scary at that moment in time, but I was so filled with anger and resentment towards him that I couldn't even fathom what either of us were capable of. "He served your damned food to you like you two are a newlywed couple! He waited on you hand and foot! *Your glass is half-empty? Here, let me fill it up for you*!" His eyes were on fire. His jaw was squared. His accusations...were true.

"Weare friends," I hissed through clenched teeth. "Nothing more."

"What, you and I?" He glared at me. "Or you and him."

His words stung. I wiped my cheek, and felt my heart sink. "Well, I guess you have a point," I uttered brokenly. "You said it yourself... No one even knows we speak," I croaked. "What I feel is between us is apparently only in my head, anyway." I lowered my eyes. I couldn't even look at him anymore.

"So all of this is my fault?" he chuckled madly, and shook his head, looking at me like I was ridiculous. "You play girlfriend-and-boyfriend with Preston at the dinner table, pick a fight while you were mad at the world, and now it's my fault because I didn't make out with you at the table and come to your rescue. Is that what you want? Would that have made you happy?!" he argued.

"Yes!" I cried. "Yes it would've! But you didn't! You let me down, Trent! No, I don't want you to *make out with me*," I recoiled, forcing myself to be calm. "I don't expect that from you, and in this situation. But dammit I just want to feel like whatever this is between us isn't just some dirty little secret, and tonight I felt attacked, and I can't help what Preston did, or how he reacted to the situation. I only wished it was you instead!"

Both of us stared at one another for a long moment. I silently pleaded with him to understand where I was coming from. And that I may not exactly have the best reasons for being hurt and upset. I just wanted him to understand my plight. His eyes were still dark, and full of emotions I couldn't recognize. His stance was still standoffish. His hands were in his pant pockets now. His jaw was still squared, and tense. He didn't know how to handle what was going on in his head any more than I did.

I dared to step towards him. His eyes watched me, and his jaw softened enough for his lips to part slightly. He was at least jealous, so that in itself was flattering. As if he could actually think that I'd choose Preston over him... Not when my body responded to him in such a way that it did. Even now.

My hand went up to his arm, and my fingertips lightly cascaded down from his shoulder to his bicep. I loved how strong he was. I heard him inhale a sharp breath... and then hold onto it. My touch slid over his stomach, and they drank in the feel of him over the fabric of his shirt, before roaming upward over his chest.

The stubble over his jaw cast a shadow about his face that made him look raw and hot, as his eyes traveled all over my face. His lips looked so inviting that I just couldn't resist myself. I pulled his mouth down to mine, and he didn't offer one bit of protest. Warm and soft, I loved the feel of his lips on me. I wanted more.

I wanted all of him.

His hands were at my back, and he matched the heat of my kiss with his own. A whimper escaped from me when he pulled me tightly to him. My hands eagerly worked at the buttons on the front of his shirt, and I couldn't get them undone fast enough. His hands were beneath my shirt, and he had it over my head faster than I could get his off.

His mouth was all over every inch of skin that his hands could free up from my clothing. I had never wanted something or someone so badly in my life as I wanted Trent Forrestor, and the moment I unfastened his slacks and sent them to the floor, we surpassed the point of no return.

I savored every kiss he bestowed on me, and every touch he gave me. It was sheer bliss. It was do-or-die, as we collapsed upon my bed and enjoyed the sensory overload that we both bestowed upon one another. He was strong, he was beautiful, he was tender, and at times he was rough. But all the way around, he was utter perfection, and the entire time we spent as one entity, there on my bed, was nothing short of perfect.

"I don't want you to leave," I spoke afterward, snuggling against his bare body under the bedcovers.

"I don't have to." He brushed the hair back from my face and draped his other arm around me. "My mother thinks I'm staying here at the house, tonight. I want you to open your gifts before you fall asleep."

"You brought them?" I looked up at him. "Even though you were clearly upset with me?"

"Can we not talk about that, anymore?" He leaned over and grabbed one of two gifts I hadn't even noticed were sitting on the opposite nightstand. "Open this first."

Reluctantly, I took the small square box in my hands. I slowly pulled the burgundy ribbon loose, and then peeled back the gold wrapping to expose a velvety box. I opened the box, and inside was a beautiful necklace, glittering under the dim moonlight that seeped through the curtains.

He reached over and turned on the lamp, and muttered something witty about being able to see the sparkling diamonds, but I didn't even hear him. I just stared at the gorgeous circle of glittering diamonds hanging from a white gold chain. "It's beautiful," I muttered breathlessly. "You absolutely didn't have to—"

"I don't *have* to do anything," he interrupted. "Here," he reached over and grabbed the other box. "I thought about doing something cliché like painting you something, but..." he paused and watched me unravel and peel the second box open. "After you rambled about never having been to a Broadway show, I knew this was what I had to do." He watched me rifle through the crumpled tissue paper, and pull out an envelope with two tickets. Front-row and center. "Phantom of the Opera."

My birthday weekend.

Chapter 19

"Happy Holidays"

"Hey, wake up. Everyone's downstairs already and they're waiting on you," was the whisper at my ear.

I turned over in my bed, and moaned, wondering if I were dreaming or not. I wasn't. I opened my eyes groggily, and Preston was sitting upon my bed, beside me. Startled, I looked up at him wide-eyed, and then looked over at the empty, other side of the bed "How did you get in here?" I asked, pulling the sheet tightly around me.

"The door. It's really quite simple, you turn this round knob-thingy, and—"

"I know how you open a door," I snapped in a panic. "My door was locked."

I came in through the balcony," he said, nodding toward the terrace doors. "I'm sorry—I didn't mean to scare you," he apologized, frowning.

I shook my head, wondering what happened to Trent. "It's okay," I waved aside, confused. "I'm alright," I assured him, managing a weary smile. "I'll throw on some clothes and be down in a minute."

He stood up, grinning. "Okay—but hurry up," he urged, excited. "We're all dying to open everything up!"

Before he was even out the door, I wondered where Trent had gone off to. I stared at the pillow his head had rested upon through the night, and then scanned the room to see if perhaps he had leapt up from bed at the sound of Preston coming in. Was he hiding in the bathroom? Or the closet? There was not a sound coming from anywhere in the room, even after Preston was long gone. Instinctively, my eyes darted to the night stand, where my envelope sat beneath a blue velvety box. I then reached up to touch the circle of diamonds at my neck. It certainly wasn't all just a dream...

I jumped out of bed and scrambled for the bathroom, where I then showered, dressed, and slapped on a little make-up. I was rushing down the stairs when I heard someone say, "I think that's her coming!"

When I walked into the ballroom, it appeared I was the last in the house to arrive for the festivities. Kate, Redd, and Charles were seated about the room, and Vivien was seated in an armchair, examining her nails. Even Trent was seated on the floor by the stacks of gifts, smirking up at me.

"Come and sit, Hope!" Lawrence was beaming brightly beneath a big Santa hat, as he addressed me entering the room. He didn't appear to be the least bit upset over last night's fiasco, at dinner, but Vivien surely didn't acknowledge me from her couch. Slightly overwhelmed, I quietly took a seat where he instructed, and once everyone was settled, he started dishing out all the presents to each person. Earrings, expensive perfumes, and diamond necklaces—the gifts kept flowing. Everyone was jolly, and buzzing with excitement. I got more gifts than I could've possibly imagined. Everything from comfy pajama pants to expensive diamond earrings! Preston presented me with stylish black wool pea coat, which was nice, and unexpected. I knew he spent quite a bit on it upon looking at the designer label. He absolutely didn't have to do that.

"I almost had a heart attack when Preston came in and woke me up until I realized that you weren't in there," I muttered to Trent, the first chance I got to be near him.

"Did he get a thrill from seeing that you were naked beneath your sheets?" he asked, grinning wickedly. "I bet it turned him on."

I blushed. "I don't care to know," I answered, making him laugh. "I'm sure he didn't even notice."

"I would've," he admitted honestly.

"I don't mind it coming from you," I said with a wink.

Even through Lawrence's surprising normalcy, I couldn't help but feel awkward. Maybe I was the only one with the problem... Hours later, we all sat down for an early afternoon dinner that Redd painstakingly prepared to perfection, and it actually turned out to be a light-hearted and delicious meal, much unlike the one we had the night before. Everything was perfect; except that it all passed by so fast that at the end of the day it seemed like a blur.

After dinner, the men decided to retreat to the parlor to play cards and smoke cigars, and Kate decided that us girls should follow for a change, and lounge with them. We all entered the big, dark parlor across from the ballroom, and Charles, Trent, Redd, Lawrence and Preston sat around a card table while Vivien grabbed one of her romance novels and found herself a chaise. I took a seat which afforded me a clear view of Trent. Lawrence removed a box from one of the many shelves that were built into the walls, and everyone took a cigar from it. Preston chewed on his, while Lawrence and Trent lit theirs up.

Lawrence dealt the first hand, and all five men were transformed into serious poker players in a matter of minutes. Kate brought in several bottles of beer that were passed around amongst them, and it wasn't long before cigar smoke clouded the room and pervaded my senses. It was impossible not to stare at the man who slept in my bed the night before, all the while that they played. Testosterone proliferated throughout the air as they tossed their money into the growing pot, while they puffed on their cigars. Trent won several hands in a row, and I silently cheered him on. I could've watched him for hours... He would often look over in my direction, and our eyes would meet for one brief, exhilarating moment before he'd place his bet. The tiny, knowing smiles that we would exchange were a thrill-and-a-half, at every single stolen glance.

Kate kept making runs back and forth from the kitchen for beer, or to empty the ashtrays for the men. At rest, she took a seat next to Charles, and joked that she was his good luck charm. Vivien was too engrossed in her novel to notice anything going on around her, and I just sat and observed everything. It wasn't "lights out" until close to midnight that evening, and overall I think it turned out to be a wonderful Christmas after all, despite the circumstances that surrounded us.

Christmas had come and gone; now just a fading blip on the radar. My birthday was creeping up, and the excitement and anticipation of something real, and shameless, developing with him palpitated through my veins. He was perfect. Everything was perfect. Surreal. Falling asleep in his arms and waking up in the early morning to sneak back to the main house... I wouldn't have traded it for anything... except a lifetime of it with no one to scrutinize.

Vivien went into planning mode the day after Christmas, and Lawrence was scarce, if not altogether obsolete. If Preston hadn't been there to keep me company, take me to lunch, go to the movies, or just laugh and chat on the terrace outside our bedroom suites during the daytime, I would've surely thought I were invisible in that massive stone-cold house.

The same crew that came in to transform the manor into a Christmas Wonderland returned to take everything back down, and Christmas was completely undone. Vivien kicked her masquerade plans into full gear, and suddenly I had to find a "costume" of sorts. I enlisted Jackie's help, and she came to pick me up at the manor two days before the ball so that we could go into the city and check out some of the shops in the area. Knowing that she knew more about the whole ordeal than I did, she showed me the kinds of things that most of the women wore to the gala every year, and I had an epiphany halfway through our excursion. She picked out a deep purple, shiny, satin two-piece gown, and its top was a corset with all the old-fashioned boning, and the skirt flared outward. Her mask covered only her eyes, and it had rhinestones and feathers to make it flashy.

She arrived to the manor at six, and her hair was already done up in a mass of curls piled atop her head. She unzipped her garment bag and pulled out her dress, and it was officially go-time.

My gown was made of flowing pale pink silk and chiffon. It went off the shoulders, and it had crystal beading going across the bodice. "Bravo!" Jackie grinned at me approvingly when I held the pink and white feathered mask I'd made myself, up to my face. "You look fantastic! Not bad for your first masquerade!"

"So what is the point of all of this?" I asked Jackie as we put on our strappy heels.

She smiled. "A lot of people have masquerade balls on New Year's," she explained. "Some people believe that the first of the year signifies a clean slate, or something to that effect. So people have these parties and dress up in costume, and then at midnight they celebrate the metamorphosis of shedding their old skin and bad habits, and taking on the new." I was still confused, and she caught my bewildered look. "Never mind," she said. "Just look at it as a way to dress up in disguise, forget about all your worries and who you are, and have a good time," she said, standing up.

"Now you're talkin'," I joked as we headed for the door. "So, is Chad going to be here tonight?"

She smiled at me. "I don't know if "Chad" will be, but I know that there will be a handsome guy in a masked costume here to whisk me away and dance with me all night," she hinted.

"Oh, so I take it we don't even use our real names?" I shook my head and laughed.

"You just need to let loose and have some fun," she urged, giving me a playful shove on the arm as we approached the bottom of the staircase.

When we passed through the ballroom doors, all the men and women in various costumes, suits, and gowns astonished me. Lawrence had hired fortune-tellers, band of musicians to provide music, and even those people you see at the circus who eat fire! There was so much to take in, and honestly, I couldn't recognize anyone through his or her masks! It was a little intimidating!

As if he were waiting for her, Jackie's 'handsome guy in a masked costume' approached us immediately, and he did whisk her away to dance, leaving me standing there by myself. I headed for the bar, and met Charles's cynical eyes, as he zeroed in on me, poured a glass of white wine, and then pushed it to me without either of us saying even a single word.

"Thank you," I politely accepted, taking the glass into my hand

"No problem, Miss." His words were as sarcastic as his smile that followed. Whatever. I just turned and uncomfortably headed away from him. I just wandered about the floor, and drinking in how happily everyone was dancing and swinging around the ballroom, while I sipped my wine. This clearly looked like a scene stolen right out of Mardi Gras, or even a party from some bygone era. One very admirable quality that Vivien possessed was her ability to assemble a fantastic party.

"Excuse me. Would you like to dance?"

I looked behind me, and it took me a second to realize that it was Preston, behind the black mask covering his eyes. "Sure," I welcomed, allowing him to lead me across the ballroom.

"I was wondering when you'd get here," he told me. "I haven't seen you all day."

"It takes a while to get this pretty," I said with a smile.

He shrugged. "It doesn't matter. You're here now," he said with a satisfied smile.

"So, what are you supposed to be?" I narrowed my eyes as I looked over him.

"I'm just dressed up enough to be considered 'in disguise'," he answered. "I'm not really good at the whole costume concept," he admitted.

"I definitely understand," I conceded.

"But *you* certainly look good," he said, looking me over. "Maybe I should've asked for Jackie's help too," he joked. His words were then lost on me. Suddenly I was preoccupied by the man in black who stood off to the side, watching closely. He was wearing the mask of The Phantom, and it caused my heart to flutter within my chest.

"I agree," I quipped absently, to whatever Preston had just said..

"Are you trying to say that I don't look good?"

I snapped back to attention, and back to our conversation. "Never," I scoffed, smiling innocently. I shifted slightly in his arms.

"Good, because I could make anything look good."

"I'm glad to see that you haven't dropped your ego for the evening," I teased, glancing over at the now vacant spot where Trent had been standing. "I guess it just seeps into any character you try to assume."

"I wouldn't want it any other way!" He grinned.

"May I?" Someone stopped us, wanting to cut in. I stopped, and looked up at the man in the Phantom mask. His hair was pulled back into a ponytail at the base of his neck. His face was clean-shaven. His face was half-hidden behind a smooth, white mask that made his black eyes contrast strikingly.

Plus, I knew those sensuously-shaped lips anywhere.

Preston stiffened immediately. I don't even think he was going to give Trent the time of day until he felt me step back a little, which certainly did not escape him. "Sure," he snapped, clenching his teeth as he released me. As Trent took my hand and led me off, I felt Preston's eyes fixed on us. He was visibly displeased by Trent's interruption.

"What a coincidence that you are dressed as the Phantom of the Opera," I mused lightly.

"Not any more a coincidence than you dressing as Christine," he countered.

"This was on purpose."

"I made this mask, myself."

"You did a wonderful job." He took me into his arms as if I belonged in them, and began to lead me backward. "Did you also leave the roses for me?"

He looked perplexed. "Roses?"

Now I second-guessed my inquiry. "After the Phantom performances. On the windshield of my car?"

His one free eyebrow rose at me. "Not I, milady. Seems you might have an admirer. Perhaps the same gentleman friend that hasn't stopped glaring at us since I took you away from him?" He glanced briefly over my shoulder. "Do you think he has a touch of the green-eyed monster?"

"I have no idea," I waved aside.

"Of course you do," he insisted. "Clearly, he's in love with you. Even a blind man could see that. Did you ask him if he left you the roses?"

I looked up at him in surprise. "No he's not," I adamantly denied. "And he doesn't know anything about me participating in 'Phantom.'"

"You might not have told him, but don't discount the fact that he takes a keen interest in what you do." My eyes met his dead-on. He wasn't being malicious. He wasn't being ugly. Trent was just being truthful. .

But I wasn't prepared to face that. "We'll just agree to disagree," I pushed aside.

"You can keep acting like you don't see it." He shrugged a shoulder, and then pulled me tighter against him, uncaring of who might've seen us. "It is of no concern to me. At any rate, you do look incredibly delicious tonight, my love. I have the urge to pick you up, take you upstairs, and then ravage you." I smiled up at him, more thrilled than anything of his openness to keep me this close to him, so publically. "I never thought Phantom could be such a turn-on."

"Perhaps I'll have to make a late-night visit to your opera house for a rendezvous," I suggested with a coy smile.

"I think I'd immensely enjoy making you sing like a canary."

I blushed profusely at his innuendo, and in return he grinned devilishly. "Aren't you worried that people might think something's going on if we continue dancing together?" I asked him.

"With your not-so-secret admirer standing off to the side, watching our every move, the only care I have in the world right now is that he doesn't start running his mouth and making a scene," he muttered with a frown.

"I still don't understand why anyone would want me to stay away from the only person in this house that makes me truly happy," I muttered.

"Probably because you're seventeen," he answered. "And, they view me as a womanizer, for reasons I cannot explain. I don't bring various women around the house. They've never caught me in the act with a female anywhere on the premises. In fact, they know nothing about my personal life, except for whatever they might read about in the newspaper. Oh, by the way, I'm having that picture they ran of you taking your clothes off at the bar awhile back made into a poster," he declared, making me gasp in embarrassment. "Why don't you do anything wild like that at my place?" He didn't even care that I was so humiliated that I was beginning to sweat under his raillery. "Do I not get you liquored up enough?—Because I can serve you something stronger, you know."

"You saw that?" I whispered, suddenly embarrassed.

"Yes I did. Why, are you ashamed?"

"I just... Yeah—I'm not proud of that, no," I stammered.

He laughed. "I'd just prefer you channel all of that naughty energy into other acts," he poked.

"You're awful," I muttered with a laugh. "You didn't even want me back then..."

"Just because I didn't rip your clothes off doesn't mean I didn't want you," he shot back with a grin. "Complications, remember? Complications that you seized control over in recent evenings." He winked, and I wished I suddenly had a full-body mask to hide how red I was. Then he threw a glance over my shoulder. "Alright, well Preston is starting to blow smoke from his ears, so I'll let him take it from here," he said, releasing me from his grasp and backing away. "It was a pleasure, my love," he said, taking my hand in his, and bringing it to his lips. "I'll see you behind the scenes at my opera house."

My eyes followed him as he strut away from me. I could've danced with him all night. But I had no time to revel in my daze. Not with Preston so miffed.

"I can't stand him," he muttered, approaching me from behind. "You need to watch it around him," he advised, casting a dirty look in Trent's direction as he made his way to the bar. "He's such a jerk. He's probably been planning getting into your pants since you arrived here..."

I wanted to snap back at him angrily that he didn't know Trent at all, but I kept my mouth shut. Preston's eyes hatefully followed him all the way to the bar. "All this anger isn't necessary. It was just a dance. Don't get your panties in a wad," I chastised jokingly.

Realizing that he was allowing too much emotion to surface, he immediately softened. "You just know how I feel about him," he said quickly. "And I was uncomfortable with him dancing with you like that."

"He was very polite," I assured him, as my eyes followed that Phantom's movements while he mingled with some older gentlemen. "So quit looking upset."

"You mean a lot to me, Hope. More than anything. I don't want to see you get hurt. Especially from getting involved with an ass like him."

My eyes snapped upward to his. "I'm a big girl. I can take care of myself, Preston. There's no need for you, or anyone else, to look after me."

"Instinct, I guess." I felt myself stiffen as he continued. "To keep the ones you care about away from harm." As he looked down over me, he went quiet, and looked thoughtful for a moment. "Remember the day I arrived back here at the manor—the day you and I met?"

"Yes," I replied with a chuckle. "How could I forget?"

"Do you remember when I kissed you, down by the river?"

"Of course I do," I recalled.

"I don't regret doing that," he stated softly, causing my lips to part in surprise. I didn't know what to say in response to that. "My only regret was that you didn't kiss me back."

My eyes flicked upward in shock. I didn't know what to say to him, and I froze in panic, hoping he wouldn't try to repeat that episode again, *here*, at the party.

"You really look amazing tonight." His eyes scanned over me with appreciation, before he winked to soften me up again. "You didn't have to dress up for me, you know."

"You like how I can manage to look nice sometimes?" I smirked up at him.

"How much are you dreading going back to Springcrest next week?"

"I'm not," I replied deftly. "Why, are you dreading going back?"

"Eh," he shrugged. "I've really had a blast just hanging out with you over break," he confessed. "Kind of sucks having to go back to reality."

"It's not like we are never going to see each other again," I teased, trying to lighten the serious tone his eyes had now taken. "It'll just go back to the way it used to be." My eyes scanned the room busily for Trent. He was nowhere to be found.

"You are really awesome," he spoke softly. "You kick ass, actually," he added, causing us both to chuckle. "I don't know. I just really like you, Hope. I like us. I like 'this'." I felt myself stiffen a little bit in alarm. *No, Preston. Don't do it.... Don't bring things up...Don't force my hand...* "I was just thinking, maybe we go out. On an actual date. Dinner, whatever you want."

"I think you've got just a touch of cabin fever," I blurted with a nervous laugh. "You've had too much time here, but once you get back to college life, and all those girls, this will just be a hiccup—"

"I really don't think you understand what I'm saying," he cut me off, exasperatedly. "I haven't even dated anyone since you and I became close. I have no desire to."

"Why ruin a great thing?" My heart was racing, and I felt panic. "We're such great friends, and we have so much fun together..."

"Nothing could ruin what we have now," he insisted, trying his hardest to convince me to view things his way. "But why not try to see if we can make it even better? I'm willing to wait for that, and work for that," he vowed.

"Preston, I can't let you do that," I insisted. "We're friends—and good friends, at that," I reminded him. "I feel like we've come such a long way from when we first met, and I don't want to let anything spoil that! I have so much fun when I'm with you, without worrying about feelings, and adding the complexities of a relationship to that." Now he looked crestfallen. "I just don't want anything to change, that's all," I finished weakly.

"What—do you have someone you're already interested in, back at school?" he asked. His eyes were displaying a despicable amount of sudden anger by my rejection that made me glance around us in concern. "How come you haven't brought him around?"

"Preston, I'm not even saying that I have someone else." I needed him to calm down, before this got out of control. "I'm just saying that what we have right now is great, and I don't want to alter that in any way!"

"Exactly. And I'm attracted to you." The reality in his words sucked the breath right out of me. Everything Jackie had warned me of, advised me against, every flirty glance I'd ever cast Preston's way.... *I deserved this.* "You have no response?" He appeared genuinely stunned as his eyes pierced me. And he just might've been that stunned and surprised; Preston never had to work for a female in his life. They all just kind of flocked to him.

But I was not one of them. I was emotionally taken by someone else.

I spotted Trent, off to the side. He was engrossed in conversation with three older gentlemen. But as soon as my eyes landed on him, he looked straight at me.

"I think that would make a huge mistake." I tried to sound firm, but it came out weak, and broken. "People look at us like we are related. I mean, we pretty much are. It would just be weird to everyone."

"I was adopted! There is no blood between us!"

My head was spinning. "It's just not feasible, Preston."

"Wow, and here all along I thought that maybe we were on the same page." He took a step back and anxiously ran his fingers through his tousled hair as he just stood there awkwardly. I had sufficiently damaged his ego. He looked wounded, and so hurt that it made my heart ache for inflicting that feeling upon him. "I'm not buying it," he dared to muster up. "I have seen the way you look at me. There have been moments when I know you've felt the same way, Hope. I don't get it. What is really going on, here?!"

"I'm in love with Trent," I blurted softly, without even a chance to re-think my decision.

But, no. It was too late. He literally looked as if he'd been punched in the gut. His face contorted out of anger, turning red as he shook his head in confusion. "What?!"

"I'm sorry," I tried to take a small step towards him, but he stepped backward instantly. "I just—"

"When? When did this start? When do you have the time?" His eyes panned the room, but Trent was off behind him, completely unknowing of what was going on now.

"A few months," I answered meekly.

"When the hell do you see him?! Are you just sneaking around behind everyone's backs? Does anyone know?!"

I shook my head. "No one knows but you," I answered. "Please... don't tell anyone—"

"Don't worry. I won't speak another word." His words were pointed as sharp as the edge of a sword. His eyes went cold. He just simply turned and walked away from me. I felt defeated. Horrible. Guilty.

I even felt a little heart-broken.

I knew, too late, the damage I'd done to Preston. But I had felt cornered, and panicked—and against my better judgment, I leaked out the very bit of information most detrimental to not just him, but to *us. Trent and I.*

So now I felt panicked on an entirely different level.

I exhaled a deep breath, and lowered my head tiredly. I wasn't going to chase after him. Clearly he needed some time away from me, and there was nothing I could say to try and fix this right now, anyway. I headed to where Trent was now standing, taking turns talking with Charles, and eyeballing Preston and I. "You were right," I told him resignedly. "Preston just told me how he feels about me."

"I see that he stomped away from you like a two year old who was just denied a brand new toy in the department store," he observed, turning to face the bar, like myself. "What did you say to him?"

"I told him not to wait around for me."

"'Wait around?' Is that what he said?"

I nodded. "He's really upset...."

His eyebrow lifted. "Wow. So he has a heart after all," he muttered.

"You two do nothing but badmouth each other," I said, irritated. "I don't want to hear anymore. I need another glass of wine."

"I apologize. So what did he say about me?"

I turned and gave him a look. "I'm not saying. Can we just drop it? I'd like to forget that the last five minutes never happened."

"Alright," he agreed. "Besides—I think Preston's already beaten you to it. Forgetting." He nodded over my shoulder.

I turned quickly to see Preston dancing with a petite brunette, who was smiling up at him, and looking at him coyly. The look upon his face as he gazed down at her was charming. As if what took place two minutes ago never even happened.

I sighed, and shook my head. "Whatever makes him happy," I muttered. Maybe a little bit more bitterly than I had intended. And while I did turn him away, it made what he said all the more cheap, and not meaningful at all, when he turned around and had already begun flirting and laughing with someone else.

That is, until I saw him glance over at me, and his eyes met square with mine. They locked and held, and then he broke the glance to look down at his pretty dancing partner. It was then made more than clear that he was driven by a motive to make me jealous. To invoke some kind of similar emotion in me, that he felt. It did peeve me slightly, but I turned my back and made it a point not to turn my eyes his way for the rest of the evening.

Trent was waiting outside in the gardens for me at eleven-thirty on the dot, and he threw his coat around my shoulders to keep me warm as he took my hand and walked with me through the woods. Kissing me was the first thing he tended to, upon our arrival inside the safety of his quaint cabin. A fire was the second thing on his agenda.

"I absolutely love that dress on you," he spoke gently, as he stood from the fireplace and continued to admire me from head-to-toe. I smiled, looking down at it.

"I borrowed it from the theater wardrobe," I told him, curiously picking up the white mask he had tossed aside upon our entrance.

"I know," he acknowledged with a wicked smile.

And that's when I felt compelled to tell him, whether it changed things, or not, what had been on the forefront of my mind all evening. "When Preston asked me why we couldn't work," I began; catching his attention as he curiously tilted his head.

"Yes?" He was watching me closely.

I stopped a few feet from him and looked to him helplessly. "I told him I was in love with you."

They went blank for an instant, until his eyes blinked back their surprise. I mean, I knew what I was walking into. I was standing before the very man who had once declared his opposition to love, and all the trappings of it. He didn't believe in it, and here I was—opening myself up to getting my heart broken. It was clear he wasn't ready to hear it.

But I had to say it.

"I looked like an idiot in that thing," he spoke, eyeing the item in my hands as he approached me. His words were barely above a whisper, and my heart was in my stomach.

"You did not," I argued softly. "You looked stunning."

He cupped my face and tilted it upwards, with his face just inches from mine. His fingertips were entwined in my hair, and my heart was in his teeth. *Just do it already,* I silently begged. *Put me out of my misery...*

"I love you too," he spoke quite sincerely, while looking me square in the eye.

Chapter 20

"Looking to the Future"

After the masquerade party that catapulted us into the new year, I began my last semester of high school, and now graduation was a few short months away. That diploma that went hand-in-hand with my freedom was so close I could almost touch them now

And for every wonderful moment Trent and I shared together, there was a hurt and wounded glance shot in my direction from Preston, until he returned to his school. His calls every evening to my dorm room never happened again after the ball, and they were replaced by Trent picking me up after my afternoon classes to go to town for some coffee. A few of the times, he was nice enough to invite Jackie along if he saw us together, and she even admitted after spending a few hours with him that he was one of the most charming people she'd ever met.

It was a shame that Preston completely shut me out from his life, but at the same time, could I blame him? I knew I had to be patient. I knew it would take time for him to come around, again. Every attempt I made to try and talk to him went ignored. To be fair, I had to give him his space.

And though I think Lawrence sensed that something really wasn't right with me when it came to him anymore, he never addressed it. I couldn't help the fact that I snapped at him in private conversation, even though I humored him in public, or at parties and dinner affairs. If for some reason he would start to charm me, and melt away my cold, hard feelings, I would remind himself of all he must've done to my mother to drive her from this house, and it would harden me against him, again.

I turned down his suggestion to host an elaborate party at the manor for my eighteenth birthday. I told him I had plans to spend it with friends, and not to expect me home at all, over that weekend. He tried not to reveal that he was hurt by my brush-off, but I saw it briefly before he replaced it with a forced smile. "It's alright," he dismissed. "Your present should be ready by that time, though, and I'll at least expect you to come around so I can give it to you," he insisted.

I'd long since given up on Vivien, but even she, lately, had a slight change of heart. Instead of walking right past me with her nose in the air, she would smile, and say something like "Oh, I love that shirt on you, darling!" or "Did you do something with your hair? It looks so nice, dear! Are you going to my stylist?" *Too late, Grandmother. I gave you multiple chances, but you flushed every single one of them down the toilet.*

Kate, however, seemed to talk to me less and less, every time she saw me. She no longer flashed me her pretty smile every time she passed me. In fact, if she did pass me, she would pretend to be busy with something so that she wouldn't even have to look up. If she had sensed that there was something going on between her son and I, she certainly didn't like it. I wasn't sure if she didn't like the idea of him choosing me, or perhaps the age difference—but it did worry me enough to confront Trent about it.

"Don't worry about it," he assured me. "She knows nothing, except for the glances she sees you and me exchange in passing, and those could mean anything."

"I don't know... I think she knows something," I insisted. "She hardly speaks to me, anymore!"

"You're paranoid," he told me. "But I do intend on talking to her about it before summer, if we are serious about traveling abroad."

I gave him a panicked look. "What are you going to say?"

He stroked the side of my face. "She's my mother. She has to find out, sometime," he told me. "Don't worry about anything," he ordered. "Everything will turn out fine."

I believed him, and tried not to think another thought about it again as time went by. I'd begun a journal, and wrote in it sometimes several times a day, about everything and nothing in particular. My feelings, events that happened, plans for the future—I wrote it all down, with the intention of presenting it to Trent when it was finished. I was already halfway done. He loved to read autobiographies, and to learn about different people. So I decided to write my own.

"I have reservations at a great place before the show next Saturday," Trent boasted about my impending birthday.

"Any hints as to where?" I implored.

"Of course not. You already know too much. You'll find out where, when we get there."

"You have to at least let me know how to dress," I told him coyly. "I wouldn't be able to show up at a nice restaurant in overalls," I pointed out.

"You don't wear overalls."

"I know, but I might decide to wear them, then," I insisted.

"No you won't," he denied. "I'll take care of that, too," he told me. "All you need to be aware of is that after class Friday, you belong to me, so make sure you have no other plans."

"I don't know," I playfully went on. "Since you have been so secretive about everything, when Jackie asked me if I wanted to go out with her, I told her I would."

"I don't think that's a wise idea," he said, chuckling as he sat down on his couch beside me.

"Why not?" I asked innocently. "You have something really special planned?"

His hands took my face between him, as his beautiful face stared down into mine. "Woman, you drive me mad. Do you know that?"

We talked constantly about going to Italy, and he teased me about getting me over there and not letting me return home, which I told him I was more than fine with. As soon as I turned eighteen, I was going to get my passport, and he promised upon receiving it that he would take care of travel plans, and that everything would be all set for us to go for that summer. I had a list of places to visit, and he had a list equally long of places he wished to show me. Finally— some plans between us becoming real.

Finally, *this* was becoming more real.

In the meantime, I allowed myself to become preoccupied with the school's Spring production, which was another work of Shakespeare's. I had never filled Cleopatra's shoes before, but I was elected to play the role. I walked a mile in that beautiful woman's shoes, and I felt her pain. The play got so much attention, that we were asked to do two encore performances. "Cleopatra" would become my last play for my high school career. Honestly, there was something a little depressing about that.

Lawrence and I never had another discussion about colleges. I received several academic scholarships from the high school, and then there was still the partial scholarship to performing arts school in New York City. I had already decided that if I went anywhere, that would be the place. But I wanted to buy myself some time before I committed myself to anything.

Jackie had gone ahead and accepted her scholarship to a school in New York City near to the one I was interested in. At least if I did go that route, I'd have her there. Meanwhile, she still didn't know about Lawrence being my father, but she was aware of the situation with Trent, and told me that I would love Europe, because she loved it when she went with her parents, the summer she turned sixteen. She was excited for us, and I needed that. I needed someone on my side of the ring, and she truly was my best cheerleader. Because she knew how much we cared for each other, and the hurdles that we overcame to get to the point we were at.

She also told me that she would see Preston out in the clubs every now and then on the weekends with a group of his college friends, and he would have a different girl on his arm each time. It really bothered me that he reverted back to the old way that he was when I first met him, and sadly, I didn't think there was any way I could change him back. I couldn't even reach him, anymore.

Friday, after classes I headed into the dormitory, and the receptionist at the front desk told me that I had received a package. She handed it to me, and I went upstairs to my room to open it. Inside the box was a sleek, floor-length silk gown in a lovely pink shade. There was also a pair of shoes to go with it. "Your ride will be waiting outside for you at five," the note read. "And don't forget—I love you. Trent."

I smiled, folding the note and sticking it in my purse for safekeeping. I had approximately an hour and a half to bathe and get myself ready to go meet my "ride". I jumped into the bath, set my hair in big curlers, and I meticulously applied my make-up. In record time, I was transformed from frumpy schoolgirl to runway material, and as I looked myself over for the final time in the mirror, I admired the dress that Trent selected for me. Good taste, indeed!

I grabbed my bag, and my purse, and I went downstairs, not exactly knowing what to expect. I half-expected to see Trent's shiny, black Mercedes outside, but instead there was a long, shiny black limousine, and a man standing outside of it, waiting.

"Miss de Havilland?"

I nodded, approaching him. "Yes."

He opened the door, so that I could get inside of the car, and I was pleased when I saw Trent in there, already waiting for me. The door closed, and we were both alone in the backseat. There was a partition up for our privacy. "I was right," he said, leaning in to press his lips to my bare neck. "You look amazing in that dress."

I closed my eyes and sunk back into the plush, leather seat. "Thank you," I accepted softly. "The dress is gorgeous."

"Happy Birthday, my love."

I looked into his eyes, and took his beautiful face into my hands. "Thank you," I repeated gratefully.

"Are you surprised?" He asked, looking around.

"Yes," I admitted. "Where are we headed?"

"Dinner first," he answered. "At one of the top restaurants in the city," he said. "And then I have tickets to a Broadway musical, if you're interested," he told me with a wink.

"Is that so?" I smiled coyly. "I think I might be interested."

"Just sit back and relax. It'll be almost an hour before we get there."

Over the course of time that I had known Trent, I learned that he was one of the most generous and considerate people I had ever known. If there was something you wanted to do, he was eager to introduce you to the experience. If there was something you wanted to try, he would bring it to you, or *you* to *it* so you could try it. But if he offered it to you, and you didn't accept it the first time, he wouldn't offer it to you again.

I loved him more than words could describe, and we shared a passion for one another that burned brighter and hotter than any wildfire you could imagine. We shared a love for the arts, whether it be paintings, drawings, or sketches all the way to performing arts, and theater, and all of which meant a lot to the both of us.

When finally we arrived in the city, where I'd never been before, I was completely, utterly fascinated by it all. It was profoundly impressive. *The city that never sleeps.* And I could see why! With so much to see and do, who had time to lie down? "This is Broadway," Trent told me, as we passed through. "This is where we'll be in a few hours," he reminded me.

We finally came to a stop, and then my door opened for me to step out. Trent was at my heels, and he buttoned up the jacket of his suit before he took my hand, and led me inside the building. We entered a grand lobby, and I was led straight to one of the several elevators in a row. Once inside, I felt us start to go up, and we continued to go up for several minutes before we stopped. We stepped out, and he took my hand again, and we passed through some darkly tinted glass doors, landing us inside a restaurant.

"Forrestor," Trent told the man at the desk just inside the entrance.

"Ah yes, Mr. Forrestor." The man smiled pleasantly. "Right this way, please."

He led us through the main area, where soft piano music played, and we got a small table in the middle. Trent waited until I was seated before he seated himself, and I looked around at the cozy, candlelit atmosphere. "This place is beautiful," I told him. "How did you know it was here?"

"I met a client of mine here, once," he told me. "The food is superb."

Every table, including ours, had a small vase of fresh roses sitting on its crisp, white linen, but while every other vase there had red roses, ours had purple—my favorite. Coincidence? I think not. "Did you ask them for these?" I smirked at him, before leaning in to smell them.

"Specifically," he affirmed, just as our waiter approached our table. He greeted us and told us what the special *du jour* was, before he placed a menu in front of us. When he asked what we wanted to drink, Trent turned to me.

Blankly, I looked back at him for a moment, before flicking my eyes up at our waiter. "Water, please," I ordered meekly.

"Two glasses of your finest red wine, please," Trent asked of him. The man nodded, and walked off. "Water?" He scoffed, looking at me in amusement. "I can't let you sip on water. Today's your birthday for crying out loud."

I laughed, glancing over the menu. "And suppose he asked me for my ID, and here I am only eighteen?" I proposed.

"I doubt he would've asked, but it doesn't matter now because I took care of it," he dismissed. "What will you be having for dinner?"

I shook my head. "Honestly, I have no idea," I muttered.

"Do you like calamari?"

I made a face. "No."

He laughed. "Have you ever tried it?"

"I don't plan to," I admitted.

"Will you allow me to order for you?" he asked.

I looked at him skeptically. "I don't want any calamari," I warned him.

"I'm aware of that."

"What if I don't like what you order for me?"

"Then you're free to order another dish, if you like."

I smiled as I pretend to ponder his request for a moment, and then nodded. "I'm going to trust you. Just please don't get me something that was once a slimy creature in its living years," I warned him.

"I won't," he promised.

Once the waiter arrived, he brought us our glasses of wine—and my glass of water—and he asked us if we needed a few more minutes to look over the menu.

Regardless of whether I was going to like the food or not, it was incredibly nice to have a man order for me. I'd never experienced that, before. It was just another way that

Trent made me feel pampered, and taken care of when I was with him. It was just a good feeling.

"This place is very nice," I commented, looking around again. When I caught his eye again, he was giving me that sly look. "What?" I asked him, narrowing my eyes with curiosity.

"Nothing," he answered, leaning back slightly.

"You drive me crazy when you look at me like that," I told him. "It makes me think you're up to something."

"Here is your appetizer." The waiter appeared, setting down a large platter between Trent and me, and then a fresh, leafy salad for each of us. "Your food will be out shortly. Is there anything else I can get for you?"

I shook my head. "No," Trent answered. "Thank you."

It was a rather large platter of many piles of different things. There were several selections of crackers, and a few different cheeses, olives, and nuts. Following Trent's lead, I picked up a cracker and started putting different things on it. "This is pretty good," I told him after taking a bite.

"Very much so," he agreed.

"What kind of desserts do they have?" I asked him, smiling.

"Whichever kind you want," he answered, grabbing another cracker.

"Aren't you going to eat your salad?" I asked him, stabbing at mine.

"No," he replied swiftly. "I'm saving all my room for the delectable slab of meat coming out shortly."

"Why do you keep looking at me like that?" I demanded with a laugh.

The smirk on his face was so obvious, but he tried to put on a more serious look. "I have no idea what you're talking about," he insisted. "Can't I look at the beautiful woman accompanying me this evening?" he said innocently.

"There's a difference between 'looking' and 'smirking'."

"A smirk is a look."

"Be quiet and eat your food," I ordered playfully.

"Can I tell you about the play we're going to see?" He asked, still smirking.

"Yes, but I'm going to ignore that silly look on your face," I told him. "I'm not even going to look at you."

He laughed. "We have magnificent seats, milady. 'Phantom of the Opera.' Did I mention that?"

"You did," I couldn't help but laugh at his boyish silliness. "Thank you so much again, Trent. This means so much to me!"

When our food arrived, and it was more than I could possibly consume. Trent was right, though—the food was divine, and my first taste of Atlantic salmon was a good one. I had to ask Trent what the other things on my plate were, and he told me that they were horseradish, sun-dried tomato risotto, crispy parsnips, and leek butter. They still would've tasted wonderful even if I hadn't known their names, but I told Trent that whatever it was, I wanted to have it again—soon—because it tasted so good.

When dinner was over, Trent decided to pass on dessert, but insisted that I go ahead and try something anyway. I opted for the white chocolate tiramisu with toasted hazelnuts, and the waiter promised me it would be just a few moments before he would bring it out.

Trent eyed me very seriously for a long moment, and then faintly smiling, he said, "Were you really serious when you said that you could leave this place forever?"

His question took me by surprise, but I answered a very quick and confident "Yes. Why?"

"I've been doing a lot of thinking, lately," he said, leaning forward. "About us, about Italy, about everything in general," he went on. "Nothing bad," he assured me, putting me at ease. "But if you're sure," he continued, "that you could leave this place and never look back, then let's do it," he stated.

My heart began to pound, and I looked at him in shock. "What?"

"I'm saying that we could go to Europe and not have to return," he put out there, throwing me for a loop. "We could take some time to travel around, and then we can purchase a villa on the water somewhere, and build a life for ourselves."

"Are you serious?" I asked him in awe. "I thought you said you'd never—"

"I know what I said," he interrupted me, reaching into the inside of his jacket, and pulling out a small, black box. He opened it up, and said, "But I changed my mind."

I gasped at the sight of a beautiful diamond ring glittering in the candlelight. I was stunned. I couldn't wrap my head around what was unfolding before me. "What is this?" I whispered in shock.

He rose from his chair, and then he knelt in front of me on one knee. "I'm not one for public displays of affection, but I firmly believe that this should be done right," he spoke with a charming, self-assured grin. Everyone around us was watching now, and it felt like the entire restaurant was holding its breath. "Hope," he began. "I offer you this ring, along with a promise to love you for my entire lifetime, if you'll do me the honor of becoming my wife. It doesn't have to be anytime soon. We have all the time in the world. But I've made up my mind that I want you by my side, as long as you're willing to have me."

I blinked, shocked. Stunned. "Of course I will," I accepted softly, my head spinning. "Of course I will!"

I was still at a loss for words, by the time the waiter brought our check and congratulated us. I just kept looking from the rock on my finger, to the man who continued to surprise me on a daily basis. Such a long way we had come, several months. So much. So fast. So soon? All I knew was that it felt right, and if Trent and I had anything in common, our impulsiveness was the biggest.

"Trent, this must've cost you a fortune," I said in awe.

"I won't tell you how much."

I glanced up at him. "It's perfect." And so wildly unexpected.

For the rest of the night, when we walked, and I held his hand, it somehow meant so much more. Every look, every brief glance, every word… everything was different and more profound. The play was wonderful, but I couldn't tell you a thing about it. I couldn't tell you what the costumes looked like, or what the actors looked like, or sounded like. All that I could think about was what tonight meant.

On the way home, we agreed there was no rush. It was just important to Trent that if we were to begin to live together after we went away to Europe, that to marry would make everything "right". He wanted away from the manor and its shadows as much as I did, and he put it into motion in the most romantic of ways. We spent the night in the city, in a luxurious hotel room with a view of Times Square. How surreal everything was. How much different it felt to touch him, and to make love to him.

The stars were finally aligning for us.

And for the time being, purposely kept my ring off, at the manor. I planned on keeping it a secret until I had at least graduated. I wanted Lawrence to know as little as possible about my life, or my plans, so he wouldn't be able to gain control, and take everything away from me.

And so, after Trent brought me back to the manor, I went up to my suite, got ready for bed, and had some of the sweetest dreams I'd ever dreamt, that night. I was on top of the world.

Chapter 21

"A Future So Bright"

I was engaged. The idea absolutely blew my mind, and I still couldn't figure out what sparked this idea in Trent. My Prince Charming had every intention to take me far away from the dismal castle where I resided, so we could live happily ever after. I was floored, and the only person I told was Jackie, who looked as if she was going to faint afterwards.

And then again, after I showed her the ring.

I had to get through graduation, first. There was an exciting buzz around the senior dormitories, and there was only a month and a half left of school. It was announced that I would be the Salutatorian, which was both an honor, and a reward for my hard work, and I had to start preparing a speech to read on graduation day. I had plenty of inspiration. I just had to work on putting all of it into words.

Trent's cabin turned into a maniacal array of brochures, papers, magazines, and miscellaneous sheets of notebook paper with random bits of information written on them. Phone numbers, hotels in Europe, points of interest we wanted to visit—you name it, and it was scattered about somewhere. It was exciting. It was a whirlwind. I couldn't wait to leave!

But all of everything in my life that I had been so excited about came to a screeching halt, the day I came home to find Lawrence patiently waiting for me in the foyer, upon my return home from Trent's, a few weekends later. Having a bad feeling right off the bat, I shifted awkwardly on my feet.

"Where have you been?"

My back stiffened. "Out," I answered quickly.

"Come here, Hope," he beckoned, stepping aside to leave me enough room to enter the parlor, past him. He saw my hesitation, and then barked his command once more, echoing off of all the walls and floors. Fear is what had a hold of me as I did what he asked. Reluctantly, I slipped past him, into the same parlor where they all played poker on Christmas night.

He closed the door behind me and took the cigar from his mouth, setting it in the ashtray. "Sit," he urged. I did so. In the very same chair Trent had sat in to play poker. Lawrence paced for a few moments, stewing, and then he stopped and looked at me, arms folded across his chest.

"I believe we've had this conversation before, Hope," he began. "However, something tells me that you didn't heed my warning the very first time, and that there is a need for me to reiterate what I said." He didn't bother to sit. He now began to pace as he spoke. "You must think I'm stupid if you believe that I don't know where you came from," he went on, keeping his voice cool. "I believe I've told you before to stay away from Mr. Forrestor, Hope. So tell me—why are you disobeying me?"

Coldly, I tossed the notebook into my hands onto the card table. "He helped me write my speech, Lawrence," I told him boldly. "In case you didn't know—which I'm sure you didn't, because really, who pays any attention to me around here—I'm graduating as Salutatorian of my class," I told him sarcastically. "And since I was quite positive that you would be too busy going out with Vivien, or locked away in your office, or maybe even gone for the week, or weekend, I knew of a place where I could get some intelligent help, yes— I went to Trent."

He looked as if his head was going to explode! "What have I told you about using that tone with me, young lady?" He charged at me until he was only inches from my face, and the breath I had sucked inward now held fearfully in my lungs. *"This is not your house,"* he bellowed angrily. *"I don't care who is around, or not around! When I tell you to do something, you will obey it!"*

"If you're going to kick me out, then so be it," I spat at him, standing from my seat. Immediately, his hand shot out and grabbed my arm, forcefully pushing me back down into my chair, and taking me by surprise.

"If I want to kick you out, I will—believe me," he growled through clenched teeth. "But while you *do* live under my house, you will live by my rules. I will not have you seeing Trent. He is too old for you!"

"Once graduation is over, I'm gone!" My yell was angry, jumping up from my chair. "I am so tired of stupid rules that you make for no apparent reason! I'm tired of being treated like nothing, and not even being acknowledged as a member of this family!"

"You're playing with fire, girl, *and you don't even understand,"* he raged, his eyes wild with anger. He was hardly recognizable. *"You just don't get it!"*

"That's right, Lawrence! *I don't!"* I cried. *"Because you never tell me! You don't tell me anything!* Just like now— you're telling me not to do something, but are you offering up a valid reason to back that up? *No!* I can't get answers from you, or anyone else here! Ever since I've lived in this house, I've felt like I'm all alone! I'd have better company just sitting in my room, talking to myself than I would have trying to have a conversation with anyone in this house. I hate it here!" I raged.

"And where do you think you would go, if you left here?" His lips curled upward in a twisted, ugly smile. "You have nowhere else to go."

"I would sooner live on the streets than think that I'm forced to live here with no other alternatives," I told him. "And believe me—after graduation, that idea sounds very tempting!"

His laughter was more demented and evil than any other I'd ever heard. "I'd watch my step if I were you," he warned. "I know every move you make, and if you make another wrong move, there will be consequences," he promised cruelly. "Just know that if you go back and see Trent, you're seeing him at your own risk."

"Is that a threat?" I challenged boldly.

"It's a promise," he answered. "Take it as such. You're in over your head, kid. If you keep this behavior up, you'll see what I mean," he said, opening the door for me to leave.

I wouldn't know what he meant by that until later. I wasn't going to let him get to me, though. I couldn't wait to get the hell out of there! It would've totally been worth giving up every scholarship and Broadway dream to run away to Europe and never have to deal with him again. From that point on, I would live a happy life. I would be with Trent. That's all I had to look forward to, at this point.

"I'm going to tell my mother about our plans."

I looked up in dread. "Are you sure?"

Trent poured himself another glass of wine, and joined me on his couch. "Yes," he answered confidently. "It does need to be done. And she wouldn't chastise, or judge. My mother is a very warm, open-minded person," he insisted. "You have nothing to worry about."

I shook my head. "I'm just so afraid that the slightest move will change everything," I sighed. "Aren't you the least bit worried?"

"No," he said, putting his arm around me. "We've come this far. I doubt anything can ruin our plans at this point."

I wanted so desperately to believe him.

I continued to steer very clear of Lawrence when I returned home for Spring Break, but when he would actually see me, his glare was so sharp that it could cut me in half. I was so miserable living in that house that I counted the days—not until graduation, but until I would be gone forever. Half of the time, on the weekends when I came home, I didn't even bother leaving Trent's cabin. I would leave my car parked off to the side of the entrance, and not even visit the house.

No matter how fast the day was approaching, it was still too far away. I felt like I was going to go crazy there!

It was only a matter of time before Vivien and I had our moment, as well. Vivien was sitting on the back patio, reading one of her romance books one morning, when I went to the manor out of necessity. She looked up from her book and narrowed her eyes, watching me.

"Where are you coming from?"

"The river," I lied.

She closed her book. "What is it that you're after, Hope?" She addressed me calmly, though the smile upon her glossy lips was tight. "Love? That fairy-tale romance that these things are made of?" She lifted her book pointedly, and then set it down upon the patio table. "You can forget about it, because love isn't what matters in life. Wealth, power, respect... Those should be your ultimate goals."

I shook my head. "I'm not looking for anything," I denied, not knowing where all of this was coming from.

"Aren't you?" she countered. "I see the wistful look in your eye when you play princess at the affairs we throw around here. You dance with Preston, with Trent, or anyone else, and you get starry-eyed. If you were smart, you'd give up on the idea of love. Love won't take you anywhere in life. Money will."

"Was that your reason for marrying Lawrence?" I challenged boldly. "For money? Did you leave my grandfather behind because he just wasn't making that much—or just not nearly as much as Lawrence?"

Her eyes widened. "Why I left your grandfather is my business only," she snapped.

"It's mine too," I insisted. "Because it brought you here, and it brought my mother here," I said, eyeballing her. "And my mother became so unhappy that she ran away. Why is that?" I asked her, knowing full well why. I just wanted her to acknowledge it.

She looked at me defiantly. "I don't need your disrespect," she hissed. "Your mother left because she was foolish enough to get pregnant and I told her that she was too young to have a baby. We argued, and then she was gone!"

"What did you argue about?" I demanded, pushing her limits even further. "Did you argue because she was pregnant, or because of whom the father was?"

Her eyes widened even more, and she shook her head. "I no longer want to discuss this subject," she whispered, looking downward.

"Do you mean to tell me that you knew your husband was sleeping with your daughter, and you turned her away anyway?" I demanded. "Your teenage daughter, and your much younger husband were having sex, *in this house*, and you turned the other cheek!" I yelled at her. "What other choice did my mother have but to leave here?" I demanded. "And what kind of mother were you to let this go on? Why didn't you leave Lawrence? Why didn't you take your daughter and leave?" I was yelling now, as I could plainly see she was beginning to crack. "You have resented me and made it a point never to talk to me unless you wanted to criticize me about something since I've been here!" I raged. "Why? Because I'm a reminder of your husband's betrayal? I'm a living reminder that your husband preferred your young daughter over you!"

"Get out of here!" She screamed, standing up. "I want you to leave! I want you to get away from me! I'm going to

Lawrence as soon as he gets home," she threatened. "I want you out of this house!"

Satisfied, I ran upstairs to grab some of my things. She wanted me gone? So be it. I cleaned my bedroom out of every single item I arrived to the manor with, and left everything else behind. I piled it all in my car and left for town to met Jackie for plans we already had in place, prior to all of this. Fine, I will just spend the rest of my time at Trent's cabin, until Spring Break was over! Whatever!

"I love you, and I support you, but I also gotta tell you when I think you're being hasty."

I shook my head and gave Jackie a bewildered look. "I don't know what that means," I muttered. "What else do I have, here?"

"Your dreams. Your friends. *Me*," she rattled off quickly. "You have dreamt of nothing but being an actress. That's all you ever talked about. Now things get deep at home, and you both want to just drop everything you've ever worked toward, and the scholarships, and opportunities, to run away?" She was looking at me like I was absolutely, ridiculously insane. "You two are both young! Why do you have to run away? I'm sure he has enough money—"

"You just don't understand!" My tone was cross. More cross than I had intended. "As long as I'm here, Lawrence will always be watching—"

"And so if you take off somewhere overseas, you would suddenly fall off the Lawrence Van Steenburgh Radar?!" Jackie's frustration had her nearly yelling at me. "What the hell are you doing, Hope? Engaged? Running away? You've never even been to Europe—what makes you think you want to live there?"

"You were fine with it at first!"

"Yeah, when I thought it was just a vacation!" We stared at each other for a long moment. I had no words. She, however, seemed to have more than enough to say. "I want you to get it out of your head that running all the way across the ocean isn't going to solve everything." She calmed her voice. "He won't be able to stay away from his family. Family that he has, *at the manor*. Not for forever. And what are you going to do—peddle things on the streets, for a job? Be a bored housewife? There's no Broadway over there," she said in an offensively mocking tone.

"I'm sorry I even said anything to you," I uttered bitterly. My head was swimming, and I forgot what my last words were to her, but I left her standing on the sidewalk, and I briskly ran back to my car. I was over it. All of it.

I just wanted to go home.

Chapter 22

"So Much to Lose"

I was so upset at Jackie, feeling like she had betrayed me, and didn't support me. I didn't want to see Vivien. I didn't want anything to do with that huge, forlorn castle. Instead, I drove the little path that disappeared into the woods, eventually landing me in front of the cabin.

I got out, and for some reason I felt that something was different. My heart actually started to pound before I even walked up to the front door. I was poised to open the door, but faltered for a second. I didn't know why my heart skipped a beat. After I closed the door, everything was completely silent, except the clock that hung in the kitchen. *Tick, tick, tick...* "Trent?" I called. No answer.

I set my purse down cautiously, and looked around. It was warm in there, and the ceiling fans were turned off, whereas they were usually always turned on. Obviously, Trent wasn't here. Maybe he made a run for the store? I hadn't had a chance to talk to him all day. He knew I was around for the entire week. A run to the city for business, perhaps?

All the drapes were drawn, which was odd for the time of day. He only closed them at night. I closed the door behind me and proceeded to the living area before I went to the kitchen. There were no dishes in the sink. The living room was completely picked up—the pillows were set on the couch very neatly, and where he always set his glass on the coffee table... the coaster wasn't there. I passed by the bathroom on the way to his bedroom, and the towels were hung neatly on the rack, but something disturbed me immediately. His toiletries—shaving cream, razor, soap, shampoo... they were missing. My heart started to pound.

I went into his bedroom, where his bed was made neatly, but his closet door was open. I approached it, and looked in horror when I saw that every shirt, every pair of trousers, his shoes, coats—everything was gone! There wasn't a thing in there! I felt myself start to sweat, and I hurried over to his dresser. Pulling open every drawer, I found that all of them were empty as well. The pitcher he kept by the bed with water was empty, and clean. I was beginning to feel dizzy, and frantic. *What was this? Where did all of his stuff go?* There was nothing personal left behind. He hadn't been robbed, because surely they would have taken the valuable things, such as the expensive art, the oriental rugs, the furniture, and the books..

The books!

I ran back out into the living room, and checked out his bookshelf. Nothing was taken, or removed from the shelves from what I could tell. I stood there, staring and trying to make sense of what I was seeing, when it dawned on me. I reached out and touched the place where the book he had been using to brush up on his Italian language was placed. It was gone. There was just an empty hole in its place. There was a lump in my throat.

I went back out into the kitchen, and looked frantically for any sign of him. The refrigerator had been completely cleaned out and emptied. Same with the freezer! The cabinet where he kept his favorite wine was empty. Even the trash was empty! I didn't want to believe it. I had been there only several hours earlier. I didn't even feel like I had been gone that long. What happened?! I didn't want to believe that he might have left... I looked for any little sign of him... anything that he may have left that could bring him back to pick up, but there was nothing. My eyes were clouded with tears, and I collapsed in the middle of the floor, letting out a sob. He left no note... why wouldn't he have left a note? Why would he have left without me? Without telling me?! Couldn't he have offered me an explanation? Or let me know that he was going? What could I have done to make him want to leave me? I was so confused, and hurt, and I felt so betrayed. I felt like I was trapped in a nightmare.

I finally forced myself to stand up, and I left the cabin. I was full of rage as I fled back through the trees, and it was building so that when I stormed back into the house, I was sobbing and shaking horribly. The sound of my footsteps resounded through the foyer as I made my way down the hallway, and I shoved the door to Lawrence's office open with such force that it slammed against the wall, scaring the both of us.

Lawrence stood up from his desk and his eyes were wide, but something told me he already knew what brought me to him. My fists were clenched at my sides, and I was fighting back tears. "What have you done?" I growled angrily. "Where is Trent?"

"I don't appreciate you making my wife cry to the point of hysterics," he said, eyeing me. "I had to listen to her for over an hour, and it wasn't my idea of a fun afternoon," he said coolly.

"I don't care about that," I snapped. "Where's Trent?"

"He's gone," he answered sternly. "And probably will not return, to answer your next question," he answered snidely.

"Where did he go to?" I demanded.

"I'm not sure, exactly, but I think he mentioned Italy," he replied with a vicious, self-satisfied smirk that silently begged for me to slap it off of his face! "Isn't that where you two were planning to run off to?"

"Look, I don't even know how you know that, Lawrence, but you had no right to do whatever you did!" My panic is what caused the tears to release from my eyes. "Why did you make him leave?"

"I didn't. He left of his own free will."

I broke down, leaning against the doorway. "He wouldn't do that," I whispered. "I don't believe you!"

"He did," Lawrence reaffirmed, stalking around the desk and approaching me. I got out of the doorway and he shut the door, locking it. Then he stopped a few inches from me. "I had to do it," he growled at me in a low voice, letting his anger surface. "I never wanted you to find out about this, just as I didn't ever plan to reveal to you that I'm your father. Trent's my son. He's mine—not Charles's," he revealed, and I felt like I'd been hit in the stomach. "Do you know what that means? Do you know what that makes you both? He's your half-brother," he snarled. "That's incest, Hope," he hissed, making me collapse into the chair that sat behind me. "I warned you, didn't I? I told you time and time again to stay away from him, didn't I?" He reminded me. "Why do you have to be so damned pig-headed? This is all *your* fault—if you hadn't kept running over there every time you got bored here at the house, this wouldn't have happened, and he'd still be here!"

"What do you care?" I shouted at him, a hint of paranoia in my voice. "He was much better company than you and Vivien! And don't you dare blame this on me! Why don't you blame yourself, because if you hadn't ran around trying to have sex with every woman you crossed paths with, this entire situation wouldn't exist! Let's not forget that!" I threw in his face, getting up out of the chair. "Now the affair you had with your own maid is what's become *my* problem," I tossed at him. "And then eighteen years ago you slept with a girl who was not yet even seventeen years old and got her pregnant!" I screamed with rage, hoping not just everyone in the house would hear, but everyone in the world. "You drove her from this house, and now Trent—next, is me," I told him hatefully. "I despise you Lawrence, because you're the real creator of this mess! You just took the only thing away from me that made living here bearable, and I hate you for that!"

"You sit down and hear me, girl," he growled, shoving me back down into the chair. "You don't think I've suffered for what I've done? I married a woman twenty years ago who didn't love me then, and surely doesn't love me now... Kate was a one-time thing, and it was mutual, believe me," he said smugly. "And as for your mother..." his look softened slightly. "I couldn't help but to love your mother—she was everything Vivien wasn't. She was sweet and wonderful, and she wasn't completely into herself. She was honest and outspoken, and was so incredibly charming," he told me, pacing in front of his desk. "I never meant for this to happen, and I didn't even know for sure if you were mine when she left, even though I had a strong suspicion. And you want to know how I knew absolutely everything about you? It's because I always knew where Lindsey was. I knew every move she and her new husband made since she left this house. I knew when you were born, and I even sent your mother flowers to congratulate her. I kept up with you, as well, Hope dear," he said smugly. "I knew you were active in theater. I knew what subjects you excelled in. I knew quite a bit. Just as I know everything that goes on around here. You discovered that. And if you would've gone a few folders behind yours, and your mother's, you would've seen Trent's file, as well," he said, taking my breath away. He even knew that I'd been in his office! "But, I guess you were in too much of a hurry to get out of there," he said with a smirk.

"I had to do it," I offered meekly. "No one would tell me the real reason my mother left here," I said bitterly. "But it's obvious. The reasons are obvious, now," I said, glaring at him hatefully. "It's because you're insane."

"Oh please," Lawrence scoffed. "If your mother didn't like it, she wouldn't have kept coming back for it," he hissed with sick satisfaction on his face. *"Because she did keep coming back,"* he rubbed in. "It certainly wasn't a one-time thing."

I felt sick to my stomach. "How did you know we were going to Italy?"

"Because my son went to his mother, as he told you he would, and told her all about your plans to run away to Italy, and get married. He rambled on about love, and eventually starting a family," he told me, leaning against his desk arrogantly. My heart was aching. "Naturally, Kate panicked, and as soon as Trent walked out, she came to me and told me the news. She begged me to do something. Of course—I am expected to come to the rescue." He sighed. "You go ahead and create a mess that I warned you to stay away from, and then when you ignore my demands, I have to go and unravel this mess that you've created." I glared up at him hatefully. "So I went to Trent. I visited him at the cabin. He already knew that I was his father," he revealed to me. "Obviously, he never cared to divulge that important secret to you during pillow talk. He'd overheard that many years ago as a child, when his mother and I were having a conversation about him in private. Anyhow, I told him that you and he had to cease, and cancel your plans. When he asked me why, I told him. He was pretty devastated," he went on. And to think about Trent hurting made the tears spill from my eyes again, and I ached for him. "I'm surprised that you didn't tell him after you found out about my relationship to you. What secrets to keep from one another! Of course, he only has you to blame for all of this, but I didn't tell him that. He probably realizes that on his own," he added, watching me shake as I sobbed. "Anyhow, he took it very hard, Hope, and he began to pack his things immediately to leave for what I was guessing to be Italy."

"I hate you," I sobbed into my hands. "Why couldn't you have let me tell him myself?" I cried.

He tossed a box of tissue into my lap. "Hope, you couldn't even handle simple orders such as staying away from him in the first place. Why would I give you the responsibility of telling him something like this?" I couldn't even say anything in response to him, because honestly, I knew I wouldn't have been able to bring myself to tell him. "Since you've come to live here, you've done nothing but turn the order of this house completely upside-down," he seethed, beginning to pace about once more. "Going against rules I've set for you—*and,* for the record, I shouldn't have to offer you any excuses as to why I make rules, Hope. *I'm* the elder, here. I don't answer to you," he added snidely. "And yet, every rule I've set, you've made a point to break. Lying, running around town making an ass of yourself dancing on bars, sneaking around!" He shook his head. "Let's also not forget Preston," he added. "I'm not sure what you've done to him, but he hasn't returned back to this house in months! I have a feeling I know why, and you're foolish for not accepting his kindness, Hope. A fool! That boy has fallen head over heels for you, and you probably never even noticed, because you're too busy worrying about yourself and stealing away to see your half-brother," he rubbed in viciously.

"And you must be out of your mind to think that you could get away with running off and marrying, the way you were planning," he continued. "The both of you have barely been together for any amount of time, and yet you think that this would work? That's what's insane! 'Happily ever after' doesn't exist, Hope. Remember that. If you're smart, you'll just forget this ever happened, and move on. Call up Preston," he urged. "I'm sure he'll take you."

I stood up, furious, and not wanting to hear another word. "I have to get out of here," I said, trying to keep myself from going hysterical. "I need to leave!"

"You'll do no such thing," Lawrence ordered.

"Watch me," I dared, standing up.

I stormed from his office, wiping tears away with my hands. After the rock on my finger grazed the skin upon my face, I looked down at the ring I wore now on my left hand. I hadn't bothered to take it off before I stormed into the house to confront Lawrence, and now my heart ached just to see it.

The heavy wooden door slammed behind me as I left, and as far as I was concerned, I'd never look back. Lawrence didn't come after me. I didn't expect him to. I ran to my car at the edge of the woods, and took off, with all of my things in the trunk.

I couldn't stop sobbing as the realization of what was going on really hit me, turning onto the main road, and leaving the manor—or, more specifically, the cabin—behind me, forever. I would never find the solace, and sense of sanity that I always found in that small space, ever again. No more would I walk in there after trekking through snow, to find him waiting for me with a fire burning. No more would he take me into the bedroom and make me his. I would never be held in his arms, or feel his lips against my ear. Never again would I feel the span of his back, or the firmness of his chest beneath my fingertips.

Never again would I love someone even half as much as I did Trent.

My foot pressed down on the gas pedal—roaring the car into motion as if the harder I pressed, the more distance I'd put between myself and my shame.

My world was crumbling all around me. I didn't know where I was headed long-term, but I definitely had to get as far away from the manor as possible. First, I was headed for the closest bank. My plan was to withdraw the sum of money that I had in the "allowance" that Lawrence had set up for me, and wipe it out. It would be enough to get me somewhere, for the time being.

When I parked in front of the bank, I took one look in the mirror and begged myself to calm down the best I could. I couldn't go into that bank scaring everyone with my wild, frantic look. I wiped my face clean and reapplied fresh make-up. I brushed my hair to sleek, soft strands, and then I went inside the bank. My plan worked. The account Lawrence set up for me would be my saving grace. With that good-sized amount of money, I knew I could live off of it for enough time to get myself a job and get on my feet.

It wasn't until I found my way back behind the steering wheel of my mother's former car that I realized I was shaking like a leaf. My eyes were glued to my trembling hands as they fumbled and then started the engine. Fear plagued me for more reasons than I could even count, and I had to make a quick decision. *Where was I going?* North, or south? East, or west? I needed to find a highway, and that was my main concern. So much so that I wasn't paying too much attention to anything else—stop signs, lights, or other drivers. My biggest mistake was not seeing a light turn red as I proceeded to go through it. It all happened so fast that all I knew was one minute I was driving, and the next minute I heard a loud bang, and my car was spinning.

Everything went black after that.

Chapter 23

"A New Life"

      I woke up in a hospital bed. At first, I wondered if I had died, but I was positive I wouldn't feel as much pain if I had... The moan that passed through my lips didn't even sound like it came from me. I looked about the room, to find that I was all by myself. The rhythmic beeps of monitors close to my bed caused me to look downward. My head was killing me. Groggily, I stared at the IV poking out of my arm, I knew I had been in an accident. I shuddered as I remembered the impact, and the sound of metal smashing and crunching all around me. Mercifully, I blacked out after I was thrust forward in the driver's seat. I think my head hit the steering wheel, but I wasn't sure. I had realized almost instantly that I had run that red light, but it was a split-second too late...

      The door to my room opened, and I heard voices. My eyes were trying to focus, and my tongue felt too thick for me to even try and speak out. "She hit her head pretty good, and she's got some bumps and bruises, so we want to keep her for at least tonight just to observe her." He must've been the doctor.

"When will she be able to return home?" *Lawrence*. My headache instantly got worse.

"I'm not certain. It depends on several different things. We just completed the sonogram and found out that the baby is just fine," he said, catching my attention. "But we also want to make sure the mother is fine, as well."

"The baby," Lawrence spoke softly. "Of course..." He was silent for a moment.

The baby. Were they even speaking about me?

"I will let you know more details as they come," the doctor promised. "Hopefully you should be able to take her home tomorrow."

"Thank you," Lawrence acknowledged him, in an odd voice. I heard the doctor leave the room, and my eyes now settled upon Lawrence, as he sat in the chair beside my bed. He smoothed the suit jacket he wore, down over him, and picked a stray piece of lint from his shoulder, before letting it fall to the floor. Then he stared straight back at me, silent,

I was terrified and I was tired, all at once. There was no way I was going to let him take me back to the manor, as he had implied to the doctor. I couldn't let that happen. The throbbing in my head was so intense that I had to just close my eyes and shut him out. But try as I might, I couldn't actually make him disappear

"You've been in and out of consciousness for a few hours, now. The doctor says that you'll be alright," Lawrence assured me softly. "He said that you'll most likely be released from the hospital in the next day, or so. Do you remember anything about the accident?"

I swallowed hard, opening my eyes again. "I ran a red light," I answered meekly.

"What were you trying to do, kill yourself?" His tone was as sharp as those dark eyes of his that were burning into me.

"I'd rather be dead," I answered flatly, "Than to go back to that house."

His eyes flicked at me, surprised at my answer. "Is that so?"

"Yes."

"You will need a place to recuperate," he insisted. "Where will you go?"

"I'd rather stay here."

"You can't," he denied.

"I'm pregnant," I said, looking at him. "Aren't I?"

His jaw tensed. "Yes."

I laughed bitterly, feeling the tears well up in my eyes. "It's Trent's," I told him, though I was sure he already knew. I was so stunned by the idea that I was pregnant... There were so many things flying through my mind!

"We'll have it taken care of," he said firmly.

"Have *what* taken care of?"

"You can't honestly think you can keep that baby." He shook his head and dared to eye me with amusement. "It will have a million problems—not to mention the possibility of being born with two heads, or grossly deformed in other ways!"

"It's not your decision to make," I fired back softly.

"Don't be stupid, Hope!" He tried to keep his voice down. "We need to take care of this *now*!"

"*Leave me alone*," I commanded with a threatening look, before turning my head away from his direction. "Just go. I want to rest."

"I'll be back tomorrow," he warned, getting up. "And I'm taking you home."

Not if I can do anything about it.

I waited until I knew for sure that he was gone, and I picked up the phone. I got an outbound line, and dialed Jackie's number.

Then I thanked God she was home.

"I was down at your hospital room earlier," she told me. "But you weren't awake, yet."

"You visited me?" I asked, surprised.

"Yes. Lawrence sent me home and told me that when you woke up, he'd call me," she informed me.

"Look, I'm leaving town," I told her, lowering my voice. "That accident—I was trying to leave, but I was so upset that *I caused that accident*," I confessed to her. "There is so much that you don't know, but you've been such a good friend, Jackie. I don't know what I would've done without you, and—"

"What do you mean, leaving town? Running away?"

"Yes," I answered firmly. "Trent's gone, and I found out that Lawrence is my father. He is the reason my mother ran away."

"Oh no," she muttered. "Where did Trent go?"

"He left for Italy. Without me," I said, on the verge of tears again. "Look, I can't go into details, but I found out by listening to the doctor that I'm pregnant, and I can't stay here a minute longer," I told her. "I'm going to New York City, and I'm going to accept that scholarship to that college for performing arts. I have enough money to get me set up in an apartment long enough for me to find a job, but I have to leave fast, or else Lawrence plans on taking me back to the manor," I told her fearfully. "I can't go back there, Jackie," I cried softly into the phone.

"Hey calm down," she soothed. "Have you thought this through all the way?" She asked. "Do you have some sort of plan?"

"I know I can make it work," I whispered into the phone. "I'll get a cheap hotel room until I can find an apartment, and I'll get a job to pay rent and bills—"

"What about the baby? Doctor bills are expensive."

"If I get a job, I'll have insurance," I answered her back. "Look, I'm *not* staying here. There's nothing you can say to change my mind," I told her defiantly. "It's not going to work."

"I'm not trying to change your mind," she said gently. "I just want you to think this through."

"Don't worry about me," I told her. "I'll be fine."

"How are you going to get there?" she asked me. "You totaled your car..."

"The bus," I replied. I'll buy a bus ticket."

She was quiet for a moment. "There's no need for that. I have a car."

"I can't take your car," I denied. "That's crazy—you just got that as a graduation present!"

"I don't mean for you to take it. I mean... I'll come get you," she volunteered. "And we'll figure this out together."

She held true to her promise. It didn't matter that I had gotten mad and left her, the last time I saw her. She didn't care about how ugly I had talked to her, at the time. She didn't think I was so ridiculous that she didn't want anything to do with me again. Instead, she was at the hospital at eight a.m., and I took the liberty of talking with the doctor myself, who said that I was fine enough to leave. I checked myself out. When I asked where my bags were, the doctor told me that Lawrence took them home with him. He had my purse, my two packed bags—everything. I needed those things, so for one last time, I headed back to the manor. The very place that upset me enough to cause this much damage to myself, my mother's car, and my pride. I ducked down in the front seat when Jackie drove up to the house, and waited for her to tell me if Lawrence's town car was parked out front. It wasn't.

I hurried inside the large, stone palace, and ran up the stairs without being noticed. I was sure I heard the vacuum going inside the ballroom, and it provided me enough noise to get up the stairs without anyone noticing. I ran down the hall and went into my suite. My suitcases and purse sat neatly at the foot of my bed. Thankful that Lawrence hadn't asked Kate to put my things away, I grabbed the bags and my purse, and ran back out. My heart was pounding, and the adrenaline pumped through my veins at the thought that Lawrence could return any second.

Fortunately, he didn't.

Jackie rescuing me from the hospital meant more to me than she even knew. Her talking me out of skipping town, and just instead returning to Springcrest, was probably the best thing she could've done. There was indeed a little life growing inside of me, and it created a much bigger picture I needed to stay focused on. No one at school knew, besides Jackie. No one could even tell. As graduation approached, my belly was just starting to take on a different shape. A shape that more loose-fitting clothes easily disguised.

And I missed Preston. I hated myself for hurting him. Our friendship meant more to me than I even realized. His adoration, loyalty, and devotion were qualities I loved so much... but no longer merited. I didn't deserve him in my life, anymore. It was time to move on.

The longing I felt for Trent depressed me. I was saddened by thoughts of him. I was sickened every time our relation was in the front of my mind. I felt wrong for missing him, but it didn't stop me from doing so. It just felt... different.

I worried about the little life growing inside of me. I tossed and turned every night with thoughts of horrific deformities and handicaps that might plague my child. I tormented myself wondering if Lawrence was right. That I should've terminated the pregnancy. Was I just being stupid and selfish for trying to hold onto something that obviously wasn't meant to be? Conflict continued to plague me.

It kept stopping me in my tracks, and making me question everything around me: *I was eighteen, and having a baby*. What a wake-up call.

I would never again return to Van Steenburgh Manor. I had no reason to. Trent was gone. For good. Preston wanted nothing to do with me, understandably. I screwed it up. All of it. School provided just enough of a distraction; however it didn't fully keep me from being an emotional mess. I cried at the drop of a hat. If I didn't make a perfect grade, I cried. I cried when I was alone in my room, alone in my thoughts. Just alone, period.

My heart was aching, and I couldn't do a thing about it. I had to just go through the motions, get through the semester, graduate, and leave it all behind for good. It wasn't an option – it was a must. But I was a zombie. I was on robot-mode. A shell of my former self. Jackie was a God-send. She did everything she could to keep me occupied when she wasn't studying. She even insisted I go home to her family's house on a few weekends. It was nice. But it didn't feel like home. And when they would ask how Lawrence and Vivien were, it made my stomach turn to have to smile and pretend all was well in the world. Inside, I was dying.

It wasn't for lack of trying to get over everything... I just found that I didn't care, anymore. I certainly didn't want to go back to Van Steenburgh Manor. I half-expected Lawrence to stop paying for my schooling, forcing me to make a move. Whether it be returning to the manor, or just taking off. But he didn't. Maybe he wasn't entirely a menace. Maybe he really did have my best interests in mind.

Or maybe I just wasn't worth the trouble. Maybe it was just best to let me go.

"Are you excited about prom?" Jackie asked, the first time I accompanied her to find the perfect dress.

"I probably would be more excited, if I didn't feel like I already dressed up for prom so much in the last several months," I joked. "I'm probably not going to go," I revealed casually.

"You can't *not* go," she insisted. "It will be fun, and I need you there."

"You will be busy with Chad," I replied lightly. "And I wouldn't want you to worry about me being entertained. I'm too fat for a dress right now anyway," I waved aside with a smile.

"You're not fat. You're *pregnant.*"

True story. But I let her think I was going to go, all the way up until two days before, when it was too late to get a dress. Too late for hair appointments. Just... too late, altogether. She seemed genuinely sad, but I honestly knew she would have fun, regardless. I helped her get ready. I was there to share in her excitement, and it did feel kind of empty when she left to go have fun. Something in me wanted to dial Trent's phone that evening, but I refrained. As if hearing the lady on the other end telling me one more time that the line was disconnected would further break my heart. It couldn't be more broken.

As time went on, I began to wonder what drove Trent to propose. Out of absolute nowhere. He started off as a celebrated bachelor when I met him, unbelieving that marriage and family life was for him. Over time, he acknowledged our connection, and ultimately succumbed to it, but really... What changed his mind so suddenly? Was there something else behind it? Talks of a vacation spurned into starting a new life together, thousands of miles away, and essentially disappearing from everything and everyone we knew. It all happened so fast...

And then it disappeared even more quickly.

I was confused. Not even a good-bye. No note. Nothing. Everything was just gone in the blink of an eye. I was left behind to deal with all the repercussions, while he was able to get away and make a fresh start. It wasn't fair.

I danced on a thin wire separating hurt, and resentment. Every day had its high and low points. I felt guilty and shameful for missing him, but I did. I struggled with that. I couldn't help but feel abandoned. I battled the ache in my heart, and the emptiness I felt with having neither Preston nor Trent in my life, and I just couldn't wait to move away, in hopes to finally clear my head of the clouds and spider webs accumulated there from living at Van Steenburgh Manor.

Of course Jackie had been right; I had been so blind, willing to give up everything to run away with Trent, and just never come back. What was I thinking? And why would he make such a tempting offer, knowing it would sacrifice the biggest of my aspirations? It scared me to conceive how ready I was to abandon the passions that had always embodied me... for another person. Maybe that's what true love felt like. Maybe it was supposed to turn you selfless. Whatever the case, I would never find out just how much our plans would change my life.

The morning of graduation, an overwhelming sense of anxiety grabbed hold of me. I couldn't distinguish between the flutter of butterflies in my stomach, and the strange gurgling I was becoming accustomed to, of having a baby inside me. My heart was in my throat. Boxes were all around my dorm room. Jackie's room. Everybody's rooms. It signified our time to leave. Where to, I wasn't sure yet.

That day was nothing but a blur. Fifty-three seniors sat on a stage, and we listened to our peers speak. My eyes scanned the crowd of endless faces as I said my speech, and I was stunned to find Lawrence sitting in the third row. Strangers were on both sides of him. He had come alone. My heart didn't stop racing, and I didn't stop sweating the remainder of that time. I fidgeted in my seat, eyed Jackie nervously to see if she saw what I saw in the crowd. I never caught her eye. My eyes jumped around the crowd, and they were disappointed, but not surprised, that Preston was nowhere in sight. Waiting anxiously until they called my name, I avoided looking again at Lawrence. I was shocked he even cared to come. Keeping up appearances, perhaps? Or maybe he did care on some level.

Or maybe it was a reminder that just as he never left my mother's life... he wouldn't completely leave mine, either.

I rose from my chair when my name was called, and on shaky legs I walked, as practiced, across that stage. Diploma in hand, I finally made it. I smiled as I had been instructed, shook the dean's hand, and when I was walking back to my seat, I nearly stopped in my tracks when I could've sworn I'd seen Trent's beautiful face in the sea of people seated. I almost passed up my spot to stand in and got distracted for a moment, but when I looked back again in that direction, I couldn't find him. Tears welled in my eyes for the sheer fact of not knowing whether I had imagined seeing him there, or if he actually was. The second we were permitted to file down the steps from the stage, I disappeared into the crowd. Desperate to find someone who obviously didn't want to be found. Tears stung my eyes when I realized my eyes had probably played a horrible, mean trick on me. He was nowhere around. His car wasn't even in the parking lot as far as I could see.

And I needed to avoid Lawrence.

I ran out to the grounds, and down the paths winding around and through the buildings on campus. The breeze gently blew my gown, and I took my cap off my head before I wiped the random fallen tears from my cheeks. *I was so scared. So alone. So confused.* Everything was so uncertain....

It was the first time in a long time that all I wanted was to have my mother back.

I sat at the picnic table where I had first met Jackie, and I cradled my head on the table. I just needed to be alone. I needed to wrap my head around everything that was happening, had happened, and was going to happen. This was not how I imagined my life unfolding, when I was a little girl. Even when I first arrived at Van Steenburgh Manor, I never in my wildest dreams expected to be in the position I was in, right now.

I needed to get myself together.

My time at Springcrest had officially come to an end. It wasn't just time for a new chapter; it was time for a new story, altogether.

At the start of the summer, Jackie and I packed our belongings into her car, and we were ready for whatever was ahead of us.

"So, was that the thing that you couldn't tell me about, months ago?"

I looked at her, confused. "What?"

"About Lawrence being your father. Was that the information you found out that you weren't supposed to know?"

I nodded, looking back out the car window. "Yes," I answered. "It is."

"I'm sorry," she expressed softly.

"You didn't tell your parents any of the details about me, did you?" I asked her in alarm.

She shook her head. "I just told my parents that you were going to the city so you could start taking summer classes," she replied. "I think that's what helped me. I'm pretty sure if I told them the truth, they wouldn't have let me go," she said with a smile. "But I couldn't let you go alone. You're going to need help," she reasoned. "I'll be Aunt Jackie," she declared with a wink.

I don't like to think of what could've happened to me if I didn't have her.

From that point on, I wasn't going to waste another thought on that cold, stone palace I left behind. What had looked so enchanting at first glance turned out to be anything but. My heart ached for the one that I loved, but couldn't have. My beautiful Trent. I knew he was out there, somewhere, and I knew he was hurting just as I was. I couldn't bring myself to tell Jackie that I learned he was my half-brother. I was ashamed, and I didn't want her to look at the baby I was carrying deep inside of me any differently. Lawrence instilled something deep in the back of my mind that made me fear any deformities, or lack of intelligence in my baby, and I knew that when I visited the doctor for the first time, I would hold my breath while we looked at the sonogram.

The truth was, I knew I couldn't have Trent, but he really had left something behind for me to keep forever. He'd left nothing of significance behind in the cabin, or no explanation, but he left a big part of himself, growing inside my belly. It was a gift I would be able to love forever.

I looked out the car window at the scenery passing by, and I was ready to accept whatever else Fate was intending to throw our way. I wondered if it was the same feeling that my mother had, when she fled Van Steenburgh Manor eighteen years ago. I wondered if she looked at my father like a hero, her knight in shining armor to come and save the day—much like the way I looked at Jackie. Yes, he was still my father. He was the one who raised me. He treated me like his actual daughter. I wondered if he even knew the truth—that he wasn't. Did my mother hide that from him? Did she feel as ashamed as I did at that very moment?

I'd never know. One could only speculate... or let matters rest. *"Don't drive yourself crazy over a mystery that may never be solved,"* I heard Trent's voice in my head. He was wrong. The biggest part of the mystery had been solved, and that's what destroyed us. I was very bitter. For once, I had wanted everything to fall completely into place, and we would end up far away from here. Selfishly, I looked back and wished that Trent and I actually had ran away earlier than we planned so that the entire mess could have been avoided.

But I realized that it couldn't have been. He would've still told his mother, who would've told Lawrence. All plans still would've come to a screeching halt. It just wasn't meant to happen. Our Fate was written for us before we were even born. Unfortunately, it was written by Lawrence.

Epilogue

Everything happens for a reason. I firmly believe that. My parents were taken from me so that I would go to Van Steenburgh Manor. I was sent there to learn about my family... About my mother, and then about my father. *My real father...* I was so confused as to where my future was going to lead me from this point, but anything would be better than where I'd just come from.

My time for happiness was surely up ahead of me. I knew I could survive. I would survive. How, I didn't yet know. That would become another story, in itself.